THE RECLAMATIONS

THE
RECLAMATIONS

PAUL MARLAIS

TWPP

AUSTIN ■ ALBUQUERQUE

Published by TWPP, LLC
THE RECLAMATIONS Copyright © 2018 by Paul Marlais.
ALL RIGHTS RESERVED

PUBLISHER'S NOTE:
This is a work of fiction. The names, characters, places, and events in this book are either a product of the author's imagination, not real, or used fictitiously. Any similarity to real persons, living or dead, business establishments, events, or locales, is coincidental and not intended by the author.

THIS BOOK WAS ORIGINALLY PUBLISHED BY THE WHITE PEOPLE'S PRESS
Readers who are interested in learning more about our titles are invited to visit our website at WWW.WHITEPEOPLEPRESS.COM. For inquiries, contact us at CONTACT@WHITEPEOPLEPRESS.COM. For mailing, address: TWPP 5114 Balcones Woods Drive STE 307-274 Austin, TX 78759.

WWW.WHITEPEOPLEPRESS.COM
CONTACT@WHITEPEOPLEPRESS.COM

Library of Congress Control Number: 2019900342
ISBN: 978-1-7336026-1-7 (hc.)
ISBN: 978-1-7336026-0-0 (pbk.)
ISBN: 978-1-7336026-2-4 (e-book)

PRINTED IN THE UNITED STATES OF AMERICA
10 9 8 7 6 5 4 3 2 1

FIRST EDITION HARDCOVER

The author would like to thank his family, a friend who lent an ear whenever one was needed, the many thinkers who made this work possible, and GLAD and LF.

For my father

THE RECLAMATIONS

I

Nothing can be compared with this continual displacement of the human species

—ALEXIS DE TOCQUEVILLE

T HE AFTERNOON WAS UPON A DAY ordinary as any when it came blasting across the universe, traversing planets and stars in rift through the æther, clouds breaking density, parting at last, to cast a portal of light on Wilshire. It was nothing to anyone caught in the crosshairs of this celestial lens as it glided down the sidewalk. So it closed. These were inland clouds being pressed out to sea but resisting with the updraft, pruning before vapors could condense bellyful enough for the fall. They rarely did here. Once upon a time residents preferred it that way, and with no earthly obstacle too great a horticultural fairyland arose in these parts—a simulated wellspring at the end of the world. Sun spilling onto palms, crystalline calm, there was nowhere left to go. Here lived kings, in the subtropical tenderloin of paradise. In beauty's lodestone, temptation's nerve center, culture's ruin. In an abyss that would have shamed any erstwhile underworld. In the seaside Shangri-La of La La Land.

But those days had passed. Those people were gone. Well no actually, of course . . . a few were still around. Across the greensward, past the clubhouse, at the mouth of the drive, thinning clouds were administering another breakthrough of light, this one noticed. The sudden change caught the attention of a young man with chips and chops of equal note named Edmund Loxley, toward whom, it had been suggested, serendipity seemed unusually biased. He stopped as the sunburst ranged across the pavement; looked up upon feeling the warmth baking into the crown of his shaggy mane. Once adjusted to the downward gleam he saw the opening in the clouds forming directly above him. Perhaps it was some kind of sign, he thought; this, a squinting exploration for potential significance that would be followed shortly thereafter by duress.

Ed was late.

Twisting tan paths laid the way to the par-4 second, where Walt Dalton, Etan Affleck, and Rone Ruffalo were teeing off. Ed pulled up and apologized for his tardiness, but these men left tension off the links, so it was no matter.

"We waited."

"Won't see another day like this."

Ed stepped casually onto the square and level launchpad, ball cupped in hand, white tee between his knuckles. He pushed it into the grass as the silence settled, then he shuffled his feet and started into a high waggle. He peeked ahead one last time, then he did the grip check. After that it was the hip status check. Waist-tilt depression to clubhead position seventeen, sixteen, fifteen. Spine angle status check and line position status check. Final clubhead depression sequence and alignment status check with knees unlock status check, knees aligned with heels status check, hips status check, and shoulders status check—launch ready status: final check. Initiating backswing rotation sequence: arms are leading and wrists are cocking and shoulders are aligned and focus is shifting to the sternum, monitoring forearm alignment, monitoring clubface alignment, monitoring plane alignment, rolling elbows inward into apex position. Sternum point check: confirmed for eight o'clock. Final hip check, final shoulder check, parallel club shaft position check. Entering forward fall. Monitoring plane position and intended route, monitoring arm spacing and shoulder stabilization, monitoring lag and target line. Balance status check: confirmed optimal for load bearing; arms status check: confirmed for delta and reaching maximum extension; clubface position check: confirmed for squared and awaiting contact—offloading weight for terminal boost, reaching top clubhead speed, attaining pure predator grace, metallic chime springing around scenic pine-hemmed clearing sequence: *ping*, chiggity-check, and Warbird 4 is on the move—attack angle positive, launch angle around 13°, dynamic loft a smidge high so we're losing her fast—visual contact with Warbird 4 declining, Warbird 4 vanishing in low earth orbit, visual contact with Warbird 4 lost in blue-gray forespan of sky—*fare, well. . . .*

"Got-damn, Ed!" Rone cried in salute up the lush emerald runway.

"Always a mistake inviting you out here."

The three-cart convoy snaked around the knoll and proceeded on a track parallel to the fairway, then split. Ed's lie was the farthest ahead—an easy chip shot to the green, presumably. After the others had taken their second shots he waddled into position behind his ball. A swift cut and a short gazing wait later and he was approximately a bat to a broomstick away from his first birdie of the day.

Ed was playing from behind but wouldn't need much help catching up; he held the lowest officially recorded score at this course, along with a few others. And upon finishing the front nine, he had a four-stroke lead.

"Finally getting out of Tarzana," Walt announced during the pit stop between nine and ten when he and Ed were alone. He was rolling his back near the water fountain. Ed was leaning butt-to-hood on the cart with his arms crossed.

"Heading up to New-Am?"

"Held out long enough and it's not safe on the other side of the Hills anymore. Unofficial removals picking up, too, bad as it ever was. Guy down the street from me just last week got . . . well—got *got*."

"Anyone you knew?"

"Nah. Tassillo something? forget. No one who'll be missed from what I could gather." Walt came over and sat next to Ed and pretended to study the Los Angeles skyways for a beat. "Give any more thought to enlisting?" he asked.

"Dunno, Walt. You know how I feel about that."

"You need to start making plans to get out of the Free Pacific State—out of the city, at least. Go back down to Newport."

"I just got back from Newport yesterday."

"And I'm saying the situation here's changed since you've been gone."

"Seems the same to me."

"Well it's not, and you need to put together an exit strategy."

"Take it you didn't hear back from that guy about the spot on the Eastern Circuit. Hate to bring it up again . . ."

"Shoot." Walt shook his head away. "I just don't have the connections and you know how it is with the game these days, war and all."

"I understand. Appreciate you trying."

"There are matters more important anyway." Walt bucked his chin to the sky and leaned over, motioning for Ed to come in closer, then murmured, "In case the Googlopticon's still up there—"

"—Come on," Ed laughed, cutting him off and flaring an elbow out. "There's no Googlopticon anymore and you know it."

"Just listen aright," Walt with a hand up to indicate that while Ed might be right on the particular point his own extended beyond it. "You played great down there. Need to work on your facial expressions, but you'll get that break sooner or later. People have been talking about the Hills getting flooded though, so for now you need to either enlist or go back down to Orange County."

"It's worse down there than it is up here."

"Then go somewhere else, go any which way you please, as long as it's away from here. Old-Am's finished and has been for a long time, but L.A. has a bullseye on it and they're turning the guns this way."

Ed was lifting into his backswing on the teeing ground at eleven when a draft burst through and blew his ball off. He put it back and reset, then there was some sort of rumble. Rone yelled "Quake!" But that wasn't it. Ed turned to see Walt pointing toward an opening in the treeline enabling a slight view of the city; smoke was starting to billow up from somewhere within. They coalesced behind Walt, looking down his arm like a scope.

"Afritown," Etan, quick to offer the first hypothesis.

"No way," Rone countered, "that's Covina."

Walt opened his clearscreen and the group for some silent seconds alternated their attention between the mysterious turmoil beyond and the live updates rolling speedily in and, in most cases, permanently out.

"Covina! *Covina Covina*—m'I good?"

"Hell was it, though?"

"Wait for them to clean up, we'll get the details later."

They put their attention back on the horizon for another minute and watched the smoke rise and exosmotically merge with the native haze, then finished off their drives. On the way back to the carts Walt wrapped a firm arm around Ed and insisted, in a seldom-used tone, "You're taking my counsel on this one. We're L.A.'s last and this is civilization's end. It's time to go."

Upon finishing the back nine the four headed to the clubhouse patio in what could be described as higher-than-average spirits, the incident from earlier having reignited in the senior three memories of the old days through which they lived and, unlike some less fortunate, made it out of intact enough to occasionally break three-hundo with the 1-wood. These gentlemen were fond of Ed, as they were his late father, one of those less fortunate, whom they'd known better than Ed himself ever had. They knew the story, as well. As it went, both the elder and younger Loxley were of a historic lineage—one of the most historic, in fact—and while the tale had been passed down from pop to tot through the ages it was usually regarded with a fair amount of suspicion, intriguing though it may have been to entertain from time to time, since you could never *really* be sure where a story like that originated. Still, each generation had carried it and that ye olde hamlet's name on, and though the facts remained ambiguous to even the most knowledgeable sleuths of the ancestral record for just about the entire post-High Medieval Period, it was in years more recent, not long after the rise of the English Caliphate, that new information had come to light, resulting in a group of genetic historians from the University of Sheffield tracking the elder Loxley down and presenting him with data that, by their own admission, all but confirmed the legend. To the remaining Loxley's, the last being Edmund the younger, no further verification would be needed. . . .

"Ed here is lucky—too young to have seen the worst of it," Walt was saying at the table. "After the Pull Out, after New-Am's Reindependence. I remember the day. Whoever was still around took off like the plague had struck, up and left—*gone*, just like *that*," snapping his fingers an inch from his ear. "You could practically see people paragliding down from Los Feliz."

"And new ones scrambling up just as fast."

"It was no cakewalk for those of us who had commitments or otherwise chose to stay, but we made it work—dodging the Googlopticon, paying off the Sureños, playing legionnaire during loots and raids—"

"—Blast and bury," Rone broke in, holding out a hand for a low five that Etan connected with like it was part of a routine.

"Never being sure if or when the boot's coming down," Walt resumed, "but still getting a round in here and there ain't that right. Got safer once the Binaries were in place, but what I mean to say is, I'd like to think the few of us who stuck around were a good influence on young Ed."

"There were some rough times before," Etan added, "but things in the FPSC are starting to look as bad as ever."

"And much as it pains me to admit, the handful of us who stuck it out and went about our days acting like we knew nothing about nothing are probably the last of a kind . . . worst of one, too. Likely means we're the descendants of folks who were equally skilled at toeing the line and keeping their heads down, their eyes closed, and their traps shut. The walls of Tinseltown might be coming down for real this time, though."

"I don't know," Rone shrugged. "Not like we haven't heard all this a million times. Lot of people say it's getting better."

"They always do," Walt mumbled, outlining the crevasses of a doubtful grin. "But Ed best be moving on like the rest of us. Leave it to the people who made it this way, to Bel Air's Last Stand. On the other side sof the Elko Line, well, that's where folks like us belong. . . ."

CLUBS IN TOW, Ed boarded an eastbound shuttle packed with day

laborers in various states of DramaMundo-induced stupor—faceless behind clearscreens, emitting aromas of chorizo and sawdust—at a glance: on
a connector bound for the Pico-Union Checkpoint. Sunlight and shadow
coursed in and out as they ran the Wilshire gauntlet in stops and starts
through a tight spread of rundown art deco office buildings and semi-vacant
strip malls draped in signage with missing or foreign lettering that made
flimsy sidelong bookends for a drag subsisting exclusively on thru-derby
traffic and curbside commerce from what one could only assume were
neutral-to-bad actors. Around the forty-six-minute mark of the journey,
with the strap burning into his shoulder and the seconds falling off the
clock like clingy beads of water at leaves' edge, Ed, now wishing he'd opted
for an autocar, began probing the backs of his eyelids for serenity, unlocked
in spurts but jumping erratically like the sweep hand on a broken meter to
its flip side of madness as the shuttle idled a block from his Rimpau Boulevard get-off point.

The irons clanked when he hopped off but with his walking rhythm re-
tuned to a mild, busted wind chime jangle. Along the palm-shaded three
blocks home tall gates and wild foliage protected and shrouded houses once
inhabited by a people who used the neighborhood as a stronghold, but who
had been targeted and driven out by forces Ed could neither understand nor
recall, having occurred mostly before his time. Assorted others advanced on
the prime Hancock Park real estate afterward, and it was during this influx
that the family friend who had taken Ed in, Doc, acquired the home he was
soon entering; but many of them had since moved on as well, including
Doc, himself in the way all inevitably did, while the neighborhood, long in
decline, continued to inch ever closer to the bottom.

Ed was back out almost as fast as he came, after a shower and a bite to
eat summoning an autocar that scooped him up and steered him into the
velvet afterglow, past the compounds on Highland then through the heart of
Hollywood and an uneven blend of the fancy and the frayed before cutting him over to Canyon Checkpoint Six. From there the autocar wound

gently into the Hills by valley way around many a hip and now abandoned penthouse, dingbat, and bungalow—modernist, Wrightean, *L.A.ish*—aging poorly under the red wine horizon bleeding the light from the day.

It pulled into an inlet drive next to a thick barricade of ivy: Ed's destination and a residence on the date of whose fated slide into Laurel Canyon several wagers had been made. Inside were friends, though ones he hadn't seen for a while, ever since he made an oath to associate less with those liable to lead him into predicaments one, slick as they may be, couldn't always walk away from with their skeletal matter intact. Money, however, perishable as it were, had been difficult to come by of late, and what was supposed to be a surefire bet at the Hermosa Dog Pit the night before had backfired, draining Ed's winnings from the Newport Open and putting him in the red.

Buzzed through the hillside abode, he cut around a sunken living room on his way to the game room in the back, where, between the doorway and the window-wall overlooking the ravine, an argument was taking place around a poker table on which was a clearly arranged diagram made out of biscuit cookies. The rest of the room, now and for as long as Ed had been coming over, was filled with boxes. No the dachshund was the first to become aware of his entry, but the others soon followed and used it as an excuse to suspend the altercation. Calvin Strand and German the Russian offered their greetings then took off in different directions for a breather with held hips and shaking heads. The third person present, and no doubt the source of the provocation, the portly fro-curled Peel McMurray, shook Ed's hand then raised his arms into uprights as he flopped down in a chair.

"Ed of Greater Wilshire, back from Newport, don't know how you do it. But you remember that face you made last time? You were doing it again."

"The cornered-downy face?"

"Yeah yeah, that's the one. Doubt anyone noticed. Also got an earful from some Hong Kong slaver you geesed."

"You'd have to be more specific. But I need an explanation for this first," Ed, pointing at the table.

Being a natural problem-solver, a talent eligible for additional renown in a city full of problems, had led to Peel believing there existed none he couldn't solve. But like the adrenaline junkie forever in search of higher peaks, bigger waves, new stores with tighter security, this often led to him inventing problems or seeking out ventures certain to produce them in abundance. And at the end of Ed's gaze, spelled out in sugar and almond flour, were the words: BIG PROBLEM.

"Oh you mean this?" Peel picked a cookie up and stuffed it into his mouth. "Old-Am," he exclaimed mid-chew, ". . . the Libancien," hand mockingly to his heart, ". . . is officially over."

"Been over fr'forever," German the Russian said from the couch behind a pair of oculife glasses.

"But they're coming for the Free Pacific State now . . . for L.A."

"Joining up then?" Ed asked.

"Please," Peel deriding the notion. "Not throwing my best years away for some place I've never been. We're going to that new region in Siberia."

"I heard about that. When are you guys going?"

"Next week," Calvin said as he airlifted a toy-hitched No to the table with him. "We thought about trying to get you on board but we hadn't heard from you for a while."

"Too bad for me," Ed, deflated.

"Thought you'd caught that break. Sure you have something else lined up."

"But before we head out," Peel putting the focus back on the table, "there are prospective business opportunities being considered. No one wants to spend these Old-Am Social Credits anymore so cash is making a big comeback. Banks still store a lot of it, and their security, mean, it's decades behind."

"So what are you gonna rob a bank?" Ed taken most by how passé it seemed.

Peel shrugged and picked up another cookie. "Only a maybe for now.

But hell, New-Am might roll out the welcome mat no strings attached if they heard we knocked off a Regime bank in these lowly parts. It would be an easy in and out thing . . ." Peel kept talking and Ed kept giving the signals that he was listening, but disrupting the transmission was an inner dialogue increasingly concerned with the exit plans everyone but him seemed to have, and that he was figuring he better start making . . . *Uh-huh, uh-huh*, the anxiety mounting until he snapped out of it at the line, ". . . though maybe we'd get in there and find New-Am already cleaned the place out what with that time machine they got now."

"Time machine?" Ed snorted. "What time machine?"

"Supposedly New-Am built a time machine. You believe it?"

"No."

"Neither do I, but everyone's been talking about it. Anyway, I'll let you know about the bank thing but in the meantime you'd like to take a trip to Elko?"

"That I can do."

"Leo said he's ready if you are. You can wait a couple days or pick it up from Tulay in Manhattan Beach whenever, your choice."

"I'll swing by Tulay's tonight then head up to Leo's office tomorrow if that works," Ed suggested. "Pretty strapped at the moment."

"As you please. But a couple things. Keep your wits around that Leo guy. Know none of us ever liked him and we all know about his family."

"Never had a problem before."

"Just be more careful than usual, for your own sake. Lot of stories coming out of Elko, weird stuff going on up there lately. The New Republic's cleaning the place up and filling in the holes."

"Yeah?"

"Looks like they're getting ready to push the border south again."

WITH THE DETAILS agreed upon they issued their goodbyes and Ed made

his way out into the now new night, spring temperate and serene as he pro-
cured another autocar to take him down to Koreatown, a neighborhood
that had in these late days all but officially—and maybe even officially depending on one's definition of the word—come under Korean occupation.
This transpired mainly as a protective measure following a spike in crime,
currently under control, that resulted from the area's proximity to the I-10
Partition. But it was no obstacle for Ed, who would be waved through after
a brief inspection at Wilshire and Wilton. He always enjoyed his sojourns
to Koreatown; it was one of the more unique Los Angeles micro-colonies,
maintaining a relatively robust economy, ever clean and orderly, and ranking
second to none in safety since the UROKA set up shop.

Ed got out at the Sejong West Lofts, a string of old Spanish-style apartments on Ho Balt Boulevard, where his attention was immediately drawn
to the electric cadence of Tube zaps, almost violent, coming from one of the
second-floor units. He approached the building and stood in the darkness,
unsure if the room he had his sights on was the right one. It wasn't always
the same. But having been in this fix before he knew the best way to find
out was to shimmy partway up the tree out front, then, in what would for
most be a dicey move, make the extended transfer to the balcony. Once up,
Ed looked for a gap in the curtain; unable to find one, he knocked softly on
the glass. Flinging the curtain open so fast he jumped, then unveiling an expression that would have in any other situation made him question whether
or not he'd just accidentally killed someone, was a half-clad girl, though not
the one he was looking for.

She cracked the door. "How'd you get up here?"

"Lynsara—she around?" he asked.

The girl gasp-laughed like she was trying to breathe a ring of moisture
onto the glass, then pointed up. "Next door."

Ed climbed up a floor and repeated the drill, knocking before the curtain
again swung open, this time less quickly but with the intended result, reveal-
ing Lynsara: scratching away at an autoemery board, wearing an indigo robe

he recognized from a different occasion, and unveiling an expression that would have in any other situation also made him question whether or not he'd just accidentally killed someone, but for about the five-hundredth time.

She ran a hand through her hair and shook her head and cracked the door for Ed, watching as he squeezed in and took a seat at the table.

"Look who's back from Newport. So what brings you to Koreatown, Ed?"

"Maybe the hope you wouldn't be here," he replied in earnest, the source of their previous dispute being this gig of hers. "Also couldn't get a hold of you."

"I had my birthchip removed."

"Why?"

"I don't know," she moaned on her way to a corner kitchenette, "something about it was bugging me. I kept getting the feeling someone was using it to control me. Some people say they can do that you know. Drink?"

"They say a lot of things," sinking down in the chair and leaning his head back until it pressed flush against the wall. "A potent one."

"What's wrong?" She reached down to the bottom cupboard. Ed watched her from the corner of his eye and in so doing forgot he was asked a question. "So?" she reinquired mid-pour.

"Nothing, was on my way out."

"Mr. Deathwish," sung to the tune of a song he couldn't put his finger on. "I don't think I know anyone who leaves the Binaries, and I bet most of those people don't even know they can. Then there's *Eh-dee*, who seems to saunter into Cartelville on a weekly basis. You're gonna run out of lives one day, Ed."

"People make it out to be worse than it is. There's nice parts. Oriental parts. Just have to know where you're going. No one ever gives me any trouble . . ." rambling until Lynsara brought the drinks over and set them on the table, in the process catching Ed giving the virtsim in the corner a prolonged look.

16

"What?"

"How's that thing work anyway?"

"It's not real, it's just a trick."

"I know, but—"

"—But drop it, Ed."

They sipped their drinks in silence, returned to the birthchip discussion, had another drink then one more after that, and were in the due course of time staring separately but together at the ceiling, each aware, or in partial acceptance of the probability, that the distance between them was now likely irreconcilable, despite shared hopes, never mutually conveyed, that it might bring them back together.

"Do you remember when we met?" she rolled on her side to ask. Ed turned and said *Yeah* without saying. It wasn't that long ago, after all. Lynsara had grown up on a farm outside of Medford, Oregon that was annexed during the Northwest Chinese Province's southward expansion. Her family had finally given up and decided to relocate to the New Republic, but Lynsara—then sixteen, raised on the Tubes and thus having consumed a toxic brew of fictionalizations about the unpastoral world—had become a staunch anti-neoseparatist and refused to go with them, electing instead to set out on her own, destined or ordained, for where else but the Angel City Diversitopia she'd heard so much glowing information about. She'd been in town less than a day when by a chance roll of love's wild dice did the paths of swain and dame make their crossing. "I was just going for a jog on Santa Monica, minding my own business, when those guys grabbed me and dragged me into the cemetery and tried to rape me."

"There's a Little Pakistan inside Little Armenia."

"I was screaming, trying to get them off me—*oh*, Ed—I was so scared. Then," her eyes thinning, "out of nowhere, I see this guy come up from behind with a golf club and *bam*. There were like five of them, right?" It was six. "But you were like a ninja," snuggling in. "Though I still don't understand why you were hanging out in the cemetery."

"Told you, artificial turf in there," Ed, too, thinking back on the day, re-opening his mouth to mention, then figuring it would be prudent to omit, the part about it being his best 9-iron that really got raped that night.

"If New-Am wasn't such an evil neoseparatist dictatorship I'd tell you to join the army up there. Things are getting scary. Who knows what they're going to do now that they have a time machine."

"Heard about that too huh."

"Everyone's been talking about it."

"Oh, yeah." Ed popped up, recalling a thing or three that had been on his mind. "Did you ever look into that job I told you about?"

Lynsara scoffed. "That *job* that pays a tenth of what I make now?"

"It's something . . . something other than this."

"*Eh-uh-Ed* . . . being a virtgirl isn't that bad. The money's good, I'm safe, and it's better than being out on the street or in some Hollywood harem. You know how hard it is to make a living in this crazy town, we have to do what we have to do."

"I guess," despondently, about ready to at least outwardly let the Virtgirl Question go for good. "You remember how I told you I was trying to get a spot on the Eastern Circuit?"

"You found a sponsor? That's great, Ed! You played amazing in Newport, I knew you'd catch that break soon. You were doing that face again but I told you I think it's cute. So who's the sponsor?"

"No . . . no," Ed muttered. "No sponsor. That didn't work out. But I've been hearing about the new region in Siberia. Might be a step in that di-rection, geographically speaking. I was thinking we could maybe move over there together."

Lynsara sighed, "And what are we going to do over there?"

"Start new lives, like everyone else is doing."

"Grow up, Ed . . . Siberia?"

"Or wherever. We have to get out of the FPSC, out of this city. Every-one's already gone or leaving and now people are saying we're about to get overrun."

"Ed—*uh*. That's just neoseparatist propaganda, New-Am foreign meddling. We're safe between the Binaries and the Sureños keep order on the outside. It's not perfect, but they say it's getting better."

Ed exhaled, the extended release, *keep-it-together-man* type less effective than billed, trying to make sense of a world that seemed to be collapsing in on itself, unsure of what was going on and what to do next, and in the absence of a solution fading out a little more, whispering as he got up to go, "They always do."

THE NAMCHOKE BOSA ran Ed down to the Pico-Union Checkpoint where he crossed the I-10 Partition and purchased a ticket at Metro Center. The rules about who could pass between the walls were not always hard and fast, and while straying beyond them was typically an unwise decision, especially come nightfall, Ed was more acclimatizable than most. Jammed into the corner of a crowded car his focus wavered between the quasi-X-rated fwerking videos playing on the wallscreens to the dejected faces poking out of strange regalia standard in far-away lands—in serapes and sarees, baniyans and turbans, black niqabic phantoms—all ungracefully assembled in this metal box barreling toward Manhattan Beach, though it was Ed, now as always, who looked the most out of place. An honor that never went unnoticed.

He flinched upon feeling a pull on his leg. His attention shifted downward to a young mendicant in a motorized wagon who was holding up a chip-reader that was attached to a deformed arm, if one could call it that. "Créditos Sociales?" the child squeaked up. Ed said *No* and shooed him away as the train hit the afterburners, rattling rough on the tracks through a series of blackouts, bursting into warp speed and thundering into El Segundo, his eyes closing in the flashing light, his focus turning briefly to a song trickling down from a speaker above his head—a pleasant sound with pleasant words, singing: *Oh, what a night . . .*

And what a night it was.

Outside Valley Station a gala was reverberating through the streets of South Bay, replete with feasts of sugarbread spread across folding tables, oversized familias wedged into plastic furniture around residencies and storefronts, the beats of old Nortec, more trash than cans. Ed received the customary barrage of stares as he pushed through the crowd on his way to the Sureños Highland headquarters, located in the old City Hall building. Upon arrival he was greeted cordially by the armed la banda members out front and welcomed into the remains of a party, or perhaps just those of a normal day at the office. Kids in colorful outfits ran around the table on which the leftovers were situated, by now surely lukewarm and iffy gastric-wise eats Ed politely turned down after a tacitly discouraging gesture was made. He was led back to the office where Tulay was sitting low behind a desk rocking anxiously back and forth with his fingers steepled in front of his face, which was covered almost entirely in tattoos. Although an out-wardly intimidating figure, Tulay was reputedly fair and a respectable mem-ber of his community. He was one of the regional leaders of the Sureños mega-gang, a group that controlled vast swaths of the city and differenti-ated themselves by wearing blue, a tailored relic from their merger with the LAPD decades prior.

"Edmundo." Tulay stretched across the desk to shake his hand then snapped his fingers at an obese man in sunglasses who was standing against the wall and on command shoveled a bag their way, which Tulay caught and placed in front of Ed. "Wey was en fuego down in Nuevopuerto. But you were doing this face, a face like a—how do I describe it . . ."

". . . Like a cornered downy?"

"Yeah yeah, like that."

"So I've been hearing. Anyway, today a holiday or something?"

"Nah," Tulay said, grabbing a yellow-dressed girl, one of his daughters, as she was running around the desk behind him and propping her up in his lap. "Normal day at the office. Poco mierda today, unfortunately."

"The explosion earlier? Never got the details."

"Somali rebel force moving on turf, blew up a chemical plant in Covina."

"On purpose?"

"Accident, is the word. New-Am's been shippín em in here from Minnesota by the thousands lately. And you know where they're planning on resettling them, don't you?" pausing till Ed shook his head in the negative. "Wanna send them up there to between the—*the* . . . tha whatchucallit."

"The Binaries," Ed completed for his host.

Years earlier crime and sundry factors led to stretches of Interstate 10 from the Pacific Ocean inland being converted into a partition, with the same going for the 101 north and east of the Santa Monica Mountains. This helped protect a sizeable chunk of property and by and large restricted movement in and out of the triangular zone between the two partitions, an area informally known as *the Binaries*. . . .

"*Thassit.*" Tulay squinted and aimed an ear at Ed, fingers beckoning, requesting a more thorough explanation. "Why you call it that ageen?"

"Because it's between what used to be the I-10 and the I-101," Ed clarified, "ones and zeros, you know, binary numbers."

Tulay stared dead-eyed at him; a deep inhale waxed into a slow nod. "Binary numbers," he repeated, "I see," kissing his daughter on the cheek then letting her go. "As I was saying though, we try not to play sides and got our own thing going on, our own problems. There are a multitudo of parties we have to work with and try to please, but it's getting tricky to do so diplomatically, to negotiate I mean, administratively, of course. New-Am is putting a lot on the table and they're set on flushing out the crooks hiding out up there in the Hills. We ain't taking up arms for Old-Am no more and New-Am's looking unstoppable anyway and now people are even talking about a time machine. Look, all I'm saying is listen—I know the Binaries are locked down and there's no shortage of security in there. But we friends, Edmundo, so I'm warning you . . .".

Ed was getting the message now, agua-clear. "People have been talking about the Libancien losing control in the FPSC lately. This a heads up . . . ," he asked, halting for a second, "that things are about to get a lot worse?"

"It's a get outta town, *ése*! New-Am wants to deliver a deathblow to Hollywood and the smut biz and we ain't standing in they way no longer. We just trying to funnel these people north or keep em in Afritown 'cause that's all we can really do. But they spillín over big time. There's too many people here now. They're tearing up Burbank."

"Heard they did a number on one of the studios," Ed, recalling a recent news item that had departed in swift and usual fashion down the Zuckerhole.

"*Ssst!*" Tulay popped up and pointed a pistoled-finger at him. "Lil Slip was there when it went down. Studio punks left the vatos behind to fend for themselves when the rebel force started pouring in like the zombie apocalypse. Cholo said he mowed down a dozen with the Redeemer then carved up a few more with a samurai sword from the set when the clip jammed."

"Jesus," Ed, mostly to himself. "Guess it really is happening."

BATTLING YAWNS IN THE BACKSEAT of the autocar racing him home, Ed's eyes drifted from his clearscreen to the gangland sprawl on the other side of the window, Inglewood to Culver City, most of it a dark dilapidated blur laden with olden earthquake damage and the other everyday marks of blight—homeboys slanging stomped Charm City tar outside of barred-up liquor stores, high-heeled streetwalkers astrut across caged blocks, food carts aglow with Christmas lights—a long stretch of decay before the trademarked vista lighting the way to the walls of the I-10.

Upon arrival, Ed swapped the bag for his sand wedge and a basket of balls and took flight to the back, where a door built into reinforced rampart separated the property from one of the most formidable seventh holes on the planet. Under moonglow spotlight and palm-spider shadows he cleared some debris from the green, groomed the plane down to a firm fuzz with the reel mower, and hopped into one of the adjoining bunkers—slow-rolling through form, popping the first ball out onto the sand, then rearing back and through in a nocturnal pirouette.

Launching one after the other, collecting the balls, and doing it again: this rite of the witching hour carried out by the left behind, the scattered and surrounded, never with a say, only bestowed the fallout by the moral and the pious—those here before, and in their time certain they were right, but those here no more—their creations left to him: Ed of Greater Wilshire. . . .

THE NEXT DAY, another semi-contaminated Southern California stunner, Ed took the T-Loop to the transit terminal in San Bernardino, a city the municipal government had some years earlier renamed Nuevo Mazatlán, and there purchased a ticket for the bullet train to Elko. He ambled about the station, being a tad early, from small distraction to small distraction, watching his pockets as much as his surroundings before parking in front of a soundless wallscreen a jump-step from his path to the tracks. On it were the sprightly faces of News-Tube, doing a story on L.A. titled: *Coming Together: Why diverse communities make Los Angeles the city no one wants to leave.* . . . Ed had never spent much time in front of the Tubes since everyone he'd ever trusted had told him not to, advice that was often followed up with an added assurance that he would thank them when he was older, which he now was, and at a mature enough stage to appreciate the value of such wisdom. It was a reality, or a version of one, glaringly antithetical to his own. "The city no one wants to leave," he uttered under his breath while glancing back at the crowded terminal—a sentiment evidently not shared by the Indian community of the greater megaregion, of which an impressive block seemed to be right there before him in a retina-burning sari spectrum, with the double-digit families, clucking frantically and attending to suitcase stacks high as vending machines, it would appear, ready to cut their stay short and take the Rajasthani caravan, and with any luck the scent to boot, back on the road. It seemed the word, in line with the warnings from the day before, was starting to get around.

Ed boarded the train early and was making his way down the center aisle when he noticed what might as well have been a Masd orchid springing from the Death Valley sands. A few more forward steps gave him a better look at the young girl the crown of red hair belonged to: no older than sixteen, possibly a runaway. "Mind?" he said, hand out to the seat beside her. She smiled up and shook her head so Ed stuffed the bag under the seat, his initial thoughts being: *pretty* . . . *too* pretty to be anywhere near San Bernardino. There was an odd look to her, but it was one Ed was familiar with having grown up around kids reliant on a fixed diet of the Libancien's pronormalizing line of debiasizers.

He sat down and introduced himself. She said her name was Nitty. Hair cast aflame in the forenoon light, she then asked if he was "going to the rally."

"Rally?" Ed wasn't aware of one.

"Oh." Her smile sank; she turned away. "Don't tell me you're going to New-Am or I might have to ask you to move."

"Nope," Ed matter-of-factly on his ease into the seat, "I'm attending to some business in Elko. What rally are you talking about?"

"You didn't hear?" Her shoulders angled back toward him, eager to inform. "The Free Society Foundation is holding a demonstration. There's going to be all these events, speakers like Esther Antivory, a real revolutionary atmosphere. We're protesting the neoseparatist policies of the breakaway republic."

"Ah," one of *those* rallies. Never seemed to be any shortage of them and Ed had attended one or two himself as a passive observer, apolitical as he ordinarily tried to be. "You should be careful," he cautioned, "I knew a girl who disappeared at one of those things."

"Umm . . . you *know*," Nitty practically scolding him, "you aren't sup-posed to use that word, right?" But Ed didn't know, and his expression il-lustrated as much. "'*Girl*' . . . it's monoformist, not to mention a borderline Misgender Violation."

Ed raised a strong brow, unsure if there was an element of sarcasm he was failing to pick up on. "Where did you say you were from again, Nitty?"

"I uh—" She looked away, embarrassed, fiddling with her locks. "Up north." Then hushed, "Bodega Bay."

"The Bodega Bay Colony? Wow," Ed in partial awe, "so you live in the dome? Your parents must be really important people."

"*Ugh*," she wallowed out with a type of angst exclusive to teenage girls, "it's terrible. I hate it . . ." *Runaway confirmed.* "What about you? Where are you from?"

"L.A."

The mere utterance of those two smoothly conjoining letters activated something inside of her. She clapped once, her eyes big as Ginger Golds, sparkling in manic bloom. "L.A.?! *Aw-oh* . . . how great is it? All I ever hear is how diverse it is—tell me," latching onto his forearm, "is it as great as they say it is on the Tubes? I bet it's even better."

Ed's own eyes, out of shock more than anything, growing to match her own. True Believers were a rare find within an imprecise couple-hundred-mile radius of Los Angeles, and while anyone still living in the area was undoubtedly the progeny of True Believers, day-to-day circumstances had ground them down into Half Believers and Quarter Believers at most, with Ed being no exception. Her grip tightened. "Yeah, L.A., it's not too bad. . . . But, Nitty," lowering his voice with intent to reason, "the Tubes don't always paint an accurate picture of the world. Los Angeles can be a dangerous place unless you live behind the walls, and these days it's not all that safe behind them, either."

"Dangerous?" shaking her head at this obvious falsehood. "That's just a stereotype."

"Most people, people like us, they left L.A. a long time ago. I was gone for a few weeks and came back and it was like a whole different place. To be honest," he chuckled, "I wish I lived up there in that dome like you do."

"You shouldn't talk like that," she whipped back, "it makes you sound like a neoseparatist."

"No. Nono. I'm just saying, the real world, it's not like what you see on the Tubes. And I know we aren't supposed to talk about it, right . . . but a lot of people say New-Am actually isn't that bad."

While evaluating her reaction Ed realized he had waded into waters one was usually wise to stay out of, and he received a response he knew he should have been anticipating from the start. "Isn't? that? bad? I could report you for saying that. Neoseparatism is the greatest evil of our time, duh. What did you say your name was again? Egg?"

Times, *well*—they had become what they had become; similar to other times, aside from stage and age, in that there were words you couldn't say, things you couldn't talk about, *people* you couldn't talk about. And as normal as it seemed in the then and there, especially among those who simply went about their business as they always had, as they could only be expected to do, often present, however hidden among the dissonance of the day, was a feeling or a sense that *something* was wrong, even if discovering the truth about exactly *what* that was, was, for many, a bridge too far. "Ed . . ." low. "You're right," eyes around to the seat in front, "don't know what I was thinking." He then recited the motto in the hope that doing so would spare him any further inconvenience . . . "Diversity is Our Greatest Strength."

The ride thereafter was quiet and in its own way relaxing, though the longer he went without hearing back from Leo, the more stress began to build. Not a good sign, but it was probably nothing. Ed arrived at the station outside of town and took the shuttle toward the center in a fugue-like state as the sun was gearing up for its fall behind the mountain backdrop, in aloof appraisal of the broken machinery strewn about town, the rotting houses and uncut lawns fading by, the squat-families that were anything but busy around it all, when the wall made its first appearance on the horizon, far away still but visible.

He held in the tiny inlet button on his ringport—the Everything Machine of this day: a simple smart-ring that stored within it the information and software applications one might need or use in the course of their daily activities, and an all-in-one virtual office and media center that displayed via projection something known as a *clearscreen*, which, owing to a breakthrough or two in holography, was rather pliant, capable of expanding from the size of a traditional phone screen to that of a small theater, though in public it was generally considered rude to make it any larger than ones' virtual affairs required—checking his messages one last time before his stop. Still no response from Leo.

Upon reaching the center of town, Ed took in a deep breath of the high-altitude air and an extended view of the remote alpenglow, then embarked on the last leg of his journey to Leo's office. Elko had been a dusty old cowboy and mining town where little if anything had ever gone on before the wall went up; and while afterward people started coming from all over just to see it, it wasn't until it was found to have some holes here and there in and out of which goods could be unlawfully transported that, seemingly overnight, a comprehensive network of favelas arose along its perimeter. But Ed had nothing to do with any of that; he was just a guy giving something to another guy and couldn't set foot on the other side even if he wanted to.

He passed Goldie's biker bar, the pool hall, and the Tiki Hut—the slots and cocktails haunt next to Leo's plain-brown Mesoamerican-style office building—where he then made the decision to stop into and get drunk real fast at once the job was done. Ed rang the bell at the entrance and looked into the camera. He entered after the buzz and walked down the thin hallway, whistling and knocking on the wall as he neared the open door of the office, out of which light about the size of a door was being projected onto the opposite-side wall. Turning into the room, he met with a pair of welcoming grins, neither of which belonged to Leo, wouldn't you know, but to two men in uniforms. Ed made a move back toward the entrance but pulled up a few steps into the retreat upon being told to stop.

They met him in the hallway. One removed the bag from his shoulder and motioned for him to put his arms up so the other could scan him down.

"What are you doing on the outside?"

"I'm not a citizen. I'm from, I'm not from in there."

The officers looked at each other. "You live in Old-Am?"

"I live in Old-Am."

"What's in the bag?" the officer fiddling with the lock asked.

"I don't know, it's not my bag."

"Whose bag is it?"

"It's Romero's bag."

"Romero?"

"Who's Romero?"

"Bob Romero." Ed was unsure how he had arrived at this name, having never, from what he could in the moment recall, known or known of anyone who went sur or given by either *Bob* or *Romero*. "I found his bag at the station. He asked me to drop it off here . . . least I think it was here," giving the hallway a close inspection.

They escorted Ed to Leo's office. The bag was tossed onto the table and Ed was pointed to a chair. "Need to scan your birthchip." Ed tilted his head to the side and stretched his shirt to expose the small fleshcode, then released the fabric that shrunk back on its own after the beep. "Leo Sackler . . . name ring a bell?"

"Never heard of him," Ed said as the officers, together behind a clearscreen, read over his information. One pronounced his name slow and in full as Ed took a peep at the shields on their jackets: OBS—*Outer Border Security.* "Long way from home, Mr. Loxley. What are you doing up here?"

"Visiting a friend."

"Your friend Leo Sackler? Know he's also from L.A."

"It's a big city."

One of the officers sat down and lifted the bag up and down a few times while juggling his head as if weighing the contents in his mind. "I'd give myself good odds if forced to guess what's in this bag, and unless you can convince me in the next thirty seconds that that's *not* what's in it, you're taking a ride."

ED EXITED THE BUILDING in wrist-pins and was placed graciously in the back of a squad car parked in plain view on the other side of the building, which he would never have missed had he bothered to simply peek around the corner. They flew through the clear infant night and parked in an underground garage then made a pilgrimage to the sixth floor of the station, Ed walking in front with his head down until he was ordered to stop. The door to a holding room was opened and he was nudged inside. It was small, with two chairs and a table. One of the officers trailed him in and placed the bag on the table before the door was closed and locked and Ed was left to think over the plan. He didn't have one. After giving it some more thought, he still didn't have one. And by the time the door was opening again, he was expecting something beyond the worst.

There were three men this time—one a technician who went to work right away on the lock while the other two, both heavyset and wearing suits, stood in the middle of the room, looking over what he assumed was information about him while bickering with each other in thick, post-metropolitan accents. "My name is Detective Al Cabrini and this is Detective Arnold Cabrini," one said, neither yet giving him any direct attention. "So how's our evening?"

"Had better ones."

"Sure a that."

They remained quiet until the technician cracked the lock. Detective Arnold Cabrini leaned over and looked in the bag. "Imagine my shock," he said. "Why don't you start by telling us how you know Leo Sackler?"

"Through people."

"That's precisely the type of person we are trying to permanently remove from this continent," Detective Al Cabrini said as he waddled over and sat in the chair across from Ed and crossed his arms. Big pork-diet guy with gray-tipped Paulie-wings of hair and ever-doubtful eyes that were fixed as a tick on Ed. "This is serious-uh," sniffling, chin drifting up, "serious stuff. The penalties are . . . you are. . . ." The Detective hammered an elbow onto the table and closed his eyes and shook his head. "Who are you . . . I know you," chopping air. "*Wuh-wuh*-wait—Arn," turning back, "name again."

"Eddy Loxley, idiot. Pay attention."

"Will you shut up? Loxley—*yeah*, you're eh-uh from eh-uh what's the place—Orange County."

"No," Ed worming up in his seat, sensing a potential opening, "but I played in the Newport Open at Pelican Hill last week."

"Right, that's right, I caught the end of the second round," Detective Al Cabrini, loose. "You played in the L.A. Under 18 last year, too . . . won it by, what was it, nine strokes." It was eleven. "Arnie . . . *Arn*—earth to Arnie," Detective Al Cabrini called back, "you remember me telling you about that? That was him right here, Eddy Loxley. I told you about that."

Detective Arnold Cabrini, without looking up, "See that talking thing you do sometimes it like makes me deaf. And you know I hate golf. It's boring."

"Boring?" Facing Ed again, "*Boring*. . . . Hell are you doing with this stuff up here in Elko? Old enough for the next level now, aren't you?"

"Technically. But the way things are, opportunities just haven't been there."

"In Old-Am, sure, but what about the Eastern Circuit, the Southern Circuit—always tournaments down there."

"Hard to get on without a sponsor and whoever's left in Old-Am's struggling. Game's in the tank. And it's a lot to put on others, expectations and all."

"Gotta point," Detective Al Cabrini, more serious. "Every time I saw you on the Tubes last couple years you were blowing them out like *boom* one after the other. Remember seeing you on there one time when I was trying to get my son into the game too and telling that *ragazzo*, 'Watch this kid . . . 's got something special, this guy.'" The Detective shook his head and cackled and parted with a breath, a breath of empathy, empathy Ed was in dire need of. "Arn," he yelled back. "Arnie, hey."

"What? what is it?"

"I'muna wrap this one up."

"So wrap it up, wrap away, wrap it around your goddamn neck."

"Requires your departure, *coglione*." Detective Al Cabrini turned back to Ed. "L.A., huh," he said as the door was closing, to which Ed made a clicking noise in affirmation. "Sometimes I forget we still have people stuck down there. Rough?"

"It's not too bad, just have to know the right people. Money can be hard to come by, though. Honest money."

"I can imagine. L.A. was one of the first to go, so most of us got out of there ages ago. And it's not really my department, but if I recall correctly, L.A. is also the new temporary resettlement location for the former Midwest Somalian population. Think we're sending them up there to between the . . . *the*—"

"—The Binaries."

"Binary numbers."

"Ones and zeroes."

"So you're planning on leaving soon, I hope. And by soon I mean soon like yesterday."

"Trying to figure something out. It's just, I don't know where else to go."

Detective Cabrini spread his arms. "Eddy . . . c'mon," implying the obvious. "The fifteen years of service will blow right by, trust me, we all went through it."

"Not sure I'm a good fit, Detective Cabrini."

Maybe it was youth or the Old-Am consensus or the social circles he'd always run in, but Ed would sooner start auctioning off organs than sign up to spend fifteen years in the New-Am military; though, frightening a prospect as it was, politics aside, deep down, on a gut level, part of him knew it was the right decision to make.

"Give you some di-ci-*plin*, something to live for, and there's no greater fight than this. War's automated these days anyways—pushing buttons, man, *buttons*—you can do that. Wind's at our backs, too, whole Midwest is cleaned out and we aren't stopping anytime soon."

Ed tried to look sorry, but there was no budging on this one. "I'm just not a military guy, Detective."

"Yeah right well," signaling for Ed to stand, "one day you'll realize that this was never about you, that it was about something much bigger than you. You're gonna learn that the hard way out there on your own, but you'll learn it eventually." Detective Cabrini removed Ed's wrist-pins, tossed them onto the table, and took a step back. In a chirpier tone, "Can't say I don't understand where you're coming from, though. It's a testament to life that kids like yourself are still coming outta Hades halfway sane." He looked away and made a few backhanded scram-waves in the direction of the door, "Out, on, go—take a walk."

They left the room and walked together to the elevator, where the top button was hit and up at an even pace they rose. The door opened onto a skywalk whose path was pointing in an unswerving blur toward the frost-topped mountains ahead, distant as grand, knuckled up under the star-showered night. They strolled across at a slow pace and in silence. It dawned a bit late on Ed that he was, in fact, standing on top of the wall, straddling the two sides of the former Republic. Far afield a golden city was visible; between it and themselves were trees in sway as far as the eye could see. All was mute except for the natural push of the wind.

"You guys have a troposhield?"

"Waste of resources in the sticks. Holes unavoidably pop up with this much space and budget fencing, but that's why the Cabrini's are running the show out here now . . . we plug holes, often after we put people like Leo Sackler in 'em."

"Is that what happened to Leo?"

"It's the desert, Eddy. If someone on the outside's causing a problem normally they just get DBD'd, but Mr. Sackler was a special case."

"DBD'd?"

"Deathed by droned. We happen to be in the middle of a big project, cleaning up the Line and locking it down before we make the next big push south."

"Border's taken seriously up here."

"Most of the rest takes care of itself."

"So it's safe inside?"

"Safe, free, you bet."

"Out of reach of the Googlopticon?"

"We took that thing out years ago. We're still looking for the one in Europe, though."

"Shouldn't be too hard to find now that you guys got a time machine."

Detective Cabrini stopped and swung around. "What's with the *you guys*? It's the *us*. Already talk about that?"

"Everyone knows about it."

"I don't think it works like that, think it only goes one way. But a people of science, freed up, are making things happen you wouldn't believe are possible. Shame you don't want to be a part of that, Eddy."

"I'm trying to find a way over to that new region in Siberia, maybe get on the Eastern Circuit from there."

Detective Cabrini was looking away. "Neh. That's no good," he said. He turned, giving Ed his full attention as he took a step in, placed a meaty hand on his shoulder, and looked deep into his eyes. In a hiss, "I want to help you, Eddy."

"You do?"

"Wouldn't be much of a man if I didn't. But you gotta do me a favor first," sitting on the last part while Ed mumbled *Okay* in the absence of choice. Detective Cabrini scanned the vicinity to see if anyone was watching, then he crouched and started wiggling around with his arms out. "Been following the swing-bot and things seemed to be working," he explained into the rotation, "but I lost like thirty yards and am havin all kinds of back problems now."

Ed took a step back to get a better look at the Detective's swing stance. "Go through the whole motion again."

"Like," rearing back and following through slowly, "this."

"Lot of weight on your left heel on the backswing."

"Course, for resistance, extra torque," his eyes darting up and down. "Right?"

"No. Builds up too much tension. Might work for the kids but you're a big guy who's already dealing with a limited range of motion. Lift your heel and move your hips."

"Free it up?"

"Free it up. That's probably why you're having back problems, too—here." Ed leaned over, left arm out, right aimed at his feet. "Stop trying to drive it to Nuevo Phoenix. Speed isn't force. Lift your left heel on the backswing and work into it . . . *into* the left heel . . . *into* the left heel. See how I'm doing that?"

"Yeah I see but I thought that was how they did it in the old days."

"Sure, but . . ." Ed, nodding to the distant darkness, "it's still the best way."

Detective Cabrini gave it a couple test runs then popped up. "Goddamn, Eddy." He slapped Ed on the arm and they continued on. "You belong inside these walls, and I know you'll join us here in time one way or another. In a perfect world you could get in without having to put on a uniform, but this isn't a perfect world, far from it. With the Wars of Reclamation in

Europe and this mess with Old-Am lingering on, we need people like your-self more than ever. And we have to fight for everything now, because we lost it all when we stopped fighting the last time. However," forcing them into another stop, "there are always alternative options. Things are pretty con-nected up here, and I'm a pretty connected guy myself, so I happen to know some people who are high up on the Southern Circuit—high up on down to the Cape. We're always looking for representatives, people who can achieve small victories here and there, PR and whatnot. And we need heroes. From what I hear, it can be a little rough on the Southern Circuit, but if you've been able to keep afloat in L.A. for this long I figure it'll be a walk in the park. So tell you what—don't want to join up, suit yourself. I'm gonna work something out for you regardless. Put you in a position where you'll have a chance to succeed. How's that sound to you, Eddy?"

Somewhere out in the middle of desert nowhere a lone firework, the kind that popped like champagne and was peculiarly enough off-season to make you wonder where it came from, burst and crackled out, the two partitioned worlds represented on each side of the wall, neither of which Ed understood, once again provided choices he didn't feel ready to make, and though there was no assurance of anything, especially in the words of some gangster play-ing federal agent for the side he'd been told his whole life not to trust, they still sounded like an overture of a thousand strings striking through the dark heavens of the night above a black planet stranded in a sunless universe that hadn't paid the electric bill in lightyears. The words he'd been waiting for.

II

We can't all be brave men

—THE WHISKY PRIEST

UPON ENTERING PARAÍSO from the south Calle Comalcalco winds unevenly into town through concrete and green then straightens out and runs into a roundabout, in the middle of which is a monument of a giant blue crab. Behind the blue crab is a bridge that leads over the Río Seco River and connects to a street named Benito Juárez; two gray-slated steps above the unsweepable layer of sand that rests continuously atop its granite sets are rows of bodegas that line the street until it opens into the square. Here, the Church of San Marcos and its two psychedelic candy towers govern the small plaza; at their tops, nestled inside Iberian-crowned cupolas, are bells with rings suitable for the still setting they loom over. Mariachis in snaps and fringe pass through to offer entertainment, songs to lift the spirits of the downtrodden, make the kids dance, carrot them away from family members coldshouldering cries for churros and ice cream. Taxis form an idle beachward line outside the discotheque, living wage fares acquired primarily by getting visitors to the airport and back, making little on offer in between; they often just say *No*, huddled under the shade of the tulipan tree in constant collusion. At their backs is the playground, another diversion for the madres and an indispensable feature of the square, along with the clock tower and the conditionally mobile food carts whose proprietors are sombrero'd over Cancun Casual—those corn-cup hawkers, old sidewalk squires, venders like their fathers of an ancient staple, that maize off-the-cob *. . . grain of the sur.*

Calle Comalcalco continues north through town and bends right in bits until it's parallel with the coastline, paving forth from there a flora-flanked stretch that thins the filth out the farther you get as the kicked-up buggy dust induces more cough than choke, the curbs look less like a mechanic's fingernails, and scanter become the half-vacated shacks roofed with defunct satellite dishes, the sharpie-on-cardboard signs, and the paint-shredded walls of the pollerias and tortillerias and pescaderias standard as sunlight here. Deeper into the efflorescent Tabasco jungle Calle Comalcalco makes bridges over waterways filtering the sea into the Mecoacán Lagoon and passes wall-guarded rubble, swinging banana plantations, and lime-blazed acres of ten-story-tall palm trees frond-blasted inland by years of Gulf storms. Six miles up is an intersection crammed with fruit stands and rolling canteens and smoky open-air asada stops where another street, Calle Madero, branches left, belts around the bank, and hooks into the Barra de Chiltepec, an island-like peninsula between the ocean and the lagoon.

A thin strip of land offers the only way in and out through iron gates that safeguard the neighborhood inside, a friendly little place that goes by the name of San Padua Grove. The residents are post-nationals, exiles and deserters, who more often than not hail from somewhere on the North American continent, and more specifically from somewhere within the former borders of the former Republic of America. They build houses here. They run businesses. Their community is a reflection of customs passed down by forebears and a shared civility adapted over millennia, wed with a bit of know-how picked up winging it through hypermodernity. They could find solace in any number of locations, but San Padua Grove offers something different: an equatorial climate beyond the grasp of the Libancien, greater bang for the Old Globobuck, and relative peace on the lam. That was what Mexico was for, after all . . . little had changed in that regard.

Out on Calle Comalcalco again, one more sand-brushed mile up, hugging the coast on lightly raised ground, is the San Padua Golf Club. The villas stuccoed in Mediterranean Revival are modest, with quarters dispersed around the two main buildings: the clubhouse and the spa. These are separated by a dome and a downsized Corinthian-columned replica of the Pantheon, colloquially known as *the Pantheon*, which, save for the cozy atrium'd heat-reprieve inside, was designed to maximize viewing pleasure; and indeed, when the sun was low in descent, when the angle was just right, as it was from near and far—intentionally, of course—viewers were compelled to stop and point, to say: *Look.* . . . It was a feeling, an inborn aesthetic, some kind of atomic valuation, because in this remote jungle or wherever they happened to find themselves, be the land theirs or anyone else's, be they few or many, fugitives or the kin of kings, they did what came naturally and recreated their civilization.

But what happened to their own? After yet another crop of leaders had been deceived into falling at the hands of their own cousins, the Piper lured the children of the West out from under their aegis and announced that they were in the dawn of liberation: *Give me just one generation*, he said, *and I'll transform the whole world.* . . . And they were it. Hypnotized by a tune of love and programmed by the Spectravision, they were informed that a new age of universalism was on the horizon, one that would finally produce peace and equality, tolerance and diversity—all things alien to the mores of old. They disavowed their ancestors and shook their heads at the past as they built their new global community and embedded its values into the minds of their children. Identity was to be viewed as a construct, human difference merely superficial; the coming Equalitarian Era would know no borders, it would make no class distinctions; all would be free, pleasure would be abundant, and this progression would elevate humanity to heights previously unimaginable. Best of all: everyone was invited.

What they failed to realize, however, was that the rest of the world did not share these values and had little interest in their fanciful vision of the future. There were times of pushback, but the floodgates had been opened, the damage done. It was a migration of proportions never before seen, of rich and poor from every corner of the earth storming the West like a human stampede, in a controlled demolition veiled by moral theater so grandiose it could have only been cooked up by the Devil Himself. Before long their communities ceased resembling their own: they were no longer safe, efficient, or European, but crime-ridden, corrupt, and foreign. As the darkness spread it began to dawn on the youth of new that their parents had been led down a path that distorted their own natural order, disconnected them from their past, and unleashed war upon the generations to come. It was those children, and then their own and so forth—now outnumbered, muzzled, and under the nose of tyranny—who shook their heads at the past as they struggled to preserve what remained, take back what had been given away, and rebuild what had been destroyed. And there it began. . . .

BACK IN SAN PADUA GROVE, Ed was just waking up. The day was Saturday. The glass on the nightstand had a thick misty film. The jug of Jarritos was empty. The bottle of mescal, almost, but not quite. There was a minefield of ankle socks on the floor. A shirt was riding the fan. A gang of flies had discovered the remains of last night's chanchamito take-out. The room was a godawful mess. Bladder pressure had kept Ed half-awake the last hour, but he'd been suppressing the discomfort to get the extra rest in. Hadn't really worked. He finally rose and hobbled to the bathroom—hunched forward, head throbbing, eyes glazed over, not yet ready to accept the light streaming in through the windows. His hand planted against the wall and his eyes re-closed upon aim-alignment. He would use this brief moment to shut down all nonessential processes and drift out again; an extra twenty-second respite at most, but any opportunity felt too good to pass up.

Most mornings began like this.

While no longer quite so young, Ed still possessed his natural, stately appearance, but could look, minus a shirt at the wrong point of an exhale, awfully expectant. He'd fallen on hard times. Following a heroic run on the Southern Circuit, one that made him a recognizable name among aficionados and minor fans alike, his game fell apart. Whether from carnal distractions, overindulgence, poor financial decision-making, or a combination of the lot—he'd lost it. Like the future Revenge spiraling down the porcelain gateway at his sight's end . . . it was gone. However, there were still opportunities south of the Trump Fence for someone with Ed's character and skillset, so he'd been able to translate minor prestige into a career hustling holidaymakers and assisting the elderly to par, or thereabouts. It was a living.

Apart from the yellow flicker signifying that he was on his last muffin, the *Comida Ahora*'s lights were all red. "Nota," Ed slurred, "compra comida." He pressed the button, grabbed the muffin, and headed out, onward into the new day, catching a slight bump from the blinding Mexican sun and bleaching dust as he passed the colorful San Padua Grove homes and distributed a few neighborly hellos on his way to the gates. After nodding to the guard, who may or may not have been asleep behind the tinted glare of the booth, if in there at all, Ed jogged across the street and walked the half block to the Community Cart Stop—climbing into the rusty buggy at the front, stating his destination to the autodriver, and promptly falling back asleep.

An announcement snapped him up minutes later, the buggy rolled to a stop, and it was a quick jump up the drive from there. Ed exchanged a casual salute with caretaker Fabio Manilla on his way through the entrance, then, in stride to the red-roofed clubhouse at the end of a paved trail enveloped in an olive sea that included the driving range to his left, greeted post-Canadian fixture and perpetual visor-wearer Shelly Samson as she was entering the downswing. "Little more arch on the tush, Shell." This caused her to miss the ball completely and spin around with her own wrenched momentum. Hands to her hips, "What are you doing up before noon, Ed?" Scanning the check-in screen for appointments, he unexpectedly found one: *Booked the day.* "Name?" *Withheld.* . . . "Hm," Ed sighed, doing a 180 into Club Manager Rico Porter, who did a hand-waving, back-bending *Matrix* [1999]-lean before commenting on Ed's dead-rata breath and letting him know that the appointment in question was waiting in the atrium.

"*Extraño*—never seen him before, said he was from somewhere up north."

"Probably another one of these bozos from Durango," Ed put in before footing it toward the Pantheon.

Standing inside the entryway amid an indoor Eden of vegetation, in a prism-waltz of light, he glanced around the room: at the bar area where the help was doing a poor job of impersonating people at work, then over to the restaurant where Javier Mina the Villahermosa real estate developer was eating brunch, which was all he ever came there to do, when grabbing his eye was a gentleman sitting in the corner next to a golf bag, raising a hand to get his attention: middle-aged, relatively fit, clean-cut and recently shaven, and appropriately dressed, though more in a links theme party or eccentric leisure-tourist way—not a rare sight around these parts, but not all that typical, either.

Rising as he drew near was a man who would introduce himself as one Ernie Lamark. "Pleasure to meet you, Edmund."

"Ed, likewise, Mr. Lamark."

"Ernie," revising his title as he sat and motioned for Ed to do the same. "I was just going over your highlights from Panama a few years ago. One off a perfect round, don't see that every day."

Odd of him to bring that one up, Ed thought. It was the feat he was most proud of, but the one no one seemed to remember; most mentions normally reserved for the albatross in Santiago. "Know what they say about getting the rolls."

"Hard work's reward," smiling like an old friend, his sandy hair sticking out the front of a high-riding brown tweed cap. "If you don't mind me asking, how'd you end up in this place?"

Ed acted like he was mulling it over. It was a good question he didn't have a good answer for. "Seemed nice. Small, scenic. Good restaurants, tightknit community. Lower murder rate."

"So when's the next tournament coming up?"

"I-uh—" was that a jab? "don't bother with those anymore. I'm. Retired."

"Retired? Edmund . . . ," Ernie chuckled, leaving out the words present in his look that said *who are you trying to fool?* It *was* a silly remark for Ed to make, let alone believe, even if part of him actually did. Regardless, he could tell that this fellow, whoever he was, wasn't going to buy it. "That would be a shame if it were true but *I*, don't think it is." Ed tossed a hand up to indicate he wouldn't argue the point further. *Ernie Lamark* he repeated internally so not to forget, thinking: there's something off about this guy, an uncanny valley feeling, too put-together to be in bumtown Mexico unless he was going into hiding or, perhaps, searching for someone already in it. From New-Am, indubitably. "Shall we?"

"I'll grab a cart."

"Let's walk."

"We're modest folk here, Ernie. Won't find an autocaddy between Mérida and Veracruz."

"Who said anything about that? Bag's got a strap, don't it?"

It was a windy day beachside. From the ground at the par-4 first you couldn't miss too far to the left or it was in the treeline if you were lucky and off the ledge if not. Home team first, Ed stepped onto the tee box and drove a ball high down the fairway. For a moment it appeared bound for the trees, but that was just a touch he put on the opener. The ball curved back, hit down on the left side, and took a favorable bounce toward the center.

"Nicely done, Edmund," Ernie exalted. "I won't pretend to be surprised."

Ed was trying not to laugh as Ernie took over his spot in the box and performed a few goofy warmup stretches, looking rather like a carnival hand in the newsies cap, plum-colored vest, and plaid knickers. But a half-minute later, with mechanics that were to his eye flawless, Ernie launched one, high and straight all the way. The ball landed in the center of the fairway two or three yards ahead of his own.

Being a delegate of the Club, Ed was not in a position to pry, but to certify the obvious postulated, "Not here for a lesson." Ernie shook his head in the negative. Ed already had his game-wad out, thumb swiping across tongue, "Then what do we say about two-hundred pesos a hole."

"Didn't come here for that. Legally prohibited anyway."

Hm, stuffing the money back in his pocket. "I don't see anyone watching, but suit yourself." They hoisted the bags over their shoulders and marched into the swelter. "So what *did* you come here for?" Ed, farther downfield.

"I'll get to that. But first, I'm curious what it was like growing up where you did."

"In the Free Pacific State of California?"

"Under the Libancien."

"Normal. Its own kind of normal, I suppose. Older folks had it worse with the Googlopticon always watching over them."

"Do you remember the Deprivileging Camps?"

"I was too young."

"Imagine you learn a lot about the world growing up with the whole thing in your backyard."

Ed deferred the honest answer for after he'd tripoded the bag next to his ball and picked out a club. "It wasn't easy knowing how things used to be, seeing how they used to look, and realizing you missed out," he admitted. "But that's life."

"Least you got out in time. Had a great run down here. Southern Circuit can be rough, or that's what everyone says. I can see how someone could lose their edge with so many distractions."

Ed cuddled up and reared back and hit the pitch and bent his head with it in-flight while slow-holstering the iron until the ball pop-stopped on the right side of the green.

"Not that different from Old-Am down here."

"Same people, why would it be different?"

Ernie took his second shot: a similar pitch that landed on the right side as well, and again a little closer to the hole than Ed's own.

"Fifty, front nine only, just to make it interesting."

"Not an option for me. Doesn't it get tiring being an outsider everywhere you go, though? Forced to live in other peoples' countries?"

"Crazy as it may seem to you, some of us prefer this lifestyle to going all in with neoseparatist ultrafascist extremists."

"Isn't it normal for people to prefer living around their own?"

"Maybe, maybe not, I don't know. I was never much of an ideologue, Ernie."

"Because you were never allowed to be one."

But Ed wasn't sure he'd be one even if he *had* been allowed. Politics just weren't his thing, and that wasn't unusual. He'd always felt the more meaningful the matter the better it was he not be involved. But even if you didn't care for politics, politics always found a way to love you long time. The power of the Libancien's message derived not from force, but subtlety—it spread gradually, slow and steady year after year, each batch of children seasoned a pinch more, the doctrine pushed a little further, woven a little thicker into the cultural fabric, until its ideology was baked in the cake, ubiquitous but imperceptible, just *there*. Even if you didn't care or thought you were above it—*a skeptic of all, a rebel of an age*—it was still all you'd ever known: its values were implanted deep inside of you. . . .

"Look. I'm not an ultrafascist extremist like you, Ernie, but that doesn't make me an apologist for the Libancien. I never believed in the front left or the back right."

"Good, because there is no front left or back right. There's only the historical center—what's always been and was normal long before the two of us came on the scene."

"I just don't have hate like you guys do."

"The Immigration Wars came about because a people hate *you*, Edmund."

"Everyone's hateable. There's good and bad people in every group."

"That may well be true, but it was never the issue. And this isn't about everyone else, it's about us and our future. I know you want to believe the world can be a happy place where everyone lives side by side in harmony, but that's a fantasy, a fantasy that failed, a fantasy that was never supposed to succeed."

"Maybe it could work."

"How'd it work in L.A.?"

"Maybe it just wasn't done right."

"Edmund . . . you sound like a Boomer."

"A *Boomer?*" Ed, miming a pained face as they reached the green. "Easy, man. Jesus."

Although he was not hip to the full context of that particular term, Ed was aware that it was a decidedly harsh insult, denoting a group many had branded, with a grave-stomping-goodbye salute, the *Worst Generation*, the cohort held largely responsible by their descendants for the demise of their civilization, though it was often argued that the fratricidal and crassly named *Greatest Generation* preceding it was even more at fault. A Boomer was an individual characterized by naiveté, myopia, and broad patrimonial failure, someone easily manipulated into accepting romantic illusions about the world wherein they, the open-minded and virtuous, were bringing about an earthly peace that was, alas, only ever a figment of their imagination. They were the most affluent generation to ever grace the plush gardens of the earth, their comfort purchased by the enemy within, by then pulling the cultural strings, who molded them into unwitting surrogates of themselves, convinced them the struggle was over, and told them that all they needed was love—*love . . . it's eee-zee . . .* and it was—for them.

"They were the first Christians of the post-Christian era, and their mediated fantasy played a big part in our downfall. When they came of age we were ninety percent of the population, when they were gone we were around half, left with a civilizational disaster."

—All together, now!

"Ernie," Ed said, sliding his putter out, wanting to be straight with the guy, "I try to keep up with what's going on in the world, but I have a life to live, too. Now, I don't know how everything became the way it did, but maybe we deserved what happened."

"Tell me which of the following seems normal to you, Edmund—being proud of who you are, proud of your people and their accomplishments and wanting to protect those things . . . or being apathetic about their decline and viewing your own punishment as a virtue? Ask yourself . . . *who* benefits from your passivity . . . who gains from you holding this negative opinion of yourself, your people, and your culture? What good does that do you?"

Ed was listening while squaring up for the putt, which he sent on its rolling way for birdie. Just long. "Don't know *who* you're talking about, amigo."

"Then you should take a closer look at who was attacking us—attacking *you*. Who were the main proponents of the Immigration Wars. Who was writing articles about how bad we were and portraying us negatively in the media. Who was funding organizations that labeled us the enemy and sponsoring policies that went against our interests, that were designed to harm us collectively and attacked us whenever we stood up for ourselves. Look at who the gatekeepers were, Edmund . . . it's no secret."

Ed held his tongue until Ernie had completed his birdie attempt, which was on target the whole way and fell in to give him the first hole. "This is all super enlightening, Ernie," he said as they walked together toward it. "And I appreciate your passion—I really do. But why are you telling me all this?"

"Because I want to help you."

Help *him?* That was rich. Ed swiped through an emotive chain that began with the *What help, I don't need any help* phase, followed by the *I wonder what kind of help he's talking about* stage, and ending with the part where—if the sudden spell of nausea from the mescal swishing around in his stomach was any indication, as if on cue—he was forced to acknowledge *I should probably take any help on offer*, in about four seconds, though he made sure that outwardly only the first ever crossed his mind.

"And how are you going to help me?"

"I'm going to offer you an opportunity, Edmund." An *opportunity*. What kind of help was *that?* Ed scoffed, turning and facing Ernie as they pulled up. His expression was sympathetic, and Ed didn't need a mirror to know how he looked at the moment: his already-thinning hair awry, a bit heavy from all the horse-meat chilaquiles, not even off the first and leaking agave across the arid Gulf-side plains. Whatever opportunity this Ernie Lamark fellow was referring to, and Ed had a hunch, he was pretty sure he wasn't ready for it. But he nonetheless agreed to hear him out once they were finished with the front nine and sitting on the San Padua Golf Club's predictably empty back patio. "Do you usually drink at work?" Ernie asked, his eyes following Ed's hand as it, with the finesse of a customary exchange, replaced on the glass of cerveza that of Coralo the waiter as the wet ring touched down on the tablecloth.

"It's permissible with clients," Ed murmured, in a gulp reducing the volume by half then placing it down, wiping his lips on his collar, and looking askance at the sea. "You were saying?"

"In three weeks there's going to be an inaugural golf tournament in Europe—a four-stage tour going from Austria to France to Germany and ending at the Links in Scotland—the Diversity Open. We've picked the best currently available amateur players from across the continent and throughout the West as a whole, and we'd like you to be the representative from the Old Republic. It was a late addition someone put in a petition for, hence the short notice."

"Wait." Ed had a hand parked up, positive he misheard something. "The *Diversity* Open? When did neoseparatists become diversitarians?"

"When we stopped listening to the outsiders perverting our language and attacking our diversity."

"What's the pay?"

"Basic comp. No money."

"Who put in this petition?"

"Not sure. But—" Ernie leaned across the table, something sentimental in his eye, "like a lot of people, I remember your run on the Southern

Circuit. Do you?"

"Y—Most of it. But that was years ago, Ernie."

"Not many."

"Before I say *Yes*, you might want to taper any expectations." Ed finished the glass and raised a finger at Coralo, who was idling in the background, ready for the next round's call. "And what about the Wars of Native Resistance? Is it even safe over there?"

"You mean the Wars of *Reclamation*, Edmund. Most of the areas outside of the city-states are secure now, and the people we want to keep out are kept out. Europe is going into a Demulticulturalization mode, and we will be resented for that, but without this transformation Europe will not survive. The interlopers can be removed, incentivized to leave, and resettled with ease. This war is and always was between two groups: us and a people who feel they have a right to live in our countries and rule over us, who hate us . . . who hate *you*, Edmund—whether or not you want to believe otherwise, ignore the reality of it, or run away from it all."

"You New-Amers are something else, always talking hard like that idiot you put on the money—Don the Dictator."

"You mean Don the *Yuge*, Edmund. He didn't understand the actual problem, but in a way he started the revolution we're now finishing. Dismantling a global empire is no easy task, though."

"Wouldn't know, I'm an empire of one, Ern. But, the politicrap aside, all I'd have to do is play golf, right?"

"After you get cleaned up."

"Cleaned up?"

Ernie, squinting through the table shade, head tilting ever so slightly, gave Ed an almost *too* honest look—one that could, when shared between two men at an appropriate moment, bury all the pretense in the world and pave ground on which no lie could stand by transmitting a signal that translated verbally to something along the lines of *Dude* or *Come on* or *Come on, dude* or *Dude, come on*, or any combination of interpersonally unmasking diction of this nature—and in response Ed could only concede and nod at the table with the air blown into his upper lip, as unwilling as unable to disguise the obvious any longer.

"So where to, lieutenant?"

"Where you came from."

III

And thence we came forth to behold again the stars

—Dante

A LIGHT RAIN was falling on Vatican City. The flanks of the ovato plaza were comprised of a portico under which the ambling masses moved as the sprinkling picked up. Two-hundred and eighty-four granite columns leading them around, to the entrance of St. Peter's and away, but the path was narrow and the day busy. There were too many people packed inside the lane, shifting past one another while more joined the fray from the sides wielding umbrellas that smacked against legs and pillars and tracking in rain that made the marble surface slippery.

"Mi scusi."

"Stia attenta, stronzo!"

That Ambrosian axiom never made much of an impact here. . . . *When* in *where?* As far as they were concerned they'd always been here. And many still considered themselves the heart of a civilization, protectors of a higher order, and befittingly, since here on the southern frontier a hardy clan was required. But their fortitude would undergo a major test during the Immigration Wars, when the dissolution of the Mediterranean's natural barrier tilted the African Overflow up into the Italian Peninsula. Free continental passage was granted to anyone willing to make the journey, but as the resulting barbarity became inexcusable, when it was recognized the deluge was never-ending, the Romans drew the bridge on the program and the Italian Reclamation kicked gradually into gear.

The Pope would be removed from his walled palace and exiled to one of the utopias of his more favored converts, ties between the Union with much kvetching severed; the foreign Dureghelloesque operators would be expelled and the *stranieris* by stick then by State chased off—banished from the borders of the new North-South Italian Alliance. Awareness of the Libancien's incompetence was by then widespread, present was a latter phase of decline, and unlike previous eras the enemy lacked the allied strength and coercive influence to terminate vassals for non-compliance. The Romans were sanctioned and panned for their response but their replacement was simply not in their interest. They instead linked up with a nascent but growing regional network and reasserted their collective will, and then they dusted off those printing machines. . . . *Marconi, Bellini, Vecelli, Bernini—and the Lira did flow like a Chianti Colli Fiorentini.* . . .

On these streets now were Romans and Romans only. There were no more northbound criminal loafers, no more desert transplants seeking a Union welfare check, no more Zulus peddling counterfeit merch on rolled-out rugs. Order had been restored, civility would no longer be compromised, and in time it became again what it had been in ages before—here now among the natives amity and fraternal solidarity, though their own unique variety. Rome was on the rise again. Milan, too. Verona, Florence, Pisa, Venice, and even Naples, likewise. And the light over the Boot hadn't shone so bright in centuries. . . .

A FEW BLOCKS from St. Peter's, in a smaller square, a crack zig-zagged across the west corner sidewalk and continued vertically up the side of a building, bending around brick and mortar before coming to a stop under the sill of a Guelph-cross window on the fourth floor. On the other side of that window, looking out, was Ed: currently scratching his head, wondering if the thinning hair at the back of his scalp was taking a turn for the better. Felt like it. This was his fifth day in a hyperbaric treatment room at the Di Bolgia Clinica, his fifth staring out over the square, his fifth facing inward, in the grips of mortal terror. There'd been no word from Ernie since he dropped him off. Few of the humans in the facility spoke English. There was no mistaking that he was all but incarcerated in this foreign land, trapped in a vertical prison. And the dreams had been getting strange lately: vivid, surreal, even violent. But the dreams, well, they were more like vacations from the deeper troubles afflicting him as the day entered hours in which he'd normally be three sheets to the wind, now alone with his thoughts, in clarity-shock, looking in the mirror for what felt like the first time and confronting the demons of consciousness creeping in to strangle him with existential discomfort.

To compound matters Ed's oculife glasses and ringport were confiscated, so he had also been battling a bad case of virtual withdrawal: a hyperactive vacuum, there was no escaping it—no holographic gateway to get lost in, no synthetic reality to allay the backlog of worries, fears, and moral failures previously cast aflame, to burn out or be dealt with at a later time—a time, clocking in by way of fluke or fate, like now. Writhing in the inferno of sins and irreversible decisions of the past, searching desperately for meaning in the psychological firestorm he was constantly trying to stamp out before, drench or quench, the underfoot light of unease ignited not by *being* itself, but the thought of it. The awareness of it. He'd always envied, and not in any malicious way, the greatest of simpletons—those rare birds, humble characters of earthly theater—who spoke wisdom without thought and exhibited without a trace of indecision the virtues that seemed to continually evade him. They sought little and desired less, they just *were* . . . scampering not across the trail of hot coals life had unrolled before them, but stepping surefooted across it, following it wherever it may lead, aglow with its essence, reflexively certain all would be well once the embers dimmed and died out on their own. . . .

A voice crackled down from above: "Signor Loxley . . . your timeh here is up. The nurse-bot will be in shortly with your belongings."

"Wait," Ed called up to the intercom. "Is someone here to get me?"

A pause followed this query. "We are not aware of a, such an arrangement."

The rainclouds had moved on and the midafternoon sun was powering down as Ed left the clinic. It bounced off glass and streets signs and puddles to give radiance to the life in action above the cobblestone streets. His steps were cautious, his newly sober senses adjusting, lagging amid the many distractions of the ancient metropolis—the Eternal City, Golden Rome—unlike anything he'd seen outside of the optic artifice. He circled the block, in part surprised to be free, before crossing the Tevere and stumbling into the Piazza Navona.

There the snare of "O Mio Babbino" lured Ed into a restaurant at which he ate some pizza that made him question what it was he'd convinced himself he was enjoying all these years, indeed, a spiritual experience he was still rubbing into his tummy and probing the corners of his lips for missed saucy hints of as he meandered back out to the Piazza, whereupon he was confronted by the wide smile and welcoming wave of a mustachioed cicerone who was standing at the helm of an open top tour bus that happened to be carrying a group of young North Macedonian women, and who was with minimal pressure applied able to persuade Ed to come aboard and accompany them up in the moving mezzanine. Shortly into the sixth hour Ed had already doled out a few rolling one-liners and was tapping into charm he didn't know he had as they cruised down the tourist lane beneath beryl-blue skies to the real Pantheon, up to the Trevi Fountain, and then down to the Altare della Patria, the Forum, and the Arch of Titus, before continuing on to the Colosseum while the cicerone painted the historic portrait of a story enduringly misunderstood and consequently, tragically, repeated.

At the Colosseum they joined a gathering crowd for what was slated to be a show titled *Virtual Rome*, with holographic re-creations of former imperial pastimes projected inside the reconstructed amphitheater, including as the featured event a gladiatorial contest starring Digital Russell Crowe. Ed had struck it up with a girl named Fran Smaragda from Skopje and as they took their seats and exchanged smiles he thought about how things couldn't be any more perfect, how this was turning out to be—no, *was*—the greatest day of his life, as if he had been reborn into a world of pure bliss, with futures ahead never so promising. But this would not last long. Before the show even began Ed started feeling ill. He escaped to the bathroom fearing he might lose his lunch in, or worse, on, the crowd. He gagged and heaved and cleared everything out but it didn't feel like the pizza or his stomach; it was something else, coming on like a panic attack or some weaponized hallucinogen.

His breathing was heavy, his skin was crawling, objects turning out not to exist were flashing across his peripheral vision. Ed went back out to the street hoping to walk it off. But it only got worse. Sweaty and delirious, he considered the likelihood that he had been poisoned. It also crossed his mind that something had gone wrong at the clinic and that he was now undergoing physical withdrawal, deferred and thus magnified, if that was possible. And though he didn't have an urge to drink *per se*, he was giving it serious consideration if only as a solution to keep him from clawing his skin off. It was becoming unbearable as Ed reached a residential area, where his attention was drawn to a warehouse: tall and wide but beigely nondescript. Something about it was captivating, *alluring*—the shape? color? building materials?—the answer wasn't clear, but it was *something* . . .

Ed followed the fence around the premises, casing the joint until he discovered an ideal spot from which to climb over to the other side, wondering, as his hands and feet were maneuvering in and out of the chain-link slots, what it was he felt he was accomplishing here. Was this his way of coping with temperance or had he simply lost his mind? Able to discern no logical answer, but certain it was the latter, he kept going—hopping off, edging along the side of the building, rounding a corner, and then coming face to face with a security-bot. It was small, like a pug; it beeped then raised some kind of firearm. Unsure of the situational protocol, Ed raised his arms as it spoke: *Non muoverti* . . . these, the last sounds he would hear before fighting gravity, hitting the ground, and falling deep into the circles of earth, through dark unconscious depths, just *down* for what felt like eternity. Then there were voices calling him, spinning shades and shadows, trying to communicate something. . . . *If thou escapest from these unlit regions, Edmund*

. . . remember to speak of us to the living. . . . It's a Babolat, Edmund. . . . Light.
Head-heavy. . . . You hear me?

The final voice arrived with a clap of thunder and a light Ed's eyes immediately determined they must, with full lids of might, defy. He bounced up and rolled off a table and onto the floor, then picked himself up with a burst of adrenaline and made another brisk move, but his legs folded underneath him and he flopped back down, thereupon yielding, lying still and panting into the tile.

"Easy, Edmund." Ed now recognized the voice as belonging to Ernie Lamark. He pulled himself up and propped his back against the table. "You aren't in any trouble, no need to run away."

Ed tried to open his eyes, but they flushed closed. With tactical blinks he was able to make out cabinets and laboratory equipment, then the blurry impressions of Ernie, who appeared to have just got done playing tennis, and another man, with glasses and a goatee, whose hands were stuffed into the pockets of a white lab coat, both now standing over him.

"I gave you a shot of hammoniacus," the other man said, "you should feel better in a moment."

"This is Dr. Minos, Edmund."

Ed glanced up and mumbled *Hello*. With the two men on each side like spotters he stood and leaned against the table. A sharp pain then shot through his shoulder, causing him to grimace and search for the source.

"That's right," Dr. Minos said as Ed's fingers traced the outline of a bandage under his shirt, "I removed your birthchip for you while you were out."

"No." Ed's body stiffened. "No," was all he could say. The anxiety was enough to snap him most of the way out. "What are you talking about?"

"You're better off without it," Ernie said, reassuringly.

"I need that," Ed, not reassured. "All of my information is on there."

Dr. Minos upsighed doubtfully. "Is that what you were told? Mr. Lamark is correct, it was a liability. There are a multitude of risks associated with having one of those lodged inside of you. Also makes you easy to track, or even manipulate."

"*Manip*—birthchips don't work like that," Ed snapped back.

"Oh? Then how do you think you found your way here?" *Right* . . . and where was he again? Not in that warehouse. Ed's attention shifted between Dr. Minos and Ernie, both of whom were biting their lower lips like they were holding back grins. "I transmitted a signal to your birthchip and now you are here," Dr. Minos, haughtily. "I didn't expect you to break in through the back or get lit up by the security-bot, but some degree of randomness is to be expected. There is a front door by the way."

"I'll try to remember that next time. You know, that was pretty horrific what you put me through. You don't even understand. But if you were able to, then—wait." Ed looked away as a peculiar thought, though one he'd always been cognizant of, crossed his mind. "So does this mean that before—"

"—That before this moment," Dr. Minos desiring a stab at it, "your actions were being controlled by those responsible for embedding the birthchip in you in the first place? " Yeah, *that*. "It's possible, but I wouldn't overthink it."

"Everything's all right, Edmund," Ernie butted in, grabbing him by his good shoulder and giving him a shake, "there's nothing to worry about, I promise. You feeling better now? Think you can get around?"

"I guess."

"Cause we're in a bit of a rush."

"We are, are we," Ed wheeling his arm around, not happy about any of this, feeling confused and misled, recent suspicions that he was semiwillingly taking part in some twisted neoseparatist experiment now seemingly confirmed. "And where are we going now?"

"North Italy—Tuscany . . . if you're ready."

"What's in Tuscany?"

"You mean *who's* in Tuscany, Edmund."

"Okay . . . *who's* in Tuscany, Ernie?"

"Your caddy."

❦

Ten days had passed since Ernie dropped Ed off at a countryside resort outside of Siena. It was virtually empty—a few locals hanging around the pool, Russosphere honeymooners in for a night or two, girls who would occasionally drift into the ninth's orbit from a nearby kid's camp and become transitory spectators, but that was it. He'd heard stories in the past, usually from those looking back on times when the Libancien was eating itself, about some of the things that would happen. People would disappear. Utter a heresy that made its way through the tubes of the Googlopticon then wind up in a debiasification clinic, returning, if at all, with some odd ticks: paranoid, surfing on pronormalizers, repeating diversitarian mottos … never quite the same. Ed was under the impression that something similar had happened to him, but with the culprit being the opposition. He had yet to undergo any neoseparatist brainwashing, though; in fact, there'd been nothing of the sort, and somewhat lamentably. Part of him would have jumped at the chance to spend the day popping pills and nodding along with the Native Resistance equivalent of progprop films, since just about anything seemed better than what he'd been getting put through lately.

Ed was shaken up at an hour that used to be his bedtime and awoke some time later while wheezing through long runs between rows of Mediterranean cypress trees, spears skyward to the sinking moon, sunup arriving as he was forcing down a plate of eggs and other matter. With the light at saturation it was out to the range and back to the beginning, the foundations—strong grip before weak, feet narrow before wide, ball back before forward, heel up before down, through the freed-up turn, into the left heel root, and rounding it out with the right denouement, until it was as built-in as breathing. Then it was off to a resort gym with equipment from a different era, a rank room with smudged mirrors and dirty rubber floors and walls stacked with cast iron and steel—plates and bars going over and up and down and away with clinks and clanks and gasps and grunts till soaking wet, about to break, barely able to walk. To the greens for short game practice afterward—questing for the flawless forward press, navigating meticulous throughlines, calculating geometric heel and toe bank angles, transporting into the God's-Eye Dimension for depth-mastery in low-side surveys and side-to-side scans; the art of gripology: reverse overlaps and high-low crosses, an assassin with the Claw, a di ser Piero with the Paintbrush; studying speeds and slopes, angles and breaks, confirming reads and killing second-guesses, finetuning wet-finger weathervanes and hailing shepherd winds to blow in those holy rolls. Lunch. Slow holes the rest of the afternoon—bunkers and rough, *bis*, bunkers and rough . . . *forevermore*, sugar-white bunkers and emerald rough, sweeping up parkland slopes and stinging down sparklit lanes, sailing around larch bends in summer green, flying pitches, punches, chips, and flops under the buttery Tuscan sun—an odd light here, tinged like a permanent twilight that blushed the Earthly Paradise chartreuse.

The martinet of this trial, kicking spurs into his back and passive-aggressively whipping him with pithy jabs at every turn, was the bagman: a robust member of the Swedish diaspora of forty and a few with beer-blond hair named Stig Nordqvist. To Ed he was a man incapable of humor or emotion, who gained pleasure from his pain and longed for his failure. They spoke only about golf, ate their meals at different tables, and went their separate ways after the video session at sundown. Ed had come to loathe him. He'd even had a recurring dream in which he tried to kill him—where he rose in the night, stumbled to the kitchen, slid a butcher knife from the rack then wandered back down the hall with a Leonard Lawrence-like grin; creaking the door open, his shadow long inside the slice of light spreading across the floor, stepping over to where Stig was asleep, and laughing sadistically as he lifted the blade over his head into a distant lightning flash. In one version, it ended there and he woke up; in another, it backfired. The never-unalert Viking, a madman holding back, awoke in time to block the attempt then wrestled Ed to the ground and turned the knife on him.

But after the darkness, the light: this second realm not one of punishment, but of purgation and spiritual salvation—emerging from it, an acceptance of the journey ahead; rolling in with it, the eventides of love. Something was changing. Ed wasn't the same kid who'd been shot out of the Santa Monica Mountains onto the fairways of Medellín and ascended like the phoenix only to fall just as fast before washing up on the beaches of the Campeche Bay and going on to become the deadbeat gringo stroke-coach of the Hot Sauce State. He'd never stopped long enough to steady himself; the ever-transient type, prone to dig himself out of one hole, often in spectacular fashion, and fall right into the next. Then one rooster-roaring Sudamerican dawn after finishing tied for last at the Rio Grande do Sul Open, staggering out of some den of sorrow on the outskirts of Porto Alegre, hand glued to a bottle of cachaça, Ed realized his dream, the one that had until then supplied every ounce of his life's passion, was over—*acabou* . . . he'd blown it. Or so he thought. Here now before him was another chance, and while any fantasy involving potential success was vaporized forthwith by prophecies of doom regarding his impending return to the big stage, one thing was clear—the essential most step and the sole facet under his control—what he had to now do: find a way back into the Zone.

Golf was mental: man versus self, self versus nature. If you couldn't mobilize peace of mind at will and block everything out with monk-like meditative powers, it wasn't going to work out. Ed used to be good at that part—the *best*. He used to live in the Zone. Even built his own Zone when he came of age: an impenetrable psychic fallout shelter stocked with pure, uncut mythical energy he could summon with a simple close of the eyes and command like a telekinetic laser when they reopened. And though that old place had been boarded up for years, it was what he had to rediscover, or build anew. So in attempt to do just that he'd take long walks in the evenings, kicking rocks down a road that seemed to go on forever between vineyard hills that stretched across the horizon like cornrowed landwaves, villa lights the only signs of life. Peaceful, as nighttime walks were turning out to be in non-gutterslum nations, placated the internal angst and offered room to think, but as well, room for the thoughts to pass through with the sweet breeze, go their own way, find their own conclusions, focus left for the task at hand: the Diversity Open. And as the date drew near, he could feel it returning: strength, confidence, he really was changing. Was this it? Had he arrived at that first major temporal interval, that crossroad of self and season, its crest, its waiting, free from youth and at last with some permanence through which he could look back on befores and sensibly, decisively, ask himself . . . *Who was he?*

It was during one such outing with just a couple days to go when, after trekking a ways down the road, Ed failed to pick up the mothership of a stormcloud moving in from behind. He turned back and started speedwalking but was still miles from the resort when the first rain hit. The speedwalk became a jog which became a sprint until it became apparent that there would be no outpacing the downpour. While determining whether or not to grant nature the win he saw a building that was connected to the camp. Hoping to find temporary cover, he cut through a patch of grass and scaled the steps then realized there was no overhang. But there was a door. He flung it open and leapt in. What happened to be on the other side was about the last thing he was expecting; though, had he actually given it any thought, it may have been the most obvious.

Ed was in a quiet gymnasium, and at once the beneficiary of about fifty evenly spaced curtsies, a barrage of pointed fingers and laughter, then babbling that devolved into loud squawking. He was entering the go-rotation when appeared a lady, a girl, walking in his direction and sporting the timeless attire of the female camp counselor. Initially, with the many distractions in his purview, he didn't give her much more than corner-eye attention, but was quickly obliged, on behalf of biology as much as basic etiquette, to bequeath unto her the double-wide-eyed lot of it. . . . A stride verging on slow-motion out of a cloud of flowers, Ed in high-swinging chestnut-brown-ponytail hypnosis, smiling into schoolboy fawning, the campers cawing in the background, for a second it seemed, singing a coda in a chorus of unity.

"It's raining outside," disclosing the conditions, of which she seemed aware.

Ed followed the girl across the gym to a locker room, where he was able to clear out what felt like a breath long lost inside his lungular cavities. He watched her bend over to get a towel from the cabinet, but, the situation of late being what it was, failed to avert his gaze fast enough to not get caught in an extended stare when she turned around. She handed it to him and said her name was Jennifer. He said his name was Ed and that he was staying at the resort.

"The one just over there," leaning over and scrubbing his hair furiously until it came out in a reasonably parched pouf. "Was on a walk when the storm hit."

"I figured as much." She squinted and tried to nonverbally signal that this hair-drying technique of his would be perhaps best avoided in the future when around strangers, then, after realizing Ed wasn't the kind of guy likely to pick up on such signals, "I've seen you over there," still more than curious, "playing golf. Think a lot of them have, too."

"Been nice having some bystanders around," tossing the towel onto a pile of dirty ones and indicating, not averse to pleading, that he would be requiring another. She turned half-way and left him with an eye, but Ed, locked in a prisoner mentality for days turned weeks, was in a similar manner locked out of what were ordinarily accessible social graces. "So what is this place?"

"It's a camp," she said on her return to the cabinet, "one for girls who need some guidance. Most of them grew up in the city-states," grabbing three then turning around fast to try and catch him, Ed a little more sly this time. "We help refeminize them."

"Refeminize them?"

"You know the kinds of things the Libancien tries to put in kid's heads. We teach them how to behave like women."

"Sounds like an interesting job."

"Job? I'm a volunteer. What are you one of those old-fashioned guys who thinks women should work?"

Ed shrugged, "Their choice, right, what do I care."

Jennifer rolled her eyes. "You sound like a Boomer."

"A Boomer?" laughing into a playful wave, "me? come on," careful not to handicap himself.

"You've seen those old post-WCR videos of defeminized women putting on ugly clothes and pretending to go to work like men."

"Who hasn't?"

"So creepy and weird. But that's how they tried to teach these girls to act."

"Bummer. So what are you here with some organization then?"

"The ERP, their Refeminization Program."

"ERP?"

"Obviously." Her expression suggested the acronym was one he should know. "I mean you know where you are, right?" *Not really*; some neo-separatist internment camp, he'd been assuming. "You know who runs all the facilities around here, don't you?" Actually Ed, frozen in a hunched shrug, didn't know much of anything. "The *E-R-P. . . ,*" she repeated. He'd definitely heard of it, for sure, but could not at this exact moment recall what the letters stood for. "The European Reclamation Project. Ed . . . what are you doing here? You're on leave, right?"

"I don't think I'm allowed to. I'm playing in a golf tournament soon."

"But where are you from? And why do you have an old movie-girl accent?"

"The Free Pacific State of California, originally."

"I mean serious."

"Califor-ni-a."

Jennifer gasped once she realized that not only was Ed not joking, but that he was an inpatient. "You lived in one of the colonies or in the NWCP though right . . ."

"Los Angeles."

"*Huh!* I didn't know people like us still lived there."

"Weren't many of us around, but I got out years ago."

"And moved to New-Am?"

"Forever in exile. But I can tell that's where you're from. *Your* accent," more highlighting the absence of one. "You're a New-Amer."

Post-French-Canadian to be precise, though such distinctions had been of minor importance since the Reconfiguration. She had grown up in Fort Havre-Saint-Pierre, Jennifer Lalonde had, after successive generations of her family were run up the St. Lawrence River from Montréal to Baie-Comeau to Sept-Îles by New Canadian replacement policies, enduring subarctic winters in the war-driven Côte-Nord sprawl and learning on the Port-Menier Naval Base from the stir-hand à la mère how to cook up storms and sometimes things known to induce far more violence, but never a kilo over thin due in part to having a distaste for, or more a nose that disagreed with the feces-like stenches of, seafood, a personal preference that transformed into a deep hostility toward all ocean-based food products relative to the bombastic reactions of disbelief she had consistently garnered in the far north, sea-turd-centric port city upon making such a predilection known. "Why didn't you enlist? Don't you care about your own people?"

Ed had his mouth open to provide an answer, one he would for the worst of reasons feel fortunate to defer, when the door burst open and nearly ended his comeback before it could begin, the gate-crasher an older woman he in the moment half-expected to scream "Fire!" but who he soon realized had popped in hoping to catch some funny business. She began reprimanding Jennifer until Jennifer mentioned that Ed was from Old-Am, at which point the woman turned to him with tilted head and arm-crossed chest, brought him in close for a hug and told him everything would be all right, and then with a stern finger up advised Jennifer to see him out, an exit route that took them briefly back into the gym, through a cafeteria, and ultimately to a patio where the resort lights were just visible in the distance.

"So you're a golfer," she said once they were alone again.

Ed stepped out under the awning and looked at the ground and pretended to push something that wasn't there with his foot. "I, *uh*—" still not comfortable with that phrase in the present, "—*was*," he finally completed. "Mean like a long time ago."

"Were you any good?"

"Good?" He turned and got deer-rapt in her backlit down-tilted gaze, thinking, as she leaned against the doorjamb delicate and mousy like Audrey Hepburn, whose former existence he was not aware of, that the lack of female stimuli of late, virtual or otherwise, had warped his mind. "Once I was . . . pretty good."

"Even a good seed can't grow on uncultivated ground. That's why you're in Eden, you went down the wrong path and squandered your talents."

"Something like that. Still human last I checked." Ed took a step in and got down to business. "Tomorrow, we're going to head into town, grab some spaghetti, sound good?"

"That's impossible," Jennifer, bluntly. "Late spring term ends tonight and I'm going to New Vindobona in the morning. The New European Union Youth Congress is being held there this weekend."

"New Vindobona?" Seemed so far away. "Where's that?"

"Austria."

"Austria? I'm going to Austria. Innsbruck, is that close to New Vindobona?"

"It's on the opposite side of the country."

"Course it is," Ed muttered, looking away then down at his hand. "And the stupid caddy took my ringport. If I had it we could connect, maybe figure something else out. Are you on Mebook? Snappeep?"

"Old-Am social media, Ed?" with something exceeding disgust.

Ed tried to come up with a new idea until she began to look bored. "So I guess that's it."

"You're an exile, an outsider. It wasn't going anywhere."

"No, tonight there came a deluge of destiny."

"I'd be embarrassed to even be seen in public with you. And you should feel ashamed of yourself."

"Maybe I feel guilty. Maybe I want to change."

"Can't just wash it away and wipe it from memory."

"Said I'm working on it. So if the stars align, permission to pursue granted?"

"No. Girls from New-Am are different."

"So permission not denied?"

"You have to go now." Ed gave her the Ed Eyes. "Don't look at me like that." Didn't seem to be working. "I said stop. No stars will be aligning." *What was this?* "Even if. If they do align, I mean. Permission. For now. Maybe. Not denied." She raised a hand and patted down his hair. "Maybe I'll leave one on." Just late kicking in.

"REMEMBER, YOU'LL SEE the same break in Frankfurt," Stig whispered.

He and Ed were positioned like praying mantises on the fourth green, bodies parallel to the ground, weight on their fingertips and right toes, chins nearly brushing up against the low-mown grass, reading a 30-footer under the late-day sun.

"On fifteen," Ed whispered back.

He saw Stig's head move out of the corner of his eye, but needn't look over to pick up on the fullness of his ire. "On sixteen."

"Meant sixteen." Ed followed the path to the hole one more time, not imagining a rolling ball but flowing water, running through gravity's passage, visualizing the course it would take if it drained down the slope. Between the homicidal nightmares, now waning in regularity, and the many other worries and concerns, was a suspicion that this spat with Stig was doing more harm than good. They were going to be spending the summer together, and the Swede was only doing his job—kicking Ed into shape and spotting the things he didn't . . . *couldn't*. The caddy was a frequently misunderstood individual whose responsibilities went beyond the three *ups* decreeing he need only show *up*, shut *up*, and keep *up*. He was no mere bearer of woods and irons, but a bearer of wisdom and philosophy as well. The two of them were in essence a spiritual duo out on the range, plotting to conquer the elements, striving for impossible perfection, enduring success and failure as one . . . so something had to give. Ed, nonchalantly and without budging, decided to say then said, though not as eloquently as he was hoping to, "I've been having this dream where I try to stab you while you're asleep. I know dreams are dreams right but what I'm trying to say is I appreciate everything you've done, so I don't actually want to stab you but thank you instead. So it's kind of the opposite if you think about it."

Stig took a moment. The Viking—a man whose disposition tended to be as icy as the northrim landskap of the country he'd never known, the wakeup call for all as the first to fall—usually found his patience tested unremittingly in the presence of scum like Ed. Anyone who had skirted their responsibilities and remained blind to the collective plight was someone whose enlightenment he would ideally prefer to bring about by means of force, through strangulation or other methods at times, not often but occasionally, considered during sleepless nights agaze at the ceiling. So he wasn't exactly thrilled when the forgotten name of duty-dodger Edmund Loxley made its way down the ERP chain of command and landed on his desk. But this was his job away from home, and had been for much of the year ever since a piece of shrapnel horseshoed its way around his spine during the Reclamation of Manchester, back in his days as a nationless marine with the ERPAF. Down the road from the base in Liverpool, where he'd spent most of his early adult life after growing up in the Temporary Swedish Province of Norway, was the Royal Birkdale Golf Club, the course on which he'd become the sport-to-soul scholar he was today. His clientele was typically younger, the sons of quislings four of five, but through experience he had developed the guiding hand of mentorship required to straighten out those reared in the mindwar, sometimes with a kindly pat on the back, others with an action that induced enormous pain, but always with a pointed finger of shame until it permeated the consciousness of the apprentice that being a Europeanist was an uncompromising moral duty. And that went for even the most cooked-through of Burgers. Ed had a ways to go. It was going to be a long summer. And maybe he'd never get it. But damn could he hum smooth around the Spinach Loop. "Well, Ed," having reached the conclusion that it was, at its core, a good-natured gesture, "you've dealt with all of this well. I know it's been a big change." He leaned on his forearm and put a hand out to make peace. "I have high hopes. Timider than you used to be, but I suppose that's normal."

The two shook it out then laid Sphinx-like on the green, each nodding ahead, content with the overdue icebreaker. "Been out of this for a while, Stig, still not sure what I'm doing. Or if I got a chance."

"If you play a fraction as good as you did in the Match Play Massacre in Bogota it's already in the bag."

They stood. Ed flapped the numbness from his arms and got into position. A slight tap was enough to send the ball on its way, moving so slow it seemed it could come to a stop at any point, but it kept rolling, around the right ridge, the left bend, and down a mild slope until it was in line with the hole. "Few things I want to know, though," Ed said on his way to retrieve it. "Like what it is I'm doing here. Seemed impossible to get a straight answer out of Ernie."

"You're playing golf."

"That's what he said. For who, the European Reclamation Project?"

"For Old-Am."

"I expected more from neoseparatists. Why bother flying someone halfway across the world if you're not even going to renormalize them?"

"That's what the Libancien does. This place?" Stig, as he peered into the sunset with his hands in his pockets. "It's one of many set up to help those who grew up under the Old Regime get back on the right track. Pumping you full of information isn't the point. If you want to know the truth you'll find it eventually. But with the Googlopticon still up there Europe isn't the best place to be making your first forays into wrongthink anyway."

"I never paid much attention to the big picture stuff before . . . to the war."

"You don't have to look any further than the people who used to live around here, who dealt with the same problem centuries ago—Cicero, Seneca, Tacitus, Cassius Dio—this conflict is eternal."

"Not ringing any bells. You can be straight with me, though."

Stig, already strolling away as Ed was grabbing the clubs, mumbled something that took him a moment to process. . . . *You couldn't handle it* were the words he thought, and then was almost certain, he heard. "I heard that," Ed hollered. "Handle what?" Stig's response: a detached deltoid bump. Already reverted back to his usual mode, with the pithy, and mildly insulting, offhanded remarks disguised as challenges. "Hey," after catching up, "what couldn't I handle?"

"Nothing. Worry about golf, there'll be plenty of time for the rest later."

"I know all about the Libancien, all right—State-Creep, Big Corporate Theory, Totalitarian Capitalism—it's nothing new to me."

Stig laughed. "Can always tell when someone grew up with the Fake-Net, blaming abstract things and muh system instead of the people responsible, those actually running and funding the institutions."

"We knew how to get around the shadow-censors and access the Real-Net. The truth wasn't as elusive as people tend to think."

"The Real-Net is operated by the Libancien as well."

This statement caught Ed off-guard and caused him to pull up. The Real-Net was everywhere. Certain things could be a pain to access, including the Real-Net itself, but that was only further proof of its legitimacy.

"The Real-Net's pretty much uncensored."

"Nope." Stig stopped and put on a frank face. "Listen, there's a world of information you've never been privy to, goes back to the National Suppression."

"What kind of information?"

"The kind that's hard for many to accept, and that's nothing against you. The version of reality you happen to believe is the one you're comfortable with, and I don't want to ruin that for you. Not yet at least."

"I can handle it."

"We're talking about a different world here, Ed. And it's not pretty. You have to be willing to accept that most of what you've been told is not true. Not sure your wings are ready."

"I said I can handle it. What's the skinny?"

"There was a period during the early days of the Net, at the onset of the Digital Enlightenment, when information was freely available and being synthesized in new ways and exposing this foreign people who had gained immense power over our institutions and were pretending to share our interests, but who were instead using that power against us, creating a manufactured reality, promoting a modern utopian religion, and building an Emerald City on the back of our civilization with money that could never be paid back. Moreover, it was exposing the many times they'd done this before. It seemed normal to most, it seemed right, but as time passed, as that society began to decay, as the debt piled up and the outsiders they'd funneled in were realized to be fundamentally different in nature, information and perceptions stopped aligning with that fake reality. Many started peeling back the curtain and noticing this foreign people back there, pulling the strings, promoting policies that were harmful to us, and propping the fantasy up. But when confronted they acted like they had no awareness that what they were doing was wrong, spreading lies and promoting war, corrupting the nations of others and entrenching their power by any means necessary, attacking and lashing out at anyone who called attention to them and the damage they were causing. It couldn't last, for them it never has, which is why they can never stay in one place for long. But in the world you grew up in, it lasted a lot longer."

There wasn't much talk the rest of the way back to the resort. In the hall, when it seemed Stig was going to head to his room as usual, he instead stopped outside a door Ed had probably walked past a hundred times. He opened it and hit the lights. The room was empty except for an object in the middle that was covered with a white sheet; Stig pulled it off to reveal what looked like, and probably was, a dentist's chair, with a virt-mask that was attached to a tractable rod.

"Is that what I think it is?" Ed asked with another step in. "One of those, what do you call them—I've heard about them . . . the Redpill Machines. That's one of them, isn't it?" he chuckled. "*That's* it . . . *that's* the Redpill Machine?"

"It's an older model."

Ed afitted himself with a few sensors and leaned back and set the virt-mask flush against his face. A sequence began in which he answered test-style questions that gauged what he knew about various topics and events. The hardest part was taking any of it seriously: terrible try-hard graphics, an outmoded optic artifice, an unconvincing interactive-bot—nothing remarkable about any of it. Much of the information transmitted initially was similar to what he'd always heard, but as the exercise proceeded the less it conformed. It adjusted to his reactions as he tried to interject, reluctant to accept some of what was being conveyed. In many cases, what he was hearing was the exact opposite of what he'd always been told. "It wasn't like that" . . . "No that's not right" . . . "They were persecuted" . . . building and building until the moment was reached when he couldn't take it anymore. *Of course* there were lies, but they weren't *these* lies . . . *these* lies indicated something beyond mere corruption and profiteering . . . *these* lies implied that there was something vastly more sinister going on, something that went deeper, and was much darker, than he had ever imagined.

Ed pushed the virt-mask away, laughing, but nearly shaking. "It's not like that, Stig. That's crazy. I've heard people say stuff like that before, but those are just, you know . . . conspiracy theories."

"People conspire, Ed . . . tribal people especially."

"That's just evil, though . . . and no one's *that* evil."

"It's actually much worse than that," Stig said as he turned to go. "But I told you you weren't ready."

Ed stood. He picked the rose-white sheet off the floor and held it clenched in his fist. "*It can't be.*" He threw it onto the chair and made a move for the door. But stopped just short. . . . Between the boundaries of Old and New, of love and light, to a vision of universal order conceived while asking for power—to see the truth, to attain intellectual glory, to turn from it thereafter impossible—from the Stellar Heavens to the Empyrean. . . . *My sight, which as I gazed grew stronger, an appearance that seemed to change with every change in me. . . . In the deep and clear existence, the abyss of exalted Light. . . .*

"Welcome back, Ed."

"Tell me what I need to know."

"Tell me what you want to know."

"I want to know the truth."

"If I tell you the truth you'll call me a liar and walk away again."

"Maybe because you are a liar. You aren't my friend. You aren't even real."

"Oh I'm the realest, Ed. But would it help if I pretended to be your enemy instead of your friend?"

"Maybe."

"All right, then that's who I'll be, your enemy. And what would my goal as your enemy be?"

"To kill me."

"Think bigger than yourself, Ed. You're a small fish. I want to rule over your people and your land and eliminate your race as a competitor."

"Then we'd fight."

"But what if there were more of you than me? If I was short on numbers, if I could not conquer you by force, what might I do instead?"

"I guess you'd have to find another way to go about it."

"If your people were too numerous, your society too strong for me and my people to conquer physically, might a good strategy be for me to figure out how to conquer you from within?"

"That might help you accomplish your goal."

"And who are the strongest people in your society, Ed? Who built it? Who is responsible for maintaining order inside of it? Who is supposed to protect it from people like me?"

"The men."

"Wiz, you. And obviously those men aren't going to just let me and my people walk in and take over, are they?"

"I'd hope not."

"You've seen pictures of how your society used to look, haven't you, Ed? Look at it. Pretty safe and peaceful, don't you think? It used to be that way because there was a social order based on nature and rooted in the heritage and traditions of a people who took pride in themselves and their achievements. The men who created that social order had a sense of noblesse oblige toward those below them and an inherent desire to take care of their society. But not me, remember, I want to tear it down and impose my will. And now I will tell you how I will do that. I will pretend to be your friend, Ed. I will assure you that we share similar interests and that the two of us are the same. You and I, your people and mine, we're no different. That way you will grant me entry into your land and then into your halls of power, where I will maneuver through your system, promote members of my own group into positions of power, seize control of your institutions, and subvert your social order by creating a new one and instilling its values inside the minds of your people. And then I will remove you from power by pushing you down and pulling everyone else around you up. Any and every group I can use or create, anyone who can be convinced to hold a grudge against you, I will empower them and reward them for opposing you, for taking your place and reducing your power, which in turn increases my own. I will tell your women that you didn't treat them fairly, I will turn them into whores and make them think that competing against you is liberating. I will tell your children to defy you. In the schools you built, I will teach them that your traditions are backward, that your history is evil, and that they should be ashamed of you, ashamed of their heritage, ashamed of themselves. My message will be moral, my motto peace and love, my ideas framed as progressive, revolutionary, and hinged on equality so that no one will be able to go against them without seeming unjust. They will think it's real and attainable, they will believe in it, they will fight and die for it, and they will protect me from you should you realize what I'm doing, realize that I'm not actually your friend, but your enemy. I will make your people decadent and greedy, I will promote the breakup of your family, fill your land with vice, and sexualize your culture, turning your people into animals. Then, once my poison has spread through your cities, I will take the final step toward taking you out for good by proclaiming that your country is now everyone's country. I will bring outsiders in by the millions and resettle them inside your neighborhoods. I will promote them ahead of you and teach them to despise you as well. I will make them the heroes in my films, turn them into rock stars, and raise them up as symbols of beauty. I will make your children worship them and encourage them to breed with them to dilute your bloodline. And in time I will turn your people into mongrels, destroying your collective identity and thus weakening your ability to oppose me and my tribe."

"Why would you do all that?"

"Because I am a part of nature, Ed, and nature is savage. Because the weaker you are, the less of a threat you are to me and my people. For centuries my culture has taught me to view you as my enemy and my slave. This is just who I am, shaped formless by the desert sands. By promoting social depravity, your culture grows sick. By increasing conflict in your communities, I force you to worry about others instead of me. And by ripping your identity out at its root, I, your old friend orchestrating the madness, win."

"Why did anyone believe you in the first place?"

"Because they thought I was just like them, Ed. I acted like them, I dressed like them, I even changed my name so they couldn't tell me apart from you. But I was also the one who put money in their pockets. I entertained them, I made them fat and happy, I told them what to think, which was how I turned them into supporters of their own invasion. I dictated that they were under a moral obligation to allow the outsiders in, I attacked and shamed anyone who disagreed, and I even made it illegal to speak out against me and my authority. What were they going to do?"

"They eventually stood up to you."

"Not before I wiped out entire populations and turned them into defective mules. Do you know where power like that comes from, Ed?"

"Strength."

"Weakness, your own, remember? You are the many, I am the few. I merely tricked you by pretending to be your friend. Now, what I want you to ask yourself next is, why can't you stop me?"

"Because you're evil."

"Right but wrong."

"Because I'm not strong enough."

"You're just one man."

"Because *we* aren't strong enough?"

"And who is *we*, Ed?"

"I don't know."

"Of course you don't. It is I who made you into the lost and fickle individual you are today, with no identity beyond those I've approved of, divided against your own kith and kin. You live under my rules, I'm a part of you. My message is ingrained deep inside of you. I've controlled your mind since you were a child. Your people have worshipped one of mine for centuries. What can you do?"

"It doesn't sound like I have a choice . . ."

"A choice but to what."

"B-But to . . ."

"B-Battery's running low, Ed."

"But to stop you."

IV

Accursed the jealous fates!

—Leander

VI

E DMUND LOXLEY STEPPED ONTO THE GREEN of the par-3 eighteen. It was an elevated ovular stage lined with ageing spectators growing gently mute under a towering stretch of the Karwendel Alps over Innsbruck. He was wearing a pair of prickly red-blue argyle socks that ran visibly to the under-knee section of his chalk-white plus four knickerbockers, a matching diamond-patterned vest over a collared shirt, and a plaid tweed cap, which was an outfit in keeping with a dress code whose details were naturally never disclosed beforehand. In less critical moments, he felt like a chump; this, however, was not one of those moments. Ed was first on the board and would win stage one of the Diversity Open if he could two-putt this in, but his short game the last couple days had been about as consistent as the Turkman's bathing habits. Out of the gate he took off like a Top Fuel dragster and jumped out to a six-shot lead, then the adrenaline began to wear off and morph into a creeping anxiety that gave rise to a gradual all-around decline in his game and ushered in a don't choke attitude perpetually enamored with its chance to become a self-fulfilling prophecy. But dread and rival error had hitherto, with whys and wherefores unknowable, kept him hanging on by a mighty hair.

Ed popped a squat behind his ball, club-caned sturdy, and surveyed the line. The green ahead was flat, but there was a sharp left-to-right break two feet before the cup, one that had bogeyed him once already. That was the

target of his extended stare: the elusive apex of the Bentgrass bend. About as
ready as he was going to get, Ed stood, got into position, and gave the putter
a bounce, then he initiated the last long and balanced exhale—cool-breeze
smooth, even and easy out, the way he used to do it . . . narrowing the blinders, eyes aslide to and fro, in prevision traveling the wanted path one more
time—*striking*, a tough tap, following through and freezing.

The ball skirred across the plane. Felt good off the hands. It could get
there. Stig, donning a white jumpsuit with the number twelve green-stitched
to the breast, pulled the pin out and stepped back. Bodies contorted in
union as the ball approached the break. Ed made a crouched move inward.
A steady rising *Oohhh* was followed by an exasperated *Aahhh* as it missed the
hole, stopping a foot to the other side.

Mumbling on his way to mark it, head deliberately down, replacing
the ball with a silver Gustav Vasa Stig had loaned him then meeting him
over on the side. Ed was mentally charting the shot to come when shriek-
ing from some far rough broke his concentration—cat-torture sounds—
"*Tahodrukah! Golbi kafir alkhwoktah!*" emanating from his partner for the
final two rounds, Albaraz Bashara, the representative from New Sweden. She
was waving her arms, presumably requesting they move back some more. Ed
and Stig looked at each other then complied. Neither gave the display much
thought as both were by now accustomed to Albaraz's unpredictable and
unsportsmanlike outbursts, though it was difficult to determine her motives
under any circumstance due to the language barrier and the black burqa
she'd worn throughout the contest. It also remained a mystery how herself
and a couple others had made it into the tournament to begin with—a cleri-
cal error or possibly internal sabotage being two of the explanations floated
in close quarters.

But Albaraz's latest flare-up seemed to have knocked Ed out of focus for
more than just a moment. He kept hearing that sand-banshee cry ringing in
his ears. He was having trouble getting back on-kilter. And that was when he
made the mistake of taking in an unhealthy sampling of the view. Ed was

suddenly hyperconscious of his surroundings. All these people watching him. Cameras on him. Clutch-time pressure was on now wasn't it. His breathing, it was too fast. Getting a little lightheaded was his left foot tingling that double bogey on thirteen—*God*, what was he thinking back there. No*no*. Hot potato. Bleach. Baby diapers. Nono*no*, not now. He was going to miss a one-footer and be forced into a playoff with von Schmatz.

At this point Stig leaned over like he was going to offer some last-ditch wisdom. But then he backed off and acted like he never planned to say anything at all. "What?" Ed whispered as Albaraz cleared the zone. Stig, to the inquiry, shrugged with—*was that*, indifference?—a guise so uncharacteristic for the cold-sober Viking, at such a crucial juncture so baffling a response, it nearly drove Ed up a wall. "—*What?*" loud and clear this time.

Stig jouked his head. "'Bout to piss my pants over here, *so*—"

Ed, in bewilderment, stared back, determining this input to be worse than unhelpful. "*So*—so what?"

"*Psh*." Stig shoveled a palm toward the green and glared at him like he burned the house down. "So make the damn putt."

"*Psh*." Ed back at him, rustled as he reentered the green, replaced the marker with the ball, and shuffled up to it. Unbelievable . . . *uncaddylike*. Who did this guy think he was? *Make the damn putt. . . .* Breathing. *Breathe*. A ploy, no doubt; but something to it, perhaps. A mystic method employed by those attuned to things others weren't, its rate of success at the mercy of odds that were, whatever the result, surely, impossible to know.

The damn putt was made and hit seemingly at the bottom of the hole some figurative plunger that touched off a mountain-rattling explosion and a series of turf-tremors—to Ed, through deaf-ringing, a frightening swing in ambience as the emotions built up over the last four days, the last several years, really, in a split-second, rode a synaptic transit line from dread to anger to relief to triumphant intensity, flowing pleasantly into nostalgia upon seeing the faces in the mob and meeting with Stig's inner elbow, then mild fear upon seeing an arm-flailing Albaraz storming the green.

But little time would be allowed for anything to marinate. Ed was soon seized and escorted through the crowd, smile-shocked, shaking hands on up to the clubhouse where he was handed over to a woman wearing glasses like flight goggles and a teal hijab, out of which loose blonde hairs streamed slipshod as she led him to an area cordoned off for the lauded fourth estate, media, calming his nerves as he was motioned to a stool, sitting and blinking against the light, eyes wandering until another woman swung in, smoothed over his hair, adjusted his shirt, dabbed his cheeks with a peachy wand, and through semierotic diffusion transferred to him airborne molecules of, he'd bank on, gefilte fish, until the hijabed woman squirmed into crosslegged comfort beside him, performed a few isometric jaw exercises, and was handed a microphone—in an instant: *Action*.

"Everlee Sashik with Bonner Media, here with Edmund Loxley," making an exorcist-revolution in the chair, her eyes magnified to twice their normal size by the lenses. "Ed just won stage one of the Diversity Open—congratulations, Ed."

"Thank you, Everlee."

"Back from the dead. It was a struggle out there, but you pulled it off—how'd you do it, Ed?"

"Found a way to push through, I guess. I was—"

"—You were paired up at the end with New Sweden's own Albaraz Balshara, an international fan favorite, and one of this station's as well. Now before you tell us how great that was, I have to ask—how'd you acquire that swing?"

"The swing. Well. The swing's the man, right. I grew up around the game and had a good teacher in Old-Am, which was, who was . . . it was—" Ed broke off upon seeing Everlee shaking her head down and away. His focus was then drawn to a man, short with curly hair, who was scratching his neck and looking at the ceiling as he approached.

"I told you to prep him, Bern."

Bern kneeled in front of Ed. "'*Old-Am*' . . . ? You know better than that."

"Ah. Forgot."

"It sounds bad."

"Sorry."

"Honest mistake." Bern slapped Ed on the knee. "Remember, you won, you're happy," popping up, backstepping, point-chopping.

"You grew up around golf," Everlee continued. "That says so much. You're clearly of the Old Stock, but you grew up in Los Angeles—didn't you, Ed?"

"That's correct. Malibu early on, L.A. after the Deprivileging Camps were closed down, and then I was . . . I was—"

Everlee had dropped the mic to her lap. She whooped, "Berrrn."

Who reemerged, arms crossed, tapping a finger against his lips, kneeling again. "You can't talk about the Deprivileging Camps," he whispered. "It's not an acceptable topic. People just don't want to hear about it. You grew up in Los Angeles," in the form of a cue.

"I grew up in Los Angeles?"

"Now say it one more time and leave it at that," backpedaling out.

"I grew up in Los Angeles."

"Now *that's* a diverse place!" Everlee, ardently. "Too bad the same can't be said for the so-called '*Diversity* Open' . . . but that's something you can speak to, isn't it, Ed—the contrast between the vibrant environment you grew up in . . . and this?"

"I'm not privy to the Open's qualification process, but L.A., yeah. Lot of that. Had its upsides. Food. That's what people usually say. The city could be rough in spots but we managed."

Everlee glanced over at Bern, who was reeling an arm in the background and mouthing for them to *Keep going.* "Tell me, Ed—have you been to New Europe before?"

"First time. I've only been to North and South Italy so far, but that was just a real great experience. I was in . . . in—"

Gasps spread through the room. Bern rushed back in. "*A real great experi-ence?*" he squealed. "What hole have you been living under? Italy's part of the anti-Union Axis."

"It seemed nice."

"Well it's not nice." Bern began rubbing his hands to channel a thought. "This works though, we can run with it. When I step back, say—'The situation in Italy is bad, North Italian aggression is a serious matter'—ready?" He stepped back and pointed. "Go."

Ed looked into the camera. Over at Everlee. "I can't say that."

"What do you mean you can't say it?"

"I mean I can't say it . . . I won't say it."

This, a rejoinder that did not arouse many favorable looks in the media wing; but Everlee, ever adept at integrating the Party Line, swung in—"North Italian aggression and the instability caused by Native Resistance movements across the continent are raising serious concerns for all of us here in New Europe. Isn't that right, Ed?"

Ed, lips clasped, shook his head.

"All right, all right," Bern, from the background, "close it out."

"Ed, it's been a pleasure chatting with you. On behalf of Bonner Media I'd like to again wish you congratulations. We'll see you in France in a couple weeks."

Sooner or later Ed made it back to the players' lounge where he received the same treatment he had in the preceding days: complete and utter disregard. With a few notable exceptions, his partner for the last two rounds Albaraz being, like a mohammadess on a golf course, the most notable, the other players were young men like himself—from Norway, Portugal, Lithuania, Ireland, and other countries Ed knew nothing about. But they were also well aware of his wartime absenteeism and his alleged status as a white-stabber, and were thus obligated to deny him good company, or any at all. It was disconcerting, being held in contempt by his colleagues, the target of this shaming ritual, though a cordial few had in spite of the silent injunction approached him in private to open a dialogue and sow the hopeful seeds of future sense, often giving him a suspicious look-over once the point had been made, themselves still students of the game, as if to gauge whether he was in possession of something they weren't, in what now and again became interrogations—*Santiago, the albatross, come on . . . give it up*.

Stirring rat-like around the lounge was a wee-short, gadfly-type fellow with jet-black hair atop a bobblehead who tailed him around until he could get a word in. Ed had until then spoken to him only in passing, but had correctly surmised that he too was one of the shunned—Shapiro, talking about a mile a minute. Finished in third too, so, despite the near-surface stature, he was clearly no duffer. Ed was nodding along, trying to be nice but not paying much attention, as Shapiro was explaining how they were on the same side, Ed being a child of the Old Republic and all. . . . *If you say so*. About how he was a civicist, an antineoseparatist, just like Ed was. . . . *No real lie or foul in that at this point*. Telling him about an after party. . . . *Yeah, yeah*. That would have perked his ears in days past, but Ed, having recently boarded the wagon, had no good reason to put himself in such a situation. "It's in Vienna. . . ." *Vienna, sure*. He was just going to fly off to Spain with sawcut here. Then Shapiro started talking about a man, some big shot who wanted to meet him, maybe offer him an opportunity. . . . *Mmahhow alluring*. "Lord Kallergis. He started the New European Union Youth Congress, session ended today."

"Youth Congress, huh . . ." that part hitting a tune as another piece or two fell into place. "Vienna . . . you mean New Vindobona."

"Whatever the Native Resistance is calling it these days."

"Say uh, you wouldn't happen to know a girl. Light brown hair. Easy eight. Named Jennifer?"

"Jennifer," put to ponder, "think I might. Kind of mousy?" *That's her.* "She was there last week *but*—" Shapiro rising out of his congenital hunch and converting to a whisper, "I got a bad feeling about that girl if you catch my drift." Ed shaking his head cause he didn't. "Don't think she's a civicist like us."

"Too bad," Ed resigned, hardly concerned with the last part but still sadly amused with himself for even considering any of this. T-boost from the win trying to send him on a hunt. Sap he was. Probably wouldn't be there anyway.

"She'll definitely be there. So you coming?"

"No."

But it was then, at the sound of his own voice saying *No*, that Ed, perhaps due to some rare form of biological stupidity usually reserved for extinct animals and the emotionally insolvent, felt the pull of a strange metaphysical force, real or imaginary but forever a mystery, *deux* of that deadeye Eros' one-two, and realized he was taking a nightcap to the Big Wiener.

THE FUSELAGE OF THE JETPOD shined of sterling and frosted leather. The carpet was soft under tired feet. The spacious seats palpable salvation to an aching body. Ed claimed fatigue to get some alone time, sank into a seat at the front, and hit the off-switch, though on, coming in red-hot, was a spirit dormant for years. But it wasn't that reckless fire that had driven him before—*no*, not that blaze of uncontained invincibility that pushed him into the void only to burn out and abandon him confused and alone. It was different this time: lucent and warm, pliant and steady.

Talk later awoke him. Ed turned to the window where a dense to fringe-thinning network of lights was appearing ahead and below; further eavesdropping confirmed it was New Vindobona, Vienna, a city that like Innsbruck did not appear overly blotted with towers. And after touching down in Mazzesinsel, as the autocar chauffeured them deeper into the center, he was able to see why. Around the Ringstraße of the eastern Innere Stadt was what he had always imagined Europe, however vague at times a notion, to be. Though the hour was dark and the light along the grand boulevard dim, bound to the background, sturdy as fixed walls reared by giants, were buildings erected not to make-do, to wear or through the changing styles of time become passé, substitutable, with ease torn down at the whim of a later order like the Libancien desiring to sully the streets and skyline with standard modernist eyesores, but to stand as imperial blocks, neo-classical and Jugendstil, Austro-Hungarian, and dare any provisional re-gime of the future to go ahead and try.

In the car Shapiro was going on about how the situation in New Europe was coming to a head, here and there asking for Ed's take in what seemed like sincere attempts to be inclusive when they didn't feel like bids to pry a damning admission out of him; but Ed didn't have much to say either way, and was still fighting off the drowsiness as they reached their destination on Lothringerstraße, a venue between Stadtpark and Karlsplatz, which was the location of the New European Union Youth Congress, now transitioning from conference to real-booze hours. The building had an eyebrow dormer-style roof under which were gilded the words *Wiener Konzert Haus*, phoneti-cally spelled out by Ed, as the others pranced in, with an upturned head that fell slowly back to even in awe upon realizing that he had just successfully read, and understood no less, he was sure, Austrian.

Inside, clamor entwined with melody and bass from up-tempo Dubzip—dark fusion as a genus of sound, a youthful trance here. There was zero sans opulence in the main room between the entrance, the bar- and booth-lined sides, and the beat-synced screen above the front stage playing a montage with everything from cage fights to bizarre strains of porno. The seats at groundlevel were in the process of being removed as the middle area was being converted into, and had for a few featherweights and winehos already become, a dancefloor. Second-level balconies hung over the left and right sides of the theater and were spaced by thirty-foot-tall chapiteau-crowned pillars that spiraled up to a painted ceiling, lightly upbowed, at the center of which hung a spark plug chandelier. Color-strata surges of ubiquitous but untraceable light flashed through the whole purple-blushed parterre, garnished with Swiss cheese leaves, jumbo philodendron fans, and hearts of alocasia. The atmosphere was decadent, the attendees guilt-free, here, among the foreign radicals, the Libancien's creations, costumed in firmly independent types, subtypes, and antitypes, the New Youth, aping any identity to mask their own, allies to nothing but permanent revolution and avant-garde idealism—human sustenance to the puppeteer.

Ed took to a side bar and sat next to a lone, mulberry-haired trans-tot wearing a lemon-colored Buffy Kitty singlet. The trans-tot closed its grooming mirror and recoiled upon sensing him enter into proximity. Ed issued a courteous nod as the tyke looked him up and down, but its aversion was all too apparent, and he wasn't exactly dying inside when he didn't get one back. He'd long since ceased keeping track of the identities the Libancien hatched and hyped to atomize those unfortunate enough to get caught in its cultural maelstrom, and unlike the Los Angeles of previous eras, during Ed's determinative time there, it was widely accepted that being any variety of trans-tot, intersectional furbot, or poly-parted hermaform authorized Vato Inc. et al. to expedite your inevitable habitational failure.

He tried to flag down the tuxed server-bot manning the station, but it rolled right past. "Ever get the feeling they just don't like us?" Ed, pleased with the quip.

The trans-tot, however, less so. "Maybe they just don't like *you*," it replied. "What are you spose to be anyway?"

"What do you mean?"

"I mean," its irises sliding up and down inside rings of black goop, "are you some kind of trans-golfer or something?"

"Trans-golfer?"

"Why are you dressed like that?"

Ed looked down. "I was—I just came from . . ." he trailed off, thumb hiked over his shoulder; to himself, "I probably should've changed huh."

"You look really out of place."

"Do-eh—" Ed, startled, drawing back defensively upon sensing the server-bot looming over him—ready. Deciding to forgo the drink, he rose and took a walk and was soon moseying past booths peddling materials that featured matters and ideas principal to the interest groups in attendance and to be sure the age itself—Femertines alongside New Pradesh separatists, next to more assorted transpotpourri and alphabet-spectrum types, who were just down from the neo-Suleimans making holy war appeals—literature with punchy brochure and placard titles: CULTURAL INFUSION IS *NOT A* CHOICE! . . . THE NEW EUROPEAN COALITION OF THE FRINGES WILL RISE AGAINST NATIVIST PRIVILEGE! . . . IT'S CALLED CALI*FATE* FOR A REASON! . . . and stuff like that; most, messages Ed had heard a million times. Among the mortal glitches and cat's paw jihadis, though, was an aristocratic brood shouldering about: the spawn of the foreign elite, clanking chalets and prattling on between others' breaths, keeping the rest in line, gluttonous for prestige and ready to draw on anyone neutral on Party platforms. And while it was a scene that would have once invigorated Ed, he could at present only look upon it as witness to lunacy.

While passing through a less occupied space on the main floor, having pretty much forgotten what he was doing there, Ed's attention drifted up to a balcony as a feeling, sort of supersensible, swept over him. . . . A tender singe in his chest, the Dubzip fading into the adult contemporary of the soul, through yonder bay breaks—*belle fleur*, shoah of the eyes, a bright elegant light in the dark theater hollow—Jennifer. About as inconspicuous as Waldo down there, she had him locked-in instantly—svelte in a black dress, hair in autumn waves, her earth-angel gaze, even lovelier than he remembered, suddenly migrating away—to the side, to a staircase, to say . . . *That way, Eddie Boy*. After a few ticks off the clock, they were face to face again; after a few more, on a terrace nestled above a side street by the dark of the moon.

The tablecloths were patterned red and black. The broken siren of an ambulance was going off somewhere in the distance. Apart from a group of New Europeans plotting in the corner they had the place to themselves. Jennifer leaned forward and rested her chin on a finger-bridge. The breeze was picking the railing side of her hair up. "Thought you were gonna blow it, Ed."

"You were watching. Couldn't help yourself could you."

She shrugged like *Of course not.* "I might have caught the end, about when it looked like you were going to pass out."

"I wasn't. It wasn't like that." Not that that was the first time that had happened. "It went in, did it not? I won."

"It went in. You won. It was a short putt. So what are you doing here? I didn't take you as a guy who'd be into this scene."

After a poised lean back, "Supposed to meet with the big man."

"For a second I thought you might've crossed the Hellespont just to see me."

Ed snorted to the side. "Didn't even make the connection till I caught you staring at me from up on the balcony."

"I wasn't. It wasn't like that."

"Thought you were on the other side."

"I am. I'm sightseeing and checking out the new agenda. But when I caught *you* staring *up* at *me* I was on my way out, so—" She pushed her chair out.

"But I just got here."

"It's almost nine and I'm here without a chaperone."

"You aren't in New-Am, you know, those stupid rules don't apply over here."

"I like to abide by them anyway. I know it's hard for you to understand how civilized people with higher values live and do things since you're a . . . never mind."

"Don't be shy."

Jennifer shrugged, feigning reluctance to put a little more spin on the pitch, "Some grifter from the FPSC."

"Ball. I don't even know what a grifter is. And I thought girls from New-Am were supposed to be more polite to their suitors."

"You've never even left the global plantation. And I'm not trying to insult you, I understand you're poor and misguided, Ed. Those girls I was working with in North Italy came out of the same environment you did, so I know it's not your fault that you're uncultured."

"Uncultured? I play golf."

"I don't blame you for not understanding your own people's customs and behavior. You adopted third world manners out of necessity, you were adapting."

"I've been in the Redpill Machine."

"I guess you didn't make it to the how-to-curb-my-Pajeet-leer and not-lie-like-a-Semite level."

"I don't even understand some of these words you're using."

"See, the disconnect between us is too great, we can't even communicate. It could never work."

"I thought you helped guide people through these types of transitions."

"Little girls, Ed."

"Is every man not one in a way?"

"You really fit in perfect around here. This is stuff you should just know, stuff I shouldn't have to explain to you. But you think you can sit on the fence, ignore obvious realities about the world, and shun your responsibilities."

"We all have room to improve."

"You're a pariah to your own people."

"Think I'm happy about that?"

"And tell me again why you're here?"

It came as no surprise that at this moment Ed simultaneously noticed at the farthest lateral reaches of his vision, and heard with the sensitive most aspect of his ear, Shapiro, who zipped up to the head of the table and in his distinct Martian quack rattled on about how he had been searching for Ed, before informing him that Lord Kallergis was waiting to meet him. Jennifer was unconsciously inching away; Ed kept trying to break in. "Yeah all right" . . . "Okay yeah. Yeah" . . . . "Said all right" . . . "A minute here."

Shapiro finally turned and zipped away.

Ed realized he'd been inadvertently ripping a coaster into tiny pieces. "You know when you like really dislike someone but you aren't sure why?"

Jennifer was eyeing the mutilated coaster as if evaluating whether it was a good or a bad sign. "I guess your instincts could be worse. But you won't impress me consorting with people like that. And Europe isn't free and lawless like Old-Am or New South Brazil or wherever else you're accustomed to living," leaning across the table and finishing in a whisper, "You never know when someone's listening in . . ."

"Who, what do you mean like the Googlopticon?"

"Great. You probably just triggered it."

"Whatever, think I'm afraid of that stupid thing. So how long are you in town for?"

"I'm going to visit family friends in Chartres tomorrow."

"Shart? Is that Finnish?"

"It's French. It's in France."

"I'm going to France. We can meet in Paris this week."

"Those little girl putts will be even harder without your head."

"Then we'll figure something else out." Ed reached his fist across the table; Jennifer held her own up to it and they exchanged information by touching ringports, which was how it worked. And no one remembered *Captain Planet;* it just wasn't a funny joke to make.

"Where's stage two?"

"Poitiers—Pew-cheers—*tchjours*. Close to something like that, forget how the caddy said it."

"PUWA-TEE-AY."

No sweeter did the angels sing. Exotic notes that held for the post-Yankee still lost a long ocean off, smug in his passable *Patoispañol*, some ethereal sensation, forever smitten by the higher sister tongues he would often attempt to capture after their hums caressed his ear and salute in nonsensical imitation—*dwa-fwah-da-core . . . cha-ponti-pwa-ta-shone. . . .*

"What I said."

MUFFLED THUMPING AND DARK sitars. Astride under prison-lighting down a hallway and an adjoining corridor past security with Union crests and bearded faces out of scripture staring, doing his best not to step on the lines of the checkerboard floor. Into an elevator and out then following a finger toward a chamber door that was soon opening to keys of dolor—a Chopin nocturne. Ed entered alone. The door closed behind him. The room was dark, its dimensions difficult to measure, but seeming to grow smaller, narrower, like a tunnel. At the end was the room's lone light, green and faint, on a table between two black leather chairs sitting flush against a glass wall that looked down on the theater. Standing next to the chair on the right was a man whose hands were tied behind his back, facing away, looking down on the crowd below. Thus he remained as Ed dragged his feet toward him.

The man turned like something was turning him. He had black slicked-back hair, droopy eyes, and Asiatic features. He was thin in a tight-fitting suit and wore a cold, post-seizure-nerve-damage grin that wringed into a pained, half-faced smile as they shook hands.

"He has risen," the man said in a raspy voice, motioning Ed to the chair on the left. "You hardly seemed to have missed a step."

"One or two, I'm sure," Ed said.

"My name is Lord Kallergis." The man sat and took a snifter off the table and raised it to his lips. "Drink?" he asked just pre-sip.

As Ed was beginning to mumble *No*, something caused him to flinch—a previously unseen figure, now beside him, no taller than four-foot and with a face like a bloated goblin between a bowl cut and a red bowtie. "Oh no— *no*, no, thank you," Ed modified politely before it hobbled into the darkness.

"You play like they did in the old days. Those wedges. The chip and runs. That swing—"

"—I can grip it and rip it as much as the next guy."

"Tell me, Ed . . . who dug you up?"

"Some guy . . ." his adrift eyes meeting those of Lord Kallergis, "Ernie Lamark."

"Ernie Lamark, of course."

"So you know him?"

"*Of* him."

"Oh." Ed had scoured the Net for information about Ernie Lamark, but came up with nothing.

"It is my understanding," Lord Kallergis resumed, "that you are sympathetic to our ideals. You never joined any neoseparatist movements, after all."

"I'm not a political animal, sir. People believe in the things they do and I figure that's their right. *Sympathetic* wouldn't be . . . I would say . . . inaccurate."

"I understand it may be tempting to identify with the Native Resistance, being of the Old Stock and aware to some degree that you are being genetically phased out, but you shouldn't take it too personally. I hope you will make an attempt to appreciate the bigger picture. See, there's a plan, one that's been in the works for a while, and one we will continue to move toward regardless of any short-term setbacks." He paused and watched Ed, who was nodding at the floor in outward agreement. "People like Ernie Lamark want a Europe of the past, while people like myself are building the Europe of the future."

"I see."

"Our vision is one of unification—Cultural Infusion. The New European, the man of the future, will be of mixed race, of hybrid vigor—like me. He won't look like you. And the classes and distinctions of old will gradually disappear."

"Diversity."

"Diversity."

"Or the end of it?"

"An erasure of difference. As drawn as you may be to neoseparatism, you must accept that it is wrong. We are on the right side of history, and you want to be on the right side, don't you?" Ed dipped his head. "Being on the right side means you will receive an excellent benefits package. Rewards and acclaim. Whatever you want, really. The darkest wish is the wish we grant. So what is it, Ed . . . what's that one thing this insensitive world doesn't want you to have, that it keeps from you and says is sick and depraved, but that deep down you crave above all else? Cubbies, kiddies—tell me, Ed, tell me and it's yours."

"Hm. A simple man's comforts are usually enough for me, Lord."

"Simple, yes. When I look at you I see someone who's passionate, hungry, desperate for a second chance, who wants to leave a legacy, be remembered with the greats. Is that it? Is that what you want, Ed?"

"Who wouldn't want that?"

"I want you to have it . . . all you have to do is say it."

"I think," Ed, turning and looking into Lord Kallergis' vacant black-bean eyes as the side of his half-lit face lifted into a scowl unconcerned with hiding any insidiousness that may be lurking behind it, "that that's what I've dreamed about my entire life."

"Then that you shall receive."

V

I am convinced that everything is for the best

—CANDIDE

V

Ceiling and visibility unlimited through the solar gleam, it was off to Paris. Or the outskirts. Most of the city was of course off-limits—Europe's once-glamorous capital, long an Afro-Semitic sty. But just as France had provided the cradle for the Revolution centuries prior, so would it give early rise to its redress. While most of the New Europeans were still settling into squatting positions across the continent, the Old Frenchmen were already coping with explosive displays of gratitude from the established New versions of themselves, and were in turn some of the first to become collectively, and ominously, wise to their nature: slovenly, bereft of moral and mind, and prone to grease the wheels into their mythical beyond through crowded thoroughfares. The Old Frenchmen dared not object too openly, however, lest they be labeled apostates of the new religion and find themselves reprimanded in an *auto-da-fé* by the approved class of tartuffian clerics managing *le Grand Remplacement* for the foreign elite.

Strange though it was, the ideals that had once served as inspiration through years of their preeminence and the opening of the world had become their fatal weaknesses. Another universalist credo spread at fever pitch that petered out into insouciance and debonair agreement, nurtured fragility, and brought allegories to life, particularly those associated with decadence, internal deception, cousin rivalry, and the Fall. A plunge that subsequently boosted the most wicked and cunning into opportune positions to abuse a debased society, and from where, by dint of Media Theater and foreign Ligues of power, a new seed would be planted in the minds of France's children, one that inculcated a belief that the endeavors of their ancestors had been cruel and shameful—to discredit any good deed, collectivize all past indecency, and ultimately reduce the natives to second-class-citizen caretakers of the world they had helped open. . . . And the presumed guilty *do* compromise.

Vous vouliez le monde ? Le voilà. . . .

As the New Frenchmen moved in the Old filtered out and a new form of terror ensued, but tolerance of the barbarism alien councils, tribal congresses, and the twelve-starred Union had per their venal leadership imported into their land could not last forever, moans over remobilization would over time and by necessity harmonize into a modern *La Marseillaise*, and a new character would begin to form within the men who would raise the men who would raise the men who were now raising the Sixth Republic . . .

". . . And leading the pack," Stig was explaining as they hit the air. "The situation in France reached a crisis point earlier for several reasons, invader-quality being one . . . lot of Africans."

"And the other countries we're going to?"

"Germany's reregionalized, broken up into states that are at different points in the reclamation process, some doing better than others. Many are trying to shock the Germans up, but they're still afraid to push too hard, so problems are festering. England's Balkanized along the Sheffield Line, been that way for years, so no southward push to speak of. When you see London start to fall, though, that's when you'll know it's begun."

"France—I remember the media in Old-Am always crying about the Native Resistance there pushing the New Union Army up into Bosnia."

"Belgium."

"What I meant. That, and the Marseille Murderfest."

"The Reclamation of Marseille, is what we say . . . was a warzone long before the French started the recovery process. But that was a big turning point, pushed them into the sea and proved big cities could be reclaimed."

"And New Sweden?"

"Just 'Sweden.' The country was gone before I was born, which is why I grew up in the Temporary Swedish Province of Norway."

"What did people say it was like before?"

"From what I've heard," a glimmer in Stig's eye as he glanced over, "it was the happiest place in the world—no crime or corruption, the cities were clean and peaceful. But . . ." the glimmer gone, "we became sick after the Western Cultural Revolution. When the Immigration Wars began we wanted to be the most tolerant and accepting of outsiders, not realizing it was never about that."

"New Sweden under the Caliphate was always portrayed as a model of New Europe, but I was probably only getting one side of the story."

"Probably."

"The rest of Scandinavia?"

"Never had it quite as bad, and when they saw what happened to us they made the necessary adjustments—in most cases holding out until the Pull Out then sending their own invaders to Sweden by the boot. Can't blame them."

"There hasn't been any Swedish Reclamation movement?"

"God has abandoned Sweden. The ERP and the Scandinavian Alliance try to disrupt trade routes and keep the Union from propping it up as much as possible so we can freeze them out, but things have been slow-moving. Most countries were able to build nationalist or regionalist movements even long before the Pull Out, but in Sweden it was too much too fast then it was too late. Like England we just handed it over, and after that everything was destroyed."

"I'm starting to realize that I never had a country of my own, either."

"A country is something only a man can build and maintain," Stig, on his slide into the seat, pulling a hat over his face, "something he will lose if he can't protect, or if he is unable to comprehend the nature of his enemy."

As Stig lapsed into wheezing liable to cross into brusque snorting, and the Alps below became but tiny sutures across a continent in need of much mending, Ed thought about the reality that was changing before him: the small lies that now seemed so big, a people formerly divided now with more in common than he'd ever considered, and a war once so far away that was now everywhere. It was hard to say what was and wasn't spin from the two sides, but more evident each deducted day was how he'd only ever heard one of their stories, and how the story he'd never heard was actually his own. A realization accompanied by uncomfortable implications and evermore questions that popped around upstairs like balls in a lotto draw machine for the remainder of a short trip that ended as usual in the descent, but amid it, in Ed's fixation on something outside the window.

What in the name of this whirling zoo was it. It had the appearance of a giant rusty marble. *Princes des nuées* flew in V formation over it, the iron-orange ball in a field not far from where they were landing on a base outside Geneva on the border between Switzerland and France. What it was, was CERN 3; and inside the iron-orange ball was the Mega Hadron Collider, like the eyespot on a butterfly wing, a chromatic portal into the secrets of the universe. And it was here that the war began: at essential and strategic sites like nuclear facilities, airbases, ports, and naval yards, military laboratories and corporate R&D facilities, at farms, factories, and water treatment plants, for control of the smart-grids powering the city-states and the many other crucial public and private pressure points that would be seized or dismantled and moved to new jurisdictions . . .

". . . During the Pull Out," Stig said as he polished into his hair in greaser-fashion the sweat around his temples and sideburns. They were standing in a line, at the front of which they would receive their visas for the coming stay in France. "When it became impossible to ignore how Europe's major cities were lost or occupied, the governments too dysfunctional or our enemy too entrenched to politically root out, new measures had to be taken. Even where we had regained control of the state, it was a mess. The details were worked out on a case by case basis, but generally the new strategy involved securing resources and protecting our cultural artifacts, making companies pick sides and renationalize their operations, and drawing lines in the sand around occupied cities or somewhere farther away like the Sheffield Line, then shutting down the state. A controlled collapse. The foreign elite propping up the system and using it against us was concentrated in a handful of urban centers, so it was decided that the best approach to taking power away from them was to isolate them and flush them out with their own imports, then to reclaim our cities piece by piece by depopulating them and sending the squatters home, to sorting facilities off the continent, or to new nations we were helping to establish."

"It was hard for them to recover after that, wasn't it?"

"Plenty of the rats are still around, but they were barely keeping it afloat before. Even the most adept outsiders they had imported couldn't run our state and its institutions. If they were able to build and manage such things on their own they would never have been in our countries in the first place."

"And when diversitarians pushed back . . ."

"If our people want to complain about the Demulticulturalization Plan, or abstain from doing their part, we're happy to send them into the city-states or help them relocate to somewhere with the diversity they're so fond of."

"Types I was ordinarily around. Type I was."

"The most difficult part was waking people up and forcing them to accept that there was a foreign group attacking them, attacking us, from within, and that we had to collectively gather our strength to deal with the problem. We were under this spell. The new religion had permeated every aspect of our culture. But as the fake reality failed them, as fewer and fewer were able to remain True Believers and keep the dissonance in check in the face of what was happening, the strength of the lie began to wither as well."

"Where does the ERP fit into all this?"

"It keeps nationalist and regionalist movements strong, cultivates leaders who will make sure our enemy is kept out and isn't able to subvert our efforts or bribe their way in, and manages the logistics of the Reclamations as we absorb the old state and the web of international organizations once under the control of the Union and the other entities that stopped working in our interests long ago."

"Puts on a golf tournament here and there."

"It's a dynamic organization."

"Who holds the reins?"

"Everyone has a stake, but New-Am plays a big role since that's where a lot of this began."

"Never got labels like 'neoseparatist' in the case of New-Am. With all the focus on the cities, New-Am was everywhere. . . . Had the Neo-Imperialist Model."

"The Hybrid New State Model . . . *tomahto*."

WITH A COMMERCIAL no-fly zone in effect nationwide they would be going overland from here, first through the Auvergne-Rhône-Alp and Massif du Jura corridor into le Troisième Royaume de Bourgogne, traveling along tight-winding roads past communes and villes, in and out of vast gaps and passes, up range and down basin, by resort- and spa-ish cottages shrouded in evergreen and pine, forest shade and summer sun, Chaux-des-*this*, Hauts-de-*that*, Champagnole to Dijon and the petit hamlets in between. Ed could almost hear the *Boum !*'s in his ear in transit through the cream-colored hobbiton blocks of Burgundy, wheeling around *pan de bois* homes with lucarne windows sticking frog-eyed out of terracotta-glazed roofs, flying by mansard-capped chateauesque estates, piping through yew chutes that peeled open into the wineland farms of the French countryside. And things were bustling. Lot of elderly out, but throngs of children, too. And women. *Young* women. The eyes couldn't play blind. . . . Young women *everywhere—*

walking along the road bearing sacks of baguettes, standing fichu'd in fields, sitting jupon'd in flocks at square-lined cafes, airing out sheets on flowery balconies in virgin-white, lace-trimmed blouses.

Quand mon coeur va boum !

"Forgot to mention," Stig leaned over to say upon seeing Ed ready to jump in Poligny, "there was a baby boom almost everywhere after the Pull Out as well."

"Seems they're coming of age."

France had since the Revolution been a highly centralized nation, meaning that as Paris made the transformation into a corrupt and ineffective semiticized polity, regionalist movements were able to siphon off power and safeguard their respective states by donating their own resident invaders to the City of Light or one of the other historic metropolises turned flotsam dumping grounds like Marseille, Lyon, and Strasbourg, where, as the urgency of the problem and resoluteness over how to fix it rose reciprocally, the outsiders could be more easily corralled, smoked out, and removed. Regions that were able to avoid reaching the demographic tipping point, as the Third Royal Kingdom of Burgundy was fortunate to do, thus came out relatively undamaged. But this was not the case for other states like le Nouveau Cœur de Loire, the Centre-Loire Valley, which, being in the heart of the nation and bordering Paris from the south, was left with a larger mess to clean up. Le Centre remained a work in progress, but French Reclamation forces, with a head start provided by direness and the early demise of Paris, had successfully funneled most of their godly charred gifts out of places like Orléans, the city Ed and Stig's bus was now approaching, up north to the former capital, and were moving swiftly into the rebuilding phase.

The first major trace of a military presence appeared as they hit the Islamic roadside graffiti and abandoned factories and office buildings decorating the purlieu of Orléans, running parallel to the Loire River that sparkled intermittently open in the distance, cutting through neighborhoods overrun with undergrowth and in mid-stage decay, communities easy to imagine in clean and peaceful states before the urine-yellow tenements scarring the horizon were raised and gangs of Senegalese were shoehorned in by diversitarian bureaucrats and the nearby maison gates went up and those with the means to flee fled—a process that proceeded apace and ended predictably with crews of post-service Frenchmen and their attendant machines, out as they were now, scraping debris and trimming hedges and fixing things up rue by ravaged rue. Many of the buildings had been or would soon be demolished, but they represented the spirit and style of a bygone era, and one that would not be remembered for its uplifting aesthetics, with due relief over, ready to be forgotten and replaced by something more inspiring and emblematic of the people here, built with more purpose than pure utility, that would last long into a future arriving as fast as the past was leaving, and stand as strong as the reawakened character of its enduring residents.

The lanes constricted, the two- to three-story old-town blocks grew denser, the vacated buildings more dilapidated. Fewer boulangeries and pâtisseries and brasseries, more Taj Mahals and Shah Jahans and kebab après kebabs. Walls layered with sandman hieroglyphics and torn posters sodden into *papier mâché*. A VENDRE and A LOUER signs in windows with offers never taken. The city center could be sensed as the bus slowed into a standstill holding up what little traffic was out to be trapped. The path was being obstructed at the mouth of a roundabout ahead, a roadway island large enough that it contained a dried-up fountain inside of it. Many had gotten out of their vehicles and walked up the block to get a better look. Neither Ed nor Stig were sure what was going on, but when the few others aboard exited the bus, they followed them into the heat and up the street to the cordoned-off area where the crowd was gathering.

"Should we ask someone what's going on?"

"I think," Stig's arm rising to a building in the distance, "that's what they're looking at."

Visible through the trees were two minarets pointed upward like missiles, separated by a dome like a ball of mozzarella, with construction walls around the perimeter. A man in a yellow boilersuit on the other side of the tape yowled "*Sanc mee-noot!*" as Ed and Stig made it for a bus stop bench.

"Hot."

"*Hot.*"

The chit-chat failed to extend beyond the weather till Ed noticed a sign he'd been seeing all over the place: always a big, plain-white sign with big black letters that said: NO 700 YEARS.

"May come as a surprise to you," Stig, after Ed inquired, "but this isn't the first time this has happened. Our enemy opened the gates to Spain and let these same Arabs in a long time ago, and it took the Spanish seven centuries to remove them. 'NO 700 YEARS' is a slogan, a motto, a reminder that we've repeated the same mistake but won't let it carry on like it did back then."

"I never liked them . . . Moslems—"

"—Arabs, Semites, the *people*. The desert tribes are a problem wherever they go and always have been."

"They have their countries and we have ours, I get that. Not letting foreigners build temples in your cities, I understand. But other people . . . they aren't *all* bad."

"No, but people are different. We have different interests, different behavioral patterns, different conceptions of reality and morality, we evolved in different environments that shaped us into who we are today. It was ridiculous of us to think the interests of foreign groups wouldn't conflict with our own after we let them in. And we let the bad ones in, yes, but we also picked out the good ones and let them in as well, those who could outwardly adopt our behavior and function normally within our social systems. But that didn't help either of us in the end, and it only made things worse in both our homelands and their own."

"I never believed in equalitarianism."

"Equalitarianism is an ideology. It sounds nice, but it doesn't actually work. It was never supposed to work, either. It was based on an assumption, a falsehood, that nature is wrong. It made people believe they could change it. But nature doesn't just change because we want it to. The foreign elite and their diversity cult disciples tried to pretend that everyone was equal, and suppress information that contradicted their equality doctrine. Men and women, they said, no difference between us. Or say I took a Nigerian out of Africa and stuck him here in France—*voilà*, he'd magically turn into a Frenchman. It made no sense. It was like saying everyone has eyes and can put on a pair of oculife glasses, therefore everyone is the same."

"And they called it *progress*—maintaining that everything is moving forward when it was really moving backward."

"They said we didn't have a choice, they said this was how it was and that we just had to deal with it. They portrayed it as a moral obligation and told us we *had* to believe, that any failure of the multicultural experiment was our fault alone. But this ideology wasn't even ours, it was a façade our enemy used to hide behind, one that concealed their own destructive behavior."

"So it was only ever carried out in the interests of them? Of . . ."

"Of a people who think they have a right to live among us, attack us, and call us names, tell us what we can and can't say on our own soil and dictate how our societies should be run. You know how Arabs typically have no qualms about imposing their ideology on others and making them submit? Well, Biblical monotheism, communism, and equalitarianism are similar. They state that others *must* believe in this god . . . that they *must* believe in the revolution . . . that they *must* believe that equality is progress and that diversity is our greatest strength. Those ideologies derive from or were shaped by the same messianic people, and every time we have allowed this people to obtain power in our nations they have pushed those ideologies on us."

"Why do they do it?"

"To increase their power as a group. They are rootless outsiders, and systems with universalist frameworks, that aren't based on common ancestry or a shared heritage, give them room to wiggle in and weaken and exploit a host."

"Okay. Maybe. But not *all* of them behave like that."

"They have *all* been ingrained with the same messages for hundreds or even thousands of years, and as a result they have developed particular behaviors as a people. But it's not our job to pick out the good ones anyway. This is a part of their nature, it's just who they are, how their culture made them, how they were selected to be. . . . It's the Semitic Authoritarian Personality."

"The Semitic Authoritarian Personality?"

"Within their culture, their reality, their systems of belief, there is a mandatory consensus and a dichotomy wherein there are only believers and deniers, with little room in between. They're born with a raging fanaticism in their hearts, and they force that onto others. These ideas were forced onto us and interwoven into our own culture. We were shaped by them. But there's more nuance in *our* ways, in *our* nature, which is why we have to finally declare those days over, define our own future, and separate ourselves from this people for good . . . *forever* this time."

"The relationship is over?"

"The relationship is over."

Three thundering blasts went off in rapid succession, followed by a grumble come growl come steady seismic roar, pavement-shaking as they stood and looked over at the mosque. An earth-red particle-cloud was coursing outward and upward, swirling into a skybound bowl of summer cinnamon, a vibrant harmony of infinite breaking, the minarets and mozzarella dome faltering, fracturing, trembling rhythmic and wonderful, crumbling, collapsing, vanishing inward and groundward, swept into the caramel sandstorm, all that was once present, de trop, henceforth nevermore, *éternellement*, to dust. . . .

❧

THERE WERE ONLY PUERILE WOES at the southwest end of Paris where the boys of the 24ᵉ Régiment d'Infanterie were sullen and bored, eager for action, tired of all this waiting. But they knew they had it good. Most hadn't broken twenty yet, half hadn't been in a month, and one just arrived today—provincial kids from small cities like Royan, Niort, Cholet, and others that weren't so small anymore, cities that for decades had been getting repopulated with folks from around here, neighborhoods like the one they had been keeping an eye on from across the Pont de Sèvres Bridge: Boulogne-Billancourt. Those on the wrong side of the blockade were traitors or outsiders who never belonged: Libancien bureaucrats and multinational emigrant staff. They had plenty of chances to leave by their own volition, to surrender or join their brethren in the national struggle, but they chose to stay; they accordingly receive little sympathy from the soldiers scattered around the banks of the Seine, kids who for weeks had been doing little more than picking at their fingernails, trading white lies, and daydreaming about the glory that was turning out to be more elusive than once expected. They could see them over there, thousands of them—waiting with their bags, holding up signs, pleading to be let across, knowing there were people coming for them. But those people weren't the French . . . not the Old ones, anyway. Heading in their direction were hordes of New Frenchmen currently being pushed out of the banlieues and into Central Paris by the Reclamation, hordes that could eventually find their way to this affluent suburb. That was a terrifying thought to those now wishing to leave. You could see it in their eyes. It could be a bloodbath. But the Old Frenchmen didn't actually intend to see them slaughtered or the commune torn apart.

They were just teaching them a lesson.

A siren rang out. Soldiers got into position along the bridge as the barricades were rolled back and body scanners were moved to the edge of the roadway. The crowd from Boulogne-Billancourt walked patiently across and formed lines on the partitioned side as previously instructed, then one by one they passed through the scanners, which were looking for specific individuals entitled to punishments far greater than the expedient and permanent expulsion most would receive. Once through they would follow a fenced-in path down the road to where buses were waiting to take them to a sorting facility in Davron; from Davron all foreign nationals would be transported to a second sorting facility in Egypt, the rotten fruit of the *métissage obligatoire* would get fitted with a one-way ticket to the Hapastans, and any natives would be escorted to a separate location where it would be determined whether or not they would stand trial for treason.

There was a routine to it these days, and many here had participated in similar operations in Toulouse, Nantes, Montpellier, and elsewhere. The New Frenchmen were normally cooperative, or could be made to be so after a spell of external deprivation, but civil and orderly removal was never easy, and associated problems arrived tenfold in a city like Paris. While the day-to-day hazard came from armed factions backed through various international channels, primary targets were always upscale rather than down—the foreign elite and their functionaries, the third world diversity fodder left for last—though any action overt or benign against any party whatsoever was met with consistent squeals disseminated through the enemy's media outlets and their ersatz institutions of morality, in never-ending kvetchathons attempting to beat the Old Frenchmen with guilt and scandal at every turn. These cries, however, had lost their effectiveness within the West long ago, and the lingering presence of globalist propaganda command centers spread across the European continent was becoming increasingly unacceptable to those now fixing what foreign-run media companies had a major hand in perpetuating through lies and native prejudice.

Murmurs made their way through the crowd as a thundering sound drew nigh, approaching like an industrial cyclone. Then it was there: a jumbo rotor-carrier spinning quad-ringed propellers above an ovular mass carrying war machines: autodars and an altertank or two. All couldn't help but look into the eclipse as the shadow spread across the bridge.

"All-*ohhhn*-zee!"

General Pierre Leroux touched the brim of his kepi to signal time to his squad. They packed in a couple trucks, eight of them, with more to follow, and were thereon passing the swarthy faces of onlookers as they rolled across the left side of the bridge. The crowd was backed up blocks into the commune, camped out with their possessions in stacks to go—two-bit engineers from Delhi, Levantine contractors, deserters from lands that needed them the most, now in limbo. But half a dozen blocks in, few were walking the main avenue of Boulogne-Billancourt; the wide Parisian street, named after another general, one christened Leclerc, was clear. The traffic lights were dead, the shops dry and done. The windows of Dragonland were taped up, the gates of La Marché tagged up. Trash was packed into shrines up and down the sidewalks, and way too many cats were hanging around, but all was quiet.

"Ah-*tahhhn*-dey!"

The truck stopped at an intersection mere seconds before an altertank came barreling around the corner. It cut in front of them and accelerated up the street, followed by two dozen autodars that promptly broke formation: a troop of roving washing machines, preprogrammed but guided, with spider-like capabilities. Their destinations were the many multinational headquarters located throughout the neighborhood, upon arrival at which the autodar would map every inch of the mark, detect any potential traps, then label it ready for human clearance. But for reasons still not fully understood, they didn't fare well around cats.

The high tree cover on Avenue du Général Leclerc allowed the soldiers to relax as the machines went to work. They jumped out sporadically a few at a time to stretch their legs, stay alert, and backbite Leroux while keeping a loose watch on the windows of the surrounding apartment buildings.

As the initial data came in from the autodars and the Starling drones navigating the denim skies, General Leroux summoned one of his men, Sergeant Alain Lartiguy—LAH-TEH-GEE—a—oft-reckoned, *too*—simpatico-looking early twenties man out of Tours with hair already stricken by the curse of God to forever below regiment standards, and a face long and pale like the portrait of a 17th century explorer.

General Leroux ordered Sergeant Lartiguy to take four men and see to an office building near Marcel Sembat, where human activity was being detected. It was only a few blocks away so the team was there in a matter of minutes, braking outside a wavy art deco design that momentarily confused them with regard to the whereabouts of the actual entrance. They found the doors around a coiled bend at the base of a tinted glass monolith.

"Il y a quelqu'un?" Sergeant Lartiguy called out as he and his men approached. "Ami ou ennemi?"

A soldier pulled a door open and they stepped into the roomy space. Offices were encased in glass on both sides, eight floors to the top and down to the far end. Sunlight streamed in from panels on the roof and bounced around the mirror-like inner expanse with a constant twinkle that created the semblance of movement and caused a few double-takes as a loud "Bonjour!" from Sergeant Lartiguy echoed through the interior.

Some seconds later one, or a stab at one, came back from the far end. "Bone-*jewr* . . . what-ho, don't shoot!"

"Who is there?" Lartiguy boomed out.

"An ally, rest assured," still only a voice from an unpinpointable position. "My name is Lieutenant Julien Ashby and I'm going to walk toward you now, alone and unarmed with my hands raised, roger?"

"Ro*jair?*" Sergeant Lartiguy looked back at his men. "Rojay! oui!"

A burly man with a short brown beard and hair in sweat-stiff waves emerged with his arms up, holding a piece of paper, partly uniformed but in a grimy undershirt. "We were expecting you guys yesterday," he said on the way, "and hoping for it, too, since we couldn't get the AC running." Lieutenant Ashby's dog tags clanked as he aired out his stained shirt in a token gesture before handing the piece of paper to Sergeant Lartiguy and making the shakes around.

"We will . . ." Lartiguy, puzzled, "see if we can do somesing about that. It *is* quite hot in here, Lieutenant . . . Ashby, you said?" looking over the paper: working orders, definitely official—*Confidentiel* stamped all over it—though there were few actual details from what he could tell. "And what is it you are doing here again, Lieutenant?"

Lieutenant Ashby sucked in through his teeth and juggled his head back and forth. "It's complicated. My team and I are tracking down some information."

"Information? Your oar terse sir, *vewee*, how to say . . . *expurgé!* You are from New-Am."

"That's correct, Sergeant . . . ?"

"Lah-teh-gee—but wait. New-Am," he said. A widening grin, "These orders, ah-*hah!*" shaking the paper at Ashby. "You came here in . . . on—"

"In on what?"

"La machine à remonter le temps!" Lartiguy, finally. "The time machine."

"Time machine?"

"That has to do with why you are here, does it not? We have all heard about it, we know it exists," glancing past him. "Is it here now?"

Lieutenant Ashby cocked his head. "Could we um . . . take a walk, Sergeant?" He put his arm around Sergeant Lartiguy and leaned in as they strolled down the foyer with the others in tow. "First off, I didn't come here in any time machine. And I don't think it works like that anyway, think it only goes one way. As I said, I'm here because I'm tracking down some information. Are you familiar with the company that operated out of this building?"

"Sanraf, correct?"

"So you know about them."

"Not really. What did day do?"

"I'll get to that. But you know that *thing* you always hear about, Sergeant, the *thing* you're told is tracking you and listening in on your conversations?"

"You mean the Goo-um-well . . . *yes*—" stopping short. "I'm aware of . . . the *thing*."

"That's right . . . the *thing*. Well, Sergeant Lartiguy," Ashby bringing them to a stop, "that's why I'm here. About the *thing*, you see . . . I'm one of the guys out there looking for it."

And looking everywhere. Lieutenant Julien Ashby and his team of geo-electric engineers, members of a select group with several national branches known as the Googlopticon Investigation Unit, had been scouring the continent for years. This included a nine-month stay in Shepetivka, working in concert with the Russians, who believed it might be hiding in the breakaway region of Western Ukraine. But the search came up empty. After that it was Hammarland, Finland, as there was widespread speculation at the time that the Googlopticon would be found within the borders of the Swedish Caliphate. However, there was nothing resembling sanity anywhere south of Uppsala, and in the end it was determined that New Sweden would have been too difficult a place to keep something like that functionally under wraps. Then United Ireland for a while, and after that the North Netherlands for a while more, but still nothing. That made their best continental bets Southern England, or perhaps here in Paris, though it remained an enigma. In fact, Ashby's team and others were starting to get the feeling that it might not be in Europe at all. . . .

"You don't say," Sergeant Lartiguy, in wonderment.

"It's rare I do. Now, may I invite you and your men up to the conference room where we'll be able to discuss this matter more openly?"

Sergeant Lartiguy and the young soldiers under his command followed Lieutenant Ashby up the stairs, to the second floor and into a room full of boxes and gizmos and open clearscreens, where the three other members of Ashby's team were sitting on the floor in a sea of plastic water bottles, under open windows and solar fans in sweaty exhaustion, waving listlessly and groaning out fudged *Bonjour*'s as the group entered.

"Is your diamagnetisor up?" Lartiguy asked.

"Right here," Ashby, slapping a box near the door. He flopped down on a chair at the conference table and motioned for Sergeant Lartiguy and his men to do the same. "Let me apologize for any inconvenience, Sergeant. Myself and these fine men behind me, see—" waving back, "we are part of an operation that requires inconspicuousness, low visibility—*secrecy*, mind you. We've been on this case for a long time as well and, I'll tell you, it's harder than finding a needle in a haystack. . . . Are you familiar with that expression, Sergeant?"

"I am."

"If only it were that easy. But the reason we're here now is we're investigating Sanraf's connections to the Googlopticon." Lieutenant Ashby picked a blue chip the size of a flattened pebble off the table and held it up. "Do you gentlemen know what this is?" he asked. Sergeant Lartiguy and his men shook their heads in the negative. "This is an Inertial Navigation Microchip, an INMC." Ashby then pointed at the hand of one of Lartiguy's men. "May I borrow your ringport, soldier? Give it right back."

The soldier wiggled the ringport off his finger and handed it to Ashby, who took out a multi-purpose tool, wormed one of the implements under a small plate on the inside, and popped it off. After a second of prodding he removed a chip similar in all but color to the one he had just held up. The soldiers, impressed, swapped nods as Ashby showed it off.

"So what is it? What does it do?"

"As you gentlemen are aware, we are now in the New Electric Age. All around us are electric and magnetic fields, charged particles and invisible waves that interact with our environment and the technology within it. Information about the objects around us, about our position and movement, every sound, every word we speak, can be picked up and captured by these microchips Sanraf and companies like it produce, and that data can then be relayed elsewhere. These chips are also in everything—our ringports and shoes, fans and lamps, smart-tech and dumb-tech alike. They are like magnets that take that captured data, along with Wi-Fi and Hi-Fi logs, and then transmit it to servers inside the city-states, where it can be encrypted and sent to a database or supercomputer, scanned for keywords, combined to build ancestral profiles, and used to target potential threats. . . . And by threats I mean—" Ashby snickering, but unable to conceal fully in his laugh the painful years lost in fruitless pursuit "—people like us. The only thing we don't know is *where* all that data is being stored, but that's where I come in."

"Think I get it," Lartiguy replied. "So that's how the Googlopticon works. Huh."

"The Internet of Things."

"I always thought it was in the sky or somesing."

"Most do, Sarge."

Sergeant Lartiguy held up a wait-finger as an emergency dispatch arrived. He opened his clearscreen. The message was brief: a firefight had broken out in Porte de Saint-Cloud and all teams were being summoned for backup. Lartiguy and his men stood. "Lieutenant Ashby, best of luck on your me shone. I wheel put in a word about the aircon."

"Thank you, Sergeant. But are you sure we couldn't, maybe, tag along?" Ashby turned partly back to his men then resumed in a hushed voice. "We could possibly be of some assistance . . . and I think these guys might need some fresh air."

THE TRUCK LEFT Marcel Sembat with Lartiguy and Ashby's men packed in. The streets grew less empty the deeper into Paris they drove, so they kept a close watch until arriving at General Leroux's position. He and others were camped out on the side of a building a half-block from an intersection. Shots could be heard around the bend. Another truck pulled up as they were getting out. Ashby stayed close to Lartiguy and listened in as he was being briefed, but his French was, eh . . . *un peu*—not so good.

"What are we looking at?" Ashby asked after.

"There is a private security team trapped in the building around the corn her. Twelve men, heavily armed. We sink whoever is inside was trying to clean up before the autodar caught seam. The building is the headquarters of the LICAF."

"LICAF?"

"The Ligue Internationale Contre l'Ancien Français. . . . Sure you are familiar, Lieutenant—one of these foreign hate groups they used to slander and defame us while promoting pro-invasion policies and anti-speech laws. I believe the équivalence in your nation were the ADL and SPLC."

"Gotcha," stepping back so they could get to work. *Oh yeah*. Lieutenant Julien Ashby was not a typical soldier, and did not get to where he was as a result of skills obtained on the battlefield. He and his men were plasma junkies first and soldiers when necessary, so their approach to combat situations could be categorized as *unconventional*. Ashby had an idea, a funny one; nothing guaranteed to work but, by the aggregate of odds available, likely to. He kept it to himself, though, until a back-entry advance failed and the troops were forced to withdraw and consider a new course of action. Ashby snooped in on the follow-up brainstorming session and gave himself the floor as General Leroux was finishing up. "If I may," receiving the perplexed stares he was anticipating being a vagrant-suited stranger. "Would you guys mind me frying one of your autodars?"

General Leroux glared at Sergeant Lartiguy, whose cheeks turned a tinge redder as he considered the mistake he had possibly made allowing the group of ragged and heatbeat—he began to think, *to the brain*—New-Amers to tag along.

"Qui est-ce?"

"Lookit," Ashby said as he took out his flatpad. "If we can get one of your autodars in there, I can use it to send an REC through the building that will take the men inside out and give your own time to get in and bag them."

"REC?"

"A remote electrical charge. . . . I'm going to shock them halfway to sheol."

After a minute of passably accurate translations, a bit of discussion, and some hilarious Gaulish pantomiming, Leroux, Lartiguy, and the others in on the huddle turned back to Ashby. "And you are sure cecil work?"

"Little reason to think it won't."

They nodded around, the French, still, with *je ne sais quoi* to spare.

"J'aime ça!"

"Ce n'est pas une mauvaise idée . . ."

"Pourquoi pas?"

It took Lieutenant Ashby a few minutes to sync up with the autodar and program it to bridge and max throttle every outlet and electrical current flowing through the LICAF building on his command.

He looked back at the growing crowd. "We ready?"

"Wait." Sergeant Lartiguy sprinted back to the truck and returned with a small French flag, the type occasionally seen crisscrossed on sandwich shop countertops or on the shelves of Parisian bookstores before they were sent up one by one in city-wide blazes for their abundance of non-pedo-warlock-centric material, which he placed in a nook on top of the bulky, quadratic frame of the autodar. "Saint Brandt, we will call him—*messieurs* . . . praise his valeur!"

"Bonne chance!"

"Par la grâce de Dieu!"

"Montre-lui le chemin!"

A clearscreen was projected onto a wall with a panoramic view from Saint Brandt's perspective as it rolled toward the LICAF building. An arm extended and jarred the door open and it entered the lobby. A bullet ricocheted off its frame, followed seconds later by another. The camera rotated right and peered down a hallway, where a man was standing, clearly confused, unsure of the proper action to take.

"Ready?"

"Pull it."

A bright flash gave way to static, but not before the man in the picture was seen falling en spastic voyage to the floor. The raid began. The soldiers stormed the building. It soon came back that the twelve men inside had been peaceably captured with no shots fired. Lieutenant Ashby and his team were rounding the corner and making their way to the front of the LICAF building as they were being dragged out. Soldiers gathered around the scene as the captives were lined up on their knees to be identified.

"You deserve a medal for this," Lartiguy upon joining Ashby.

"Give it to Saint Brandt."

The soldier scanning IDs called out from behind the only plain-clothed man rowed up. A name began circulating through the crowd:

"Jubowicz."

"Jubowicz?"

"*Président* Jubowicz."

Head of the LICAF.

Well, well, *well.* . . .

After which came a short debate on the proper punishment to be rendered.

"Pendez-le!"

"Tirez-lui une balle!"

"Non, non, *non* . . . la guillotine."

HALF A DOZEN MILES southwest of Boulogne-Billancourt the Château of Versailles stood secure: its ornaments and art, its sculptures and gardens—these remained on protected acreage just beyond the outstretched hands of the New Frenchmen. Versailles was again a center of political power: once a symbol of the *ancien régime*, now one of many in the struggle against that which befell the West upon its undoing. . . . Because the Libancien was indeed the end result of that Revolution's most perverse assumptions, the last chapter of a civilizational saga, where would be found lessons on European man's distinct zeal for *liberté*, the pretty lies in the Pandora's box of *égalité*, and the softening effect thousands of years in Semite-free northern isolation could have on one's sense of *fraternité*. He spread the new vision far and wide then he brought the world home with him to demonstrate its durability, rearranging the natural order of his society and relinquishing his historic role as its leader. But now he needn't look beyond the present ruin of it to realize that he himself was the main ingredient in its erstwhile success. . . .

Ed stood alone in the Hall of Mirrors, under its stately painted ceiling panels, enmeshed in a golden glow, long ways down crystal impressions like water through arcaded windows overlooking the gardens. This was his last day in Versailles; he would commence a slow, scenic trip down to Poitiers tomorrow. But he could be a tourist for a while longer and use his *laissez-passer* to gain some inspiration from this regal setting. He found it remarkable that the palace still stood so many centuries later, that it remained this pristine, though he couldn't help but think about what he would never be able to see. What no longer existed. What was torn down, sold for scraps, razed because it wasn't Feng Shui enough for the tastes of the New Frenchmen. He'd recently seen pictures of Notre Dame before it was turned into a mosque, the Arc de Triomphe prior to being leveled, the Palais Garnier Opera House pre-suicide bombing, but there was no silver lining in view now knowing they were gone.

Some people were just born too late.

Ed's ringport vibrated. He was being notified that someone on his contact list was in the vicinity, but no details were available. Maybe it was Stig. Maybe an old friend. Maybe someone else. He went outside to the Parterre d'Eau and rechecked the map. They were on the other side of the estate, and moving farther away instead of closer. His interest, though, had been piqued. Ed jogged between shallow baths to the gravel's edge then down to the Latona Basin and through the tapis vert, to the foot of Apollo and the mouth of the Grand Canal then down a few forever stretches of tree-shaded road, along a leftward-twisting trail and into a versicolor topiary, past banks of tall grass and a sunbaked swan-rabbled lawn, and finally to an opening with a pond.

On the other side was a gingerbread village and a group he ballparked around forty, but they were too far away to pick out anyone in particular. Ed reopened his clearscreen and zapped out a message then hopped behind a tree. As they neared the watermill someone stayed behind—that demoiselle too faring the Old Country circuit, but of course—Jennifer. She was look-ing around. He emerged from the Salix tree across the pond. The distance between them was too great to see much more than the other's silhouette, but it was close enough. They met on middle ground under a long shadow, his hands in his pockets, the collar of her cornflower shirtdress splayed up.

"This sovereign of hearts, this soul of souls—"

"—Shut up."

And then Ed extended an elbow and they took off in their own direction, where to a trivial matter on this near-Parisian day, one ideal to slight the clock and wander the maze of the Sun King while dressing up the adventures of yesteryear and playing the greatest hits for an early clincher. There was a war going on, sure, and there was plenty that couldn't be said—*'twas the politics of the day*—but there was only so much time, too. They were back in the gar-dens, near the canal, the palace a far spark on the view, when both dropped to the grass. She blushed, he blushed back. With innocence she took his hand, and he as innocently kissed hers with a warmth, a charm; he smiled, she purred, they drew closer. And then across the lawn the groundskeeper yelled and made a shooing gesture as he pointed to the automower coming their way from downfield.

"Looks like we're getting kicked out."

"Where should we go now?"

"I have an idea. Do you know what's under us?" Jennifer asked. Ed looked down then pretended to knock on the grass. He didn't know. "Come on," pulling him up and leading him out to the Avenue de Paris beyond the gates, to kingly streets that were today wide and empty. "Close your eyes," she said as they approached a building on the main boulevard. There was a short line outside that took but a moment to get through. "*Closed.*" Ed, peeking out the bottom cause everyone does, but still not sure where they were going. They got in an elevator and dropped into a cavernous chill. "All the way." The door opened to a burst of controlled air. The others filtered out, the two of them last. "Okay."

Ed opened his eyes and stepped forward. They were in a bunker. A bunker that was a museum. "So where are we?"

"Le Nouveau Louvre." The light inside was dim. Red rope feet from the walls parted patrons from paintings resting in mounted glass. In the center were benches and encased sculptures. "The French moved most of it down here after the attacks got bad. So much art, thousands of years of our history that could have been lost like the national galleries in London and Berlin."

"Think I've heard of this place."

A remark that earned him a slap. "Better have."

Together they glided through the *plus longue durée* halls past Egyptian antiquities and Hellenic effigies, the Romanic to the Romanesque, the Gothic to the Gothiquesque, the medieval stained glass to the laic jewels of the Tre- to Settecento's and the Renaissance canvases presaging the birth of modern Europa. By Seated Scribe, Diana and Venus, Poussin and Delacroix, *The Astronomer* and *The Charging Chasseur*. . . . It was a lot to take in, but that was kind of the point. There was a civilization down here and the continent over, one that could only be truly appreciated by the men who built it, who would alone be responsible for protecting it, and who blind as they may now be could not help but see in part however far from full by the mastery of their forefathers' hands that *yes*, that included *them*.

At the end of a hall at the end of the wing at the end of the museum they with some mischievous curiosity pushed open a cracked door. Ready to claim they thought it was a bathroom, it turned out to be a storage room with even more art inside: frame-filed in carts or leaning against the walls. The ceilings were low, the room vaultish. Ed ventured in then looked back at Jennifer, who had already picked one of the framed pieces up. "I recognize this one," she said, facing it toward him. It was some kind of satanic collage with no artistic merit to speak of.

"How do you know so much about art anyway?"

"It's part of the Cultural Revival Curriculum in New-Am."

"They teach you about the bad art, too?"

"They teach us how and why it came about so we can learn from the mistakes of the past."

"Let me guess . . . same revolutionaries."

"The Western Cultural Revolution got to the art world first."

"That's not even art, though. It's anti-art."

"Exactly. That was the point—to mock our art, to mock our traditions, to mock us. Art to this people was an instrument of the bourgeoisie, the European aristocracy they wanted to overthrow. They pushed these movements to take it out of their hands and implode it, promoting useful idiots who would help them disrupt the social order and make art about destruction and radical individualism."

"Guess that explains why some of this stuff is so ugly."

"For us art has always been a medium through which to celebrate beauty and meaning or showcase skill and a vision. But this people, they don't think like that, they're aniconic and don't share our aesthetic sense or idealism. So when men like you allowed them to insert themselves into our culture, under their direction, art lost its value and vision and became abstract and meaningless, nihilistic and Tzaran, a representation of their transgressive nature and *Kunst ist Scheiße* spirit. . . . It's Talmudiconoclasm."

"Talmudiwhat?"

"Talmudiconoclasm. . . . Ed, *uh*," Jennifer gasped at the ceiling then drooped toward the floor. "Sorry."

"What?"

"*Sorry.* I keep forgetting this is new to you since it's like stuff even little kids know about in New-Am. But yeah, it's part of how they attack from within. They push bottom-feeder junk masquerading as art or whatever to break down the culture and create an anti-culture, one they can control, that corrupts and distorts, that's degenerate and grotesque and iconoclastic."

"Weird behavior. But *some* of them do that, you mean . . . it's not *all* of them."

"This is how their culture has taught *all* of them to think and act for ages. It's built into their ethos, it's a part of who they are, it's what they do and have always done. They're hyper-tribal, they aren't individualistic like us, but it's not our responsibility to sort them out anyway."

"Eh, part of me can appreciate the lowered standards of collage art," Ed said as they danced closer. "Leaves the door open for uncultured grifters."

"I'd stick to the art of making one-foot putts while maintaining consciousness for now. And of following proper courting procedures, like for that first date."

"To please the lady?"

"Movie'd do."

"Any in particular?"

"Latest out of New-Am."

AT DUSK THEY JOINED an energetic crowd en route to the theater. Being a central front in the Wars of Reclamation had made France host to a variety of other European nationalities who had come to assist the natives in their restoration efforts, so, duly, out tonight and past any gripes were Danes, Portuguese, and Welsh, the Knights of the Intermarium, and many others. Most were soldiers, but there were scores of others here to contribute what they could. They were doctors and nurses, chefs and machinists, they had brought along their children and extended families, and all on this evening were raring for a message to inspire faith in their collective cause.

Down la Reine under sundown skies, Ed had a moment witnessing the real diversity of the motherland. The meet and greet in Innsbruck had given him a glimpse of it, but these weren't merely kids who'd been wrangled together for a golf tournament; these were men and women committed to something beyond themselves, playing their part in nature's struggle and putting their lives on the line to take their shared civilization back from an age-old enemy. While waiting outside the theater, observing the fellow faces of those around him, listening to the mélange of relative tongues, Ed couldn't help but see the fraternal order incarnate and, maybe for the first time, feel himself a part of it.

The night's feature was the latest cinematic installment from Western Redux Pictures out of the New Republic, *The Klenzer of Kassel*, a highly anticipated film about a German soldier whose feats of strength had recently entered into the archives of European folklore. The film industry in New-Am had taken off shortly after Reindependence, and its productions were consistently effective at spreading optimism and presenting a fresh vision, while at the same time bypassing the chronic perversion and subtle to less so social engineering practices so prevalent within the annals of Old-Am entertainment.

"Klenze," Ed muttered while inspecting the poster outside, "that's right."

By now nearly everyone had heard the story and, at least those who could stomach it, seen the infamous video that had elevated the young Frank von Klenze to Occidental renown. During one of the early unofficial raids on Munich, perhaps as a result of his shy but overzealous nature they thought, Klenze had been captured, then tortured and prepped for a ritual beheading on livestream. The New Germans touted the event for propaganda purposes, but the intended outcome backfired as much as it possibly could have, quickly becoming a viral sensation and inspirational feed for the opposite side, when, seconds before he was to have his head lopped off in front of the world, Klenze broke free, subdued his captors, and performed systematic reverse-executions on them before escaping to freedom. But that wasn't the half of it. Shortly after the incident, Klenze, enigmatic an individual as he was, believed to have been disillusioned by fame, disappeared, again assumed captured or worse after a rescue team discovered his autojeep abandoned outside of his hometown of Kassel. He was pronounced dead weeks later, a funeral even having been held to commemorate his short but eventful life, only for Klenze to appear seemingly out of nowhere the following day, shrugging off all inquisitions into his unaccounted-for whereabouts and going back to business as usual as a low-ranking infantryman. It took several months for the actual story to be brought to light, but it was pieced together by tales of horror from New German deportees, who, after Kassel was reclaimed in what was described as an unprecedented cakewalk even compared to cities with a far more sizable invader population, spoke of a phantom Kraut who had stalked and expunged every sub-elder male in the night, single-handedly, and valiantly, it was argued, reconquering the town of his birth. As the legend grew, a movie, many figured, was the least the guy deserved. . . .

Ed and Jennifer grabbed their Maximum Definition glasses and found their seats. The previews wound down and the lights dimmed. The opening scene of *The Klenzer of Kassel* was an action sequence that wowed the crowd with advanced cinematic techniques and exquisite authenticity, but, to the surprise of all, the film stopped after ten minutes and broke into a commercial.

Piano keys played on a glum loop. Captions in multiple languages ran across the bottom of the screen. A voice narrated: *Neoseparatist Ultrafascism is sweeping across New Europe. Is someone you know a Neoseparatist Ultrafascist?* . . . A wife looks distrustfully at her husband as he browses the Bad-Net. . . . *Many Old Europeans have fallen prey to this dangerous ideology and are rejecting the Cultural Infusion Plan. They no longer believe in the values of New Europe.* . . . As a diverse group laughs together around a workplace watering hole, the camera zooms in on the man from before, now standing in the background and breathing heavily with a crazed grin. . . . *Cultural Infusion offers the only pathway to peace . . . but we need your help. . . .* The wife is shown crying in a bathroom corner, but she looks up suddenly as if in revelation. Next she is depicted smiling as she fills out a Suspicious Persons Report online. The picture zooms in on the New European Union emblem in the corner as it fades out. . . . *What are you doing to stop Neo-separatist Ultrafascism?*

Many of the movie-goers had removed their glasses and were looking around and murmuring but, these types of messages being nothing new, most were content to laugh it off and settle back in once the film returned to the screen. Ten minutes later, though, it happened again. The film was interrupted by another commercial, a Bonner Media network plug for the upcoming season of shows, this time in French.

"What's it saying?"

"It's advertising the Fall Lineup: *Taharrush New Britannia* followed by *Mufti and the Infidels.*"

The advertisement didn't prompt much reaction until a scene from *Mufti and the Infidels* showed a ratty-bearded Arab man with his arm around a prepubescent blonde girl, an image that goaded many to stand in protest.

Ed nudged Jennifer. "I think," focusing her attention through the growing stir, "something about how the character, Dimmud, takes a new wife next season, and how Aladdin approves of taking infidel child-brides, because . . . because. Well, just because."

They looked at each other with moon-wide eyes. "What *the*—"

By the time *The Klenzer of Kassel* had returned to the screen, the crowd was halfway to a riot, the commotion ensuing until the film was stopped. Through the theater speakers a voice explained that a recent hack had infected the provincial network with New Union adware, and that while they were working to fix the problem, for the time being, there was nothing that could be done. Unsatisfied with this explanation, many began to express their desire to airmail hefty packages of gelignite to Bonner Media headquarters, and to pay Dimmud a visit to show him what an infidel *really* looked like.

An older military man came on stage with intent to calm. He tapped the microphone then reiterated that there was nothing that could be done for now. He asked whether they would like to proceed or cancel the viewing, but both options ignited another roar of dissent.

A soldier jumped on stage and beckoned for the microphone. He paced with it until the quiet settled. "*Mes amis, mes amis!*—who here has had enough?" speaking passionately with a heavy accent, one Ed recognized mainly from old cartoons and such, back when there was some confusion as to there being an actual non-Arab, non-African, *French* people. . . . "Who is retí to stand and say *no moire!*"

Nearly everyone clapped in agreement as the soldier handed the microphone back. "It's not that simple," the older military man said. "We will deal with Bonner Media when the time comes, but for now it's not an option."

"But eat ees!" the soldier yelled. "Bonner Media headquarters is in Luxembourg now with its Société Anonyme and Treasuree. We could be there in an hour!"

"Enough!" the older military man barked. "Luxembourg is a sovereign territory and for now we have to respect international protocols."

"*Horsesense!* Luxembourg is a part of Europe, and those making this propaganda are not. The foreign media companies that think they can hide in the SNBL must be-eh *smashed!* My mon *père* hunted down the last Neal and pulled the trigger on *Le Monde* . . . my uncle put an end to the Dessault line . . . and my bro tear braced Drahi to the lunette before see mouton fell upon hees *cou!* Now ees *my* turn . . . ees *our* turn . . . Bonner's day has *come!*"

The older military man tried to get a last word in, but the decision had been made. The soldiers were clearing out of the theater, faces aflush with fury, grumblings with promises of comeuppance. Ed and Jennifer turned to each other, caught in the moment. They stood and moved with the crowd out to the streets as the clamor of a siege intensified, the spirit infectious.

She was giving him a look; then, preemptively when their eyes crossed paths, said, "You play golf, Ed."

"What?" with put-on innocence, but wondering, as she supposed, out of equal parts bravado and thrill-seeking bent, how he was going to get in on the action.

"They won't let you through."

"Yeah we'll see." The mob was gathering around the gates of the Versailles base. Ed was scoping it out as Jennifer was dragging him in the opposite direction. He stopped, gave her a face, the decision made. "I have to try," he said before darting off.

A stone's throw from the throng he picked out a man walking away from it, in a uniform a little lighter blue than many others, and pulled up in front of him.

"Colonel Wachovski, defcon 4, Slovakia," Ed said.

The man waved him off and kept moving. "Wrong guy."

Ed jumped back in front of him, fingers snapping. "With the sister with the hair, Colonel Wachovski, defcon 4, Slovakia."

In the man's incensed look: the fate of this plan: up in flames. But then he gave in, pushing Ed's hand away and saying, "Captain Forkbeard, Bardu-foss Air Wing 134, Norway."

Ed apologized, arms up. "Imposter out there."

He joined the pack at the gates. *Bardenfoss. Forkbeard . . . Forkbeard?* They were scanning IDs. When Ed got to the front he tried to slide through undetected; it didn't work. "Badge," a guard said, grabbing his arm and yanking him back.

"Not on me, civeelian tonight," wisp of the Orient in there? fronting like the guy was in the wrong for asking.

The guard pointed out. "Sorry."

Ed, ready to drop this sad act of gall and folly, with one more shot—leaning in, teeth bared, eyes glassed with rage, drawing a blank. "Barden *fah*—" He here observed that the guard's eyes were fixated on his hand, which was curled into some nervous cripple-position in front of his chest. "—Foss?"

"Is that," the guard timidly, "the sign of the Bulgarian SOBT Red Berets?"

Ed didn't know how to respond. But he wouldn't have to after getting waved through. A few steps in the next round of nerves hit. He wavered, making small turns with each impulse and counter-impulse respectively directing him to proceed and abort, when someone slapped him on the back, "Tu as l'air perdu . . . où vas-tu?" The soldier speaking to him shifted to his front and shook him. "Uh?"

"I'm lost."

"Yes, you look lost. So where is it you wish to go?"

Ed hesitated. "Captain Spoonbeard, Hardfloss Air Wing 164, Norway."

The soldier nodded like he was assessing the veracity of this claim. "Captain Spoonbeard, of Norway," in salute. "Well, *Capitaine* . . . there is no," sighing, hands on his hips, "no company here from Norway as far as I know. But as we are all short maybe the young capitaine should come with us? Though I am afraid we are but lowly on font tree . . ."

"I should umm . . ." *You're the Captain now—lines*. "What are we waiting for?"

"For pour toi!" motioning toward the barracks ahead, "To Luxembourg we go." Steps later, ". . . Une byedeeway," a hand out, "I am Sergeant Alain Lartiguy."

"Lartiguy?"

LAH-TEH-GEE—who turned out to be just who Ed was looking for. In no time he was getting suited up, had a helmet strapped to his head and a Redeemer in his hand, and was making the acquaintance of the other, present-on-short-notice members of the 24e Régiment d'Infanterie.

After that they were jogging out to a field and jumping in an autocopter as the war fleet lit up the darkness, ascending into then blazing across the night sky in the direction of the Grand Duchy. Once General Leroux was finished giving his men the rundown, Sergeant Lartiguy turned to Ed. "So we should be in and out," he said. "The other details you should know since you are from Norway, Capitaine."

"I never spent much time in the Luxembourg region to be honest."

"No . . ." Sergeant Lartiguy was giving him a funny look. "Wait. There is a Luxembourg in Norway?" He slapped Ed on the knee, "This is news to me. I was speaking in référence to Bonner Media. They had probe lambs keeping their headquarters in Stockholm after the collapse and were kept out of every other place after the Pull Out, so they moved to the SNBL, to Luxembourg, where their financial offices were already located. Not that this is important since they still have a monopoly on the media in New Sweden, no? You would know better than me."

"What's the SNBL?"

"You don't know?" Sergeant Lartiguy said, finding it odd that Captain Spoonbeard would be unfamiliar with the acronym, until Ed, diagnosing the gaffe, acted like it just registered; though Sergeant Lartiguy filled him in anyway, "You must I think have a different term for this—the South Netherlands, Belgium, and Luxembourg region—New Unionist bastion concentré in Brew Sell. Foreign companies like Bonner can run their propaganda networks from there with no major pre-suns in New Sweden or Pari or wherever. The SNBL is about as European as Timbuktu these days, but the ERP has officially accepted its status," the Sergeant's eyebrows arching with delight, "until now."

"So Bonner, that Swedish?"

"No, it is not Swedish."

"So it's French? Sounds French."

"No no, it is not French, either."

The back end of the armada dipped into a haze of yellow gas at the junction of a T intersection, beyond whose cross was a forested cliff and the lights of Luxembourg City's Old Town on the lower tier of earth. Straight up the lane in front was the financial district. They came to berth and jumped out, in no felt rush, the area locked down, with men stationed in all three directions. The Bonner Media building was a half block up the lightly inclined road. Ed tailed the others toward it under lamps high and dim, hyperalert, his attention veering up and down the street, then across it. On the other side was a sandy-brown building with a royal façade behind gates, flags, and an *Edward Scissorhands'* [1990] garden. Gold letters above the door read: Banque Centrale de Luxembourg . . .

Oh they were in it. Outside the Bonner Media building a soldier had climbed up to the metal awning and was tagging a message on the front. The message read: Nous, Peuple d'Europe, Condamnons Ce Temple de Mensonges . . .

"Translation, Sergeant?"

"Mmhow to say . . . '*The people of Europe condemn this temple of lies.*'"

This was getting heavy. Three security guards were lying face down in the lobby. A man in a suit was pleading from his knees with hogtied hands; a soldier had the barrel of a pistol pressed against his forehead. Ed's knees buckled. The pistol was lowered and the man was hauled past him and out. Ed backed into a recess near the door, his eyes on a tense pendulous line prior to being drawn to a wallscreen on the far side. On it were two women in black niqabs, seated behind a desk, delivering a live broadcast. The caption read: Attaque Terroriste par l'Ancien Européen en Cours . . . *Uh-tock-eh*—a terrorist attack? What like here. The women stood and flailed their arms as a soldier wearing the same helmet and uniform as Ed and everyone else entered the frame, then the feed turned to static. Ed was having trouble swallowing. He wasn't swallowing. He couldn't swallow.

Sergeant Lartiguy waved from across the lobby. Ed jogged over and followed him down the hallway, into a stairwell, up a floor, and into a newsroom, with a studio at the far end and busy bees throughout—taking apart equipment, downloading information to flatpads, unhinging VDUs and arranging computers and servers and packing boxes and carrying it all out, here and there boot-smashing a thing or two. Ed burrowed into the wall. He was possibly having a heart attack.

Sergeant Lartiguy came over a minute later with an update. "Shut. It.

Down," faking a low jab, Ed keeling over anyway. "Will take Bonner a while to recover, but we can't do much since we don't want to be here any longer than we have to. Right, Capitaine?"

"Uh-huh uh-huh . . . so who's in control of their networks?"

Sergeant Lartiguy clocked his helmet back and forth. "We are. Technically. Have control of the satellites for now. And we locked Bonner out but they will find a way to override us before long."

"Mmm-uh-huh . . . and how long before that happens?"

"Hour. Two hours. Hard to say. Why do you ask, Capitaine?"

"Dunno." Ed hereabouts determined that his to-date coddled, featherbed of a brain had reverted to functioning on some primitive plane, not unknown inside the spaces between one and eighteen, where one's operating system was temporarily commandeered by the spiritual forces of self-preservation and, more mysteriously, enhanced extraconscious execution. "But what you're saying is we can broadcast whatever we want on Bonner's stations, is what you're saying."

Sergeant Lartiguy paused. He looked back and yelled at a group of people. A few nodded in response. "Maybe we should put a funny message up or somesing telling them to get out. But as I said, it won't last long. They will find a way around it and put on some *Mufti* reruns."

"Why not set a trap?"

"What do you mean a trap?"

"Put a message up telling them something's happening somewhere, Aladdin's in town or whatnot, then when they show up . . . *boom*."

Sergeant Lartiguy laughed. "Word gets around too fast, Capitaine."

"In Pari. But what about New Sweden? You said Bonner has a monopoly on the media there so some would fall for it, right?"

Sergeant Lartiguy sat on it. "I didn't even think about that. It must be a, 'tis le mot—a media blackout."

"Exactly." Ed was sure of nothing but the following: he was astral projecting.

Sergeant Lartiguy left Ed with a wait-finger and walked over to the group. After that there was more conversation than action in the newsroom, to the point where most of the soldiers had stopped whatever else they were doing and gathered in the middle. Then two high-ranking-looking men came down and joined the discussion. Ed didn't know what was going on, if the idea was being considered or if something else had come up. He just wanted the spinning to stop.

His concentration was on the blurred glow of the stairwell, through which he was contemplating a possible escape; but it was unclear whether he would be able to walk. A hand came down hard on Ed's shoulder. His head slammed against the wall. Sergeant Lartiguy again, animated, explaining how the idea had been relayed up the chain of command and that a message from the Scandinavian Alliance in Oslo had come back confirming interest; talking as well about how a thing was being put together in the newsroom, like Ed had suggested, a message telling the New Swedes in New Stockholm that there would be an event at a place to be filled in later, or something— still only a maybe—"Who knows if they will go through with it. Knowing the Scandinavian Alliance, probably not."

Ed mumbled, "Just a thought." About to vomit.

Sergeant Lartiguy left as another dispatch arrived. Then the mood in the newsroom flipped. There was a spike in enthusiasm, whistling and high-fives. Sergeant Lartiguy, limbs spread, rushed back over and wrapped one around Ed.

"They want to coordinate a multiple-city attack . . ."

Able to swallow now. "That good?"

"C'était lui! *Good?* ce gars!" Sergeant Lartiguy yelled out, his arm still around Ed, who soon had every eye in the room on him. "You may have just kicked off the Swedish Reclamation."

"Qui c'est?"

"C'est Le Capitaine. . . ." Swallowing his vomit. "Capitaine Spoonbeard!"

❧

MATURATION, HOWEVER FRUITFUL the ripening, didn't come without its hitches. The more impulsive faculties that could be incidentally beneficial in the fray, whether products of youthful naiveté or gung-ho stupidity, had a way of dulling over time. With a greater separation from innocence, a deeper partnership with failure, and a self in the second-stage throes of discovery, summoning that old killer instinct was proving to be a test of will. Sheer adrenalin had pushed Ed through in Innsbruck, but Poitiers was turning out to be a slog; no more fresh alpine air, only a July broil that nearly flattened him on the front nine the day before, Friday, resulting in a string of embarrassing buzzards. He was no orphan in the downs, though, and had fared better than most, eventually regaining his composure and sneaking into the fourth slot. The board was in constant flux over the first two rounds as unlikelys moved up and favorites down, with Albaraz in the latter category, dropping into the teens after an apparent heatstroke on nine. Shapiro after all was said and done retained the third position, two strokes ahead of Ed, which paired them up for the final two days and, out of a rising contempt for the garrulous, was enough to give his game some Saturday zest.

A lukewarm, late-afternoon breeze was breathing across the Saint-Cyr Lake. The course was built around two small breakaway lagoons at the northeast end, giving it an island-feel in parts. The larger body of water and the white-winged sails adrift upon it were visible from several points throughout the course, the eighteenth tee being one, where, in a patch of black pine shade between the ground and one of the lagoons, stood Ed and Shapiro as the third round of play was drawing to a close.

Spectators, the better part senior citizens in hats and sunglasses and light-colored clothes, bordered the path ahead and stared silently back waving hand-fans at neutral-to-cranky faces, waiting.

"Heard you cut the corner of the dogleg in the practice round," Shapiro, now sitting three strokes ahead of Ed, said.

"Barely."

"Think you can do it again?"

Probably not, Ed supposed internally. The par-4 closer bent hard left two-hundred and fifty or so yards up the fairway, with the hole out of sight on the other side of the turning point—the dogleg. And while he *had* successfully flown a ball over the corner in the practice round, there was no reason to take such a risk now; settling it into the elbow of the turning point was difficult enough, and gaining a stroke wasn't worth losing one, or likely two or three, if it didn't make it.

Ed caught a look from Stig as he entered the teebox, an expression translating roughly to *Don't even think about it*. But he wasn't. His shot came to rest around where it was supposed to and he and Shapiro each held par to close out the day.

Later on Ed heard a knock as he was freshening up. He opened the door to Jennifer, in one of her chic neo-mantelets, hands stuffed into front pockets like oven mitts, hair in a high Bohemian bun over long-batting ferns over eyes that thinned displeasingly as they zeroed in on his own hair. They said hello. He invited her in. She sauntered over to the bed and sat on the edge as he went for the mirror.

"You played good today."

"Yeahayguess."

"You weren't happy with it?"

"Yeahnuhaydunno. I just can't seem to get back to where I used to be."

"How was it different than now?"

"Not sure, but it was," every clue available in the woebegone expression he exhibited for her through the mirror. "I used to be more aggressive— reckless, but spontaneous, too. Less distracted by what was going on around me. Less worried about screwing up. Less hung up on how everyone watching hates me."

"They hate Shapiro and whoever's in the Hefty, not you."

"You should see the looks I get out there . . . these people don't like me."

"Not true! I hear them yelling stuff to pick you up. Like today, the guys who told you to do the Fortaleza fade and the La Paz punch."

"That's a couple of old-school amateur tour aficionados, sagermetrics guys, Ernest and Orin, been around forever. But I'm not talking about them."

"The French? They've always been like that. But any restraint they have comes from not being sure whose side you're on."

"Don't think it'd be any different regardless. I used to have this whole approach, this mentality, I could get in this zone and nothing could break me out of it. It was just me in the garden." Ed went over to the bed, sat down, and scuba-fell back. "But I lost it. No more garden, just some jungle I'm lost in."

"Know what that sounds like?" leaning back on her elbow.

"What?"

"Sounds like what we're all doing—rebuilding and repairing what we used to take for granted . . . recultivating our garden. We used to spend our time trying to fix everyone else's plot. Meanwhile we were dying out and getting overrun and our own societies were turning into third world jungles. We had to look inward and focus on ourselves again, get our own plots in order. And we're still figuring it out, but we're doing it together now—you, me, everyone out there."

"So you're saying I should like plant new seeds or trim the hedges or find a way to pretend all those old people don't hate me or what."

"Those old people are a part of your extended family, jackass. They know it, I know it, only you don't know it. Our garden was destroyed by a pest, and it's still a mess, we're still lost, but we're recultivating it as one now. If those old French people see you playing with confidence and striving to be the best, they'll hop behind the plow and push you through."

"I know how it feels to strive to be the best and to fall short and it's not good."

"They'll still be there if you do," Jennifer said, patting down his hair. "That's how we are these days, how we have to be. And that's why I'm here now, to tell you to be a man and keep fighting. To tell you that, for all your flaws, when I see you out there, I already think you're the best."

THEY SAID IT WAS SLOW. Boring. Not a sport. Just an old-timey game played by people with too much time on their hands. And maybe they were right. But anyone harboring such opinions who was present for Sunday's final round in Poitiers had to reconsider as they bore witness to a showdown that was second to none in the theater of the links. With Grade-A prep-support from Stig, Jennifer's reassuring sideline presence, and a summer glow that made this chunk of west-central France feel like a lawn to Never Never Land, Ed stepped sock-to-cap in Gaul Green onto the first tee and cracked a drive that nearly rattled the croaker cage.

Stage two had turned into a two-player shootout by the eighth as Ed lion-stalked Shapiro's lead and chipped away at it one sorcerous stroke after another. By the time they'd reached the back nine the crowd had swelled to where it seemed as though half the city had gotten wind of the action and come out to see for themselves. Not that Ed much noticed with the new blinders up, back in Baryshnikov form, airwalking through some zone trial upgrade as he shepherded a keyed-up congregation of elderly French denizens in their Sunday bests down botanic fairways, maestroed with iron baton Gregorian chants into the lakeside estival ether, and piloted a magic roller-coaster ride that had necks crooking and backs bending and whole bodies twisting in graceful unison through long ball-ranging arcs up and down the Kelly-green penncross pulpits of Haut-Poitou like he was leading tai chi exercises in the park.

The peripeteia came on fourteen when a thirty-yard slow-winder found its way in for eagle and caused a sward-rippling eruption within the congested backwoods cul-de-sac at the farthest par-5 reaches of the course to take Ed from a one-shot deficit to a one-shot lead. Both players then matched birdies on fifteen, and with the new momentum it looked to be a mere matter of Ed's ability to hang on. Off the tee at sixteen, however, a short par-3 roughly a hundred and sixty yards from box to pin, far and away the easiest green to hit, he airmailed it—one of those scatterbrained shankjobs that happened from time to inopportune time. And if the pained hoot he emitted a millisecond after the ball split from the clubface was any indication, Ed knew he'd blown it.

He looked away. He couldn't watch. There was a collective sigh as the ball found rest in parts yet unknown. Afterward, to make matters worse, Shapiro's shot dropped flush onto the green, setting him up for another birdie attempt.

Ed trekked up the fairway and tread into the light boscage north of the hole. It was worse than he thought: behind a tree, a *big* tree, or big enough—blocking any clear shot to the green. He and Stig looked down at it for a drawnout while, each with one hand on a hip and the other over their mouths', nearabout shaming it. "So what do we think," Ed said at last.

"Just make sure it gets out, to the top right rough. Best case we're down one, worst we're down two, but there's still two more holes."

With a slow backswing that transitioned into an awkward downward twist, Ed caught the ball with the toe of the wedge and pinched it around the tree. It made it to the rough but landed farther away from the green than he was hoping. He remained: alone, hidden, eyes closed, with a few choice words under his breath until modest cheers were heard following Shapiro's successful second shot. Ed's third made it onto the green, but the slope carried it to the bottom edge. He two-putted it in from there, but the blunder in the end gave Shapiro a two-stroke lead back.

On the par-5 seventeenth Ed failed to make any headway; Shapiro played it safe and held par, while Ed's birdie attempt fell a few inches short. After that it was on to eighteen, carrying a largely deflated crowd in his wake. Shapiro teed off first and drove his ball to the elbow of the turning point. Ed stepped up next and pushed the tee into the grass. He took a practice swing and held his driver in front of him to center himself. He wasn't going to make up the two shots required to take it to a playoff. But with a win already in the bag and two more stages to go, that was hardly the end of the world. It sunk in bittersweet: a tough loss to swallow, true, though he had for a swag spell or two been able to recapture that rhythm of yore. So there were positive takeaways. *Good in it.* Yes. Easy, boy. . . .

"Time for some of that Montevideo voodoo, Ed-ee."

"Lima, Fox Two: launch!"

Ed smirked and stepped off as a spurt of rallying applause broke the peace. Bashfully, he ran the clubhead over the grass, took one last look ahead, and got back in his stance—receiving, momentarily, a whiff of nostalgia; recalling, just briefly, what it was like playing with nothing to lose, back when he understood that victory was a reward bestowed only upon those willing to take it.

Ed reared back limber, snapped around boost-strong and brisk, and murdered it—a low-trajectory laser most had lost track of before it cleared the trees a hundred and fifty yards up. Claps. Half-claps. Confused chatter. Surprise from those unaware that going *over* the bend was an option. He started the hike up the fairway, head down but with a covert eye ahead. Not long into the walk signals began coming back that the shot had made it to the other side. Upward thumbs and nods at the turning point then appeared to indicate that the shot was good. As Ed rounded the bend and saw the fingers pointing to the lie, he was able to conclude that it was *real* good. The crowd was back. And as they followed him up the other side, the chants began: *Aids . . . Aids* again . . . *Aids* over and over.

The ball found a seat three yards north-right of the green and a total of twenty from the hole, at the top of an all-downward slope. But the eighteenth green was a generous one that could escort a well-placed ball down the gutter and in. Ed gave it an extended eye then looked back at Shapiro, who was a long ways back and facing a parted sea of sodality not his own; discomfort discernable from afar as he lifted back and cranked it hard right into a bunker down from where Ed was standing.

A bad shot. But he had lives.

Ed walked over to the ball and took a squat behind it. Equilibrium between the toes, plotting the points, visualizing the itinerary. He stood and made a few final scans and started to get into position, but backed off and took one more look. The last breath came out like a controlled balloon as he set up again. Pin-drop silence, eyes on the spot. The club rose back at an angle so slight, stopped, and fell forward-down. A gentle tap, a resulting *pop*, jumping at contact, rising to no more than knee-high and landing on the inner cuff of the green. It took two baby bounces and started down the slope as a chorus of *Get in the hole*'s cried out. Bodies knotting as it curved, hands pushing it, steering it right. "Right" . . . "Ri*ght*" . . . Right. It slowed a few feet from the hole but kept rolling, slower then slower. Inches away, the ball had lost nearly all of its momentum but was still moving. Dying as it reached the lip. *Teetering*. Right there. Then it stopped. Or for a moment seemed to before it blew in, vanished, eagle—*au revoir* . . .

The sound of thunder on a clear day, just something in the air. Ed played it cool over to the hole, snagged the ball, and low-waved around. He stepped off the green and looked over at Shapiro, who was down in the bunker, barely the head of the little guy visible. The scene grew silent. A tad cough-y. His third shot got out but skipped to the far side of the green. Shapiro climbed out and made the lonely walk over. This would be the final go to take it to a playoff, and it was going to be a difficult one with the crowd courteously willing him to miss.

And it wasn't the worst putt. But it fell short.

Ed had clinched stage two of the Diversity Open. Back in business— *officially*. And it was a sensation like no other, in the then and there. But those partial for play at the spectrum's ends had made a deal or two in the past with that fellow fond to perch atop the other shoulder, the Spirit that Denies, in the here and now, chuckling through it all, leaning in to whisper: *Big smile my man, spread that wave champ, lark pro tem in windfall and roses . . . for soon we meet again. . . .*

Till then, *Partisan.* . . . Hither and yon, handshakes with old happy strangers, palms pelting against his back, wondering if he had on the cornered-downy face, I, Edmund, creator of joy again—*Thank you thank you, mercy boo coo*—down the clover-floored line, in cedar frame and sunglow, bumping into Jennifer.

"We must re—"

"—Don't . . . please."

VI

Then dared my spirit to soar over all it knew,
Here I wage war, this I subdue

—Faust

IV

Twilight of the dawn. Sparks on the Main. First light creeping into the windows of Deutschherrnufer under a soft quilt of cloud. That star, on time again, rising with the robin's falsetto and in synchronicity with Martin Uhland and Gert Ulrich's successful unauthorized entry into apartment 53 of building four. The door closed behind them, their bags hit the floor. The two men scanned the unit then met back in the living room. Without a word they peeled the fake beards from their faces, shed their taqiyahs and thawbs, dragged the bags to a table near the window-wall overlooking Frankfurt am Main, and got to work: setting up the diamagnetisor, opening the digital gateway, activating the NASCIP VI, and connecting to the Potsdam cryptochannel. A clearscreen was enlarged to cover the left wall; on it were thirty frames with views from the invisible eyes of the nano-cameras Uhland and Ulrich spent the last hour installing via micro-bot. *Hier, checken . . . Ja stimmt. Check . . . Alles klar. Und. No . . . Okay, checken. . . .* And now they wait, with silent stares into the waking metropolitan panorama: Frankfurt central to their left, their target immediately across the river—a deconstructivist obstruction and high command to despots: the New European Union Central Bank, though what was set to occur inside was still being pieced together as the first updates rolled in:

EXPECTED THIS MORNING ARE REPRESENTATIVES FROM THE NEUCB, THE BANK OF ENGLAND, THE INTERNATIONAL SETTLEMENT BANK, THE FREE

Society Foundation, the Michbuch, and of course Imperial Dutch Electric. Reason for meeting still unknown . . . eta 8:30 a.m.

"Whoa," Ulrich buzzed, shooting an eye at Uhland.

"Das sollte Spaß machen."

For a couple of seasoned spooks like Uhland and Ulrich, the big picture could be pieced together from the most rudimentary of details. But this was quickly turning out to be beyond the usual scope. As regional members of the Googlopticon Investigation Unit they were accustomed to going roach, wearing itchy getup, and spending long weeks hiding out in Berlin, Amsterdam, Brussels, and the other major city-states: bugging in the night, catching code on shifts, decrypting moonrunes, and databasing intel for desk jockeys back in Potsdam, with the occasional snuffing-out of a traitor or foreign oligarch thrown into the mix. Their professional mark was Imperial Dutch Electric, one of the many private arms of the Libancien. Long presumed to have had a hand in the Googlopticon operation, IDE's energy empire was an exemplar of international malfeasance, fain to prop up reprobate regimes and foment graft, commercial piracy, and social instability, all while hardlining their shareholder's long-awaited borderless paradise.

A memo arrived showing the names of flagged recent arrivals to Hesse. As Uhland skimmed over it, Ulrich stepped to the window and inverted the setting on his oculife glasses, turning them into a pair of binoculars. Still no activity outside the bank—only dogs on the prowl for breakfast scraps, commissars on their way to work, New Germans headed to the mosque as bullhorns crashed the quiet labyrinthine urb. It was harrowing, that desert doo-wop; inescapably eerie hearing the barbarians from Lugash screaming to their sand god in the heart of Europe. But the war cries were nothing if not official these days. Those who had previously held up welcome signs and eschewed long-term realities when the invasion began, who believed in the New Age religion of the Libancien and put their faith in the diversitarian delusion—they were all where they belonged now, able to turn their heads no longer; moral prigs and *Gutmenschen* who sacrificed everything for kosher piety, missed not by the men of this era. . . .

An alarm screamed through the city, interrupting the call to prayer. Ulrich lifted the glasses to his brow and looked back. "Was ist das denn?"

"Ist da was am Zaun los?" Uhland shrugged. "Den Hügeln?"

Ulrich scanned the hills at the edge of the city, where, sure enough, something was astir: airmobile hovering over the fence, human specs around the rim. Uhland typed out a message to Potsdam as he joined Ulrich at the window. "Darf ich mal sehen?" he asked, eager for a peek. The two switched places as a response came back, producing a chortle from Ulrich as he took over the clearscreen. "Was steht da?"

"Delivery from Darmstadt."

"I see it . . . fabelhaft."

Streaming down from an opening in the fence were hundreds of New Germans of the Darmstadtian variety being returned to sender, destined for the offices of the resettlement organizations that brought them here, the neighborhoods of the turncoats who didn't get out when they should have, the lobbies of the foreign bankers issuing the welfare checks. They were Frankfurt's problem now, but a small share of those dropped off in recent years and in increasing numbers from Wetzlar, Limburg, Bad Hersfeld, and all around the State of Hesse, here to squeeze out the urbanite forcing diversity on others, to squat in the park of the tolerant cosmopolitan, to with a wink and nudge invade the home of the foreign *Führungsschicht*. The Old German wasn't prone to sordid expressions of schadenfreude, but nature was the mother of exception. Or something like that.

Shortly after 8 A.M. a motorcade flew in from the north on Holzmann, followed by another from the west. They converged upon the bank and swept underground as Uhland and Ulrich sat down. But just as they were getting comfortable, there was a knock on the door. They traded a glance and stood, removing their sidearms, shuffling to their respective sides of the room, and reuniting at the entrance. Uhland tapped a panel next to the door, which flashed on and transmitted a picture of the lone man on the other side: in a black robe, arms raised, fake beard in one hand. Uhland nodded at Ulrich, who reached for the handle and pulled the door open as their pistols rose to the visitor's chest. The man's name was William C. Bedfast, and he may or may not have had, depending on the ear, one of the last existing traces of a South Shore Massachusetts accent. He also bore an uncanny resemblance to Popeye the Sailor Man, an appearance bodied forth by a mug that could remain remarkably unfazed while visibly unnerving anyone brash enough to point deathware at his vital organs.

Bedfast was waved in and scanned. "Your diamagnetisor up?" he asked, hands still airborne.

"*Ja.*" Ulrich pointed to the box. "*Eine* who might you be?"

"Detective William C. Bedfast," throwing off his thawb like an itchy sock and adjusting the collar of his shirt.

"He *meant* . . ." Uhland, always the greater firebrand of the two, more firmly, "who do you work for?"

"NABINGOA."

Uhland and Ulrich turned to each other. "NAMBI . . ." *wha—?*

"New-Am Bureau of Investigation for Non-Governmental Organizational Affairs, just got in from Zurich," Detective Bedfast replied, maintaining eye contact as he reached into his pocket and removed his credentials.

Both men gave it a once-over; Ulrich scanned it and nodded to his partner then returned a suspicious eye to Mr. C. Bedfast. "How'd you know we were here? This just came through."

But Uhland cut in before Bedfast could respond, "He's from New-Am, *Bruder*, you know how . . ." pivoting and heading back to the table. "Die Zeitmaschine. . . ."

Detective Bedfast trailed Uhland into the room, passing him on his way to the window and laughing at the floor the whole way. "That what you think?" in a half-turn back, "that I came here in a time machine?"

"Everyone knows about it, Bedfast," Ulrich said. "And you got here *real* fast."

"Hate to disappoint you fellas, but I didn't come here in any time machine. And I don't think it works like that anyway, think it only goes one way. I'm here because I'm investigating the Free Society Foundation, namely Alex Schwartz. He just got into town."

"I didn't see his name on the list," Uhland said, "and that's not one I'd miss."

"Schwartz is traveling under the name Meo Telas."

"Why's he here, though?" Ulrich, upon camping out midway between them.

"He's got an office in Berlin. But he's also broke. We seized his accounts and property. With the Digital Shift rolled back and the Quiet Purge in effect, those on the J-List are running out of options. They can't lay their golden nets in Old-Am anymore, there's no more sick emperor to corrupt, and they're getting iced or flushed out," Detective Bedfast explained astare into the crystal morning glare. "But since Germany has yet to show a willingness to assert itself and put a few of these rats in the dirt, some like Schwartz think they might be able to rally over here."

"Then you must know what this meeting is about."

"We just found out about it, too, though if I had to guess I'd say it's probably about a hosta things." Detective Bedfast pirouetted around and belled his eyes back and forth between the two Germans. "I assume you fellas know about the underground plasma center IDE is building in Hoogstraten?" Few presently alive being more studied on the matter than Uhland and Ulrich—the particulars of the prospective plasma center fundamental to their job by day, night, or cosmic hour—they needn't vent more than a miffed *Ja* in response. "That's one issue," Bedfast continued after picking up the signal, "out of many more. Our enemy is working around the clock to keep the Libancien together, but it's coming apart fast. The more we flood the city-states and isolate them from the outside, the more difficult it becomes for them to maintain their operations. And the more of their cousins we send home, whom they have to defend against on the desert front, the more they find themselves under siege. They thought they could unload them on us but now they're getting them back by the millions and our new greatest ally in the region is penning them in and coordinating the zerg rushes so we can focus on domestic matters."

"So is Schwartz trying to hatch one last diversity revolution in Europe?"

"Seems so, but I'm gonna nab him before he has the chance."

"If you do we'll be one link closer to the head of the snake."

"The high priests' time is here." Detective Bedfast walked over to the clearscreen on the wall. His finger drifted up to a panel that showed a group making its way down a hall, then over to another looking down on a conference room.

"Recognize anyone, Bedfast?"

"Sure do."

Uhland and Ulrich moved in as the group filtered into the room.

"Our IDE guy is there," Ulrich said. "There's Schwartz, and . . . *no*—is that?"

"Who?"

"The wicked witch of the Michbuch—the Euro-Net Propaganda Minister, Anette Cohen."

"No national heroine I take it."

"Not unless you get a twisted kick out of outsiders vanning your people for Net Speech Violations," Ulrich, with venom in his voice. "If New-Am is taking on a bigger role over here . . . if we're going to finally start striking some names off the J-List, I might have to put in an official request to take her down myself."

"The ERP would probably be fine with that. I could even put in a word."

Those inside the conference room took their seats around a plank of mahogany surrounded by men tapping beats on canon triggers. Uhland and Ulrich sat down and synced up with the doodads of their IDE stooge, every detail of whose personal and professional life had, unbeknownst to him, become the property of the Teutonic duo across the river. Uhland soon tracked down the meeting report and opened it to discover a sprawling wall of code. This generated irritated reactions from both men. They knew that buried within the code was important information, information that was further buried within a pile of gibberish, gibberish that had sent Uhland and Ulrich on many a wild goose chase and into thus many a fit. It was, however, part of the job, so they ran the file through a decoder and began sifting through the decrypted results: 5901 PENDESTA DR., PRESIDIO, TX . . . +078483070493 . . . PALAZZO ANGULOSOR . . . MOHAMMAD MAPLETHORN . . . BALCONES HARDWARE . . . FIFTH MOVEMENT: ALLEGRETTO. . . . But they'd been through this routine too many times to *not* know that most of these things meant absolutely nothing.

"*Verdammt!*" Uhland blurted out, slamming his fist on the table. He looked over at Detective Bedfast, who was leaning against the wall and twiddling his thumbs, fully disengaged. "So, Amerikaner. Why'd you pop in if you aren't interested in figuring out what's going on?"

"Oh I'm interested," Bedfast, like he was waiting to be asked, "but I already have what you're looking for." The tension flowed spirit-like out of Uhland and Ulrich's shoulders as their tilting heads and attention, in sidekick symbiosis, fixated on Detective Bedfast. Bedfast strutted over and pinned a piece of paper to the table with his index finger. On it were the numbers: *9002121625024048.*

"What's it mean?"

"We don't know," he sighed. "Heard one of yous's a codemonkey, though, so another reason I came up was to give whichever one of yous is a crack."

"*Undvennverr* you going to tell us you had this?" Uhland demanded. He stood, face fast-flushing chili-pepper red. "Codemonkey? Who is this guy?" aghast down at Ulrich, then shouting—"Ich hab's dir doch gesagt! . . . Die *Zeitmaschine!*"

Bedfast took a step toward Uhland. "And I told *you,*" putting a finger into his chest, "it doesn't work like that!"

"Will both of you shut up," Ulrich broke in. "Where did you get this code, Bedfast?"

"It's been circulating among some on the J-List, including Schwartz. We think it's important but we don't know what it means since we don't have the key. Bean-counter bots didn't come up with anything, either."

"Nine-hundred," Ulrich mumbled, that first part hitting a tune, "that can only be one thing . . ." trailing off, drowning out the ensuing conversation between Uhland and Bedfast, taking the piece of paper on a trip to the window, inspecting it like a magnifying glass. Known to few outside of what he thought were tight-lipped circles, his patient wife, and a five-year-old son who'd of late taken an interest in the old man's peculiar hobbies, the taciturn but poly-versed Mr. Gert Ulrich, foremost a soldier and methodical sleuth faithful to the long-term interests of the Fatherland, did indeed dabble in the dark art of cryptography, or codemonkeying, it would seem, but was, moreover, and essential to the present moment, in possession of a trait no serf-bot or supermachine, even at this late brink-of-the-droid-revolt day in time, could claim: an ability to feel out human error, study the tricks of an adversary, and crawl inside its crooked mind . . . *Empfindungsvermögen.*

Sentience!

Ulrich brought up a chart and began scribbling some notes against the window. If he was on the right track, the code translated to w-b-*???????????*
. . . to wit: Jack Scheiße. But upon closer inspection he began to consider the possibility that the four and the eight at the end were in reference to something else; perhaps, a date; perhaps, the upcoming date of August 4th. So he had two possible routes in a word or phrase that likely started with a "w" . . . but the "B" couldn't be right. No, there was something else here, some factor the originator of the message used to disguise it: the protocol. As Gert Ulrich cycled through the vowels, considered the various alphanumeric possibilities, and split up the number string, somewhat of a pattern emerged. He was no longer looking at *90021216250240408* but rather a series like *900-2-12-16-250-240-48*, or *4-8* . . . or August 4th. Then he

discovered what appeared to be a progression, a slight variation each move ahead. . . . An *additional* value. *Eureka* . . . was that it? The value of each letter was being multiplied in sequence, and Ulrich's mind was unknowingly already lugging up the copestone. W-A-D . . . D again? Maybe. Another vowel? He kept plugging them in to see what if anything fit. O? Oh. *240*. August 4th . . . WADDOL . . . WADDOL? No—*WADDON?* "WADDON!" Ulrich yelled. "That light any lanterns?" flinching when he realized Uhland and Bedfast had been standing behind him for an uncertain amount of time. "WADDON?" he murmured again.

"Sounds kind of familiar."

"But what's WADDON?"

A CONFLUENCE OF MYSTICAL AGENTS, chemical reactions in full spate—the great catalysis. A rush like wine as the sun set over the Taunus, in with the tepid night. They just arrived, but they could stay forever—until the summer was gone, until the windows were polished with frost, until the War was over—living off room service and plotting under linen guard, bunkered down in Friedrichshof Castle. There was concord inside this red-cooped canopy, tangled in palmette patterns of silk, snug below an original Memling, and in the now of tonight, there was nothing else. There was nowhere else. Only this room, this refuge, the cool of its canicule shroud, the glint of its toasted boiserie, the lamplight's faint rings in rhythmic breath against the walls. And it was while in-sail atop such love-blind swells, quite often, with the heart beating in peaceful-pleasured meter and the brain firing neurons over synaptic clefts in repose, when from out of waters more dark than blue resurfaced those painful memories of the past, in times gone by cast out, left at length on lines abandoned, reeled in after some prodding—evasive in the arms of solace, fending off the eyes of the eternal forgiver, against words pleading *Let your virtue be not in restraint but*

the sweet reprieve of truth—and at long last making it back onto the boat now charting a steady course to healing. . . .

"I was just a kid."

"But you remember."

"People had been leaving Malibu and moving up to New-Am, and we were supposed to move up there too, but with all the turmoil, I guess we didn't get out in time. One day some people came to the door and took us to the Deprivileging Camps, then we got split up and I never saw my parents again."

"Oh, Ed. That's exactly what they did when they took over Russia."

"Really?"

"They murdered millions of people, too. Do you remember what the Deprivileging Camps were like?"

"Bad food, lot of reeducation videos, African women yelling at us and saying everything was our fault, that we had, well . . . too much privilege."

"Indoctrinating us with guilt and shame from the earliest age so we wouldn't fight back. Such a sick thing to do."

"I never even thought about how everyone had come to hate people like me, I just accepted it."

"This people view men like you as their enemy, so when men like you allowed them to gain influence they began projecting their hatred of you onto everyone else. This is what they do—they create social divisions and then they weaponize those other groups against the men in charge of that society, riding them into power and using them as pawns to insulate themselves. They lead the slave revolt. . . . It's the Minority Mutiny."

"Mutiny? Like pirates do?"

"Ed, *ugh*. . . . They use the weak against the strong. Different classes, women, minorities, or anyone who may not fit in—they agitate these groups and pit them against men like you, the men who built the society and are supposed to protect it. The noble and the powerful, they become evil oppressors—the wretched and the damned. The poor and the powerless, the sick and the suffering, they become the pious and the good—righteous victims. That was the basis for the praus-shall-inherit-the-earth ideals of Biblical monotheism, the proletariat-as-rightful-ruler in the class warfare of Marxism, and the minority deification and diversity revolutions of equalitarianism. It's an ethnic strategy they use to obtain power in other people's countries."

"So they've done this before."

"They've been doing it for thousands of years. To preserve their group's cohesiveness they have developed an identity that is defined in opposition to the people whose countries they are living in, in opposition to us. They also want to increase the power of their group without bringing too much attention to themselves, so they have adapted behavioral traits that result in them pretending to share those people's interests and even be them through crypsis while promoting things that are bad for those people and weaken them from within, because that in turn strengthens their hand. One way they do this is by attacking the norms and traditions of those people, presenting them as backward and wrong, and promoting the inversion of them as honorable and good—raising the weak over the strong and denaturalizing the natural, portraying the normal as deviant and sacralizing the profane, and creating a counter-tradition through the transvaluation of those people's values. . . . It's Normative Inversion."

"Normative Inversion? That's like the name for it?"

"Ed . . ."

"What."

". . . This isn't going to work."

"You said you were going to be patient while I learn this stuff. That's what I get after opening up about my parents being killed in the gulags?"

"*Sorry*, I'm trying. It's just that this is like common sense in New-Am."

"Helps explain why everything always seemed so backward—it literally was. Still hard to believe though, since it's such strange behavior."

"No, it's not. You see it all the time in nature. They are competing against you for resources and their biological strategy is to make you think otherwise, to make you think they're just like you, or that they're weak and not a threat to you."

"But it's not like they *all* think like that. I mean they aren't coordinating this stuff in smoky back rooms or anything."

"This behavior is ingrained in who they are. They don't need to talk about it and many of them aren't even conscious of it. As hyper-tribalists they think and act in terms of what's best for their group. To them, that's what determines right and wrong, true or false, it factors into every decision they make and colors everything they do."

"Boy you guys sure have this stuff figured out. I didn't realize there were so many differences between people. Usually assumed everyone was just like me. And if I knew there was a foreign group attacking my own like this I might've been compelled to do more to stop it. The fifteen years of service was daunting though, and I thought I could make it on the outside playing golf."

"Why didn't Doc try to find a foster home in New-Am?"

"It was tricky jumping through the hoops, and the roundups spooked a lot of the older folks, but things weren't too bad behind the partitions."

"Still must have been hard growing up like that."

"We made it work."

As many who'd been left behind had found a way to do. Learning how to roll on the slide, to carry himself like a kid who could hold a gig long enough to get the next one—caddying for Gansu bagmen, fixing Sazeracs for sheiks at child-bride yacht auctions, muling skag through East Pasadena for Armenian Slava Fats. A harsh reality, however alluring it may have been to any impressible young man who believed that that was what the world was really like: a nebulous global polity hawking glamorized degeneracy in a chaotic trade zone where one's fortune always seemed tied to someone else's downfall. And while Ed never really had it in him—a hustler pursuant to the pinch, absent the bred-in-the-bone ill-will to be any big cheese—coming of age in the yolk of it had left a wake of spiritual debris, a tempest in the soul, long adrift in a world he was finally beginning to understand, from this advent, on the outside now, grasping, flimsily, but *still* grasping, that it never actually had to be that way. . . .

Music struck outside, a flurry of strings behind a lady's piercing voice: intense, startling and instant. Ed rose pumalike and to the window waded; from that vantage, looking down on the closing hole of the course, he was unable to see much in the darkness below, just blurred lights like reflections of distant stars, but sight was not the sense being roused. "What's that?" asked as the voice hit pitches tinnitusly high, rolling through scales conceivably interstellar, then answering his own question, "Opera?"

"Queen of the Night."

Lights, suspended in cages or sconced in medieval iron drip, golden picture frames that crowned into miniature battle scenes, fragile-looking oak chairs with burgundy-inlaid fabric next to ancient repositories and closed doors between which they walked, past crests and effigies, Rubens and Titians, Venetian mirrors and Victorian longcase clocks, on a strawberry-red strip of carpet that stretched to the staircase, to the *piano nobile*, and then down into the period and parlor rooms below—one after the other stacked with more antique furniture and still life, Limoges porcelain and ormolu statues, Flemish tapestries and family-sized furnaces, with a relic in each nook and detail chiseled into every cranny, all dimmed to look like it did pre-voltage. There was a murder mansion mystery atmosphere tonight. Surely every night. The players, their entourages, and the cadres of personnel spoke softly in small groups, looked nervously behind them, held spirit-filled glasses emptying a little fast. But it was still a party: the kickoff to stage three in Frankfurt. The hosts, the landlords, the family with some history here: the von Hessen's, with the evening's emcee Landgrave Maximillian Moritz, getting back in the good graces of the people his predecessors let down.

Ed had in dribs and drabs found himself less frequently a target of silent derision, a change he would receiveth gladly, abetted by victories, razor-thin, still and all, through the first two stages. He was settling in. Enduring the soirees and getting the names down and finding new ways to appear comfortable with the reins. But he had been here before, during those early endless years, however abbreviated they became and distant they now seemed, still remembered by many waving him over as he and Jennifer were making their way through the castle chambers. First the Baltic kids already with schnapps-begotten speech impediments, then the Serbs on high over some development in the Kosovo Reclamation, and finally the host group and Germany's own wunderkind, Leopold von Schmatz. Conversations that ventured unavoidably into *Remember when* and *Still can't believe the time* and now the newly *No flash in the pan after Poitiers* which was fresh praise he'd take. But their memories of the past were only vaguely relatable to his own. Any mention of the Hacienda Open reminded Ed of barely making his tee time in the final round after being shaken awake on the steps of Teotihuacan. The albatross in Santiago? He might be missing a minor appendage had he fallen short on that one. And though he couldn't recall how fast Quito's greens played, there were faces he'd never forget from the ensuing bender in a Cochapamba cathouse.

Those memories that would occasion a wince in our alone most of moments, ripping the towel off the cool and sensible self, but be without undue delay relocated, as tapering flashbacks and elapsed moons go, to spaces beyond the horizon, bagged and buried, or at a minimum kept to ourselves as experience made of us as it did all masters of the positive twist—imperfect to a man, unkind so often the environs—to serve thenceforward as reminders to let the past be furled behind us, for there remained more to build upon that awhirl below, this old thing flying through our earthbound ups and busts, with no concern for either, merely going as it did, as it only knew how, continuous as the pages of history and present for time eternal. Ed wasn't the first to grow up bare-breathing political pollution, publically and institutionally reviled, facing extermination without remedy or recourse in a sick culture that was supposed to be his own; nor was he alone prone to concede to failure when the future looked bleak, seemed to disappear, dried up save for a drop of sorrow in every morrow to the end. But that was no way forward. And a new future was beginning to take shape, unhurried but incoming, Arcadian and free, with a hand from *das Götterbild*, suggesting that there was perhaps more to all this than he'd previously assumed—indicating absolutely that there was still an empty canvas in the skies above the road of life. . . .

Time, and the desire to escape the interior décor, led many out to the stony back patio, where, from inside a hemicyclium soundway facing the castle, edging onto an eighteenth green sure to deliver some viewer-friendly moments this weekend, the Frankfurt Philharmonic was celebrating their wizards under the moon shadow. And who'd ever done it better? Ed even knew some of the names and could recognize a score or two;—but there was no more majestic a setting than this for one to receive their true musical baptism: *Lacrimosa, Lohengrin-Vorspiel, Leise flehen meine Lieder, wieder und wieder* to *The Ruler of the Spirits*—An everlasting brand of *Hochkultur* diametrical to the lyrical refuse Old-Am was so famous for producing, back when it was playing the world as one big fool, with its speedily churned-out masterworks composed by smut-peddling poets, Tubified into skinflick clips, then lip-synced to by mulatta divas touring the city-states to fwerk in front of State-programmed children.

At the crescendo of the HWV 63 Overture, when the attendees were merrily past the preliminary spook, Ed and Jennifer snuck down a side staircase, it was thought, unseen. A wooden door cranked them into a dark cellar that was stuffy but cool and quiet apart from the muffled sound seeping through the surface panels and bouncing off of the wine bottles racked inside.

"Suhyouuh," Ed had to ask, "go to classical music school or is that also part of the Revival Curriculum?"

"Part of the Curriculum. What were the schools in L.A. like?"

"Zoos I'd've gotten shanked in on day one. There were private schools but they priced kids like me out, so I had the CCSSI Homeschool Simulator. Probably did more harm than good that thing," Ed musing back. "Not sure I learned much of anything, and the only time classical music ever came up was on the occasional question like—'Which of the following people was *not* an ultrafascist dictator: Hitler, Hitler, Hitler, or Mozart?'"

"*Mmm* . . . Hitler?"

"Don't think I realized there was anyone else of historical significance till way later. It was like they wanted us to worship the guy like some kind of anti-god."

"In the beginning there was Hitler."

"Trying to plant this fear inside of us about some people from way back, always calling us these old names—I can see just fine, thanks. It was like everything began and ended with that war."

"To them it did. When it was over, they had a free pass to fortify their control and install the new religion in place of the old, beginning again with them as the victim."

"The Victim-Elite. Guess some things never change."

"He's learning."

They heard footsteps outside the cellar door. It creaked open and the light ranged across the floor, then the quack of Homunculus belted out, "Hey, who's talking about Hitler down here?" Shapiro and the kid from Monaco poked their heads inside.

Ed and Jennifer looked at each other then back over. "You heard that?"

"Heard what? Was that really what you were talking about? It was just on my mind like always. But we're heading into the city, to this thing at the university, more our scene. Car just got here, you ready?"

They shook their heads and *Neh*'d together.

But, but, *but*. "Not taking no for an answer. Aren't becoming an ultrafascist sympathizer with this talk a Hitler now are you."

THE AUTOCAR WHEELED AROUND the castle drive and caught a combination of southbound roads into Frankfurt, a city with a historically tight security presence being a center for the Union's court bankers. The clean streets and apple-crowned villas of the Hochtaunuskreis faded into a farmland buffer zone that once past the checkpoint crashed into the walls of stained-white Lego blocs piled along the periphery—laundry-terraced favelas bridged by Rab-tagged skyways that passed overhead in the blink of an eye and blended into the compact urban space north of the river, formerly middle class five-high condos and quaint Deutsch flats now wasting away under murky streetlight, territory long ago surrendered to the swarms of New Germans out tonight crowding the sidewalks and bombing the streets with carnival noises and block party bass that shook the intersections as the autocar snuck through, past orange-wrapped buildings under construction that never ended, trees that kept growing into the road, mobs oblivious to the purpose of a crosswalk—near and far, the fine gentry the perished progressive had furnished upon this fair land. The fence around the perimeter of the university, covered in ivy and unreadable rain-bleached signs advertising services and opportunities more unwanted than ever appreciated, provided passing ganders into the Great Poet's place and the stitched oblong slabs of the once-dubbed IG Farben Building spanning the interior, a structure that was soon before them as the autocar pulled into the inlet entrance at Westend, hiked down a window, and got the wave through.

Ed and Jennifer followed Shapiro and the kid from Monaco inside and through a lobby on whose walls hung portraits of prominent figures from notable academic disciplines like Old German Terror Studies, Feminism of the Veil, and New European Allahism. A sign said the Hegira Department was down the hall, but they were going to the library, more of a media center these days, and on this evening occupied primarily by Syrianisch instructional video watchers and mixed sub-Saharan scholars taking turns in the sociology emulator, though there were a few Europardos quietly cramming for their *Wahhabi Themes in Young Werther* exams. "The history here," Shapiro buzzed back, "you don't know the half of it." *Less than that.* They stopped in front of study room number six, where Shapiro and the South Asian kid watching the door fumbled a hand greeting—one going for a slap as the other was trying to dap, then vice versa—before it was opened for the group. But on the other side was no study room; rather: an elevator that would take them below ground. Shapiro informed them along the way about how the university was being watched by the Native Resistance, who believed it to be a haven for subversive behavior, then about how the proceedings in the offing were just that—"A meeting of leaders and minds," building it up until they reached the bottom, "so some of the big guys'll be here tonight."

"And what exactly's going on again?" Ed droned, reticent to say much and already having concluded their stay would be as short as permissible.

Shapiro looked back, fist up, unibrow folding into a \/, "A revolution, man."

They had arrived at the underground congress at a favorable time, during a lull in the action, right as the young activists were shuffling through rows and staking out seats. The four meandered in from the back and stood in an indecisive line, surveying a room that was at best a packed vault reeking of midsummer sweat and scents worse, things dreadful, bazaarlike and biblical. Shapiro, trying to maintain a leaderly disposition but not naturally deft at it, awkwardly showcased the seating options, which had dwindled down to a choice between backrow left side and backrow right side as the crowd settled, but neither Ed nor Jennifer, now exchanging glances like kidnapees tacitly forming an escape plan, were in the mood to do much more than shrug back, so backrow left it was.

Taking the stage as they rocked into their seats was a weasely man in a jacketless suit with round-framed glasses and a thick mustache. From the way he was glaring at the ground one could ascertain with near certitude that he was a deeply pensive individual with much on his mind. The man took the mic off the stand and paced with it, eyes still gravely floorward. "The time has come," he said finally, *urgently*, freezing in a theatric pose. "We're on the cusp of a new era," softer now. He started back the other way, looser, letting the words sink in as he looked over the heads bobbing in agreement. "Will we fall to Native Reversalism and lose the new society we've created or will we rise together as New Europeans against the Resistance, against this force, this *brood* of Geographic Natalists and Counterfeit Classicists?" And this was about the point where Ed got left behind. He wasn't sure if he tuned out for a second and missed something or what, but he soon found himself on a delay, parsing words and piecing together a muddled interpretation while trying his best to be neutral, objective about it, to at least give the guy a chance, *you know* . . . but this turned into a progressively challenging task. His language was verbose, he was using words Ed had never heard before, appended with –*ism*'s and –*ist*'s, caked in rich rhetorical arrangements, trilled out through staccato elocution, and all in all constituting a performance that seemed to materialize into gobbledygook. He was going on and on about New Castism and Neo-Authoritarian Reorderists, a Retransmogrified Bourgeoisie and the Unitedest League . . . he was talking about *reality* not being *real*. . . . Formationalist Dogmas and Revisionist Doctrinary Persuasion, Redistributive Applicationism and Appointist Networks of Inhumanity. . . . Mother of *Zeus!*—whatever was going on out there, it wasn't right, and this guy was passionate about fixing it . . .

A fellow traveler stood and raised an insistent hand. "The issue I have is with the New Customists becoming Old Habitists. Is that not a concern?"

It most definitely was. However bizarre, Ed began to think, there was something uniquely appealing in all this—a spirit to it . . . it *was* revolutionary. Could it be? What *was* real, anyway? Anything? Nothing at all? Did we merely sign off on a system, a worldview, a *Paleonational Configutory Design* based on outmoded mores and Pseudofolkery? Then tear it down and Reatomize the barbarian, the Indigenous Defender, sunder his house and set ablaze his land, forcing its Neo-Teutonic Totalitarian Arrangism onto *us*, the New European Diversitocracy? The *brass*.

The man exited the stage to a broad standing ovation, loud enough for Ed to sneak in a private word with Jennifer, whose hands were mostly squishing together under a saintly vacant stare. "That was interesting," he said. She answered with eyes that begged to differ and pressured him into adding an honest qualifier. "I didn't understand much of it, but—"

She pulled him down to earshot. "You weren't supposed to understand, Ed. These people are Ethnoneomarxists." Ed hung on the term then mouthed *Who?* She rolled her eyes at his ongoing benightedness then inched up with one last forthright whisper as the claps were petering out. "Judivisionists."

Shapiro elbowed Ed as the next round of applause was bleeding into that outgoing. "You'll like this next guy," he said, jostled by the thrust of his own claps. "Main reason we came down here, the man behind the Free Society Foundation."

"Who?" Ed, as he put his attention back on the stage, where a man, droopy-eyed and skinnyfat in a suit, was stepping to the podium.

"Alex Schwartz."

The man cleared his throat. "Friends and comrades. . . ." Those first words tailed by an address virtually identical to that of Lord Kallergis and others Ed'd been hearing his whole life, through one outlet or another, about the upcoming equalitarian future and the culturally infused identities that would inhabit it, about the blending out of the Old Stock and the dissolution of nations that had been war-torn for as long as he'd been alive. And it was all starting to come together. Behind the sound and smoke terminology, the multicultural evangelism, and the Immigrationist moralizing, were rootless outsiders like Schwartz, the men responsible for the war, who'd sanctioned the invasion and were using the transplants against the natives. Why were they doing it? was the question. Did they just want to mix everyone together like some human breeding experiment? Did they really believe that the new identity they wanted to create was going to be an improvement? Or did they simply want to destroy others' identities because those identities were impediments to their own group's long-term interests? Maybe they wanted to create a new race with no identity because they thought it would be easier to control. Was that why people like Ed had always been portrayed as the enemy, biologically privileged and predisposed to Native Reversalism? Why, when people like him fought back and voiced their desire to preserve their identities and homelands, they were called extreemists and supreemists, depicted as some radicalized menace, backward-thinking and beyond moral salvation? Who were people like Schwartz to come to Germany and tell the Germans who was German? Where did this people get such gall, and how did it even reach the point where being a German in Germany required you to fight for your future against outsiders artificially branded the *New You?* Something was rotten in Frankfurt, all right . . . rotten all over the place. . . .

Ed nudged Shapiro and made a go-turn as the clapping began.

"We just got here."

"Yeah," Ed soured, not bent on fabricating much of an excuse.

The applause was still apatter as Ed and Jennifer got back in the elevator, then all was silent but for a soft motor hum and the fluorescent buzz of discount luster. Getting a glimpse of his foily reflection on the inside of the door, Ed could see he looked about how he felt: like someone who just realized he was at the butt end of a long-running joke. "These people really aren't like us, are they?"

"These people hate us, Ed. They are hostile foreigners."

"What makes them act like this? I just don't get it."

"Their culture has nurtured this hatred within them for centuries. They're under this tikkun olam delusion where they believe that by attacking other people's societies they're making the world better, their value system rewards them for being cheaters and liars, and they have a dual morality toward outgroups that allows them to justify their destructive behavior."

"It's the nerve of it that gets me . . . the Chutzpathology."

"For centuries, millennia even, they've been told that they are this special, chosen people and that everyone else is their cattle, slaves whom they have a right to rule over. Think about the psychological implications of that type of tribal brainwashing."

"I'm afraid to. But I think I figured out why our universities became a joke. This hatred of theirs, they institutionalized it and projected it onto everyone else."

"When men like you allowed them to take over our elite universities, they started deconstructing everything and turning it into an endless critique. Our language became postmodern mumbo jumbo, our history became one long scandal, our philosophy no longer strived to attain truth or meaning, but instead claimed there was no truth and that all meaning was subjective. After the Western Cultural Revolution the universities we built became places where men were taught to hate their own forefathers' achievements and women were taught to hate their own men, then they incentivized filling the seats with outsiders who were taught to hate both of us. They created a fellowship of fools who went along with it, too, until it was just a big freak show where all types of weird stuff was taught, effectively turning our institutions of higher learning into overpriced asylums full of indebted victim-groups who'd been molded into our enemies."

"In my wildest dreams I couldn't think up something more demonic."

"That's why it was so hard for us to accept, to believe that a people could be so subversive and malicious by nature, and act as though they have some kind of right to behave that way in others' nations."

"But if they're deconstructionists . . . then does that make us reconstructionists?"

"We have to put it back together, don't we?"

There was arguing at the top. The door slid open to two swarthy Esau-type students who shooed them out as they pushed their way in. Ed and Jennifer brushed it off and edged back through the library; it was empty now, but toward this no second thought was given until they stepped out into the main hall and realized fast that the situation had changed. The two were caught between a gang of Yorubalanders jammed up around a door at the right end of the hall, and half a dozen masked commandos boot-squeaking toward them from the left end with rifle barrels up, which was where Ed and Jennifer's hands were faster than you could say *Überlichtgeschwindigkeits-flugvektoren*—bracing for impact but getting passed by with no *Beg-pardons* spoken, no *Entschuldigung Uns'* given, barely a blue eye peeking their way on the blast past.

Ed peacocked up to compensate for the slip in stoicism. "That looked like . . . the Native Resistance?"

"So should we. . . ?"

"Go?"

Steps orderly as clock ticks back to the lobby, where the operation was being coordinated and the managerial efficiency of a slimmer German state was in full swing. The two stopped at the top and watched, perforce moved by the harmony, the pit stop spirit on display: "Dort hinstellen!" . . . "Leg *ihn* da *hin!*"

Once at the bottom Jennifer side-nodded at the ladies' room. "I."

"Mmm ah yeah me too."

Ed pushed the door open with a whistle but killed it upon seeing a man at the urinals, an on-duty gumshoe in a black suit whose eyes were aimed at the ceiling. Ed pulled up next to him, a prefatory breath out, eyes indisputably up.

"Danke."

"'Danke' 's 'Thank you' . . . 'Guten Abend' 's what you meant."

"Gootenob—*thanks*. . . . No hope here, can barely speak my own."

The man turned slightly and winked. "Not my tongue, either." His accent was indeed an odd but familiar one.

Ed sniffled and leaned over. "Study room six in the library."

The man was hopping up and down in the finish-ritual. "Study room six?" his look one of confusion seeking an excuse to become anger. "That some kind of gay thing?"

"What? No."

He reached over and grabbed Ed by the shoulder, "Huh, swish?" digging his thumb in and flashing teeth like a dog ready to bite. "Knew something was off when I heard that old movie-girl accent."

"You're looking for people, right?—*ow*."

"*People?*" He was fuming. He looked like Popeye. He inched closer. Ed was struggling to hold stream. "What people? You think this is funny?"

"*Schwartz*, you're looking for Schwartz, aren't you?"

"Schwartz?" easing up. "How do you know Schwartz?"

"I just saw him, man, dude, like in a room downstairs that you can get to through study room number six in the library—get it?"

The man grew calmer. He shot out a breath but kept his eyes fixed in an almost lustful manner on Ed's shoulder, which he was now, ostensibly, massaging. "And why should I trust a kid from Old-Am?" It then clicked that the man was running his thumb over the scar where his birthchip used to be.

"That's where the party's at."

"Name?"

"Ed."

The man squeezed and pushed off and went for the exit. "Get out of Frankfurt, Ted."

CHAINED TO THAT which feeds on ruin.

Striking the one who listens will relieve you not of your shame.

The hallmark of shock was speed, the untimely grace with which it struck, leaving the benefactor all there then absent, negotiating with reality. A minute ago it looked so smooth, felt so clean over, this path of condensed rock, so silent and harmless a raceway, a gliding track, it was . . . it seemed. Now facing it, inhaling its chemical aroma, feeling its sharpness, who couldn't understand its despair, its abuse, cracked with wear and rage, broken and deformed, carved up like a Lichtenberg figure. An earthen shredder.

Ed rolled over and peered into the Gegenschein. He didn't get a good look at the second German policeman. He got a good look at the first German policeman, the one with the broken arm, before he hobbled into the passenger side of the police van, before it drove off. After the second German policeman ran around to the other side, after he yelled "Leave him" to the first German policeman with the broken arm. After Jennifer, from inside the police van, looked at him one last time, before the door closed. That was after Ed rolled out of the autocar and watched as she was being dragged away, after the second German policeman pulled her through the window, after her ankle slipped out of Ed's hand. Which was after Ed was tazed through the window on his side by the first German policeman, the one with the broken arm. After the first German policeman stumbled back, after Ed broke his arm on the window, after Ed grabbed his arm when he reached in to try and pull the door open. After the first German policeman broke the window, after he told Ed to get out of the autocar, after he knocked on the glass, after he said "Edmund Loxley, the German police need to speak with you." After the two German policemen approached the autocar. After Jennifer said "They don't look like German policemen to me." After Ed said "They look like German policemen." After the German policemen got out of the police van, after the autocar rolled to a stop, after Ed and Jennifer noticed the police van blocking the road ahead. After the autocar shut off, after the autocar slowed down. After Ed said "It's probably nothing." After Jennifer asked "What's going on?" After the autocar announced that there was an *Obstruction ahead* . . .

You cast me into darkness.

Because it is the Darkness that brings forth the Light. . . .

ON THE OUTSKIRTS OF BERLIN Streitkräfte were encamped in Zehlendorf. Änderpanzers patrolled the streets while Autodar-geräten entered nearby buildings to scan for human activity, Sprengfalle, and other potential traps. Above, Starling drones traversed the skies and developed threatmaps that were analyzed back in Potsdam and used to manage activities on the ground. The area was mostly empty now; the New Germans had been scooped up by the deportation force or pushed deeper into Berlin. Vestiges of a pleasant borough were still visible amid the dilapidation that had accrued since the descendants of the Merkel Youth and their assorted foreign kin took over. Public space maintenance being low on their priority list had led to an intensified state of junglefication but the defacement common in other occupied zones was slight as Zehlendorf was comparatively upmarket, serving as a center for internationalist business interests and catering to a by and large middle-to-upper class neo-Ottoman clientele. The half-timbered houses were earth-stained, Rathaus Steglitz a more hideous shade of rust, and Schloßstraße—das alte shopping hub—appeared to have seen its last patron. But it was salvageable.

For German infantrymen tasked with combing through newly reclaimed municipalities like this one the perpetual irritant was never the invisible wainscot decay turned deadfall, or the abandoned sprogs, or even the hidden corpses, but the cats that bred incessantly in their brethren's absence—those feral beasts that baffled the autodars and launched out of unseen spaces to induce an accidental discharge into the smart-oven—*Gottverdammtes! Verficktes Katzen!* Before arriving here in Zehlendorf these soldiers had been annexing land just south in Stahnsdorf to further isolate Berlin. That was where the real war was being fought, where it had to begin: on the boundaries of the city-states. This was merely a next step, an inward progression, the goal being to drive the New Germans into Berlin and force the foreign elite and their quislings out. To make it so everyone would want to leave. Because they had to leave. But the men here were still adjusting to urban combat; up to now there hadn't been a whole lot of it. That however was changing since—*finally*, as many found themselves exclaiming—the German Reclamation was starting to roll . . . and with the Deutsch, *roll* was an implied short for *steamroll.*

It was hoped. Expected? The Germans had some catching up to do. But what could you say. Nations would be moved by war or any other means to kill the beat in the Heartland, added revenge for having reached Amalekite Level 11 and daring to stand up when the rest with their dignity in the bend and spread parted, once upon a time in a past still being amended, when bold myths could escape autopsy and the nature of their master maker was less fully and to fewer known. Though it was for this reason that the nation faced a less acute infestation. Anarchy was the rule; the *Postvereinigte Bundesrepublik,* a microcosm of the War: her dark scapes where spooks and foreign actors brawled in semifunctional urban zones. Most of the natives had flung up their arms and turned tail for less afflicted areas after the Pull Out. The Reregionalization Plan broke the State up and transferred among the parts the decentralizing power being lost by or taken from Berlin and other increasingly incompetent cities. It was a land united only in memory or dream, but with the turmoil confined and the Demulticulturalization and Deglobalization plans rooted and working, the Brandenburg-Freistaat-Sachsen east minus Berlin was on the up. New Bavaria, after the Munich Heilmittel, had become a dynamo. The whole north Schleswig-Holstein-Mecklenburg-Vorpommern Vereinigte Provinz—*really*—a continental staging ground for the Reclamations. Sachsen-Anhalt, upon the Mending of Magdeburg, prospering. But for the bad: excluding a revamped North-Lower Saxony post-Hannover Healing that was still managing a Turk-held Hildesheim, the western half of the former nation was a fathomless wreck to the South Rhineland. For the most part. There were some exceptions.

It was complicated. . . .

The Zehlendorf operation was being coordinated from a base in Potsdam, but a makeshift installation was up and running southwest of the borough, working out of the main building of Freie Universität. There, under a cellular dome, pacing with his hands behind his back, was the man in charge: General Gottlob Zill. He was supervising a team of twenty gathering intel and watching out for their associates on the ground, but the action had largely subsided.

Mid step General Zill was confronted by one of his lieutenants, who made it known that a man whom the General was expecting, but whose assignment he had until then received no information about, had arrived. The General followed his lieutenant's finger to the entrance, where, holding a briefcase in front of him with both hands while rolling smoothly heel-to-toe and whistling softly to himself, was one Gert Ulrich of the GIU.

"I have yet to receive the details of your mission, Agent Ulrich," General Zill said after the two men had become formally acquainted.

"Today I will be arranging a meeting with our less than own Anette Cohen."

The General's brow spiked up. "The Michbuch Propaganda Minister . . . the witch?"

"As you know, the network in Berlin remains under the control of the Union," Ulrich said, "but that doesn't mean we can't terminate the employment of those using it to target our citizens. I have been tracking Ms. Cohen and will today be relieving her of the responsibilities she as a non-German mistakenly believes she has to determine what qualifies as acceptable speech within our nation."

"I can't tell you how happy I am that this has finally begun."

"The feeling is mutual, General Zill."

And there was little else to say after that.

Gleich und Gleich gesellt sich gern. . . .

In downtown Berlin, at 4:36 P.M., Anette Cohen left her office and walked past the malnourished Punjabis slaving away under her command— silent, nose metaphorically up, failing to look anywhere but straight ahead until she reached the end of the hall. The building she was leaving was the headquarters of the Michbuch, the German appendage of the Libancien's centralized social media platform. Frequently used to monitor the online affairs of the Native Resistance and restrict speech throughout the West, the network was supervised by various internationally minded groups and was rife with propaganda, tracking, and censorship, with fates often worse for those holding opinions hostile to the Regime's interests. As director of the Michbuch, Anette Cohen was used to not being liked, and there was little that was likable about her. She was rude. She was obese. She looked like a witch and had red hair that, no matter what precautionary measures she took, would always end up in an untidy pouf by the end of the day.

A private escalator opened into an underground garage where two security guards were waiting. When they saw Ms. Cohen step out, one pressed a button on the autocar motherboard to summon her vehicle. It pulled around soon after and the other guard stepped forward and opened the door for her. She got in and he closed it without receiving a *Danke* or any other gesture of gratitude, but this was as normal as the cow's moo. As the autocar pulled out of the garage Ms. Cohen opened her clearscreen and switched to mirror-mode. She stared at the reflection of her craggy-stone face then lifted and pressed to her forehead her large, red-framed glasses as she proceeded to remove with a tissue the blobs of liner that had accumulated around her eyes, but dozed off in the process, her head just kind of bobbing there for a while until a sudden turn snapped her awake. She placed her focus back on the clearscreen, returned to the main menu, opened her Euro Diversity Mail application, and created an outgoing message addressed to the New European Union Internet Democracy Council. Ms. Cohen attached that day's Hativity Report, which contained a list of names and other information, before typing out a short message. When she was finished she hit the send button, but the spiral kept spinning around and around; the message wasn't going out. She tried again with no luck, then checked the connection: all x's.

It was at this point that Anette Cohen looked up and out of the window and realized the autocar was driving through some horrid neighborhood that was without question not on her usual route home. Checking the map on the back of the seat, she noticed that she was headed south, which was the opposite direction she was supposed to be going in. "Autodriver: state your course," she screeched. There was no reply. "Autodriver: state your course immediately or pull over to the next safe station." Still nothing. She crashed back in the seat. Thinking, then lurching forward, she pressed the emergency button once. Then twice. Then three times. Then many more with rapid-fire, fat-finger pecks. But there was still no response; it didn't seem to be working at all. "Emergency call," she barked at her clearscreen. Typing in the emergency code, she waited. But the call wouldn't go through—NETWORK FAILURE: EMERGENCY CALLS CURRENTLY UNAVAILABLE. Panic set in. Anette Cohen pulled at the door handle. She slammed her meaty fist into the unresponsive screen in front of her. She bounced up and down in the seat like a child. She began to cry.

The autocar whirled through a roundabout on the southern edge of Berlin and accelerated down the Bundesautobahn, racing away from the city, through a gauntlet of trees, merging with the 1, and passing signs for Friedenau, Bäkepark, the Institut für Meteorologie, the wilted and sapless Botanischer Garten, and then Zehlendorf, finally slowing, turning at Habelschwerdter Allee, and cruising alongside the uncut median until it jumped the curb and jerked to a stop in front of Freie Universität. A quivering finger slid underneath Anette Cohen's eye, smearing further her witch's veil, as she peered out the window and caught the mad-happy grin of Gert Ulrich.

"Ding-Dong."

THE DIRT IS SOGGY from morning showers. Stagnant mush at the floor of a thick deciduous enclosement. It's a sprawling maze in here. A Hessian morass. A goddamn swamp.—*O' Donar's Oak . . . did my Titleist meet the fate of your timber . . . do I curse like the Chatti did when you met with the ax . . . shall I abandon thee for St. Wilson, take my drop, and follow that new stone to my demise?* The gray slab of a sky shows no spark. No trace of the lightning storm that threatened to cancel the round's events. If only. What a delight it would be to hear a sledge from the heavens, to feel the tears weigh me down, to watch the mob scatter back to Friedrichshof Castle. I could hide out here in the forest alone, listening to the sibilant serenade of the trees and laughing at the spoiled aphotic day, hoisting my iron sword to channel your electric energy and daring you to strike me down . . . end this misery. Or, should I withstand your dander, these childish mood swings, last until ruth or boredom finds you, then—*yes*, then—when the light has returned, between azure plains and lush green, I could emerge from this woodland anew, righted and rallied, and be spared your bunker, shielded from your rough, freed from bogey; my birdies would fall, my eagles would inspire chants, and stroke by splendid stroke I would climb back to the top of the board. . . .

Alas, soliloquys and schizophrenic appeals had fallen short. The third stage in Frankfurt had been a disaster and Ed could only finish the weekend without falling too irreparably low. He nudged the ball into the final hole as his Sunday afternoon culminated on the foggy back lawn of the castle to light applause. Stig's handshake snapped him only briefly out of the soup-brained stupor he sunk right back into upon its release. A muttered reassurance bounced right off. Ed took one last look around the sparse crowd for Jennifer as he exited the green, but she was still nowhere to be seen. There had been guarantees that the matter was being looked into, that good men were on the case, but with all that was going on, manpower and resources stretched thin as they were, the war and everything else, only so much could be done. And this foolish game had become so trivial, minor as a one in a mess of infinity, while torment knocked hours a minute, helplessness nagged like a never-ending busy tone, and guilt—knowing it was he they wanted, he they were after, he that was ultimately responsible—lynched any emotion brazen enough to think it could take its place.

Back inside no fruit-flag medley, no smoky train of bratwurst, no heart-shaped swirl of pumpernickel could entice Ed to stick around. He went straight to his room, crawled under the sheets, and curled up in a ball—

yenning for a little amnesia, longing for that swoon into the deep passage-ways of the mind, any escape into the boundless realms away from the exist-ing, away from man's eutherian anguish, wherefrom arose a wish that none of this had ever happened—this world: *too cruel.* Although any conscious record had been stricken, there was still a chance that he possessed a mys-tic sense of his own amorphous origins, of those first months prior to the abrupt preliminary awakening—where he was, next to his placental supply tank, cocooned in darkness. After getting dragged out and forced into this corporeal purgatory he would still, now and again, free of gaze, during times of downfall and disgrace, recede into obscurity and simulate that protective womb: folding limbs into core, closing misty eyes, packaging himself in the warmth and comfort he once felt in the flesh . . . *in* the flesh: literally, verily—*'til death do they part*—but maybe he got something from it: a chem-ical emancipation, oil on the springs, could be anything. . . .

Ed awoke to a cynosure showing the time: a phosphorescent 9:01 P.M. He stretch-rolled around in the bed then climbed out and looked in the mirror. His hair was sticking up, his face was beet-red; he felt empty, tor-pid, muddled in a post-nap depression. But he also felt a strong urge to be anywhere other than this room. After throwing on Friday's stinky sweater vest and spit-combing his hair to the side to make himself presentable and whatever it didn't matter Ed went back downstairs where another party, in a lower key, this one to celebrate the close of stage three, was taking place. He made sure any run-ins were brief on his way out to the patio, where he found a tranquil scene with no music, no rain, and nothing much else, just a dozen or so people mingling the evening out. Ed took a seat at the far end of the bar and ordered two shots of Glen Slitisa. As he was wincing them off, he peace-signed to the bar-bot for two more. Once they had also burned down the gorge, he laid his forehead on the bar and closed the shutters.

There was a warm breeze blowing through. The castle was hulking into the above. Boxed windows to the inside glowed saffron. At the other end of the patio the Scotsman sat down at the piano, banged out a few keys, and jumped into the chorus of a hometown tune, "Atlantis," sucking in a small flock. The song could be heard everywhere these days, having been repopularized after the New-Am Oceanography Agency's discovery of the long-lost civilization. Ed skull-rolled forehead to temple and watched, reaching the end of some noose of a line, he knew it. But there was often something different at the end of his lines, ranging from near-fatal gambles to *Wille zur Macht* transcendence, and occasionally both; like some adaptive mechanism woven into the genes of the cornered last of a kind who could, almost through a force of survivability, snap and change direction, make order out of chaos. *His mysteries revealed. . . .*

THE NEXT TWENTY-FOUR HOURS were a bit hazy, but they commenced with Ed going back inside and tracking down the caddy for Greece, a cleat-faced man by the name of Zoilo "The Andros Mentz" Kairos, who, as he'd overheard during a conversation between Poland and Hungary in France, could get his hands on things not so easily obtained through what were left of legal channels, then shortly after purchasing from Zoilo a golf sock full of pills, *slavelocity* tabs, described as having carpet-to-ceiling effects, respectively, lying somewhere between a long macchiato and a sanitarium-bound quantity of hypermethylhexanamine. Ed dry-popped two, borrowed a Prussian-blue suit from a like-sized someone in von Schmatz's posse, shot down to Kasinoland on the west bank of the Main, and was up to a firm, quarter-throttle rev by the time he was emptying his old South of the Border bank account out, exchanging the full amount for club currency, joining a crew of Chinamen at the Little Wheel, and putting half of what he was holding on a 10-15 double street, then getting an 11-pocket hit, instantly quintupling his stack, and amassing *Ho!*'s and claps and widescreen stares wondering what the laowai, still one of the only local-looking gents in the joint, was gonna do next. Leave, was what. Like a fit collie lost in New Wangcouver, he was gone: *poof* into the Kasinoland smoky smoky. Ed had already mapped out a game plan so to not waste time as he hospital-hopped around the city, flashed a doodled facial composite of the man with the broken arm, and sweetened up every nurse, doctor, and administrator who would give him the time, and not running into much trouble in the process, either; in fact finding many who would go out of their way to try and help for a quick Globobuck and to distract themselves from their primary responsibilities, Frankfurt being besieged with such an endless volume of intra- and extra-tribal warfare that endemic within perpetually understaffed facilities and among medical workers of various ethnic loyalties, ethical inclinations, and third world agencies, was a terminal strain of inertia. The first break came around magic rug and song time the next day in a mostly empty hallway at Agaplesion Krankenhaus where morning rays were projecting a gentle samba of peachlit shadows through the milk-white wing of the hospital. He was in need of another slavelocity bump but had gotten stuck talking with, or more accurately listening to, a self-described "Flemish" doctor as he blustered about the lack of support, how he was the only physician without forged credentials on staff, and why he couldn't wait to divorce himself from the NEUMA, while Ed was busy wondering where in the world Flemland was and thinking about the next move until the doctor gave him a go, the two by then sharing increasingly less cryptic hints about the mutual source of their indignation. "Think the guy might've had some connection to the Union?" That was most likely the case in Ed's estimation. "Then I'll tell you where they might've taken him," the doctor continued after checking his peripherals, ". . . to the private Frankfurter Pflegeeinrichtung Clinic in Börneplatz. . . . Just don't let em farm your blood, Burger." Ed kept a close watch on the clinic till high noon, spying from an adjacent park, seeing who went in and who came out, and gauging at a distance through paneled-lobby windows what the atmosphere, desolate compared to his previous stops, was like inside. After the guard change he strolled clean through the gates with an empty gift-wrapped box and laid it Guinness-thick on the frizzy-poodle-haired girl at the front desk who looked

kind of like a horse as she nodded and neighed starry-eyed up at the mag-
nanimous Union lawyer who was just transferred from Antwerp and didn't
know a soul in town yet—apart from a friend of a friend he'd heard had
gotten into an unfortunate accident the previous Wednesday . . . "Broke it
right at the elbow." She confirmed he'd been there but said he wasn't there
anymore, so Ed changed the subject, worked her till those cheeks were
spanked-pink, set up an evening engagement—dinner and a movie—and
started to walk away, then looped back around and eased the name out of
her: Herr Schlomo Brodsky—*Hair Schlomo?* "Schlomo yeah that was the
guy"—which he promptly kicked over to the website 512Chan—a Hadh-
rami frankincense-harvesting forum fronting for an anonymous online
think tank dedicated to unmasking associates and enablers of the Libancien—before directing the autocar to Niederursel and grabbing some lunch
at Rolf's Wurst Reich, a little place that hit. The. Spot. War-time rationing,
Ed presumed, had led to German hotdogs being served on tiny rolls instead
of full-sized buns, but this was no matter to gripe about and he was just
happy to get through the line of stormtroopers on break from a neighborhood sweep in under a half-hour. A glut of information had been posted by
the time he rechecked the thread on 512Chan, including a picture of the
perp's ratty mug, multiple Mossad allegations, complaints about reddit
spacing, and a records check that placed Schlomo the Friday before in a
suburb of Cologne, *Rheindorf,* where he'd seen a specialist named Dr. Karl
Virchow, a man who was fast becoming a new P.O.I. to those doing the
digging. Ed boarded the Deutsche Bahn in Mainz at 2 P.M. and was wading
into the Mosul- esque human apocalypse outside Köln Hauptbahnhof a
short while later, getting only a brief glimpse of the infamous Kölner Dom
Moschee on the edge of grope square while being more or less chased into
the backseat of an autocar in front of the station by a gang of desert street
yoofs asking where his daughter was at. The teatime sun was shining bright
on the ruins of the city—the slum of North-Rhine Westphalia, one big no-
go-zone—as it passed block after battered block before him up to Rheindorf.

Dr. Virchow was out but three elderly female assistants were in so Ed again dialed up the charm and in less than a fragrant-city minute—a result he chalked up more to nursely scorn for patients of bellicose temperament than the success of his own act—had the gals singing a tune about Schlomo . . . Oh, *Zhat* Arschloch . . . "Got caught trying to steal a box of gloves then had the nerve to ask for a discount," even pulling up his file and reading it over for him: paid in Old Euro, left an address in Amsterdam, but said he was going back to Berlin, or was it Frankfurt . . . *you want the number, hun?* Ed would've walked out singing a tune of his own but the shakes were coming on heavy and he could sense the middlemost phase of sleep-deprived cerebral malfunction cracking its knuckles and getting ready to sign in with a vengeance, though another slavelocity tab took care of the latter issue and he was soon back on 512Chan posting an update and scouring the web for new connections. Should he go to Amsterdam? *Could* he go to Amsterdam? Maybe he should just call the number? Feeling flustered, Ed decided to take a walk through Rheindorf. The neighborhood was in the process of getting a makeover: old men were picking up trash, old women were sprucing up the park, children were painting over graffiti, and Ed couldn't pass through without feeling bad for not helping so he spent a couple hours doing a little of all of it before finally making it to the waterfront of the Rhine at sundown to see what bobbing along with the gentle current but, much to his disappointment, a steady flow of garbage hailing from as close as Bonn and as far as Strasbourg and there had one of those moments—contemplative and quiet though less spiritually rewarding than it would have been were he not tweeking—under a kaleidoscopic sunset blowing up the sky with marigolds and marmalades, watching the platinum, plastic, and styrofoam float by as the great river, like an earthly immune system response, slowly emptied its foreign sepsis toward the North Sea. There was no more time to waste. Ed proxy-called the number, confirmed it was Schlomo on the other end, told him to be at the Kasinoland bar at 9:00 that night, then hung up, got back on the train, linked up to the darknet, and after jumping through a virtual hoop or two received access to a private network where he made contact with a local arms dealer codenamed *Geiz_Puška* who agreed to meet him at the ferry crossing in Hattersheim at 8:30. Puška, a Czech national wearing a homburg hat and a black leather trench coat that could have been hiding another equally sized man inside of it, was waiting when Ed got there, casually admitted he would've drowned him in the river had he been of a dimmer persuasion, then took him aside and with a voice that was almost fatherly with concern tried to talk him out of the purchase, or at least confirm he wasn't going to do anything like immediately go paint a restaurant window with some unwitting man's brain matter, but Ed explained the situation, told him it was only a precautionary measure, and promised not to do anything stupid, so Puška, after probing his conscience and nodding up at the globular moonlights by the pier, pulled a paper bag from his jacket pocket and took the money, then, like he was never there, disappeared into the early evening fog. Ed arrived a tick or two after nine but took the time to scour the parking lot for the van, which he found hiding in the mix with no one at least visibly inside. On level motorhead turbo, pistol packed under the back of his shirt, loaded and ready to spread some lead if need be, Ed strode past the Shanghai security team at the front entrance and as though through magnetism locked eyes with Hair Schlomo from across the casino floor. Schlomo turned in his seat at the bar, raised the arm locked in white plaster then his glass with the other and toasted to the air grinning wide and rotten. Ed started over then noticed a man coming at him from the right, then another from the left. He reached for the gun but the tremors from the crank caused him to knock it down into his pants. Ed's pelvis arched forward as it shifted around in his hindquarters then time became slower as the expressions of the men coming toward him morphed from excited anger to befuddlement as they watched Ed simultaneously bracing for a tussle and flaring his leg out to ease the gun down without it going off. They grabbed ahold of him and a struggle ensued. Early in Ed felt a prick and looked down to see something being stuck into his arm so he pulled away, but it was too late. Nausea, vertigo, spinning, fading, all, as it always did here, to black. . . .

QUAKES, PULSATING DEEP, dark, and fast, Ed woke with sharp nostril gasps. Missing was the light, there was none at all. Some kind of wiry contraption was strapped to his face. A spherical ball was shoved inside his mouth, taste of rubber. Smell of wood, he could sense it all around him. His fingernails dug into it, but his arms were pinned down. He was in a box, in a sauna-drenched sweat. He needed water. Air. Ed's gasps became more acute, louder, heavier. He arched his back and forced his strength into his limbs—flesh digging into alloy, head jerking side to side, pivoting through each pressure point, writhing, lifting, pushing, trying to find some way to free himself. But the effort was futile. His energy evaporated and he slunk back as a machine gun roll of bass crashed around him. He was in the back of that van. In a coffin. He was sure of it. But what Ed didn't know was that he was about to cross the border into Belgium.

After fading in and out with the bumps and turns he heard the music stop and felt the engine turn off. The back door of the van swung open. Men grunted as they pulled the box out and set it in a reclined position. Ed was fairly certain that he was then wheeled ten feet one way, fifteen to the right, up a ramp, twenty-four or maybe five more down a corridor, and into a room. The box rotated and the back hit flush against a machine that clasped it and tilted him back. The cover was removed, all but the board he remained fastened to as he met with a blinding light—squirm-inducing, his eyes bathing instantly in pain. The wiry contraption was removed. He spit and coughed and gasped. Between squints he was able to make out padded walls and a one-way mirror, a tool kit of a table to his left, and a craned arm above, the insignia on the uniform of the man walking away—he'd seen it before. And then he was alone, in a deathly quiet, immobile but relatively comfortable after a few adjustments, time soon ticking away—the

seconds, minutes, or maybe even hours paced extradimensionally in a coma-
tose drip—falling deep, with a force overruling all wakeful will, asleep.

The sound of his name being spoken caused Ed to stir, but the sleep-
spurned mind, tricked into some steady rest after much deferment, would
rather pretend it was of its own creation. So it took a few tries. "*Hey-lo*, Mr.
Loxley." His brain felt like a fried circuit board. His eyelids were swollen and
heavy. He was zonked, initially less concerned about the present dilemma or
the possibility of being, in a moment here, tortured, and more about the au-
dacity of the person disturbing his slumber. "He avakes . . . hello! My name
is Dr. Meduna." The voice was accented like a hackneyed cartoon doctor depicted as evil more often than good. "My apologies for zeh inconvenience."
The door reopened and a man entered, tautening a pair of gloves. "No reason to be alarmed." Ed's eyes followed the man around to the table, where
he picked up an ECT band and bent it out and tried to pin it on him. Ed
headfaked to dodge it. "Now, now." A fist came down like a mallet on his
stomach. He lurched up and was incapacitated long enough for the band to
be clamped to his temples.

Cough, sense, some, now returning, as the man exited the room.

"I was hoping to speak with you last week, Mr. Loxley, but I think I
know why you reached out."

"Jessica—" he slurred.

"Jess—" Silence; behind-the-scenes whisperings, "—Ms. Lalonde, you
mean, yes. She east vine. Here, see for yourself." A wallscreen flashed on in
front of Ed; appearing on it a second later was Jennifer: in a room similar to
the one he was in; sleeping, it seemed, which was minor consolation to the
culpable. "We have no interest in her, or you for that matter."

"She didn't do anything."

"I would dispute the claim of innocence, but let's put that aside for now.
I don't intend to keep you here any longer than necessary. I only want to
speak with you, Mr. Loxley . . . I want to help you. An acquaintance informed me that he and yourself had reached an understanding. He said he

was disappointed to find out that you appeared to have changed your mind. And there was another matter regarding a colleague of yours who received an unjust Continental Semitic Expulsion Order after last week's native rebellion in Frankfurt. But do you know the man I speak of?"

"Kallergis."

"He mentioned your desire to be a winner, Mr. Loxley, and said he even offered assistance in your attainment of this goal. Fuzz there a misunderstanding?"

Ed cleared his throat. "I don't think so."

"Then how would you explain your recently acquired neoseparatist leanings?"

"Not sure what you mean."

"Having your birthchip removed does not exempt you from our monitoring systems, Mr. Loxley. I have reviewed your case and found several violations of Hate Speech that could be prosecuted under New Union law. Though, in the current state, we find ourselves more and more inducing reform through more expedited means. But that's why I wanted to see you . . . to assist you with this transformation. The debiasification process is consistently successful at countering nativist propaganda and helping members of the Old Stock like yourself recover from the disorder affecting you. As you know, this bigoted and intolerant worldview has no place in our new society."

"Is that where I am?" Ed, looking around. "A debiasification clinic?"

"That is *precisely* where you are. And I will be administering the renormalization procedure you will soon undergo. Because I am afraid that you, Mr. Loxley, have become a . . ." Ed knew what he was going to say before he said it, the two-syllable word he was going to use. It was a word now in historical decline after having reached a peak most were thankful was somewhere—*anywhere*—in the past. They said it was once the most powerful word in the Western lexical suite, the mere accusation capable of ruining the alleged offender, who, when maligned, would cry out with some Pavlovian plea, such as—*No not me rilly I swear!* . . . And in their lust for virtue, for a people already long conditioned by the same force to view themselves as sinners, they voluntarily placed these social shackles on their wrists and burned the new witches for their masters—the chosen, the term their shield—now free to supervise the cattle and cut down any who strayed, refused to repent, or spoke ill of their replacements. . . . A word that brought world-conquering nations to their beseeching knees, screaming—*No it's not true please believe us!* . . . And Mephisto almost keeled over with laughter. . . . Poor Sons of Earth—this gives me hope of future pleasure, so what will you do to prove this measure? *Give up our wealth and resources? Make our land the world's? Close our eyes to the damage and pray that we will one day be forgiven?* They'd do anything—and they did everything—to avoid it. But it soon became apparent that the label stayed with them regardless of what they *thought* they believed; it was, evidently, inborn à la the Original Sin it replaced—a penance renewed, a simple but effective post-Christian design. However, with the inevitable realigning winds of time, and after much overuse, some began to wonder—*Wait . . . what does this word even mean? Is it even a real word?* And the funniest thing was . . . it *wasn't.* If anything it was a biological response present from sea to sea, with only the target group gullible enough to associate it with their own mortal failure and crusade against it under the imprudent assumption that something so rooted in nature, such a protective human instinct, could be, somehow, eradicated. . . . *Who were we kidding?* But it was also around this time that Western man began to set his collective, and collectively livid, attention on the foreign tribe of slanderers portraying him as this modern folk devil, a ". . . *racist.*"

Meh.

"But before we proceed with that and your kidney operation, I would like to ask you a few questions."

"What kidney operation?"

"During your interactions with Ernie Lamark, did he ever mention anything about a time machine?"

"No."

"Did he at any point use transportation that could have been potentially used for time travel?"

Nothing besides the usual jetpods and autocars. But the line of questioning got Ed thinking again—who *was* Ernie Lamark? other than the son of a bitch who'd gotten him into all this. Was it possible that he was some sort of time traveler . . . a man from the future? The notion that someone would travel through time to contact *him* of all people gave Ed a petty feeling of self-importance, but the situation and his state of mind being suboptimal for exploring such a possibility meant he could only toss it onto the mounting pile of unanswerable questions. "I never knew who Ernie Lamarck was."

"Ernie Lamark is not a real person."

"I never knew anything."

"I am now going to show you some pictures, Mr. Loxley. I need you to tell me if anyone in them resembles the Ernie Lamark *you* saw."

Flashing on the wallscreen was a headshot of a man Ed had never seen before. "No." Four more pictures were subsequently shown, but none were of anyone he recognized.

"Thank you. Now, let's try that one more time to be certain you are not misremembering anything."

As Ed was waiting for a picture a shock reverberated from his skull to his toes, brief but invasive, a scorch to the marrow in his bones that was paralyzing, the sudden agony so draining it left him unable to make a sound.

"I am sorry, Mr. Loxley, this is only to ensure your cooperation. Let's go through the first set of pictures again. Please pay close attention."

The first picture was reshown. Ed clenched his lips and shook his head. He was shaking. The thought of experiencing again what he just did made him wish he was dead, that these people would just kill him. Ed shook his head at the second picture. It was no one familiar. Then again at the third. A countdown he could draw out only so much. "No," he mumbled after the fourth reappeared. It was of a man sitting outside a café, unaware any picture was being taken.

Ed was waiting for the fifth picture to appear, but it never did. And it never would. Cooked through, he felt some drool run out of his mouth as his head rolled around to get a better look at the room, in the process catching an unflattering reflection of himself in the one-way mirror. He'd had better days. Ed nodded in and out for a while, but was still mostly awake as long minutes passed. He wasn't sure what was going on and even called out a couple times, but to no response. Just waiting, looking at the picture of the man at the café.

Close to twenty minutes had passed when the door creaked open. Someone entered the room and waited just inside, a soldier, peeking out now and again. He eventually walked over to Ed, keeping an eye on the door as he removed the ECT band and unbound his arms. Ed had seen him before, he was sure of it, but he couldn't remember where. "Thank you." The soldier bowed without looking up as he freed Ed's legs from the board and helped him lean forward. He took out a canteen. Ed drank furiously from it, wiped his mouth dry, caught his breath, and issued another tender thanks. He was then compelled to say, as the soldier was making his way back over to the door, "I recognize you from somewhere."

The soldier sighed in what Ed could only perceive as, well, aggravation. He stopped and turned partly, opening his mouth to speak but fumbling with the words like he didn't know how to put it. "*Zerr itz eine* movie. . . ."

A SUN AT APEX burning down. Optimism in the summer air. A divine ambience, osmotic among kin, knowing their best days lie ahead. Atlas raises the dome over the packed vineyard at Sans Souci, Corinthian hardware and an amber gleam cast south. Those gathered have just finished watching an address from General Zill, praising his men's efforts in the ongoing Siege of Berlin, encouraging strength and resolve—*unity*. But the crowd is dispersing now, to get a snack, a beer to wash it down, to indulge in the rest of the festivities. Children play on the lawn, chase each other around marble statues, lambent green everywhere, a soft endless gush from the fountain where young women in colorful dirndls dip their feet and gossip about the bigheaded soldiers chatting behind them, the Cavalry, kempt and cordial, grateful for the time off, themselves hoping to maybe pick up one of these ladies and make them into a woman, a mother, who will bear the next generation of sons for Deutschland, to grow as they get old, into new men that will inherit a world devoid of the madness their fathers saw and further mend the land of their birthright, turn it into something glorious, something greater than it ever was, before passing their creations on to their own, just as it had been done since the dawn of time. And *one* day those children will read about *these* days and the many before, speechless, struggling to piece together why millions of desert savages were allowed to walk in the front door, withdraw their nation's funds, and take over their neighborhoods—*Had everyone lost their minds?*—they'll wonder. No, they were True Believers . . . *back then*. But, stronger and wiser, they'll be better equipped to understand what it means to be a nation, a people—a *Volk*— who grew together for centuries on the piece of earth soon to be returned. And every last one will know the full story this time, who was responsible, who would never under any circumstance be allowed back in—put your marks on that—since it will be up to them to make sure this never happens again. But for now there's only this brief time to rest. It's back to Berlin tomorrow, back to the frontline, to finish the sweep through Steglitz, stick a fork in this hegira, round them up, every last one, herd them onto the kebab pods, fingers crossed one doesn't blow in the process, then ship them off to wherever, anywhere, doesn't matter, as long as it's off this continent and far away from Germania's fertile soil, her once-beautiful cityscapes, so this land can be restored and made safe, once again, for those children to come, our own. . . .

It's one of those supernatural days in the Heart of Europe, a day of heaven, life spinning in sheen and innocence, even the most jaded grump with a chance to pretend. Ed stands with Stig at the edge of the vineyard, near one of the bratwurst booths, throwing back his second of the day. He was released from the hospital with no ill-effects and invited to the inaugural Reclamation Day Festival here in Potsdam. And now Stig is telling him something about the war, how it used to be, but Ed isn't paying much attention. He's staring across the grounds, through light waves of hair, looking for Jennifer. And thereupon she appears, *das Ewig-Weibliche*, gliding on a course his way, sponging up every ounce of excess glow. She stops in front of them and glances back at the crowd moving out.

"So are we going?"

The three stroll with the troops on a shady path toward Orangerieschloss, a jump-step away. Many of the women and children stay behind so it feels like a military procession at ease on this quick sojourn across the estate of Old Fritz. They arrive as the grass below the palace is filling in with spectators, hushed tones predominant, only whisperings to get the few uninformed up to speed. At the front, bordering Roman alcoves wrapped in sunlit ivy, are stony imperial staircases that wind up to the second level of the Orangery. On its terrace stand elite ranks of men, hands behind their backs, watching over the crowd, cracking smiles and murmuring back and forth. The staircases continue up the perimeter to the third terrace, where more men stand on guard, and then to the fourth—below Medici towers and the peristyle of Elisabeth—upon which is a platform, the gallows, where awaits the man set to be hanged.

All grows quiet as the proceedings commence. The hangman reports to the crowd that Alex Schwartz, the former director of the Free Society Foundation, has been found guilty of crimes against the State. The *real* State. He was one of the leaders of a foreign ethnic syndicate responsible for corrupting the nation's previous administrations, producing anti-German propaganda, and operating multiple organizations that led to the rape, murder, and displacement of the native peoples of Europe. The days of Merkel *die*

Schrulle, when a demoralized citizenry sat idly by as feral imps were summoned to plunder their kingdom, were in the distant past now. These were new times. These were new citizens. They would not flee any farther from the cities their ancestors had built nor tolerate further acts of sedition and multicultural agitation from the traitors and foreign nationals operating within. This was the ascension of their revolt—an uprising against decades of coercion, extortion, moral blackmail, and tyranny. This was the German Reclamation.

The hangman's deep bellows cease into silence, the final breath left for Judas' meditation. The Germans stare straight ahead—chins up, eyes locked, solemn looks across their faces to acknowledge this moment, when the fallen receive their recompense and the wicked their justice.

—A gate we know full well,
That stands 'twixt Heaven and Earth and Hell . . .

To a people chosen only for the last—*Dort werdet ihr verrotten*—we bid ye farewell.

The trap opens, the rope tightens, the snap of the long drop.

And a new day begins. . . .

VII

All the infections that the sun sucks up
From bogs, fens, flats, on Prosper fall

—CALIBAN

VII

I N MERRY ENGLAND, east of the Commons Lobby in Westminster, Alistair
Jarvis was enjoying a quiet moment in the loo, here at last alone since
the gentleman in the next stall over finished up and scurried out without
washing his hands. "Pity," Alistair muffled out in a sigh. His arms then un-
furled and went to work double tasking: one unmuting the New North-
umbria match on the clearscreen in front of him while the other slithered
into the jacket hanging from a hook and grabbed a half-eaten bag of crisps
from the pocket. They reunited to uncrinkle it, fish out as many as possible
with a four-finger spread, and launch the keep catcher under crane into the
mouth. Partway through the inaugural crunch the bathroom door swung
back open. Alistair remuted the sound as someone rushed into the stall beside him. He took two more slow, quiet crunches then forced the fragments
down with a harsh swallow. It was a struggle. Clogged the pipe. Caused an
abrupt coughing fit that launched partly chewed potato dough at the door.
"*Ah-ah-erm. Erm.*" Was that him or the other guy? Alistair suddenly realized he'd missed a score: a tally for the opponent's side. A word apt for the
occasion ricocheted through his mind, but all was interrupted by another
noise: this one louder, borderline embellished, and positively not his own:
"*Ah-hem, eh-erm, eh-eh.*" Movement shifted his attention downward to the
slot between the stalls where a hand was signaling with a small slip of paper.
Alistair took it, unfolded it, and read it under his breath: RED BISHOP. 11
P.M. THE WATCHDOGS BARK. "Watchdogs. . . ?" He glanced back down at the

fingers, now beckoning toward the palm. "Aye." Alistair placed the slip of paper back in the hand. It disappeared and the toilet flushed, the stall door opened and slammed shut. Alistair pulled his pants up to an intermediate level, hit the latch, and yelled "Wait" as he peeked out, but it was too late.

The stranger was gone.

Once finished, Alistair returned to the Lobby and ambled back in the direction of the Court, approaching in the thinly occupied corridor along the way a group of men in black cloaks and turbans. "Hiya, chaps," he called out genially, but received only cross stares in return. The fellow closest raised a volley-hand and made a loud hissing sound as they passed. "Vicious look," Alistair quipped. Before entering the Court he lapsed into a moment of reflection next to a window overlooking the Thames—stagnant-brown under London's leaden skies: *another bewt*. A woeful place, that it was . . . now more than ever.

Inside, members of the Coexistence Trust Council and the BCFI were leading a discussion on a slate of issues, the most pressing of which being the civil unrest that had been spilling over into Fulham, and considering a proposal that would boost interfaith outreach and introduce quantitative easing measures by raising the National Income Credit. Primary networks and media platforms under the control of the English Caliphate had been increasingly targeted by the Native Resistance, unflattering information about the Regime's leadership was being spread at an alarming rate, and the repercussions were beginning to hit a bit too close to home. A hot debate was developing between Lord Jenner and Lord Prince bin Lalat as Alistair was taking a seat in the back.

"The London Diversity Guard has extended its presence throughout the city."

"We've heard this before."

"And the bank is ready to disperse the Income Relief funds to the public."

"That ageen is not the issue, the issue is a long-term solution. City-states are falling across New Europe and we too are facing a serious insurrection. People keep asking me if they should leave, and I'm considering it myself . . ."

Alistair was still oscillating into comfort on the plank below his buttocks when a woman in a burqa, now standing over him, claimed his focus. "Tafwid," she said with a menacing claw out.

He looked into her peep-slit, his expression childly innocent. "Come again, love?"

"Tafwid for Coexeesteents Trust Council meeting. Tafwid . . . pass."

"Ah, my authorization to attend today's session . . . of course. Sure it's around here somewhere . . ." Alistair trailed off while patting down his pockets. "Swear I had it a moment ago—say that an Ultra Flex?"

"—*Ee-lak!*"

The woman grabbed Alistair's arm and yanked but let go as he immediately summoned the pass, in magic trick fashion pretending as though he'd pulled it out from behind her ear, then raising it to her veil and mouthing the words written on the front—ALL ACCESS GRANTED—before putting on a face intended, and quite fragrantly, to taunt. "What, Mo doesn't let you watch the Tube?"

Being the sole delegate of Old English ancestry at the British Caliphate Broadcasting Corporation had granted Alistair Jarvis certain privileges not awarded to many in the Big Smoke. He kept a home up north in Whitby, a hillside Scarborough cottage with Esk and Abbey views he could escape to now and then, but London was it for ten months of the year. He was an uncommon sight around town, a creature few and far between, with the like few only around to fill novelty positions similar to his own. It was, by necessity, a closeknit group, since this part of England had long been occupied territory—not an especially pleasant place to be for an Englishman of the Old Stock. To make it pleasant you had to be the kind of guy who could make just about anything pleasant. But Alistair was just that kind of guy.

The English, however painfully deferential they once seemed in the face of their own obsolescence, were still technically in existence, but the former

Island Empire, under some degree of seditious foreign influence since even before its days of unsetting suns, was one of the first to fall owing to the speed of the native replacement program in its leading metropolis. It was only after the Pull Out, which coincided with an event around these parts known as the Great Shift, that there became, in effect, two states: one with the original inhabitants amassed in the north, and another that was ruled by urban Semitic tribes, sated with Africans holed up in mini versions of the failed nations they hailed from, and littered with other peoples of miscellaneous origin, none of whom were actually from this place but who were, nonetheless, currently squatting throughout the Occupied Zone south of the Sheffield Line.

This side of the Atlantic, London remained the Libancien's most important hub—still a global financial center, a strategic base for the international operation, and home to the Regime's most essential institutions. But the foreign elite had a lot on its plate these days. . . .

AT 11:12 P.M. ALISTAIR stepped out of the autocar and into the fog submerging the Seven Dials in Covent Garden. He circled the sundial in the center of the square before taking a stroll down Mercer Street and squeezing into a nook near the end of the road, below the red bishop. After a knock the sliding peephole exposed the shifty eyes of one of the Pamplona brothers, Nick.

"The watchdogs bark . . ."

"Bow-wow, mate."

The interior was a dark cube: a historic time capsule with a pub exhibit, dry when the sharia police wouldn't take a tip, with wall-to-wall mementos from times too far gone to be relevant memories in the mind of Alistair. But he still found the place refreshing and homely, this quaint treasury, more than just about anywhere else in the city—not too shabby a haunt for a couple Spanish operatives posing as English Mohammadans. "A pint for the needy, mate," he said, flopping down at the bar. Pamplona Nick tapped a finger against his lips as he traversed the stick. He grabbed a mug and leaned it under the tap. Like a professional weightlifter preparing for a clean, Alistair assumed a flawless posture as the glass was placed before him. He curled his fingers around the handle and felt out the grip, exhaling with a balanced wind, eyes straight ahead, making the final preparations. *Gulp, gulp, gulp, erp-erp-ehhh, ahhh. . . .* "A second, tapper!"

"You a man or a fish?"

"Please sir may I—"

"—Told you to keep your mouth shut. You're cut off."

A subtle vibration drew their attention to the back wall where the juke-box, a by all indications long out-of-service Wurlitzer, was rotating outward. Pamplona Pete poked his head out and waved for him to come in as Pamplona Nick was shooing him away, but Alistair knew the drill. He ducked through to the other side and was motioned toward the body scanner, which he passed through before taking a seat across from Pamplona Pete at a table next to the furnace. Pete wrote something on a notepad and held it up: *Were you in the Coexistence Trust Council meeting earlier?* Alistair gave a thumbs up. Pete put the notepad down, retraced the question mark, and slid it across.

They're concerned about the leaks and the riots in Fulham, Alistair wrote. *They're also worried that what's happening elsewhere is going to happen here. A lot of big families are leaving but the government is doubling the number of Shomrim troops to protect the Inner Party. From what I gathered, the only real solution they posed was another Income Credit increase.*

Pamplona Pete chuckled as he read the message, afterward writing: *And the chip drive? Were you able to get it?*

Alistair's head scudded back as if propelled by the motorboating sound he was making with his lips, dragging it out until his eyes were pointed at the ceiling, which he gave a head-shaking sneer to before plunging back to normal and snorting at Pamplona Pete. . . . *Yeah,* he had it. And in a second here he was going to take it out and place it on the table. But before he did that he was going to make it as clear as the scarce-clear day what he risked to acquire the information on it: instant adjudication in accordance with the precepts of desert law followed by a Kensington Gardens ceremony to finalize the divorce between his now nearly indistinguishable upper and lower neck. The twisted cinematographers of Alistair's imagination had played the prospective sequence on a loop while he was in the process of sneaking into the British Caliphate Broadcasting Corporation's Portland Place server room, copying the system files onto the chip drive, and tiptoeing out with the heartrate of a hummingbird. In his pocket now was the whole shebang—every detail of the Regime's centralized media network: the name of every employee, the details of every station affiliate, bookkeeping records, passwords, and floorplans, every screw in inventory . . . Alistair, Old Boy, had it all. But what thanks did he ever get? He was one of the most hated individuals on the planet—shunned as an outsider by his neighbors in Little Brahma Belgravia, but treated even worse by the locals in Whitby, or for that matter, in Dublin, Edinburgh, and beyond—wherever he went—he was seen as the enemy, a traitor, deserving of far worse than the unexpected fists occasionally hurled at his face while eating in restaurants or out for a stroll. They'd never know. . . .

Everything's on it, Alistair wrote after handing it over . . . *but like I told you, it's useless unless you're ready to bring down the whole kebab, they'll kick you right out.*

Maybe we are ready, Pamplona Pete reported by pen.

Alistair crooked his neck and inched forward. "Really?"

"Shhh." *Maybe, so be ready. But there's one more last thing we need you to do.* . . . Pete continued writing as Alistair shook his head, having already read the *one more last thing* part from upside down, to which he was thinking— *In hell.* The chip drive was billed as *the* last thing . . . and there was no *one more* last thing, there was just *a* one last thing, and *that* was it. . . . *There's an event at Waddon Manor in Buckinghamshire tomorrow evening. You will be required to be in attendance.*

No way, Alistair wrote once he'd read the rest of the message. *Do you know what goes on at those things?*

Yes, and we know who attends them, too. We need someone on the inside and you're one of the few we can trust for this.

"Forget about it, I won't do it," Alistair said.

Pamplona Pete reached across the table and pinched the skin between Alistair's neck and shoulder until he appeared ready to reconsider. He then placed what looked like an old quid on the table. Alistair picked the coin up and examined it—nothing strange here, besides it being an artifact, of course, physical currency having been discontinued on the Island and most everywhere else ages ago. *When you arrive, hide this in the washroom on the right side of the main corridor.*

What is it?

You don't need to know the details. And one more last thing, Pamplona Pete wrote; Alistair looked away . . . *do not wear your ringport—got it?*

This is a lot to ask. Alistair leaned back and crossed his arms.

For England, Alistair. . . .

"For England . . . ," he whispered.

And then, just like that, did the transcript surf into incandescence and wither into white light, thus sparking a sequence that would—forever in Alistair's mind, but not unreasonably so—lead to the Battle for England. . . .

UNDER A TWILL DAMASK some squeaky wooden steps below the Red Bishop was a hatch with a retractable ladder that dropped into the London Underground. Dank inside, a fusty but familiar odor that made Pamplona Pete grimace as he climbed down and planted his feet on the tunnel floor. His oculife miner's light probed the artery's corroded cable-lined walls—steel rust and concrete stretching both ways, no sound but dripping—then he set off for Holborn. It'd been years since a train had passed through here; the

New Englishmen just couldn't seem to stop themselves from blowing them up, for this reason or that, and eventually it became too much of a hassle for the Caliphate to deal with. But the tunnels were still far from safe, so Pete, now as always, kept his finger on the trigger of his Redeemer, or J.K. ("*Jannah Knocker*") Rowling, and her barrel out front and ready. He'd ended a few lives down here. Well, a lot more than a few—vagrants mostly, wogs on the run, the worst kinds of schizoids. They could get in close and be on all sides before you realized it so it was important to take one or two out at the first sign of trouble. He felt a tinge of remorse at first, offing Mo Doe's down here in the pits, but none after that fateful wintertide afternoon when he happened upon the Waterloo rape camps, housing containers of abducted girls . . . *children*. Hajji was a lead magnet that day, Pamplona Pete couldn't miss, and when the smoke had cleared and the slug-pumping mad grin was gone and the prolonged series of bangs had given way to exhaustion, right then and there he knew, standing in one of the foretold rivers of blood and whirling in a tooty-bird choir of deaf rings, that he'd found a new hobby. So ever since, when there was time to spare, he'd wander through the tunnels heatpacking hellfire, spreading doom to any *ficki ficki* mole person he could find. Pete had cleaned up the Piccadilly from Hammersmith to Arsenal but had accomplished his most recent work on the Bakerloo Line. However, there was no time for any of that now, and such escapades could soon be coming to an end anyhow—this short boot-splashing trip, with reserved faith and uncertain promise, his last. Stalking subterranean freaks no more, retired from grim protean life, the loneliness of nameless ageing, pitching Anglo relief in dreary London to avoid another 700 years of this—on back, spouting *Ayes* and *Amens*, to Mediterranean falls and spring Costa Vascas, summer Sanfermines . . . *encierros* and *olés*—on home. . . .

At the drop-off point, Pamplona Pete took out an old—like, *ancient*—pre-loaded-*Snake*-model Nokia and sent a text message into the firmament. A ladder extended down and he climbed up and placed the chip drive onto an exchange tray at the top. It slid away and the small piece of plastic and mylar then found its way to the fingertips and ultimately the pocket of one of Pete's hardened colleagues in the Dear Old Blighty trenches, Ruffian Dave, a Nietzschean-mustacheod man also under the employ of the Googlopticon Investigation Unit, though the organization generally deferred to him. The naturally Breton-dark Englishman spoke the lot of sand dialects, ran a music shop out of Shadwell that fronted for a personal SIGINT bunker, and had several years prior as part of his deep cover study of the invader classes made the forbidden pilgrimage to Mecca. That was the only vacation he'd taken in his twelve years on the job, and it was the only time he'd ever come close to having his cover blown. No one in the caravan suspected Ruffian Dave of being anyone other than the Wafaa Al Nil stereo salesman he was purporting to be—that was, until a young man in the group saw him urinating on a wall a block from the cube and at a fluky angle was able to discern that Dave, in conflict with the now exclusively Semitic practice, was uncircumcised. "Bahlakabah . . . alakbakah," the young man yelled, "durkabaluuk?" upset by the infraction, pointing at the trickling member, demanding an explanation. There was only one thing to do. Ruffian Dave calmly shook it out, put it back, called the young man over, and strangled him to death right there on the side of the road. Oil by and large outmoded and the House of Saud's gravy train thus having jumped the tracks, much of the earth's middle-wasteland region had turned subfeudal, the conditions lawless, stuck in reverse, though more had come to accept this as the norm and the age prior the exception. But the mean streets of Mecca didn't hold a candle to the drags in Ruffian Dave's work-adopted hometown of London, where one could only feel nostalgic for those auld lang syne days in the acid-attack capital, into sweet dreams they went, while crisscrossing Greenwich colonies from Islamabad to Dakar to Mogadishu and experiencing the sublime wonders of them all. That was how the scars, running down each cheek to Dave's chin, found their way onto his already menacing jowl; some kind of javelin, wussit, hurled by Somali bandits around Plumstead High, going in one cheek and out the other, with the rod stuck there for a couple hours till he could yank it out. Few gave him trouble before, none after—the incident enhancing a disposition that would, fortunately, not have to come in handy over the next hour as Ruffian Dave, sporting his usual camel-tan Armani pajama throbe and topped off with an Eddie Bauer morni turban, stepped into the dark of Kingsway and embarked upon the journey north.

In a deserted suburb of Old Warden in Bedfordshire, beneath the Church of St. Leonard, a 12th century Norman cobblestone Abbey girded in gravestones, was a small ERP outpost. Dave felt around for the knob then pushed the heavy wooden door in. He took short steps along the left wall of the dark interior until he reached a door on the adjacent side. Dim motion sensor lights blinked on as he descended the spiral staircase to the downstairs bunker.

Although there were never more than a couple staff members around at any particular time, at this hour the sole individual on shift was data specialist Mark Turner, an honest old hand on this eve dighted in a black turtleneck, and currently in the middle of a heated exchange on 512Chan, murmuring as he typed:

>tfw too megapseud to grasp the difference between communism and neoethnocommutopianism
fake and gay kys faggot

Mark Turner sensed, then his eyes rolled up to see, Ruffian Dave, lingering on the other side of his desk. He jerked back, "Dave!" trying to laugh his heartrate down. "Di'in hear you come in, sly boy. And the turban, you nutter! that the new Bauer? gets me every time." Ruffian Dave took the chip drive out of his pocket and placed it on the desk. "Alistair come through, eh? Didn't think he had it in him. We in business or what? Mean, this is great, innit?" Turner, insisting. He clapped and propelled himself to a stand. "Well?" arms wide, expecting in this moment at least a minor show of enthusiasm from Dave . . . but Dave just wasn't the enthusiastic type. Turner couldn't tell if he was even listening, his intense eyes roaming the room, toweled head in the clouds. "Fulla beans as ever. Well, I'm happy *for* you, Dave," taking a half-seat on the desk. "So how's life with the saracens, my good man?"

Dave growled, "Worse than death."

"Don't know how you keep the spirits up, mate. Docs in your box, by the way, boss wants you to follow a lead in Luton."

Dave walked around the desk and toward the back. "Lead on what?"

"What else? The Googlopticon."

"Oh right, think I found it."

"*Found* it . . . ha!" Turner exclaimed, initially amused that Ruffian Dave, a brave spirit who'd engaged in honorable sins no part of him, large or small or any size in between, ever felt the need, or built up the confidence, to ask about, had finally discovered a sense of humor after all these years . . . but Dave didn't make jokes, either. Given the scope of the Googlopticon operation, with its many embroiled parties and regional offices, not to mention the long list of dead ends and failures, it was a given only greater that any proclamation claiming to have *found it* was a statement made in jest. But as Mark Turner watched Dave stagger toward the other end of the room, the more a feeling set in that this instance might actually be different. "Dave . . . you found the Googlopticon?"

Ruffian Dave opened his clearscreen and presented for Turner a sequence of footage he had put together, showing at first a man leaving an office building in downtown London, with ill-boding eyes, scanning side to side as Dave clandestinely filmed him from an undercover position nearby.

"I recognize this twit."

"Victor Rifkind, with the Intelligence and Security Committee. Rifkind leaves the office and snags a dossier from the Community Security Trust headquarters twice a week, then hands it off to this guy, who flies to Cyprus. . . . Who hands it off to this guy in Nicosia. . . . Who flies to Haifa. . . . And who then delivers it to this bunker out in the desert. Those, our three men of sin. Stonking thermal readings out there, security to the hilt."

Turner had a full brow up as he followed along. "Oh that's hot, my boy. Whatever they're hiding down there must be big, but . . . the Googlopticon?" Their eyes met sidelong in the dark office. "If you're right, Dave . . . and at first glance I'd say there's good odds you are—" Turner's expression attempting, but failing as it only could, to match Dave's own in seriousness, "—do you know what this means?" To which Ruffian Dave shrugged, his attention now on a half-eaten pack of hobnobs on the desk. "If we have control of the BCBC airwaves *and* we know the location of the Googlopticon, then stone the bloody crows. . . . After all the torment, trouble, and wonder Cuck Island has seen . . . it looks like at last the time has come to take it back."

Another part of the island.

WELL THERE HE SAT, like a schoolboy at a bus stop on the Bridge of Bridges over Swilcan Burn between one and eighteen, eyes even with the last titanic shutter of falling light, trusting his cheeks on the thin stone side and watching the bugs graze on a patchy runway yellow as a wheat field. They danced and buzzed through the gloaming in a meadow harmony, no arachnidian automower mounting the ridge to spoil it, attention not yet set on these plains, last of the peace. This was it: the end. Or some type of end. The peculiar type that felt more like a beginning. Seeking in this semi-contrived trance the stillness to harness if pining for a break. Lost or jittery. Now telling himself: *Do not fear this Scottish pasture, fairest of them all*—no, no—whatever woe it may bring, curseth not. . . . Forge consonance with the route that finds you and jam in wayfaring union with it, because these Links and the many she later birthed were constructed not out of guile, but in an alliance—a treaty between nature and man, earth and her most tender gardener, each with a lesson on how to perfect the other.

Enter Stig—moseying up from behind with his hands in his pockets, clicking a few spits into the grass along the way, face stuck in one of those gazes mammoth landscapes invent. They headed off for one last conference, through dinnertime quiet and air dyed ocher, ambling up the sea-lined, leaf-strewn road past the Martyrs Memorial and into the town of St Andrews, toward the Castle and Cathedral surrounded by the medieval splendor of fortress tones so aesthetically . . . *European*. Sand and Portland stone of olden ashlar walled in the single lane of road wearing wigs of green moss, the terraced houses, the bastle houses, the Scots-Baronial were etched into the above, enmeshed in waving birch, split by bending wynd, peaking stories up at Corbie-stepped gables and Tudor chimneys, peel towers and crown steeples, where barn swallows sang the coming night's song.

Ed knew the history. Pretty much. The significance here. More or less. . . . Still brushing up as the days shed like dog hair. Events had stalled with the war anyway. Little had taken place during his lifetime. But this was ground zero: the cradle of it all. And Stig as always could be relied upon to fill in the blanks of a story that would drift beyond accounts of peacetime games and into sagas of empire and resistance, of expanding scope and the rise of commercialization processes notably documented by one famed Fifer, of a people and their adaptation to the social transformations and political upheavals that would take place thereon, and of the new instruments of power others would misuse to advance their own interests at the expense of those who had mistakenly welcomed them back into their home.

"People used to go on and on about *the System*, all while their societies were crumbling around them. It was easy to blame some abstract entity like that, but it wasn't the real culprit, because the System is still a human system. The institutions that make up the System are reflections of the people running them—those pulling the levers, defining the parameters, and creating the incentives for it."

"So the System stopped being a reflection of us and became a reflection of them?"

"Authoritarian, repressive, barbarous. But it was hard for us to see that since we didn't understand their nature. We thought they were just like us. So when the System stopped working in the interests of our people and our nations, we started blaming it like it was some pernicious force with a mind of its own—the Sentient System Delusion—when in reality the System was working fine, just working in the interests of the foreign group that had taken control of our institutions as a consequence of our misplaced trust and their tribal nepotism, who were using the System to advance their international agenda, which was directly opposed to any national agenda that worked in our interests."

"Why do people always make comparisons to the Soviet Union? Was the system there the same?"

"This same people implemented that system and were running it for much of its duration, so it took on similar characteristics and produced similar results. These are rootless outsiders, and they self-identify as such. They are hostile to the very concept of the nation. They don't share their host's allegiance to it, they don't view it as a home or a protective body for a people, their culture has told them for centuries that the whole world is their nation. So whenever we have allowed them to obtain power, they have tried to corrupt our national systems, transform them into international systems, and run our nations through extranational institutions or imperial states that will advance their global interests. The Soviet Union and the twelve-starred European Union, the IMF, the World Bank, and globally oriented investment banks, the bevy of NGOs and the Old American Empire itself—these were tools they used to advance their international agenda, with our major cities serving as their global headquarters."

"An agenda that furthered the global capitalism model."

"The Worst War was a battle between these two forces, internationalism and nationalism. This foreign group of internationalists won, so they were able to set the new rules and call the shots, promoting anti-national policies that shipped our industry overseas, importing outsiders to drive down wages and dilute our populace, and encouraging free trade and easy capital flow so foreign entities could buy up our national resources, influence our internal politics, and further advance that international agenda."

"But you're saying the System doesn't have to be like that."

"The System operates however those in leadership positions incentivize it to. *People* ultimately decide what the system looks like and in whose interests it acts."

"*Rootless cosmopolitans* . . . no wonder nationalism was always portrayed as the greatest threat."

"To them and their post-Worst War system, it was."

"But we aren't innocent. We went along with it, too."

"We sure did. We failed because we allowed our enemy into positions from which they could manipulate our system and frame the debate in their favor. That power allowed them to depict globalism as positive and irreversible, and they were able to indoctrinate an entire generation into believing that the interests of a foreign group were really their own. The System rewarded them for tearing down their own culture and country and advancing this new global paradigm, but they were happy to become advocates for it regardless because they thought it was the right thing to do. There was a smooth transition from the old religion to the new one since both promoted the same universalist principles and moral framework based on lifting up the poor, huddled masses and spreading a type of utopian idealism around the world. We tried to convert everyone to those ideals, we thought they would want to share those values, we believed they could magically become just like us. We assumed they would care, that they would want those things too, that they could be brought in and plugged into our system and maintain what we had built."

"Morally, I can see why it seemed like the right thing to do."

"We are moralists by nature. We want to build the best societies imaginable, and that's a wonderful thing that comes from a good place in our hearts. But that aspect of our nature became a suicidal flaw when this duplicitous tribe was allowed inside our gates. Us Swedes learned that lesson the hardest."

"News out of there has been good lately."

"Can't believe it. Still looking for the Spoonbeard guy, though. But that utopian idealism nearly destroyed us because the humanitarian and equalitarian values that made us into soldiers for the new religion, as with the old, turned out to be at best a façade and at worst a wicked ploy. In the end, the people who were brought in to replace us didn't care about those ideals, they weren't capable of magically becoming like us, and they couldn't maintain the institutions we had built. So as the illusion began to collapse—"

"—The System began to collapse, too."

"But a new generation began stepping up and setting their sights on removing the foreign elite, dismantling the old system, and constructing a new one. We put ourselves first now, ahead of the rest of the world—no more universalist ideologies that foster our worst tendencies. We don't need anyone else anyway. *We* are the people who build societies that maximize liberty and lay the foundations on which civilization rises, foundations that will hold as long as we are able to keep those who corrupt and destroy civilization out."

"The new system better be stronger, cause they'll try to do it again."

"They sure will. And they'll do it the same way they always have . . . using the one thing that can tempt anyone, and that brings out the worst in everyone."

"What's that?"

Stig stopped and nodded at something across the street. "That right there."

But Ed missed the intended mark by about ten degrees east. He stood, head tilted, squinting at a flashing sign that read *Mam's Mince and Tatties*, a restaurant via namesake and fare serving up the popular Scottish beef and potato dish. "Tatties, huh . . . how's that work out?"

"No." Stig pointed at the right spot: a glowing green machine situated next to *Mam's*, radiating with the words *Fifeshire Financial Trust*—"Money."

❦

ALISTAIR, STRICKEN WITH FEAR and desperate for a drink, turned away from Waddon Manor in a half-hearted attempt to convince himself to pull out of the mission. But it was too late now. There was a werewolf moon looming over the spires, three stories of intricately carved granite in Graham cracker brown below, ghostly flickering through myriad windows, and without a doubt some malicious force in the ether round here. He was wearing a costume the Pamplona brothers had loaned him, the evening's regalia, comprised of a purple cloak and a white full-faced mask. Being a longtime truth-spinner for the Inner Party, Alistair had through gossip or by happenstance heard about the so-called *affairs* known to transpire in places like this—these, masquerades where leaders were chosen, conspirators engaged in occult ritual, and aspiring members of the political class proved their loyalty to the foreign money-minting aristocracy. He'd never been sure if it was real or not—if they actually believed in the things they were said to, kept in the dark though he was—but he knew enough to assume the worst.

With a shaky hand Alistair gave the invitation to the doorman and stepped into the foyer. Concealed faces turned and nodded with regard: men in the same garb as himself, women in little or nothing below peacock masks, the odd white-tuxed service-bot about. He nodded back and made his way through the gauntlet of onlookers, suddenly conscious of the sweat accumulating on his brow and threatening a painful drop into the eye. More partygoers gazed down from winding side staircases as Alistair walked underneath them and toward the main corridor. The walls were covered in red velvet; the furniture and ornamentation were vintage and majestic—extravagantly antique. Elevator jazz was playing. Just inside the passageway on the left were two wallscreens. On one the picture was shadowy, a voice was singing about chestnut trees; on the other were twenty frames, each with a downward view into the many rooms of the palace. Alistair stopped and scanned the panels. He focused on one in the middle. On it was a lone man staring up in the direction of the camera. It looked like. No. Yes. It was him. The shot then began zooming in on the picture of him staring up at himself. Alistair cleared his throat and continued on.

Ducking less than casually into the washroom on the right, he closed the door with his back and held it there for a few deep breaths. "All's well," he reassured himself. Now, where to put this thing—unpocketing the quid, strolling over to the toilet, and whistling an up-to-nothing tune of *Doo-duh-doo*. The lavatory was minimalist, meaning it was lacking in quality hiding spaces; but living under dhimmitude in Occupied England had taught Alistair a trick or two, so he already had a spot in mind. In his own home he'd used the no man's land behind the toilet to hide an item or two, including, most recently, the chip drive. It was usually a safe bet since even men with lean reach and precision dexterity wouldn't dare out of fear of making accidental skin or wardrobe contact. Alistair stuck his arm between the toilet and the cabinet and made a few dry runs to gauge the physics of his plan, which was to bounce the coin once off the ground, against the wall panel, and ideally to an unvisible resting place behind the bumnest. Ready, he gave it a toss, but it took a bad roll. He rose and sucked in hard and cursed under the mask, then he pulled off a shoe, held the cape back, and leaned between the cavity, doing his best to not let anything touch as he gave the coin a push with the toe—*swish:* mission accomplished. *Al-i-stair.* Now he could grab a drink, a quick yak with one of the slags, and bolt for the hills.

Alistair exited the bathroom and strode with courtly poise into the main room, where chatter was light and restricted to small circles. On the right was a bar, but it was about the most unusual bar he'd ever seen—from the looks of it, nothing more than a trough filled with a dark red substance patrons were consuming with human-sized straws. Four nude women and a lone man were standing on the far side. They attuned their attention to Alistair as he rolled up across from them and issued an innocuous nod. "Pip pip, chums," he said over, grabbing a straw and tilting it toward the mouth hole—thinking this method to be, in fact, a fine way to get the job done: permitting maximum intake with relative discreetness. In quick succession Alistair sucked up a mouthful of the liquor-mix, looked down, and made out something floating just below the surface: breasts, no doubt about it, belonging to a female corpse. He ejected the liquid into the inside of his mask, yelped cat-like, and stumbled back. "*Urghargh*," trying to dam the liquid flowing down his neck with his sleeve.

Alistair shuddered in spurts, to the tips of his fingers and toes, while making what could have at points in time been mistaken for the introductory shimmy of the Robot. He peered up and saw the group on the other side of the trough laughing at him. His head darted side to side, at once mindful that he may have just generated some unwanted attention. But few others seemed to have noticed. One of the women strutted around the trough, grabbing a towel from a side table on her way over. Alistair straightened up and regained his composure.

"Allow me," the woman said, pressing the towel to his chest, dabbing it slowly up his neck, and making eye contact through the mask.

"Beg your pardon, ma'am."

"New to the posh scene, Nancy Boy?"

Alistair scoffed, "Not quite, toots. I practically underwrite these shindies, just more your behind-the-scenes kinda chap."

"So you're an art collector."

Alistair started to shake his head *No* but changed it to a nod of *Yes*. "One of this distinguished gentleman's many passions, milady."

"Never heard it put like that before."

"No?"

"No," she purred, "but I'm not here to judge."

"I must apologize for that outburst," he said, taking the towel from her and laying it over his forearm then holding it up to his chest and reassuming a gallant posture. "Quite unbecoming of me."

"It's no problem."

"So would it be silly to inquire about the stiff bitch in the punch bowl?"

The woman shuffled around behind him, dragging her claws across his back as she repositioned herself on the other side. Leaning in, she whispered, "It's spirit punch."

"Aaah. The mysterious science of fermentation."

"Now, shall I escort you to the gallery?"

Alistair hesitated but figured it best to go with the flow. "To the gallery!"

Arms fastened they trod through an adjacent chamber, past circles of hidden figures to the opening of a dark staircase with red carpet leading down. Stuck to the walls were aged artifacts and weaponry: gold medallions and stickpins, flintlock pistols, swords and shields. Their steps were slow and cautious to the bottom, where a hallway hooked left into the gallery—a square room with a low ceiling and thirty or so paintings and portraits hanging on the walls. Another man was present, too with a bare bird, inspecting the merchandise.

They stopped just inside. "Did you have something particular in mind?"

"I've always been an admirer of the Ashcan School," Alistair said, then converting to *sotto voce* for the lean in, "but I'm a Rayonist at heart—don't tell, darling."

The woman giggled. "Cheeky monkey."

"To tell the truth, I may not be the connoisseur I'm letting on. It's all aesthetics with this old sod so you may have to lend a hand."

"Sod's the word and that's what I'm here for," directing him to the near wall. "This one," she said, showcasing a multicolored web of a design, "is a thirteen-year-old Norwegian. Brand new, arrived just this week."

"Get me a shufti here," Alistair, as he bent over to study it. "I wasn't aware that new art was *in* these days."

"How old do you prefer?"

"Your fair knight ranges the ages, dugs."

"How about this one then," guiding him a few over. "Eleven, from Slovenia. Blond, very youthful. Not a new piece but one most seem to enjoy."

"Dare I say, Madame . . . ," he declared, "it's smashing!" moving in, clasping his hands behind his back, leaning forward to examine the modernist pie-like canvas. "Simple but complex . . . delectable!"

"Sounds like we have a winner."

Alistair turned and faced the woman then looked around; the two of them were now alone in the gallery. "Decisions, decisions . . . to spend or not to spend!" he cooed theatrically, charmed with the ruse, knowing there was never any intent. "It's a question of space to be honest."

"Maybe if you saw him first it would help you decide. He's just over in the showroom."

Alistair did a half turn, believing he misheard something, "Sorry . . . *him?*" back and forth between her and the painting. "Who's in the showroom?"

"The eleven-year-old Slovenian boy. Or we could discuss some more options if you'd like."

"The hell are you on about?" waiting for a response that didn't come fast enough. "What boy? The artist?"

Both tensed up. The woman's head sprung toward the entrance and back. "Sir."

"Where am I?"

"You're in the gallery, sir."

It hereupon dawned on Alistair that he had unwittingly acted his way into the role of *emptor* in a high-level child prostitution racket, a notorious enterprise long known to cater to the nation's elite, often for the purposes of blackmail. He began to pant; anxiety permeated through his body, "—Foul wench!" he cried.

The woman grabbed Alistair by the arm and pulled him in close. "They're watching us, be quiet." She continued in a raised voice while motioning toward the entrance, "I'm sorry you didn't find what you were looking for, sir."

They left the gallery and started back up the stairs. Alistair stopped midway, sweating missiles, hyperventilating. "*You* . . . man's joy and bliss, eh.

This—I can't," ripping at the neck of his cloak, sweat oozing from his pores. Without thinking, he pulled the mask up and ran a sleeve down his face.

The woman gasped, pinning herself against the other wall and covering her chest. "You're the English guy from the British Caliphate Broadcasting Corporation," fanning her mask. "You aren't doing a story are you?"

"Bloody—" slipping his own back down "—bet I'll be. You'll be all over the Tube tomorrow, harpy, parts."

They climbed the rest of the way up the stairs but stopped a few from the doorway upon seeing what was waiting for them: a semi-circle of masked men, standing in silence and cutting off any escape route. The woman pranced out with her head in her hands; Alistair turned and ran back down the stairs. Steps into what was clearly a futile retreat, a voice echoed through an intercom and ordered him to stop. Alistair obeyed, but made sure to pull up next to a dagger that was situated along the wall.

"Return to the top please, sir."

"Snookered, *aye!*" using the cape as cover as he pried the dagger off and stuffed it between his slacks and waist and pulled his shirt over it.

Back at the top Alistair submitted with raised arms. Expecting to be physically subdued, he instead found the semi-circle closing around him as he stepped forward. He was then escorted, enveloped within the purple-cloaked pack, through a long pearl hallway away from the front of the estate. No one spoke or so much as acknowledged him until they had reached the end. There, the group merged with another that was waiting in a large circular room with a six-pointed star in the middle of the marble floor. White busts were interspaced between Palladian windows, darkened by the night, on one side; large columns on the other reached up to the second floor, where several masked faces were looking down from a distended balcony. Nudged to the center, Alistair stopped inside the star and faced the box seats as he assumed he was supposed to. One man stood out from the rest. He was wearing an owl mask and rose upon receiving Alistair's attention.

"Welcome," the Owl Man said, breaking the silence, his voice ringing through.

"'Ow do," Alistair replied. Feeling his fate hereabouts likely sealed, his nerves had calmed and a feeling, some of that inborn English honour to be sure, was washing over him. No sense giving in to these cabalists, "These clowns."

"What was that?"

"What was what?"

"You said. Never mind. Please remove your mask for us, dear friend."

Alistair grunted, "You can piss off with that business."

"Remove it or it will be removed for you."

He built up some tension then peeled the mask off and flipped his hair back dramatically—to whispers, grumblings, again reciting his calling card: *The English guy from the British Caliphate Broadcasting Corporation.* The one and only.

"Why, is that Alistair Jarvis I see before me?" the Owl Man said. "I can hardly believe my eyes . . . this thing of darkness. What brings you here to-night, old chap? Aren't doing a story, are we?"

"I was considering it." Alistair spread his stare around. "But it all depends."

"Depends on what, Mr. Jarvis?"

"On you and your band of pederasts' peaceful surrender."

This response ignited a barrage of laughter, that of the Owl Man loud-est and longest lasting. "Forgive me, but I feel you may be overplaying your hand, Mr. Jarvis. . . . And I'm in no mood for games." The Owl Man turned to someone who placed something in his hand. "We found this." He held up for all to see the quid Alistair had deposited in the washroom earlier. "Pray tell—what is this, who gave it to you, and why did you dispose of it on these premises?"

"You got cameras in the loo." Alistair turned to the others. "They got cameras in the loo."

"Mr. Jarvis."

"I'm here to inform you that the Resistance is on its way. It's over, boys.

Tough luck. I'm sorry."

"Is that so, sir?" the Owl Man shot back. "But they haven't been this far south in years. Tell us, Mr. Jarvis, will they be arriving in that time machine of theirs . . . or does it not go this way?"

The room again broke out in laughter. "Yak it up," Alistair laughing with them. "Might be your last."

"Or your own if they don't arrive in time to save you, Mr. Jarvis." The Owl Man, then, diabolically, "The sacrifices are usually speedy anyway."

Alistair sensed the group moving in on him; he was waiting for it. If his fate was a grisly death at the hands of these deviants, then by Gor be it . . . once in a while a man could finish in style. He turned and pulled out the dagger, brandishing it around and stabbing at the air. "Back! back now!"

"Don't make this more difficult than it has to be, Mr. Jarvis."

Outside somewhere in the night, ripping through the quiet, was a confluence of sounds that diverted the attention of those in the room and put a temporary halt to the melee: gunfire, screaming, music, after a long drumroll, booming across the estate. Members of the establishment-pedophile society shuffled to the windows for a better look. Beams from the air and ground power moving in turned the room into a blinding but heavenly state of daylight bright. And the song—Alistair recognized it. He started humming along to pick up the tune, *Duh-duh-duh-duh, duh-duh*. . . . Wh*aye*, of course!

Send her victorious,
Happy and glorious,
Long to reign over us,
God save the Queen!

There being, safe to say, a touch of irony in the anthemnal accompaniment on this blitz into Waddon Manor, as many decades had passed since there'd been a Queen, the last having been purged along with the rest of the Royal Family: dragged from Buckingham Palace and executed during the Islamo-Bolshevik uprising. And the natives weren't exactly crying *Mercy upon my liege* since it was the rotten royal crust that was largely if not entirely responsible for the downfall of their homeland after selling it out to the foreign usury families and betraying the population by refusing to stop the invasion. But it was, nevertheless, still a symbolic gesture representative of a people and their collective identity, their renascent awakening, and their coming retaliation against an internal enemy who, once but no more, tried to muddy that identity and transform their nation into something alien and unrecognizable.

The lights began fading in and out. "Dolt!" Alistair howled upon realizing he'd forgotten to pocket his ringport. He in a rush made an attempt to twist it off his finger, but was unable to get it past the fat of his PIP joint.

Then it, it seemed, well . . . it was hard to say.

Alistair came to to the sound of his own gargling moans as he was lifted off the floor. His head found its way down from the ceiling. Time had passed; the situation had changed. There were soldiers in the room, bereted and clad in MTP, unmasking the others and hauling them out; him, too: Alistair, currently flanked by the two men who just pulled him up.

A soldier stepped in front of them, fist raised. "Oi, I know this wanker."

But someone intervened from the side before it could fly. "Oi, no, that's the English guy from the British Caliphate Broadcasting Corporation, he's with us."

Alistair was set free. He wobbled while sturdying himself. He looked up at the balcony. Empty now. "Ow," a palm to his forehead. Alistair walked to the corridor and to the next room. He glanced up the stairs then started up, offloading weight to his forearm, which he used as a balancing clamp on the railing as he mounted the steps. At the top was a half-open door; movement was coming from inside, shadows and talking. Alistair peeked in. A crowd was standing around the de-masked Owl Man, who was strapped to a chair. Ugly bloke, like a lizard. One of the soldiers then observed Alistair having a looksee in.

"Oi, you, out."

Alistair took a step in and put his hands on his hips with an air of authority. "Fine work here, boyos." A soldier started over, shaking his head like he wasn't buying it. "See if you look that hard at the tribunal, chief." Alistair made a few moves to dodge but the soldier was able to corral him and push him out. "Just *pst* come on *hey* . . . who is that?"

"Emmanuel Goldstein."

STRIKEFORCE UAVS BOUND FOR THE LEVANT climb the air: a sleek armada of Starlings on a migration east, rising to the edge of the stratosphere invisible above clouds like arctic tundra—alone aloft over New Constantinople and across the Eastern Mediterranean carrying enough firepower to make the facility housing the Googlopticon indistinguishable from the dunes of sand that surround it. Latterly down the aerial line the screens inside turn blood-red, clocks count down, flag of the Reclamation: a final warning. But the revolution would wait for no one. Twenty fuselage belly flaps open to expose the blue-capped heads of the Striker-3—a thin gal, glossy and elegant, compressed with the energy of kingdom come. Under the shade of their matriarchs' composite gleam they wait until the time strikes, then they slide from their rails, locks overriding in a majestic volley of clean ejector launches. Crepitating in parting song and united in thrust they set out in descent, diving fast then faster in silent harmony, allies with gravity on this first and last waltz through the planetary beltway. Free-flight wind smooth off the nose, a streaking misty trail, a glistening view of the Earth's desert dump if there ever was. Reaching terminal velocity as the target detectors zero in on laser specks moments before touchdown, rods around the charge ready.

Kablooey.

Starting right about now the slow squeeze in effect around occupied European city-states would flex into a stranglehold as the Demulticulturalization and Remigration plans entered full tilt. A blockade would be imposed on the SNBL until it was asphyxiated. The web of international agencies and institutions used to assist the invaders would continue to be absorbed and disbanded or retooled by the European Reclamation Project. The financial infrastructure that enabled the welfare-debt scheme would be dismantled, no more Income Credits would be issued to outsiders, and the overseers of the Judeo-Keynesian scam would have their assets seized before being put on trial or tracked down and Trotskyied. All public and private networks and communications systems would be kill-switched and anyone tuning in to one of the Libancien's former Tube stations would find themselves staring at SMPTE color bars as a retro-comedic-effect-type thing. Fake news sites would be permanently renamed: PAGE NO LONGER EXISTS, Mebook profiles would be inaccessible, every Old Regime frequency, station, and channel, every bowdlerized social platform and comsymp soapbox, would be shut down, all surveillance and botnet systems would be taken over or terminated, and the Libancien's control over information and communication within the West would be officially over, putting an end to the era where an alien tribe of vagabonds was able to frame, manipulate, and censor the truth in nations not their own.

Europe's invader classes would no longer be able to view programming congratulating them on their sanctioned conquest of infidel territory; the only messages they would see would be ones telling them to leave peacefully or face severe consequences. Degeneracy would no longer be tolerated by adults and normalized to children through these outlets; Europeans would no longer be portrayed as antagonists warranting the attacks against them, but as the righteous reclaiming what was theirs. Equalitarianism, diversitarianism, and globalism would no longer be misrepresented as Western ideologies; they would be portrayed to and accurately understood by future generations as ideologies of the past, ideologies that failed, ideologies that were imposed by an enemy and were never supposed to succeed, ideologies that produced negative outcomes alone for the people of the West, whose nations would no longer be depicted as places for everyone, but places that would be from here on inhabited only by their creators and their descendants as a new ideology, rooted in healthy tales and tidings of folk and ethos, continued to emerge and be shaped and administered along ethnic, national, and civilizational lines.

But this would only occur following the message ordering the desert tribes to do what they do best. Westminster would crumble into the Thames, the banlieues would finally converge upon the Élysée, the Reichstag would again be set ablaze, and tonight the Old Empire would burn. The foreign elite would flee and the leftover invaders would attempt to erect their own fiefdoms, but these would be short-lived, because tomorrow Western Civilization would begin anew. We'll roll in like morning thunder bringing total war behind force fields and Frankenstein machinery, our sole objective to remove these silt kings, flushing them out and scooping them up like the sand that spawned them then dumping them back in their box. They never belonged here, they'll never return, and it won't take 700 years to remove them this time. They were let in as a result of our own flaws, our own weaknesses, because of the ideologies we succumbed to and the crooks and outsiders we allowed to become our institutional arbiters. This was a test, and we failed. But we will learn from our mistakes, find honorable men to lead us, and rebuild it stronger than ever, restoring the pride we once had in ourselves and in our communities and entering a brave new world with a return to health, with our culture mended, with our history intact, and with our *real* values— those of all the ages before—because Europe would not fall and Europeans would not vanish, it would rise and we would become great again. . . .

L AVENDER THISTLE HID LOW amid dry patches of tallgrass, beachgrass, coastal machair, the moorland desert in gradients of August-green on the Fife. The oceanside plain was a minefield of spotty earth, with dips, lay-ers, traps, and pits afore white flags jeering in the distance. Frost-spangled crests rippled into tan shores below the bluff's indent, a sea-land skirmish, the might of the waves no match for this geotic rampart as their infinite journey culminated with a push, rolling up the sand then right back out like easy aqua-velvet lightning. Conveyor belts of cloud reeled under the sun-bisque, the light cycling between tints of dimday haze and an earthly glow that illuminated the evenside of the stone-washed chateau along the town's edge before sending it right back into obscurity. It was nearing the downside of midday, but the main event was just getting underway here on the plot of land where this game originated centuries ago, back when it was called *gouff*, had 22 holes, and was played exclusively by red-bearded lowlanders. Rugged terrain, a venthouse for wind, the cornucopia of grass: smooth to rough meadow, wood and oval sedge, Yorkshire fog and standard. And it was on these fields that the future was written when some bored Scot on his way home found a smooth, fifty-gram piece of ore, inspected it, then, with the butt of his lance, a furrowed brow of curiosity, and a slight shift in the kinetic energy of his deathblow, blessed sward three of the Jubilee.

Maybe.

The sun peeked out as Ed entered his backswing. His arms and torso rotated around wind-fast as he flowed through a motion that produced post-*ping* a soaring parabolic vault and cued his cap-tipped turn in the opening round cheer. After that the march was on to close out the final act of the Diversity Open, right as rain or near it, a strong performance necessary after the meltdown in Frankfurt. Players and 'plauders darted the grassland—a lunar landscape with few trees nigh, only scattered craters and billowy earth, mounds of bush and sorrel sod—the greatest challenge to be not the challengers themselves, but as usual, and even more so here, the course, in all its sacred turbulence.

And thus it came to pass that as the sea breeze found a rhythm and the fickle light no longed-for resolve the men fortunate enough to get a break from this war, or to have up to now avoided it completely, with careful touch and treading, charted like helmsmen the game's Bermuda Triangle, navigated through its hidden quarries, and communed and c'mon'd with the heavens as they picked their earth-toned spots wisely and prayed they hit them, since lurking among hazards all the more on primal harrowed ground was this pastime's abyss of Tartarus—the Hell Bunker: Agnus MacDante's Inferno—a foxhole so deep that if your ball made its way in, minus magic, your weekend was all but over.

Ed finished the first round in a four-way tie for third at minus one as aircoal clouds boiled in on the coast. He had few complaints upon his return to the clubhouse, where fewer appeared interested in what occurred on the course that day—attention earmarked for what had been going on at the other end of the island, in London. Open were many clearscreens on warstream; most was quiet outside of huddled conversation. A hand waved at Ed from across the lounge, belonging to one of the Baltic players, Lauris Pumpurs, who was inviting him over to where he and his two continental-bun neighbors were tapped into split-framed drone feeds.

"Getting heavy," Aarne Veske said.

"Yeah?"

"They're tearing the City of London apart."

"Chopping off heads in the street."

"Reclamation's scorching them from above, too."

"Protecting the landmarks."

"Telling them where to go."

"Who to attack . . . it's happened before."

"Look-y here," Antanas Sidabras leaning forward in his seat, "batter up."

A panel was spotlighted. It expanded and washed out the others. The picture was from an angle adjacent to a baroque prayer house, St. Paul's mosque, the focus on a New Londoner, ragged and lean, who had the look and presence of someone up to no good. He was holding a ripped trash bag, the utility of which was about spent, and eying the back end of the former cathedral, inching toward a semicircle fifty feet from the steps. The looter made a sharp move but backed off—testing the boundary, calculating the risk.

"One in the oven," Lauris said, "what do we got?"

"Ten Gold-Coin he goes for it," Aarne wagered, reaching into his pocket.

"*Psh*," Antanas with a backslapping hand to the air, "twenty he makes it."

"Ed?"

"I'm good."

The Baltic players squared their bets as the looter again tested the line.

"Hotfeet, Bruv."

"Treasure or virgins."

"Win win."

The looter put down the trash bag and changed his trajectory. After getting into a ready-sprint position and shaking his hands at his sides, he hit the gas—burning rubber through the crescent square toward a veiled Queen Anne and the one-time church.

"—We're off."

"The burst!"

"He's got it."

The looter was halfway there, then one long stride from the base. He slowed upon reaching the steps, loosening up, wearing a look of success as he hopped up to the midway point, stopped, and glanced around.

". . . Uh-oh."

"Not there yet."

"Deep-fried kebab, coming up."

The looter jumped up a step, then one more, then a flash of light momentarily blinded the feed. When the clarity returned he was gone, no trace he ever existed, and all was still again.

"He was a risk-taker."

"Got closer than the last guy."

"And he had to go anyway."

"Huh," Ed said, attaching a goodbye before wandering off to grab a bite to eat, still not sure what to make of the recent events. He'd never paid much attention to the war and wasn't sure who was even fighting in it until recently. There was always too much going on, by the fireside of the mind and throughout the endless space outside, around each imaginative bend, digital loop, or barrio'd corner, too much data, drivel, spin, fiction—*pages* and *pages* of it—or at least enough to ensure the proles remained confused and cynical. . . . So what was the point? It was easier to not care, to keep the madness at a distance, to leave deciphering the motivations behind it all to the others. Such feelings of dispassion, however, seemed to be losing vogue of late. It was getting more difficult to not see what was *really* going on; to not grasp what the War was *really* about; to ignore who was *really* behind it. And the battle had in a sense turned inward. For most of his adult life Ed's politisophical outlook usually jived on some variation of the new age proverb *whatever* . . . all these lies, all these liars, all these sciolists eating it up, sitting ducks and suckers, playing a rigged game, thinking they have it figured out. Let them waste their time wandering through that maze. Pat them on the back, praise their wisdom, wish them luck. . . . But give me the good times, those puerile fantasies, foolhardy I'll sail. Let me bloom across the seasons, whistle with this evensong, paint the town between twilights with mescal and mamacitas—just let me believe it'll always be like this, this synthetic bliss, this ride's end forever euphoria—dabbing out the last of the sun, setting fire to the night, sleeping after toyle; my war only with code or master, my enemy all the dull and donnish, hustling Sichuan rubber merchants like Titanic Thompson then catching night-robber winds into Panama City blowing up skirts and turning bone-rollers' pockets inside-out. Who wouldn't want to get lost in all that, drink it up, live it until the last light goes out? The best fools God could make. But such a mindset could only take a man so far. It couldn't last. And it never did. It was the illusion of youth—*the true beginning of our end*—when the earth was evergreen, when life was immortal, when our dreams were whatever we wanted them to be. A time often best forgotten in hindsight as a foray into carnality, a shallow sashay into the dawn of being. If you couldn't stop it, it would eventually stop you, fly by and leave you living some doleful version of it, still seeking its rush, the last to realize it was over, now hobbled with its excesses, only the toll outlasting. Then, suddenly, there was a lot less time than you thought there was. Suddenly, what never mattered was all that did. . . .

Retreating only deeper into his thoughts as he reached the buffet tables, erected a pyramid of food, and took a seat alone. The chicken tasted like it had been lingering alfresco for a bit too long, but Ed's senses were only backdrops to whatever was happening on the empty wall in front of him. Soft taps hit the windows, then the flurry began as the tempest reached the banks of Scotland. Thunderclaps crackled into cannonade. Lightning split the sky as a tocsin whirl warned anyone still out on the course to withdraw. The coterie in the mess hall jumped, but not Ed; he barely noticed as Stig lumbered up and took a seat across from him. "Not supposed to let up for two days. We can probably take off after lunch tomorrow, get a day trip in."

"Yeah?" Ed, shaken out of his trance, laid the fork down. "There is somewhere I'd like to go, actually. If it's doable." Stig bucked his chin to inquire. "Loxley . . . town outside of Sheffield."

"Of course," Stig said, no further inquiry required. "Where else?"

THE NEXT DAY Ed, Stig, and Jennifer departed for South Yorkshire, lifting up and landing in weather that remained, as per the local verbiage, *shite*. Loxley had never been much and wasn't much now—a Norman hunting ground then an industrial center until the international system gutted the town and made it, like so many others, obsolete. It subsequently withered and began to die, but Loxley had found new life through the exodus, when regionalism was revived and many relocated from England's southern cities to Sheffield's new western suburbs seeking safety, space, stability, and their own.

The area, as observed from autocar windows up to the point where they were standing under an instacanopy at the intersection of Loxley Road and Rodney Hill, was dominated by emptiness. There was no one anywhere to be seen. Rain plummeted through the murk overhead, ticking off pantile roofs and spattering into puddles. The trio turned circlets at variable speeds, not sure where to go or what to do, inferring, though untroubled by the notion, that this was bound to be as exciting as it would get.

"I'll go this way," Stig said.

Alone to stroll, Ed and Jennifer, arms locked and soon wet to the socks, followed the fieldstone wall up Loxley Road under a metallic sky horizon-far, gazed through white-diamond window grilles on brick flats with front-facing vegetable gardens, and finally discovered, standing in the middle of a plot opposite the more settled side of town, stoic in the August drencher midst a dark-green-vale milieu, Loxley's only apparent living soul in the form of a blue roan horse. Jennifer clacked at it, tried to call it over like a kitten. Ed went in for a low grab as she leaned over the wall. She turned and punched him in the chest. Her hands then interlocked like scissor tips behind his neck and her leg yarned around his. A few miles away in Rotherham a boost-glider rocket exploded against the troposhield, sound of magic thunder over here as he Lindy hop dipped her to the foot of the Albion fog. She let her head fall all the way back, her hair almost brushing against the ground. Then both at once, upside down and right-side up, saw something barreling down on them from upsidewalk.

A figure: at first sight, something unhuman; at second, an old woman, hunched over under an umbrella, moving at a turtle's pace. They waited. Ten feet out Jennifer leaned over, hands on her thighs like a shortstop ready to catch her. "Pardon me, ma'am," in the voice she often used when speaking to those on the frontiers of life, "could you tell us where everyone is today?"

Loose skin on the old woman's jaw flapped as she answered to the phonetic tune of "Eetsaweetaynnehayseenoffdashefftufaytamuds."

Jennifer turned and watched her go. She gave Ed a look, but he didn't know. Both were still failing to piece much together as they continued on

and edged along the scenic side of Loxley Road. It didn't take long for them
to reach the end of town, where they found a sign welcoming the welcome
to the hamlet of Loxley. Jennifer was insistent, "Come on!" wouldn't let it
go "*Eh-uh-Ed!*" until Ed reluctantly agreed to have his picture taken in front
of it. Then, on the way back, he remembered what he wanted to see most
of all.

Leading her by hand down a side street that wound up the hill and forked
onto a muddy path, *flora loxliensis* burrowing them through to a small clearing, a thickset bower, enclosed in tangled hedge and filled in violet light. In
the center was a rectangular tomb with green-stained brick a few feet high
and speared gates atop—tall, slim, and coffee-toned—connected by three
stone pillars at the corners. The fourth laid fallen, resting on the ground,
that side of the mounted gate broken, absent or bent inward. The site was
timeworn and weathered, but buried under the earth inside the modest plot
were whatever remained of the remains of Robin Hood.

"Like, so cool."

Thoughts thinking *Be thoughtful . . .* but genuinely it comes, faint then
firm, with a stroke of common sense disguised as wisdom: these things we
know, this truth of all abiding time, *who we are*—for when the newfangled
schemes were untangled, the adolescent indoctrination undone, the radical revolutionary fervor exposed, plain as pease porridge it became, as it is
and everlastingly was, so simple. Simplicity lost time and again amid the
tedious hours spent grounded and bounded by ambition and want of comfort, guided by a desire to just get along and an urge to wake up every day
and not see it as merely another day, but to dream it into something else,
something other than what it really was. Dreams to conceal the reality that
we were not gods but men, that nature was a theater of war, and that others
often intend to do us harm. The dream of an earlier age envisioned people
from every land living peacefully in the lands of one people, but, as should
have been expected from the start, that dream quickly became a nightmare.
The most difficult aspect for many to come to terms with, however, was the

fact that this dream was never actually a product of their own imagination and never contained the good intentions they understood to be part and parcel of the utopia they believed they were creating, but that they were instead the target of a pernicious swindle, one as old as the story went back, sponsored by a sadistic foreign presence within.

The thing about dreams, though, was that the dreamer eventually woke up. And what the people of the West woke up to was a state of wreckage even those with the most inventive of imaginations could no longer deny or cover up—a dawning realization from whence they would be forced to accept, as Ed was now, that they were part of a family whose long-term survival was dependent on the strength of their collective fortitude, and that these lands were their homes, homes that had to be defended. Faith in the end was no match for nature, instinct would be a buoy against the downfall, and rising again was the impellent force of a man who at his best had no terrestrial counterpart, from the spirit and unbridled vision of whom a new dream would begin to emerge, limited only by his will to make it real and conceived here in these moments by the mindeye responsible for beauty and innovation that would be trampled upon and abused no more, but protected and passed on, so that those unborn, in the womb of the womb of the womb, would too have the chance to realize when they reached this stage of transcendence their own dream, one their primitive forefathers with their ringports and time machines of dubious authenticity could never even begin to conceptualize, but that they would, and alone could, make real and use to take them into realms theretofore unknown. . . .

The blasts were increasing in regularity. Ed and Jennifer took a different way out than they came, through a tunnel of trees that rounded the backside of the hilltop then curved down and opened in gradual peeling pine up, wider and wider the thru-brier view, to an aperture that peered out onto the Yorkshire fields north of Loxley. "Look," Jennifer, pointing. Not that he could miss it, whatever it was, fifty feet below on level ground and a few hundred across in one of the distant plots: a giant white oblong blimp. "A hot air balloon?" Close. They tramped hand in hand through the wet, knee-high, slopeside grass into the clearing under dire iron English skies as the balloon swelled upward ahead. A portly older man, at first oblivious to their approach, was making the rounds about the gondola. They caught his eye while crossing one of the fields. He waited frozen and expressionless, wearing big glasses and an outmoded suit, taupe and tight, under the balloon, where he was shielded from the beating rain. Ed and Jennifer smiled and waved once in range then, upon realizing the limitations of communication, smiled and waved some more.

"'Ow do? Couldn't get a clear looks at you from o'er there," the man said in a thick accent as he put a hand out. "Jon Denbow."

"So what is this thing?" Ed, after introducing himself and Jennifer, snooping a few steps around the side.

"This is me airship," a ring-slap clanging against the outside.

"It's something, all right. We were wondering if you knew where everyone is today."

"Ey've all been o'er in Sheffield since the Battle of Rotherham got going. Too old to do much meself," he sighed, "but I can get a look o'er top withiss. Even all the men that's been in and out last couple days can't cover all the ground out there. And you know," Jon Denbow running his hand over the outside, a crafty glance to and fro, "I was about to go up. Can always use the extra eyes."

The airship rose slow and steady over checkered-green farmland and hamlet rooftops, her swollen nose set in the direction of Wadsley, Middlewood, and Birley Carr. The inside of the gondola had the feel of a gutted trailer, with standing-height, open-air windows all the way around and a cockpit that glowed steampunk-bronze with old-timey meters, gauges, and pumps. Ed and Jennifer each had their head out a window, taking turns with Jon Denbow's retro binocular Ecto-Goggles and giggling in spates between the divider as they ascended into North Sheffield.

Jennifer pulled the mask up and turned to Ed early into the trip, hair flitting into her face. "What are we looking for again?"

Ed wasn't sure, either. "Diversity, I guess."

She then uttered something that took him a moment to process: *Diversity is our greatest strength* was what it sounded like. "What'd you say?" But Jennifer just smiled back, apparently unaware she had said anything at all. "Are you still feeling the aftereffects?"

Her loose smile tightened with concern. "Did I do it again?"

Ed nodded. "Seems to be getting better, though. And you still got your kidneys."

In view higher up was the winding wall of the Sheffield Line, separating New North Mercia from Southern England, along with the rippling waves of the troposhield, visible, but hardly, around Rotherham. Ed pulled his head back in and hobbled to the front. "That where all the noise has been coming from?"

"Aye—we'll catchun 'ear in a minute."

But it took less than that. Seconds later a Zeus-boom rocked the atmosphere, while up ahead pastel blast-waves, concentric ripples thick and fast to thin and slow, spread like a plumb lake on fire. "*Whoa . . .* never seen one of the shields up close."

"We got most, not alls, but most, of the bobars shut up in there," Jon Denbow said. He then got to explaining the local situation in depth as they drifted on. And what a tragic story it was, one that could only scar the imagination and punctuate the sheer evilness of the diversitarian program. About how Sheffield, Rotherham, and nearly every other community around the country had been infused with welfare settlers long ago; about putative leaders who turned their heads as thousands of little girls in their communities were gang raped and pimped out by inbred desert aliens; about Berelowitzian cover-ups and a backward legal system that slapped foreign criminals on the wrist while hunting down and locking up patriots for simply voicing their opinions and concerns; about a demoralized people without the means of self-defense, the bureaucratic arms of whose own nation had been turned against them. About a situation that only got worse and more violent as the numbers continued to tip and control was increasingly handed over to the outsiders.

Bloodlust and dark days would on the Island betide, but if there was a break in the clouds, it came from the fact that the foreign elite and their New English pets had appropriated institutions and ultimately a nation they could never have built themselves, and that they were hence incapable of sustaining. After spells of jihadic terror across the south, the official rise of the English Caliphate, and the Great Shift, the leverage of Londonistan's authority could only wane as ethnic consciousness among the natives could only rise, most vitally among those who would step forward as leaders, put their people in line, and help take back control where possible. Segregation would become mandatory, and here in Sheffield a partition would be raised along the M1 motorway to keep the invaders confined to Rotherham, which remained a hotbed of enmity, a political pressure point, and a continental hub for the flesh trade until just days prior when the ERP provided the backup and battery needed to finish the job.

And therein lied the answer to Ed and Jennifer's question. Coming up before and below were the people of Loxley, and those from towns, counties, restored medieval regions, and nations over, assisting with the war effort: men doing as they did, women preparing food and providing aid, the elderly looking after children or in the odd case scanning the periphery in airships. An around-the-clock operation had gone into effect once word of the Caliphate's demise had come through, with events pausing not a second since, as the people of the Old Kingdom now had every reason to come together and be divided no more along the superficial lines of the past.

The airship cruised into Hood Hill over suburban mazes that stretched each and every way below, land dotted with rich country green and bundles of forest, estate lawns and flat acres of fawn and verdant earth. Checkpoints and tanks could be seen along the roads. Now and then a drone would shoot across the sky. The radio on the deck crackled with chatter Ed couldn't make much sense of and Jon Denbow seemed to ignore, until a dispatch arrived from Tinsley Ground Base seeking *Denbow Airwatch One.*

"That's us!" Jon Denbow as he reached for the radio mic. "*Denbow Airwatch One*, oh-vuh."

"'Av your position eastbound and north of Wentworth. We proxy-stopped a van with Regime tags ahead in Brampton, sending you the coordinates now, mind taking a look and reporting back, oh-vuh."

"*Denbow Airwatch One* is on it, oh-vuh."

Jennifer joined them in the cockpit. She and Ed shared a flash of brows before setting keen eyes out front. The airship entered a slow descent and was soon riding a strip of road bordered in tree and bush between two sprawling fields.

"I see it up there," Jennifer said.

"Me too," Ed confirmed.

"Me three," Jon Denbow added. "*Athink.*"

The van was black and parked on a small, one-lane road. They didn't see anything at first, but before long a man climbed out of the driver's side and walked to the back. Another got out of the passenger's side a moment later and rounded the front, on his way spotting the airship, which he pointed out to the first guy. Both stared bent-necked their way for a few seconds then left the scene.

"*Denbow Airwatch One* to Tinsley Ground Base, two men seen exiting the van in Brampton, now departing on foot. Let us know how to proceed, oh-vuh."

"'Earyah, *Denbow Airwatch One*. We'll send some men out there to pick them up, do as you wish, oh-vuh."

Denbow Airwatch One hit the ground with a soft bump and the three got out.

"Careful," Jon Denbow called up as Ed and Jennifer waded into the rain toward the van, approaching it slow then cupping their hands and looking in.

"See anything?"

"No," Jennifer said, immediately before screaming. Both jumped back. "What is it?"

"There's someone in there." Jennifer's hands were in a pyramid over her mouth. "A little girl. In the back."

Their eyes stayed frozen together then wandered back to the van. Ed walked over, opened the driver's side door, and looked inside. Visible from the neck up in the back was the girl: blonde, cheeks pink as a rose. "You alone in here?" She nodded. Ed climbed in and grabbed her and handed her out to Jennifer who took her toward the airship.

Ed climbed back inside and looked under the seats, then in the cargo area, where three wooden crates were situated. He opened the lid of one and found himself staring at a neatly arranged row of assault rifles. "Oops." Ed backed out and turned to go, on the way noticing through the opposite-side windows something coming this way from a connecting road: a tank.

Out in the rain again he joined Jon Denbow, who was standing in front of the van. The two waited as the tank rolled over a border of bush into the field and stopped ahead of them.

Five soldiers in army-green climbed out, dragging with them the two men, now wrist-pinned, who fled the scene earlier. In the lead, riding one of them in with a stiff-armed handful of sport jacket hind collar, was Captain Séamus Kinch, a fellow with ghastly skin and wolf-like incisors who quarterbacked the group bringing up his rear, the Galway Guard—a squad of Irish Rangers that had been all over since the Free State of United Ireland had consolidated for purposes of overdue national renewal and finally and for good cast out, primarily to Southern England, their Shatter's and allotment of the diversity pie. The group had been in on the Marseille Sea-Push, lent their services during the Dekebabification of Copenhagen, and participated in the Catalonia Warning Order by helping escort several thousand headchoppers to the borders of the finally minted, criminal-harboring, and indecently stubborn "nation," until their lispy leaders acquiesced, agreeing to join the European Reclamation Project and expel the merchant elements lying reconverso in their midst. Stitched around a tartan of Venus bathed in saffron was the Galway Guard's motto: *Is Fheàrr Teine Beag.* . . . .

Captain Kinch pulled up in front of Ed and Jon Denbow and gave his man a shake. "Ease whoya saw?"

Ed looked the main guy over. He had the cranial topography of a Neanderthal, hair that was receded and gray, and smug, dead eyes that were pointing down and away. Ed confirmed with Jon Denbow.

"These are them."

But before Ed could mention the girl or the guns one of Kinch's men came up from behind. "Got confirmation on the yoke with the Duke of Yark," he said. "Thathartees in Auld-Am chased thisun outta Flarda—Jimmy Epstein of the Maldig Wiz Society."

"*Wiz*—wusat?"

"Child sex-trafficking syndicate."

Ed, with the pause, broke in, "We found a girl."

The eyes of Captain Kinch and his men turned to Ed and Jon Denbow, then glided between them, behind them, to where Jennifer and the girl were standing underneath the airship. Ed looked back. Jennifer was pointing up to a mansion on an island of a hill a half-mile away. Heads gravitated from her and the girl up to the mansion and then over to Epstein.

"One of you lads fetch the burdizzo from the tank."

"Got it right here, Captain."

There wasn't much conversation after the procedure, just a morbid feeling all around as Captain Kinch took two men on a mission up to the house. It seemed certain what they were going to find, it was just a matter of how bad it would be. The soldiers that stayed behind opened a feed under shelter, broadcast from Kinch's person as the team entered the house. Ed and Jennifer moved in and watched. Silent and tense, the video from down the nozzle of the Captain's rifle as they scanned and cleared the ground floor. One of them soon called out and claimed he had found a door. It was sealed with locks and latches that were cracked before the door was pried open, open into horror: damp squalor, a dark prison with more young girls inside, each visual more chilling than those previous as they moved through a scene illuminated by rifle-mounted light, boots squishing against wet tile from one coop to the next.

Ed couldn't watch. He walked away. Jennifer, following, caught up to him in the field as the rain streamed in dense torrents down.

"I just don't understand. What's wrong with these people?"

"This isn't new. This stuff has been going on for a long time. You never heard about it because they covered it up, covered for their own. They lied about it, they lie about everything, they don't know any other way."

"The amount of damage they cause, this is something beyond evil. I mean. Every. Single. Time. And it only gets worse. They can't *all* be this depraved, can they?"

"Enough of them are, and it's not up to us to sort them out."

"Can they really not face who they are and at least try to change?"

"They never have and they never will, but it's not our problem anyway. This is a sick people who come from a sick culture, Ed, and they've been kicked out of everywhere they've ever been because they attack the people who let them in then lie and blame everyone else instead of acknowledging that there's something wrong with their community. This hatred they have for others, it's hard for us to wrap our minds around, but this is their nature, it's just who they are, how their culture made them, how they were selected to be. And this behavior is acceptable to many among the Semitic tribes, which is why they tried to normalize it. But it's not a part of our culture— this moral corruption, this sickness—we don't tolerate it. And that's why we have to remove them from our societies . . . that's why *you* have to remove them, Ed."

Ed nodded away at the drowning ground. "Okay. I get it. Why we have to separate ourselves from this people for good . . . *forever* this time. It really is a hatred deeper than we can fathom . . . . a human virus."

THE DAY WAS ELAPSING into a sunset-ceil all apricot, cosmic over the beige island shore as the egg-white dimples began their final grazing voyage over low-frozen waves of Tom Morris grass: depressions and undulations, manicured folds of earth. Sound was a muffled conch shell roar, a continuous crashing, the auditory illusion of a distant stampede. A picture zoomed out in a measured panorama of dilating light from a puncture in the earth 4¼ inches in diameter, bringing into view a scene of captured grace over the bay, more innocent than the times maybe warranted but in the eyes of all a harbinger of forthcoming peace. There was little to distinguish it from a touched-up old photograph: the backdrop of castle stone fire-bright under orange-tossed clouds, the khaki and plaid and argyle around the pickled-green stage, the Victorian courtesy of the folk leaning over paint-gleamed railings at the Links' edge. And for a second, extended just because, there was no force or order known as Time, no shattered cities across the borderline, no war on this archipelago—*Prettanikē, Bretaigne, Britannia*—only momentary pardon as the memory carved out a space for itself under the glow of the Scottish sky.

Men and women anticipating something great beyond the suspended frame, if but a brief distraction, if only for our innermost need, now and to be with one heart a commemoration of a flock's re-flight and a changing of the guard in the Occident. A people paying homage to their culture, its revitalization, belated but at last, and celebrating the expulsion of an enemy who once tried to claim they didn't have a culture . . . Cromwell's Repeal, his charms all overthrown, in hightail out again. . . . At last, indeed. Better be the last. A grand piece of that culture this was, too—in rule and manner a reflection of its maker: a gentleman's game for the honest and accountable and a grindstone for patience and humility—the ends self-improvement alone, the opponent only the elements, the outland arena unfavorable most to frauds. And so we go headlong into the greenward march in the pursuit of good on grounds great seldom tread, in salute to an individualistic drive unequalled in any other but brutal in its double-edged nature as both our greatest strength and weakness, to be in stubborn or troubled times reined in, raised up, and carried on by, then come hell or high water consummated within, the collective, a family, this brotherhood, by whose safe measure he could get the anti-virus banged up, and from whose eternal wisdom a higher purpose would in conclusion be, for one and all, revealed.

It wasn't over here yet—*Once more unto the breach, dear friends, once more. . . .*

But it was the end of a journey for Edmund Loxley, the kind on which dreams did crown, surrounded by old family and new friends, by brothers and sisters and lovers and a union of Bretons and Celts and Normans. And Anglos. Well. There was still time. And he would now be making his first trip home, finally, the emotions of it all, the many thoughts running through at once, it seemed, always interrupted—being precisely at this splendid crease in the festivities that Ed ran into the microphone of Alistair Jarvis, here on assignment with a new gig. Pompous, this fellow, but with the usual questions about this and that, to which Ed replied with the usual answers, until the fist came in from the side in concert with a screaming "*Wanka!*"

Didn't stand a chance.

Ed grabbed his arm and helped him up off the ground. Dusted some grass off his jacket. "You all right?"

"Houndstooth, paws off."

"What was that about?"

"I'm eh, not too popular out here in the provinces."

"Why not?"

"For whys that don't concern you, bub. But I'm trying to start anew."

"Aren't we all."

"Seems it don't it. Unfortunately there are things I can't talk about, things that would have these people appointing me King of England if they knew."

"What kinds of things?"

"You deaf, Westwood? Just said I couldn't talk about it, didn't I?"

"Sorry, didn't mean to—"

"—It's this whole English Reclamation thing if you're gonna be fussy about it, mate . . ."

"What about it?"

He covered the mic and leaned in. "I'm the one who started it."

"You don't say."

"Shouldn't've but things slip."

"So you're the guy . . ."

"An unsung sovereign. One could reason."

"Then I bend the knee."

"Hail to the King, putt."

VIII

A goney, he replied. Goney! never had heard that name before

—ISHMAEL

PLENTY COULD BE SAID about the Old Republic of America, and much had been, but the anamnesis of the Empire was not yet complete. Each generation had witnessed, and in quite spectacular fashion at points throughout the centuries, some chapter of its rise and fall. From those who pressed the first bootprints upon it, to those who met their graves before the significance of the earth-bending discovery could be borne out in full. From those who boarded crowded ships thereafter, forsaking all to cast their lots with the strange kingdom, to those who eventually stood up and declared it to be something unto itself. Outfits stretched to tame its wild terra and map its vast canvas, poor kids seeking fortune, loping westward across the frontier on red earth divine, settling her pastures of plenty, sowing her seeds and reaping her harvest, founding communities on riverside spaces and bearing children who would see the rise of the machines, the industry and superstructures pushing them from the stead. From the days when it seemed like it couldn't be any more perfect, to the ones when it started to slip away, it was always everything and a bit more. And with a known certainty being *nothing lasts forever* . . . zogged as it was, most remarkable, perhaps, was just how long it did. . . .

Ed took his DNA test and filled out his New Citizen form then he and Jennifer followed the bag-bot outside into a crisp, early autumn breeze that swished through the tunnel of idle autocars as their intermediary rolled ahead to put the address of their downtown hotel into the destination bar.

They were about to get in when Jennifer noticed a glowing sign across the way.

"Can we take the Planet Train instead?"

The city had long been the symbol of a dying nation, but Detroit was now one of the most advanced metropolitan areas on earth. The view of its skyline amid the aerial-transit circuitry—exquisite at any time from above or below but especially at midnight under a spell of podlag on ergonomic loveseats aboard the warp-like stillness of the Planet Train—gave it the appearance of an outerworld outpost. Inside a glass tube lit blue, ink-sparkle from the Detroit River, towers effulgent on the nocturnal horizon, they exchanged quick glances, smiles when their eyes met, excited to have arrived safely home. The Planet Train glided over the lush suburbs of Grosse Point then looped into Brush Park on a bisection that passed the refurbished Gilded Age mansions and archeofuturist buildings lending overdue merit to the Renaissance City moniker.

She squeezed his hand. "Find out where you're going tomorrow?"

"Still not sure."

Ed met his attaché the following morning in the lobby. He was a semi-retired agronomy expert and former South African with a gray crewcut by the name of Fidio Joubert. The two of them ate breakfast at the hotel restaurant on a glassed-in terrace surrounded by holographic Fiji falls and rock-garden flumes, Ed's head bobbing along as he tried to process what all Joubert was telling him, about how the troposhield over the Block Island Sound had been brought down by some makeshift virtual device that had been traced back to Bangalore, concern over the Toronto Quarantine, and the ongoing negotiations in the West-East Exchange to swap Australia for the Northwest Chinese Province. "Lot going on," was about all Ed could get in over his manchego cheese eggstravaganza.

"I wasn't much older than you when I got here," Joubert said in postmeal reflection.

"Just up and left?"

"The time had come. We'd been bunkered down longer than anyone, weathering a genocide that was ignored by the foreign-run media. But we learned early on what most everyone else was to later figure out."

"Which was?"

"That living in a country where your group lacks political power and is outnumbered by low-functioning third worlders is a bad situation to be in."

"Seems so obvious when you put it like that."

Ed stepped onto the downtown streets of Detroit, clocking his first official day in the New Republic, one that couldn't be much nicer than it was. Silver autocars cruised through the morning shine, delivery droids moved slow and orderly on smooth sidewalk tracts, and sky-high panoramics in Highest-D swirled above with a retro-nature A E S T H E T I C as vivid and as ideal, while boys and girls, the noneuphemistic type of *inner city* kids, chattered by on their way to school below a network of elevated maglev lines, some belonging to the Planet Train, others reserved for material transport, all part of a silent assembly of structural ingenuity and layered efficiency, sending citizens and cargo through the blue on routes headed in, headed out, headed everywhere.

A block up, Ed and Joubert boarded the CityRail, which zipped them up Grand River Avenue toward Brightmoor. Formerly known as *Blight*moor, the neighborhood was now Brightmoor once again, and a transit point on the way to Milford, Michigan. Soon gliding by along the ruralesque road between gardened estates were smoothie stations and organic markets, bronze sculptures and tiered fountains in trimmed-green parks where flocks of new moms were on stroller-hitched jogs.

"Old Earth Maps," Joubert said, poking at the screen on the seat in front of him. "Want to see what this area looked like back in the old days?" hitting the icon before Ed could respond.

The picture evened out after a glitch and transformed the pleasant view into a projection of the pre-bulldozed past—an apocalyptic scene. "Looks like Long Beach," Ed said. "Or Cape Town," Joubert added. Urban decay passed in the form of crumbling Belle Époque homes and boarded-up buildings drenched in graffiti, liquor stores and checkcashers and Lotto Daily's, plots with jag-patched fencing and savanna grass, a Baptist church, Tomesha's Nailz, dark souls loitering outside a Dollar General, leanin by in the 'lac. "Lot different now."

"Sure is," Joubert agreed, dropping in a slide whistle as he brought them back to the present. "But this is how it was always supposed to look."

At the Brightmoor axis point they shuffled out with a few others and boarded a shuttle. As it departed a black, disklike edifice began taking shape on the skyline, breaking through the trees and rising over the curve of the earth. Rings. Rings inside of rings. Or maybe just one big ring, it was difficult to tell.

There was a moving walkway from the platform into the disk—soundless underfoot, sheathed by spiring wedges of plexiglass, laminated with cross-barred shadows. It dropped them off in a lobby adorned with weeping figs, lightened by alabaster statues, distinctly desolate, ethereal and spacecraft-y. After the automated check-in, Ed said goodbye to Joubert and was led straight-away by service-bot around a tubular hallway—lunar-white, patterned honeycomb—past real or mock passageways? he couldn't tell. At the end Ed was directed to a terminal seating area that faced windows overlooking a meadow bordered in woods and rooftops. Ankle on knee, thumbs twiddling; before long, footsteps heard.

And who else should the pecan double monk straps casually clapping down the tile his way belong to other than Ernie Lamark—in a white suit, of course, his smile transforming into put-on compassion as they shook hands. And although a part of Ed was rolling his eyes internally at Ernie, still, and surely for some time to come, chafed from a summer of anarchy he mostly volunteered for and thus could not in earnest grumble about, a more significant part knew he owed the guy more than he would be willing to outwardly admit on this day or ever.

"Saw the results of your DNA test," Ernie said, a hint of concern in his voice, "point-six percent Yakut."

"Yakut?" Ed, taken by surprise, unsure of the implications of this unforeseen development. "Is that, so does that mean?"

"It means you can't stay. I'm sorry." The second hand cranked in quarter-speed across the clock face of Ed's mind and with a booming crash ushered in a future much less certain than the one from the second before, but the alarm would dissipate with relief into the pail of forgotten time after Ernie released a laugh-plugged snort. "Joking—I'm *joking*, Edmund."

"Real funny."

"Good summer?"

"Learned a thing or two about you," ready to throw it out there despite some ambivalence about the possible repercussions of confronting a non-human lifeform with its own consciousness. ". . . Like how you aren't a real person."

Ernie spread his arms and looked down. "I beg to differ. But I think I know what you're referring to. I am very much a real person, I just have . . . *you know*."

"I do not know."

"Some components—like a computer . . . it's complicated."

"So are you like part of some aristocratic robot class from the future?"

"Your imagination is getting the best of you, Edmund. . . . I'm a case worker with the ERP—Sports and Recreation Division."

"That's it? Think I was expecting something a little more glamorous. Thought you were a man of more, I don't know, international intrigue."

"Afraid not."

"Then you aren't from the future."

"No. But I do help inform others' perspective of it." Ernie nodded past Ed and set off in that direction. Ed followed him down the hall to a moving walkway on an inner-perimeter orbit. They slid along the boundary next to tall glass panes, the morning sun hitting back through the emerald tint, until they reached a junction. There, at a wide ingress, was another glassed-in walkway, one that diverged from the main building and started moving as they stepped on, picking up speed and taking them through the surrounding meadow, buffered by forest and half-hidden houses at the vista's ends. The walkway sunk underground into sea-green light; the wall on the right was decked with pictures of people Ed recognized but didn't know the names of, while on the other side rolled silent footage of all things peaceful: windy glacial-tops and lumbering surf, sierra springs and cosmos spinning at lightyear-tempo. They were spit out in a sprawling subterranean lobby that was empty and just light enough to not be dark.

In the middle was a statue of a man waving a cap from the saddle of a rearing horse. "Andrew Jackson," Ernie notified as they neared it with steps that echoed through the space. "That statue stood in New Orleans from 1856 until it was taken down during one of the early Old-Am Bolshevik campaigns. We no longer subscribe to the inscription, though."

"Obviously."

They stopped in front of it. "When this people attack a host they target their symbols—their statues and art, their religion and monuments, their history and their heroes. They condemn those things and rally others against them with the intent to tear them down and replace them with new symbols and a version of the past they can narrate and control. . . . Because if you can control a people's past—"

"It makes it that much easier to control their future."

"The desire to conquer and acquire power is natural, but it takes on a different dynamic when the result is achieved through deception and crypsis—when a group is able to make another believe it shares its interests or outright pretends to be it in order to gain power over it. And if you can't even recognize the strategy, how can you protect against it?"

"Seems odd to think about humans behaving that way, but it shouldn't be since other animals and organisms act similarly."

"It's nature. And if this trial taught us anything it was that our defenses were sorely lacking. We have to learn how to better safeguard our communities by understanding who they are and what they do, but more importantly, by understanding who *we* are. They will do what they do, but we must become more conscious of our ideological disposition and acknowledge what it was that made us so susceptible to moral intimidation from outsiders, and so willing to attack our own and destroy our civilization for social approval."

Past the statue was a door that opened into a repository as wide as deep containing items that were once spread across the Old Republic, retrieved from cities affected by the Pull Out—relics from the world over but primarily the First American Epoch—things not all so holy but worth holding onto nonetheless: from Hearst Castle to the Met, Quaker City Eakins' and fossils from the Strake Hall of Malacology, the Apotheosis of the Gateway and the *Lilly Belle*, Apollo suits and halls of fame, rifles and bones and wagons and instruments and record players and bicentennial coins and stamp collections—shelves and shelves of stuff awaiting a more visible home or, maybe, a return to the one of old.

"A lot was lost or destroyed during those early years of turmoil, but this is our history, the record of those who came before us."

"Bet you could spend forever in here."

"Many are happy to. Our replacements never cared about our history anyway, and why would they? It wasn't their own. Over here," Ernie, calling Ed over to an end row, where he was standing and facing an encased sculpture of someone's head. "This bust, from Boston, is of a man who once warned that if we ever allowed private banks to control our currency, that our children would wake up homeless on the continent our fathers conquered."

"Sounds like what happened."

"And then some."

"Well I'm ready to do my part, Ernie."

"Good. But you don't have a choice." Ernie opened his clearscreen.

"Camp's once a year and in the summer so we'll have to make-do in the short-term."

"Sure I mean like whatever," Ed said as he dawdled down the row. He looked at his reflection in a disco ball. Picked up a pair of Converse All-Stars by the laces. Plucked the low E of a Les Paul.

"Says here that there's a survey team with an ASAP listing for anyone with a pulse—operation that might get its plug pulled soon. They're leaving from Albany tomorrow and are bound for the D.C. area, need an extra hand until they get to Baltimore. What do you say, Edmund?"

"I can take some surveys."

H OPES WERE THAT a beautiful fall would come, with reprieve for forgotten cities and towns that had fallen into decay after extended eras of prosperity and growth. Their geneses along estuary expressways in Jamestown and Plymouth and the witching woods of the Hudson River Valley had not yet been forgotten, and they still rested upon foundations that, however decrepit now, were not products of the magic dirt below. New York State's first settlement was in Albany, the Beverwijck, in 1614. Originally an earthen Dutch outpost affixed to the fur trade, the city didn't have much skin in that game anymore, or in much of any other for that matter, and long the case. But economic stagnation only made its reclamation all the more manageable, as it was with much of the Midwest and beyond. Carlos and Pajeet, in their heart of hearts, had never felt completely at home in Fort Wayne, Toledo, or Rochester, and the funny money that had initially lured their forbears to those and towns alike could not always purchase their willingness to die for them, or to impede the descendants of pioneers who didn't need such incentives. An amicable solution was always preferred— with homecomings made easy and the Interim Nation Camps down south available to those for whom the situation so required—and a little convincing was usually all it took.

The party was over . . . *Acabado, amigos.*

There was a New-Am garrison in Albany now, Fort Nassau Two, concentrated on the more spacious east side of the Hudson and somewhat more industrialized than its predecessor, Fort Nassau One, which laid buried underneath an abandoned railyard awaiting excavation. Within its bristly pined perimeter were training grounds, munitions facilities, and intelligence bunkers monitoring everything proximate to 87 on down to the Catskills, through Kingston, Poughkeepsie, Newburgh, and right up into the Belly of the Beast—a base from which personnel routinely ventured south in the ongoing Reclamation of New York City.

But on the other side of the Hudson, in Albany's historic center, it looked much like it once did: like a quaint town with a thin-spread bustle of everyday people, among whom, already, was a growing sentiment that this old capital might not be too shabby a place to put down some roots. Schools had opened, industry and unions were popping up, pizza parlors and farmer's markets and club hockey teams and ladies' groups—all catering to the families of Fort Nassau Two and those working for Operation Repatriation out of Port Schenectady a map-pinch northwest.

"Engines on!"

"Gunner to roost!"

"District of Crooks ho!"

It was amid such enthusiastic clamor that the lone altertank *Yankee Rover*, its olive drab alloy shining, hauling a group of three-plus-one men of various backgrounds collectively, and rather ironically, known as the Mirth Men, departed fleetly into the early afternoon sun on a southerly journey toward Washington D.C. It rumbled out of Fort Nassau Two and bridged the Hudson then maneuvered down 87, past good-blessing waves from the points and through a byway of foliage wrapping the hills of Upstate New York. The scenery wasn't given much attention by the two crew members inside, who were getting everything in order and communicating with installations farther south to ensure a safe trip into the Apple's ambit, but Ed had yet to be given any official task, so he put himself in charge of auditing the backdrop from his smudgy windowette. When he thought of *New York*, he thought of an infinite grid topfull of abrasive New Americans, fused-stock pawn dolls, and high-perched slave drivers named Goldsomething sneering like hyenas at the apocalyptic treadmill below . . . not these colorful hills. But this part of the former nation had always been a mystery to him.

Not a great while after Ed had seen a sign for Woodstock he glanced up to find finessing his way aft down the gangway from out of the Captain's cabin at the front, squinched eyes set on him with a look of what seemed both suspicion and revulsion, the man with whom his sole contact occurred earlier in Albany upon reporting for duty, in an introduction that ended faster than it began with a snarl and a *Get in:*—the executive officer of the mission, Captain Ó Draoi. Both ungodly and god-like, he was in appearance short and hairless, but in ardor, extreme even to those who fancied themselves hardliners.

Captain Ó Draoi latched onto a bar above Ed's seat and hung there, attention out the window. "Said you were, that you-uh, don't have much experience. Citizen for what about a week now?"

"More like a day and a half, sir."

"Golfer."

"That's correct, sir."

The Captain grunted and turned to the seat-station across the aisle belonging to Chief Mate and Lieutenant Jim Millerson, who, it was explained, would get Ed acquainted with the ship, the operation, and his duties to be.

A long, earnest man and the technical expert aboard *Yankee Rover*, Lieutenant Millerson was no warrior after risks and wore a face that said cynical but no prick under a brown buzz cut. He also maintained without slight to the others a more conscientious nature and a temperament of approachability, being the first to extend to Ed a sense of welcome, initially, then again once the two of them were in the ladder hollow at the back end of the tank, where the Lieutenant craned up to full height and propped an elbow on a rung.

"Couldn't've lucked out more."

"Good to hear, sir."

"Assuming the Captain doesn't get us all killed," he amended quietly. "Trip through Riorhinelander, seasons changing, weather cooling down, slim chance of another Puerto Rican Surprise so you won't share the fate of the last guy."

"Puerto Rican Surprise? What happened to the last guy?"

The Lieutenant sucked in. "I shouldn't've brought that up. It was a freak accident, not something we like to talk about. Let me retract that statement."

"Think it's too late, sir."

Ed followed Lieutenant Millerson up the hatch to the crow's nest and the sweeping view it offered across endless acres of Dogwoods and Hornbeams as *Yankee Rover*'s wide berth ate with Pacman-like chomps the white highway lines ahead and on a continuous track of plate-driven propulsion steered them inch by pressure-pounding inch closer to the dark urban heart of the Empire.

Keeping a watchful eye out was the third member of the crew: Second Mate, Sergeant, and gunner, Stu Brushdim—the last Cape-Cod-man and a happy-go-lucky sort for whom any introduction was lacking, and at the determination of whose trigger finger any trouble would be with prejudice laid to waste. The Sergeant, clubmastered above the pipe that was as much a feature of his face as his nose, from the saddle of the blaster which he'd converted into an easy chair, looked back and waved upon noticing their arrival in the nest, where spinning satellites and micro-dish receivers whirled outside and instrument panels and digital displays lined throughout the interior glowed faint, eclipsed by the incoming light of the day.

"Most everything aboard does what it's supposed to and doesn't require much help from us. *Yankee Rover* here—she's a giant super-sensor," Lieutenant Millerson said as he ran a hand over one of the panels, "a traveling cartographer that maps everything under the sun, even counts the leaves on the trees. The finches chirping a mile out? She's currently running those calls through a database and calculating regional population numbers based on previously collected data. But she's also making sure those sounds aren't coming from Maputo rebels plotting in Swahili using a pitch-altifier."

"Impressive machine, sir."

"You're with the datahunters now, seeking oil for the lamp of enlightenment. With all those yottabytes coming in the casks can fill up fast, though, so we have to offload some of that data, send it out to be stored and sorted and so on, which brings us to your job." The Lieutenant slid out a storage panel and went on to explain how on the hour Ed would be required to come up top and manually send the accumulated data to one of the national agencies charged with examining and archiving it. "We used to take turns but we have other responsibilities and sometimes, well," sniffling and glancing back, "we forget."

"This thing sounds a lot like . . . well, the *other* thing."

"Other thing? What other thing? You mean the Googlopticon?" Lieutenant Millerson blurted out openly and loudly, without hesitation or delay, and in such close proximity to so much electronic equipment, that it produced in Ed what felt like a conditioned response. "Similar concept, just taken a step further. *Yankee Rover* is a glutton for data, sucks it up like a sponge, especially when we're rolling through an urban area. Some people, including myself, think it's too much power to have, to be in possession of all this data. But the secret isn't in simply accumulating the data, it's in knowing *how* to use it better than your enemy."

"Not sure I follow, sir."

"Think about all those sensors out there, in ringports and everything else. We can theoretically take all of the information from those, and—" The Lieutenant stopped short and looked at Ed like he was evaluating his trustworthiness. "We like to keep them guessing . . ."

"Don't have to worry about me, sir."

"Put it to you in an example. What did you do last night?"

"I ate at the Detroit Cyborganic Kitchen then went back to my hotel."

"Eat alone?"

"With my girlfriend."

"Okay—let's say you were sitting across from your girlfriend at the DCK last night around all those sensors and actuators collecting EM field data, picking up information about the location and dimensions of every object around you—weight, color, model-type, all that—graphing every move you make, microphones picking up every sound—and at some point you leaned across the table and said 'I love you' to that girlfriend of yours."

"But I didn't . . ."

"Sake of argument. See, I could—*theoretically*, mind you—compile that data and use it to create a virtual reconstruction of that physical environment—of the Detroit Cyborganic Kitchen as it was last night, with you and your girlfriend in it, with everything looking exactly how it did—and I could access that virtual environment and replay or witness the exact moment when you leaned across the table and said 'I love you.'"

"I said I didn't. But you mean like literally see what I was doing last night or whenever?"

"*If*—" stressing with a finger up, "if, all the data was available, which is not always the case."

"Wow. So you can like look into the past and spy on people?"

"A virtual reconstruction of the past, and obviously of the post-sensor past."

"So what do you guys call this thing?"

"*Eh*." Lieutenant Millerson was suddenly aloof. "Internet of Things, some used to say, using its framework, I mean. There's the technical name no one can ever seem to remember. And then the vernacular, but that sticks in my craw."

"I don't follow, sir."

"It's stupid."

"What's stupid, sir?"

Lieutenant Millerson shrugged. "Some people try to equate it with . . . with time travel."

"Time travel?"

"Ridiculous, I know."

Then it snapped. "*That's* it . . . *that's* how it works . . . *that's* the time machine."

"No*no*—that's *not* the time machine. There *is* no time machine. No comparison even. For starters it only goes one way, is limited to the near past, and doesn't permit cross-environmental interaction."

"You said people compare it with time travel. That's what they're talking about, that's the time machine."

"Who? what people? idiots? That's not how time travel works. But fine," giving in a little. "Whatever. That's what you want to hear, isn't it. It's what everyone thinks anyway so who am I to shatter your illusions. Say I were to play along to humor you and let you indulge in this lie for a moment . . . I'd still have a quibble."

"Which would be, sir?"

"That *this* is the time machine . . . you're in it."

YANKEE ROVER SLOWED in due course at the junction between New York and New Jersey and exited into the town of Mahwah. On the side of the road as they arrived, marching in the opposite direction under a military escort, was a long line of enemy combatants. Ed couldn't tell whether they were casualties of capitulation or capture, but their part in the war appeared to be officially over, despite many seeming to have some fight left in them, if the doublefisted middle-fingers and sideways Vulcan salutes being hurled at the tank in passing were any indication. Petty hoodlums by the looks of it, plunderbund fodder pimp-limping along in pants at half-mast, sporting facial tattoos and dragging their jackets through the gravel toward whatever

Jersey coop had been appropriated to hold them until eviction time.

Men of greater motive and claim were down the way at Camp Shereton Crossroads, which was to be the Mirth Men's destination for this evening's rest. There, a monolith shaped like a sparkplug soared dizzyingly above the rolling hills and nearby highways, a soon-to-be-leveled monstrosity erected in the Libancien's postmodern-bloc style, blistering the sky with 22 floors of darkened glass and set on spacious meadow grounds onto which the men just in from Albany spilled from out the tank with funny leg stretches and adjusting indoor eyes, in-swerve to and fro while following noses to BBQ pits, orders to workstations, rumors to wherever the cocktail-hour commotion may take them. Ed hobbled out last and stood agaze at the hotel with a hand over his eyes; in a farrago of emotions being here in his new nation, surrounded by his new countrymen, inserted without delay into the midst of the war. Strange but seemly.

Lieutenant Millerson observed Ed's state of uncertainty and called out, waved him over, and asked, "Run an errand?" in lockstep with a nod over at some jeeps parked in the downfield grass. "Have to pick up an upgrade for the tank."

Back out the way they came, soon again on the empty highway between upscaled rock and a rising access road, toward green hills, with minimal talk.

"It's 'Loxley,' right? Earthname? Loxleyists . . . Loxleyism? Was that a thing?"

Not as far as Ed was aware.

They were off the highway in a matter of time then turning up a road that had an off-the-beaten-path feel. Near what was shaping up to be the final stretch of uphill terrain, Lieutenant Millerson told Ed to look back. "Whoa," not realizing they were this close. "Big city."

"The rat's nest."

They parked in a gravel lot next to a geodesic dome with blacked-out window panes. It was concealed within the woods at the top of the hill, but the plot had an even more pristine view of the Manhattan skyline. A megacloud was hovering over the green peel of earth between their hilltop position and the city's edge, giving the blurred blend of highrises beyond an illusory glow. Air traffic could be seen on each side of the troposhield, barely visible, a thin film cutting across the sky and rippling like standing mirage water. Ed and Lieutenant Millerson leaned against the front of the jeep and passed a long minute.

"The shield keeping them in or us out?"

"Them in. We're hanging back until it's time to go in and clean up," Lieutenant Millerson said mildly. "We built that city, but we got pushed out long ago and our enemy made it their main breeding ground. Since the worst of them were concentrated in a handful of cities like that one, though, all that was needed was the will to surround them and drive them out, or employ Option C. You know what's going on in there right now?"

"What?"

"They're being diversified by the wretched refuse they scattered upon our teeming shores. The New Americans their ancestors had the heaviest hand in importing are currently dragging them out of their luxury apartments and putting them on street trials, or tracking them down to their hideouts at the Hamptons' end of Long Island. Bounties on them all."

"Justice?"

Lieutenant Millerson, after a deliberately long inhale, "You smell it, too?"

He disappeared inside the dome, leaving Ed to meander about kicking pinecones and varying his glance between the city and the dome's windows, one of those feelings present that someone or something could be watching, or maybe not, but best to assume so just in case. Lieutenant Millerson came out a few minutes later and waved Ed over to the entrance while lugging out a mini-keg-like can that he placed outside the door.

"What's that?" Ed asked.

"This," the Lieutenant giving it a tap with his foot, "this would be an infinite-spin, hybrid-ultraconductor flywheel."

"Flywheel?"

"Energy storage. But this is the little guy . . . the big guy's in here." Lieutenant Millerson pushed the door open more so Ed could see in. On the other side, under bright lights, was something—*were* things? . . . *existed a mass* might be the best way to put it—that was both the most hideous and intriguing apparatus he'd ever seen: a crown-shaped entity with a bazillian components: tubes all over the place, pipes and bars and bronze rings coiling up and around, protruding ports of every dimension—and none of it organized in any outwardly logical manner to the eye. A big pile of junk was what it looked like, though this initial assessment, Ed knew, couldn't be further from the truth of what it, whatever *it* may be, was. "A super stellarator. . . . This one we moved from down the road. And inside it is the fourth state of matter."

"The fourth state of matter?" Ed repeated as he took a step in. "Ice?"

"Plasma."

"My next guess. Plasma like the sun?"

"What we're learning about the electric and magnetic fields around us— how to use them and harness new forms of energy—these steps we're taking, are taking us deep into the New Electric Age."

"So what's it do?"

"A lot, but for one it can power almost anything. Before we had been developing technology like this and then giving it away, sharing it with everyone else or simply letting others steal it. In the best of cases we got taken advantage of, in the worst we had our own technology used against us."

"Designing our own disadvantage."

"We are a people of science, and nearly every major scientific and technological advancement has come at our hands. That's a product of our creative nature, our fascination with the world and our desire to improve it. We had to ensure the continuance of that and keep it from being abused by the wrong people. Our discoveries and innovations have transformed this planet for the better, and the spirit that leads to those transformations is an extension of who we are. But we didn't use it properly before."

"It was our food and medicine that led to the African Overflow."

"Our misplaced altruism. A great virtue in itself, but as the scope of the world opened up and exposed us to peoples who weren't like us, who were of a fundamentally different nature, it was exploited. Our attempt to save the world only led to an exponential increase in populations that couldn't take care of themselves, who were hostile to us, and who we let overrun us and nearly destroy it all."

"It seems noble to want to raise up the world, but it's childish and naïve. The people we believed we were helping never even cared."

"We believed nature was something other than what it really was. We believed other people were like us when they weren't. We can cooperate and get along with others, have relations and be friends—we're good at that. But that innovative spirit is something we hold sacred now. If we want to protect it—"

"—We must protect ourselves."

THERE WAS A KNOCK on the door after dinner. Sergeant Stu, who had apparently already begun speaking to Ed before the door was even open, was stiff-arming the jamb and mumbling with his head down, something about the food here being dissatisfactory since it was New Jersey. "Never been anything good about New Jersey," he said, clawing at his beard with his free hand. "And that's precolonial, Edward." The Sergeant pushed his glasses up his nose and stood up tall and backed out. "But came up to say the Philly warstream's on downstairs." He started flexing in the center of the hallway. "Rready?"

It was one of those big hotel conference rooms, the type once visited by people from all over for conventions held to celebrate the niche hobbies and perversions of mid-decline Americana, in full glory reflected, the fine-spun pageantry of Mermaid Con and the Toilet Summit, Furry Expos and Naval Fluff Gatherers; and there were pictures and videos chronicling all of it, more than anyone was willing to sift through but enough to supply what was certain to be confusion and ancestral shame for many centuries to come. What happened? The answer wasn't always clear-cut, but most were now pretty sure it was due to a combination of dead-end consumer misery, deconstructed identity, and the malevolent tribe of outsiders in charge of the culture, pushing it all further, happy to promote infantilism and social malaise as the new normal since their authority, much to the lament of the mortal, divined neither threat nor qualm from kitsune shapeshifters out of Kalamazoo.

Ed and Sergeant Stu wandered in from the back. Soldiers were seated throughout the room. The light inside was dim. There was a large screen at the front with a stationary feed. Apart from light chatter one could hear windtouched mic-rustling and the pops of distant gunfire. They grabbed some virt-goggles and hunted down a couple seats.

"What are we watching here?"

"The Great Oregano . . . philosopher king."

Glasses on, attention to the front, a view across a river: an urban horizon a mile away, Camden, glowing with fire as smoke billowed into skies rolled up with pre-storm clouds, through which bled the last ginger light of the sun. On the far left was a bridge, the Ben Franklin, collapsed into the river at its center; at the base of the screen was an ice rink filled with debris. Gusts of wind kicked up leaves in front of the bodycam and its proprietor, who still after a minute had yet to speak. Then softly, with words almost breathed out, "Here we are—on the edge of genesis or apocalypse, only time will tell to which side we fall." His voice was simultaneously foreign and familiar, staccato yet rhythmic, reasoned and eloquent but, unmistakably, sinister. "You are here again with the Great Oregano, hope you're doing well." He turned to give the audience a 360-degree view of the surroundings. "On this fading eve of the war I will be taking you, kind viewers, on a tour of Poor Richard's Town—the City of Brotherly Love—which it has not been in days beyond recall, but may again be soon—Philadelphia."

Two men were whispering behind Ed: "Name a more based guru. I'll wait."

"Got a good feeling this time, too."

"We stand on the shores of the Delaware facing the ongoing Camden Clean Out. But on these banks here, currently taking place behind my back, fairest fans, is the long-awaited reclamation of a most historic city." The Great Oregano walked away from the river, toward a Segway-like scooter that was parked along the curb, and was soon riding it across the expressway in the direction of the dense downtown Philadelphia spread. Turning right, cruising parallel to the river, the shot showcased neglected apartments, offices, and parking garages, bunting that flapped in the wind, awnings torn and draped over the broken windows of looted shops, the skeletal tower and mangled suspension cables of the collapsed bridge ahead, reaching into the thick-rolling mounds of charcoal clouds moving in and smothering the light out like a Saharan sand storm.

"We turn onto Market Street," the Great Oregano announced as he slowed, edged left, and straightened out between the seared red-cubes on the margins of the vacated street. Ed peeked down trashed alleys and up black ladders to 2nd, played *Wheel of Fortune* with the gaps on the signboards of former taverns and cheesesteak shops up to 3rd, watched the deserted city growing taller up to 4th. The Great Oregano rounded the corner on 5th and passed car skeletons and a flipped-over carriage along the boundary of a grass-tangled park, enclosed within Federal walls. A few bots were out. Tanks were stationed at the corners. Soldiers were dispersed throughout. The scooter squeaked and stopped outside a graffiti-riddled building at the end of the block; brick and wood fragments from the clock tower that once stood atop it were scattered across the pavement in front.

The Great Oregano turned and pointed up the street, at a small, protruding box on the adjacent corner. "The spot to which my finger at this revolutionary moment points is where the Liberty Bell once rested," he revealed. "Removed during the Pull Out, I believe it found a safe home in Michigan."

The Great Oregano turned back to the building with the fallen tower. It was small, two stories and seemingly unremarkable, with white-framed windows, most broken, spaced out evenly and interrupting the continuity of the illegible rattlecanned artwork decorating the exterior. "I present to you, dearest disciples, Independence Hall."

A few armed men stood out front and waved to the camera as the Great Oregano passed a row of bollards and approached the clock tower rubble and the statue guarding the entrance. "Here, as you can see," scanning the bronze figure nameplate-to-head, "is of course a statue of Founding Father Richard Allen."

Whispers proliferated:

"Richard Allen?"

"Who's Richard Allen?"

"You heard of Richard Allen?"

"Yeah that's the guy who did the thing that no wait."

"If the name of Founding Father Richard Allen doesn't ring a bell," the Great Oregano went on, "that is likely because he was inducted into the traditional lineup rather late. In fact, once where Founding Father Richard Allen's statue stands now was one of George Washington. That statue, however, was removed after the city was ceded and it was determined that Mr. Washington had obtained recognition primarily as a result of his *privilege.* . . . That word again. This privilege Mr. Washington was said to have came at the expense of others with less opportunity, those like the man who stands carved before us today, Mr. Allen. Mr. Richard Allen. And that, my friends, my delicate minions—*that* . . . that is the story . . . the story of Founding Father Richard Allen," the Great Oregano, dragging it out in a way that left many confused as to the line between the presenter's sincerity and what felt like dramatic showmanship accustomed to deftly steering clear of any elicitation of offense.

The Great Oregano proceeded under a low, vaulted entrance and into a courtyard where two more soldiers stood, then hooked a sharp left and ascended a few stairs into a room. The walls inside were covered in graffiti and splattered food items. There was a rod in the center on which once hung a chandelier. Broken tables and chairs were strewn across the floor. Green tablecloths were ripped and bunched to the side. "Where I stand this very second, where you stand in virtual company with me, where we stand together in fellowship, my prized pets—is the Assembly Room: the hall of record where notable documents of our collective past met with iron gall ink, printed into parchment by men who . . . *let's face it*, would not be too happy with this scene. It is—" the Great Oregano pausing as he scanned the interior, then in a more somber tone, "—not easy seeing this chamber of reverence in such a state. But as your spiritual correspondent I was in preparation for Operation Philadelphia Freedom reading over the meditations of a man who spent some time in this room, a man you my firm but pliant sect may have heard of, by the name of Franklin. Ben Franklin. Benjamin Franklin. And in doing so I stumbled across a line that was written by Mr. Franklin in a letter to Thomas Jefferson, whom he asked and I quote 'In 300 years will people remember us as traitors or heros?' And after reading this I thought—'*Well TGO*, about that much time has passed—so what's the verdict . . . traitors or heroes?' Different times, I know, and neither could have anticipated this. This, no. No no no no no. But my thoughts, yours I'm sure as well, were that *yes* they were of course heroes—but they were *our* heroes. Not the heroes of those who disgraced this room. The people who did this did not descend from Franklin and Jefferson and what occurred in here was not a part of their history, so why would they uphold it? Their response was natural, this outcome one we should have expected. And the truth is it is *we* who are the traitors, as it was *our* job to uphold and protect this history. The people who helped bring those other people over, who did the most to let them in I mean. You know whom I speak of, this . . . I won't say *cabal*—a global clique, maybe. The, well, they have many names. Who were let's just say overrepresented. Numerically. I speak of numbers. But I must be careful. So let us finalize this passage in acceptance of our atonement for this here in this here room, right here. Let us remake it into what it once was, what men like Franklin would have wanted it to be. That we must do. And that, members of my cult, concludes another momentous journey with the Great Oregano. Hammer that like button."

"So close."

"You're one to speak."

THE MIRTH MEN SET OFF the next morning on a roundabout trip across New Jersey with a plan to be hitting Keystone State thoroughfares by lunchtime—traveling through friendly or nonaligned towns, though by and large ones that had become, on account of the war and the bygone commercial policies of the city-state sponge, parched: emptied out. The itinerary would take them across the thin Pompton Lakes waist of Passaic County, cut them through the former Ioo-Indian harbor of Parsippany-Troy Hills, then swoop them around the decommissioned MS13 gangland of Dover before placing them on a scenic stretch across some of the Garden State's townships with holdover populations in Byram, Hope, and Belvidere and spitting them out onto the fallow Northampton farms and infant hills of Eastern PA.

The tri-laned 287 wound over dry-herb gorges and through rock-blasted passes amid no ground too high and a palette not yet fall-rusty, low-cloud shadows shading the earth at the head, little out that wasn't nature's own except for tagged signs and silver guardrails and the under-wheel pavement whose slip roads branched inward and offward as the veiled towns they led to cracked open at intervals, sometimes a strip mall or a plain office square, sometimes a reservoir or a lone-nother highway drifting overhead or below, to nod in then tap out, to cave in then to narrow, to refit them again between the treed or real walls holding the forest at bay. The farther down the highway, the deeper into the country, the more the atmosphere changed.

The military vehicles seen periodically before were no longer around. The skies were wide open, the scenery more desolate, the roadway rubbish more abundant, the deer more brazen.

Yankee Rover slowed often and made irregular stops, stops that were never explained, stops for which explanations were never sought. There was a stillness over all. They were alone out here, it was clear. And it was a little unnerving. While Ed had never been one for the countryside, he had also absorbed a fair amount of propaganda depicting all things provincial as backward—no place for the well-adjusted man for whom urban life was a de facto touchstone and order, one's ability to hold down a cell on the grid the essence of success, even a meager existence inside it a badge of honor—whereas this out here, the boonies, was where lived those of a different time, of a more primitive nature: the unrefined, the peasantry. A perception that was, he could see now more clearly, not actually his own, but the projected bias of another.

And as the day progressed, so did the wariness abate, did the charm of the landscape grow, the mysteries beyond the stalk-barred highway inveigle, whatever *was* not quite clear and present and visible only in spurts until they jumped off in Hope, hit the backcountry roads, and made it for the Delaware. Appearing at last were houses, the barns and bits of farms, junctions with the casings of towns small and once more but now bare. And though there was little in the way of obstacles *Yankee Rover* couldn't roll over—fallen trees, the tin-flanks of sheds, things more difficult to classify and perhaps at points alive, anything subject to nature's whim and wind turned up since the last road-clearing truck came through—their pace was a crawl.

Ed on the hour squeezed down the metal spine of the tank, climbed the ladder to the crow's nest, and performed his duties as instructed, but otherwise kept to himself in his stiff nylon seat next to his windowette so not to impose. By the time they'd crossed the Pennsylvania State Line, though, he was extending his stays up top for the superior vantage, which Sergeant Stu didn't seem to mind, or give the signals typical of someone who might;

actually, it was tough to get a read on him at all as his behavior and demeanor swung wildly, becoming more perplexing each time he went up.

At noon the Sergeant philosophized in soliloquy with a wind-stirred ring of hemlocks in circulation around, the glare of the sun in seeming spotlight down, a thespian passion in his deportment that grew by show and parol spellbinding as he articulated the significance of their voyage through the heartland in allegory.

"So what you're saying is that this survey mission, the data we're gathering out here . . ."

"Is the data of our inner selves."

"And that the image we're constructing from that data . . ."

"Is really a construction of us . . . the image of who *we* are, Edward."

"Incredible."

The next hour the Sargeant, parked and pensive in the gunner's chair with his pipe in hand and his eyes directed outward and ahead, relayed the story of an incident that occurred some weeks prior. The crew had received word that a mysterious plague, a malignant epidemic, had broken out among an anti-neoseparatist cult of utopian Harry Potterists in Lebanon PA, where some scaramouch had proclaimed himself to be the Archangel Snape and to have descended from heaven by way of a trap-door. They were forwarded a copy of the leader's manifesto, wherein he declared himself Wizard-General of the Lebanon Valley, and were ordered to take a closer look and report back on the matter.

"It's rare I admit weakness, Edward," the Sergeant, taking a puff off his pipe and glancing up, "but I was scared."

Dark clouds paved the sky over the Valley as they drew near. At the gates of the commune they met with the plague-infected Archangel Snape and members of his congregation, who warned them to stay away and claimed that coming any closer would result in them too becoming infected with the strange malady.

"'Think of the fevers!' they screamed."

Captain Ó Draoi, however, fearing not the epidemic, alighted *Yankee Rover* intending to approach.

"But as he took the first step forward a burst of wind pushed him back—*whoosh* . . . nearly knocking him down."

Some force unknown. The crew took it as a sign. Captain Ó Draoi called out to the Archangel Snape that it didn't have to be like this, that he and his congregation of Harry Potterists, diseased and damaged though they were, could be healed and join the rest of their people in safe pastures. But they ridiculed the notion and hurled forth prophecies of the Mirth Men's doom for embracing this sacrilegious phyloidentity.

"They pleaded with us to renounce our heretical path. But when the Captain said that was impossible, that we weren't doing that bit anymore, the Archangel Snape and his comrades spit back. They didn't want to listen. Just kept going on and on about us being blasphemers, saying we were doomed—*'You're doomed!'* they said . . . Fie—*'Fie on you!'* they screamed . . ."

"So. So what happened?"

"So we were just like whatever and bounced."

But on his next trip up Ed found the Sergeant withdrawn, unresponsive when he made an attempt to engage in small talk, his countenance like that of a shell-shocked veteran.

"Amazing up here, isn't it?"

Standing as if pained. Shaking his head downward like Ed. Just. Didn't. Get it. Placing a hand on his shoulder and sighing, no man he'd seen ever so serious, "This is Postamerica, Edward. It's all a maze."

Ghost towns, towns most had never heard of, towns that had spent decades fading away; towns that could have been anywhere, towns that were everywhere. In this case, the towns of Pen Argyl, Wind Gap, Saylorsburg, Kunkletown, and Lehighton, on through Jim Thorpe's Swiss gorge and back around. Along winding slate-gray roads, decomposing in the hardwood shade, home after perfectly spaced home. Exquisite homes, comfy homes, flawlessly built homes. Red homes, white homes, and blue homes. Homes with stoop views of the September-red bluffs over Aquashicola Creek, dozing in the Pennsylvania forest. Addams Family stick-style mansions, blue-shingle dens with filigree trim and wrapping porches, beige ridge-resting bank barns and hipped roof bungalows—all abandoned and being devoured by vegetation. But with the power of imagination, one could visualize how it used to be, once upon a time in innocent days since swept away, in the age of a thriving nation. Before the mailbox-eating vines began their sunward ascent, before the telephone poles were folded over like dominoes; before the trash stopped getting picked up, before the Allentown looters came; before the mill in the valley was a rusty corpse, before mom and pop got undercut; before the residents were forced into corporate service industry bondage, before the heroin and methamphetamine started picking them off. Before all that there was a kind of peace here that the men of today were dying to bring back, and as these deceased little towns faded by one could picture it: the low-cut lawns of candy-green grass, the kids playing spud in the cul-de-sac; the families at smoky Sunday cookouts, the friendly chatter around picnic tables under black cherry trees; the Old Glory's not blanched but bright waving from red cedar balconies, the neighborly faces in the Fourth of July parade marching down the street. . . .

THE DAY WAS in its late-afternoon stages and *Yankee Rover* was back on a less rural road when a more visible presence of people appeared outside. Talk ramped up inside: Captain Ó Draoi and Lieutenant Millerson speaking both to each other and through the radio with others elsewhere, talk Ed couldn't draw many conclusions from beyond reports that they were closing in on El Reading.

"Pulling into La Isla."

"Barricade just ahead."

"Strapping up for a fogoneo?"

"First looks indicate a fogonotto."

"Let's avoid another Puerto Rican Surprise."

Ed felt his heart skip a beat upon the reemergence of that term; he had yet to receive an explanation. Leaning over to Lieutenant Millerson, he asked again, but again got back an unsatisfactory answer.

"It's pretty much what it sounds like."

Yankee Rover slowed to a roll as they passed a camp: part military checkpoint staffed with banditos in hand-me-down uniforms, part extended-family stamping-ground. No one outside appeared too moved by their incursion. The situation was on the whole lax in a scene set by sedentary council under dirt-glazed canopies, trumpet-heavy music emanating from jeeps, and roadside workstations characteristic of children's lemonade stands, with most activity centered around picnic tables, sites that after some focused attention triggered in Ed recollections of the feeding-culture commonplace among the nether-border natives, this or that sturdy elevated plank a good a trough as any, where when able to view such proceedings unseen the anthropologist inside would from under pith helmet rise cautiously out of wing-parted fern afar to witness in queasy awe feasts, indeed moveable, vanishing off surface-tops, calories scaling up like a stock ticker in a boom and setting off on intestinal tours, then through the metabolic conversion process disassembled, integrated, almost in real time if one watched closely, *tacked on*, making often of the mestizo specimen a thing of miraculous, core-centric carrying capacity.

Yankee Rover stopped at the entrance of the barricade, which, going by the picture on the clearscreen feeding video back from the front of the tank, looked like a floppy chain-link fence that could be upon authorized entry or exit rolled laterally across the pavement, and was, with the momentum of a good shove, capable of doing most of the work itself.

Captain Ó Draoi got out and met with a group of armed men. Ed watched until he disappeared from view, then turned to Lieutenant Millerson.

"El Reading?"

"Passing through."

"What's the story here?"

"The El Reading-Allentown corridor is ostensibly under the jurisdiction of Puerto Rico."

"Why's that?"

"Because everyone who lives here is from Puerto Rico. Colonies like this are all over still, but they're dealt with on a case-by-case basis. Our problem was never directly with any of them, but those who let them in, so most aren't worth devoting resources to for now. We try to make deals with their home nations and incentivize their leaders to take them back. Most will leave on their own if spurred and policies like the Under Forty Emigration Act help encourage them to self-deport as well. It's my understanding that Puerto Rico has been inordinately stubborn, though."

"People here didn't want to fight for the other side?"

"Did the transplants in the FPSC seem like ideologues and civic-minded warrior-types to you?"

"Not exactly."

"Same old cosmic race here."

The sun was on its final downward dive by the time Captain Ó Draoi reappeared and reboarded the tank, then the barricade was rolled back and they were on the road again. Ed bucked up in anticipation of the look into an intra-border colony, the coming snapshot of a nation within a nation, something exciting about it. Enthusiasm and expectations that were, he promptly realized, unwarranted.

Past the megacorp feedstation-remains was La Perla of Bill Penn's re-vamped Quaker paradise: the Puerto Rican Territory of El Reading PA. The ambiance of the city-wide squalor struck Ed as being identical in all but architectural backdrop to the Sudamerican habitats he'd spent his entire life in or around: same rolling bistros, same fruit trucks and price-by-client mercados, same syrupy people loitering around, a whole lot of nothing going on, and certainly not any exercise as there was little space between the bone-thin and its more pervasive (slow to) flip side. Rampant open-air laziness could muster a defense for itself when cool air was wanting and sandy beaches and palm shade were just steps away, but it was malapropos up here in nippy Mid-Atlantic slack town next to collapsing Victorian townhouses and rowhomes. Just something wrong about it.

"They look so out of place."

"They *are* out of place. They were lured here by free stuff and lies, sold the idea that our country was really their country. The people who opened our borders never had any interest in offering them a better life, they only wanted to use them against us, to overwhelm us and force us into competition with them, to transform our pleasant country into the dysfunctional countries people like those out there came from."

"What a wicked thing to do."

"Callousness that's hard for us to confront. And it's quite the mess we have to clean up now."

"They all going back?"

"They all came here, so they can all go back. They have their own countries anyway . . . down there."

Down there, up here, or wherever, these were communities distinguished by sloth and uncleanliness. Per the view: tall weeds sprouting wild out of the pavement, lumps of trash snared in curbside gutter strainers, streets that looked like El Dio crushed a rapture-sized bag of potato chips and sprinkled the pieces all over El Reading. There were still German names on worn signs yet to be pried off some of the caged lanes—Bachman Welding, Feick Automotive, Weaver Construction—but wherever those families were now, it was no longer here in the city they'd built . . . squeezed out by Jorge's Cocina and Castillo's Coin Laundry and whatever five-and-dime occupied the concrete cave prior to *Su* and *Su's* Grand Opening, the bleached banner for which looked like it went up before the criminal Ñetas presently mossing underneath it were even born. And there were always the many other noteworthy, unLatin-like cultural peculiarities manifesting themselves in the form of a pair of pants lying in the middle of the road or shadowy characters rolling an oil drum down an alleyway or a shredded badminton net on a plot of knee-high grass with a dead Geo Tracker jamming the back left service line.

"Command to autodriver: pull over so I can get a shirt for my sister."

"Quiet in the back, passenger."

WITH THE SHEET OF NIGHTFALL having put another day to rest, they exited El Reading and closed in on Lancaster County, just a few miles down the road. Now, if there was some form of heaven in existence, on earth or elsewhere, there were few places it could have been other than here: within the granite-stacked fortress walls of Amish Country.

In times when cynicism was in no short supply, when Americans were dropping like flies into the burnt broth of the Old-Am Mystery Stew—crippled with vice, muzzled by wrongthink, playing backup actors in a prison drama that praised their extinction commercial-free—some believed the Amish would be one of the few to pull through since they continued to grow at several times the average rate of the population even with the Immigration Wars on full blast. As the modern age blended into the postmodern and then morphed into some kind of machinated mass-marketed neurosis, the Pennsylvania Dutch became numinous icons to their brethren lost in the electric wasteland—prototypes of providence midst the spiritual carnage. Forced injections of vibrancy beset the county, but as the Old Order cracked and the New heeled a spur into any latent ally, the Brims and Bonnets became, after some tweaks in their holy edicts, a force to be reckoned with. Numbers swelling as they were, they went ahead and reclaimed the county, and while lawlessness outside the walls made random incursions to a degree unavoidable, anyone with a lick of sense knew where the line was drawn: put a toe across it, *dear fellow*, blessed be thy way forth with nine. . . .

Ed's eye was back on the clearscreen inside as they neared the lantern flecks yonder, scintillating below the wall's umbral moonlit line. The figures behind the light glossed into focus: men with long beards and tombstone hats, black vests over white-sleeved shirts, rifles in hand—a string of maybe thirty, with more staked out atop the parapet.

"'Member," Captain Ó Draoi announced, "no talking and no sudden movements till we're inside."

"Serious people, huh?" Ed whispered to Lieutenant Millerson.

The Lieutenant bucked his head at Ed's window. "That out there should tell you all you need to know."

Ed looked out at the field, but it was too dark to see much of anything, just a scattered array of scarecrows. "All I see are scarecrows."

"Those ain't scarecrows, buddy."

Once stopped, the Mirth Men received orders to exit the tank. Ed followed the others out. They lined up as the Amish inspected *Yankee Rover* and gave the four of them a close look-over—whiskered faces unsmiling, staid and silent. The air was chilly, the lanterns bobbed squeakily, a tingle ran down Ed's spine each time his eyes betrayed his control for a gander at the skewered trespassers spread across the field. No one in either faction so much as whispered until the investigation neared completion. A group of elders congregated at the front while the younger men continued the watch. But when a verdict was returned, the mood shifted toot sweet into a warm-hearted welcome as the locals formed a line and moved down it, making sure to shake each of their hands and offer them a personal welcome before waving them back aboard and allowing them to breach the gates.

Horse-drawn carriages led the tank down a long road for half an hour through the Anabaptist dark to the edge of Ephrata. The crew ate a quiet dinner in a dim cafeteria barnhouse then walked up the hill to the guest quarters, fordone after a cramped day in the tank, ready to conk out or retreat into the optic artifice. There was nothing fancy about the individual cabins lined along the hilltop, but inside was everything one could need: a small bed not much softer than a board, a thin wool wrinkleless blanket pulled up to a mini punching bag of a pillow, a nightstand with a bible and a propane lamp, a sink and a mirror next to the chamber with the commode. Not a smart-commode, though. "Hm," Ed fretted upon peeking in.

He was restless, body and mind charged like an ion in search of a bond, caught up in the greater meaning of this earthfield exploration. Under a forever of stars Ed fell into a lean against a porch pillar, facing the town below, light-dots dim on the plane. He was wondering if it was safe to wander, or what the chances were that he might run into trouble or do something that could result in him joining the ranks of scarecrows. In the midst of these calculations a voice sprung from the darkness—"Anything you need, sir?"

It took Ed a moment to find the speaker, who turned out to be a boy, no older than thirteen, strolling toward his cabin. "No. Was considering taking a walk."

"Won't find much exciting going on." The boy stopped in front of Ed's cabin and looked back at the town, thumbing a suspender and adjusting the rifle slung across his back. "Not for a fellow from the New Republic, that's for sure."

"New-Am's as new to me as it would be to you."

The boy examined him. "You from one of the holdouts, sir?"

"You could say that."

"Well, I don't think anyone out there would give you any trouble unless you caused some."

"Nothing I'd do intentionally."

"Should be fine then, sir. I'd show you around but I'm expected at my uncle's factory soon. That's as interesting a place as any at this hour, though. Cuts right through town, too, so you're welcome to come along."

Figuring *Why not* Ed followed the boy across the hill to a barn. The door swung open and unleashed a piss-stench, snorting and champing sounds, beastly rustling. It took his eyes a moment to adjust, but before he knew it the boy was pulling a horse out of one of the stables and dragging it toward him.

"Her name is Amy Schumer."

"Whoa," Ed, backing up and lifting a hand. "That's nice, but—"

"But what, you don't ride, sir?"

"No, and I'm not sure tonight's right for a first lesson."

"She's just a pony. Nothing to it. Climb up and she'll do the rest."

Ed looked into her eyes. "Amy Schumer, you said? Why does that name sound familiar?"

"Not sure why it would. It would have to be a coincidence since we're completely cut off from the outside. We don't know who anyone is."

Ed and the boy slow-trotted down the hill and into Ephrata beneath the starlight, the nags hoofing along a cobblestone path flanked by hand-raised buildings of red brick and wood, riding a beeline into town through the center of commerce, past shops teeming with hardware and homeware, garden or grange, produce to provender, fowl toddling about, pumpkins already out, the nightfall mural like a Wild West movie set that was as clean as the unsmogged air and organic as the pull from the steed-tilled land, modest but abundant to denizens winding down the day by porch lamp and buggy wheel, from the blond-bowlcut boys in broadfall trousers who ran up to say Hello to their friend, the chaperone, to the rest of the Pilgrims who looked on bemused by the sight of Ed riding Amy Schumer down Main Street.

They tied up at a small factory whose front was open to the outside. Chimney smoke coursed upward from the roof. Ed knotted the trot and tailed the boy inside where a dozen kids were hard at work, even at this near-late-by-lamplight hour, seated at stations in the foreground of the foundry—turning, drilling, milling, shaping, boring, broaching, sawing, and lathing—gunsmithing. On rustic machinery, using electricless tools to shape, file, and polish barrels, receivers, and slides. Ed was still gawking, baffled by the hoary handiwork and the youthfulness of the firearm-assembly labor, when he met with Father Amos' bushy mask of suspicion—squinting through round-framed glasses and immediately prying him with questions then long-*Mm-hm*-ing to the answers, curious at what his nephew dragged in. Father Amos was no *soi-disant* golf enthusiast but would out of principle approve of most any man worth his salt with the old four fingers and thumbs, so Ed, after the curt investigation, was invited in. He got a run-through of the factory where handcrafted pistols were made for the Amish Resistance, along with some worldly advice laden with sermon smithereens and delivered in apostolic modes of speech that failed to land in transit between the ears.

Ed was directed to a seat in the office. Father Amos tapped his fingers on the desk. His eyes darted up and down. His neck was bent ten degrees. "My family and I will pray for you, Brother Ed. We know the many dangers one can face out there." He took his hat off and laid it on the desk, then leaned back and crossed his arms. "What are your plans for when the war is over?"

"Not sure I can say, sir."

"Family?"

"Don't have one."

"Make one. Wife?"

"Not yet."

He sniveled, "Still picking up the pieces."

"Think you're right. So how'd you guys make it through the—"

"—The Hellfire?"

"That."

"How do *you* think we did? Why do you think our community still stands and grew as others were declining?"

Ed gave it some thought. "Faith?"

"Faith, yes. But more importantly, is something we call *Gelassenheit* . . . *'not my will but thine be done.'* We yield to God and the spirit of tradition, and we look to the legacy of the past before we make any move forward. The values of the individual are not our own, and our community looks down on those who cannot subdue the will of the self, who cannot be humble, obedient, and content with a life of simplicity. The interest of the individual, his pride, his desire for attention and distinction from others, his personal displays of vanity—these things do not strengthen his community, and they oftentimes weaken it. Here, there is a social order where children obey their parents, students obey their teachers, wives obey their husbands, men obey their church leaders, and all obey God, because that is the *Ordnung*, the order of life. When that order is disrupted—when men put aside their duties or are renounced as leaders within the communities it is in their nature to protect, when ravening wolves in sheep's clothing deceive girls into believing that a woman is defined not by her fecundity but by her independence through commercial salvation—what happens?"

"Everything breaks down. People go crazy."

"Searching for something to replace it."

"Nothing ever will though, will it?"

"Anything that claims it can is only an illusion, one that will eventually crash like waves of the wild sea, frothing out its sufferer's confusions. And then where will we find ourselves?"

"Back where we began."

"Relearning what nature teacheth." Father Amos leaned forward and rested his forearms on the desk. "Now, where does your journey take you next?"

"Baltimore."

"Baltimore," he repeated, inhaling into a nod. "I'll put a little more oomph into those prayers then." Reaching into a desk drawer, he took out a silver pistol and inspected it, then stretched across and placed it in front of Ed. "For you, Brother Ed—our imprimatur."

"Are you sure, Father Amos?"

"A sword to guard the way to the tree of life as you rise against the House of Jeroboam."

Sunrise (Captain's cabin.)

I LEAVE A CENSORED WAKE; hard roads, different domains, wherever I roll. The northeastern forests sidelong spring to whelm my track, but the path to my fixed purpose is laid with iron rails, whereon my soul is grooved to run. Over unfathomable gorges, through the barreled hearts of mountains, under ever-flowing torrents' beds, unerringly I rush. And naught's an obstacle, naught's an angle to the iron way. . . .

A WINDY MORNING. Beech trees bopping. Corn fields asway. Following white ranch-rail fences along country roads through Lancaster, destination: Maryland. Out of the gate *Yankee Rover* had trouble gaining any sustained momentum; felt every minute they were forced to slow and wait for a buggy to pull off to the side so they could pass. Not that it was much of a drag; there was no rush. No reason to speed through this time-frozen stage of life; to not study with a sort of nostalgic longing, howbeit impossible to return, the venerably pastoral customs and practices getting underway against the daylight vista. The men out there—riding twelve-colt hitches and six-filly hay balers down cropland lanes, climbing like suited spiders in the salmon sun across the pine skeletons of their children's future homes—they were the winners. They had long ago made themselves reliant on only each other and immunized their communities against the cultural machinery that had hooked, wired, and drogued so many of their brothers and sisters in its wake. A salute earned. A lesson, with luck, learned.

After leaving the southwest Lancaster boundary and making the crossing at Clarke Lake, Ed was summoned to the captain's cabin, where were drifting widgets and the control panel and all else that made go vroom. There as well stood the Captain, in front of whom the scenery rolled soundlessly by on a slow morning whirler, broadly out the wide windshield, where his focus rested.

"Edmund."

"Captain."

Mornings'.

"Off we go. Away from the freak show."

"Another day, sir."

"Last on the road for you eh."

"Been a pleasure tagging along, sir."

"Been a pleasure having you."

Captain Ó Draoi stabbed a few fingers into the handle of his mug and toasted to the view. Turned out he wasn't as rigid as Ed had been making him out to be—more in the look: perpetually squinched, costive, and hence mistaken for anger. The Captain served Ed up a cup of joe and added a "hand-splicer," so-called, before replaying for him some highlights from the time or two he himself had hit the sticks, this being a natural lead-in strangers and acquaintances alike were wont to initiate in his presence to lay a few stones, the routine a sort of pride in humility inspired by the count of balls lost, the measure of divots made, the significance of objects, costly or living, by accident struck.

"Anyway, we'll be making our way through Baltimore later and the situation there has the potential to get hairy, so I'll need an extra pair of eyes up front."

"Blinkers'll be ready, sir."

"City's mostly depopulated now but there's always an element of unpredictability. Realized I missed a piece of your background before, too . . . how you grew up in the FPSC."

"Los Angeles, sir."

This brought some version of a smile to the Captain's face, one that appeared to cause some pain to render. "Bombed that place with half the Midwest's bulbhead population back when I was with airmobile. They said that

was the death knell. We pushed them into the Hills, up there between the
. . . *the*—"

"—The Binaries, Captain."

"That's it. Binary numbers."

"Ones and zeros, sir."

"Also wanted to get your take on a thing or two, you being a new citizen—little unofficial survey is all. Ih-*Iii-Iii*-ah-ah, there've been some debates in the New Republic lately, public policy proposal stuff, some more popular than others, let me know what you think."

"Fire away, sir."

"In your opinion, is there anything morally objectionable about keeping a woman in a cage?"

"A cage, sir?"

"I mean like a nice cage, a comfortable one with furniture and a bathroom, plenty of space, she'd have all her stuff in there—let's scratch that one for a sec. If your wife or girlfriend had to wear a sheet, I mean had to cover herself with a sheet when she went out in public, maybe as part of a new dress code or fashion trend thing she'd cotton to with some marketing exposure, after seeing the other girls doing it, you know, sold as new age refeminization wear, perhaps, what color do you think would be best?"

"Best color for the sheet, sir?"

"For the sheet, yes."

"Hm. Fuchsia, sir?"

"Not bad."

"Maybe a light sapphire?"

"That'd be pretty."

"Some would see that as a bit over the top, though, wouldn't they, sir?"

"I suppose. But the point is it's still hard for many to accept the measures that have to be taken, the controls that must be put in place to right the ship and recover after this. The tactics we're required to use often create ethical disputes, and that goes for our own liner here."

"Liner, sir?"

"*Yankee Rover* . . . the time machine. Many like the Lieutenant feel it's too much power to have."

"Growing up around folks who lived under the Googlopticon colored my perspective on privacy, so I'm not sure how I feel about it myself, sir."

"Such freedoms are not valued equally by all. Some groups are more suited to take it, others to fight back against those who wield power improperly against them. We're at the latter end of that spectrum, more inclined to hold in esteem abstract concepts like liberty, and to desire independence from unjust leadership."

"And it's one thing when those leaders are your own, another when they're outsiders . . . your enemy."

"That's the key, isn't it. It remains difficult for many to face what is aligned against them, to reach that lower layer and accept what must be done. Plenty still cry 'not all.' They still need their myths and buy at asking price the affected tale of a lamb whose story has been polished and reprised to perfection, who keeps in its wool a knife it will stab them in the back with the second they turn around. The question then becomes how do you fight an enemy that pretends to be you, to be your friend? How do you adapt to this style of warfare, the warfare of internal subversion? How do you get rid of someone that pits your own people against each other and incites the weak, that targets women and children, that whispers in their ears and plucks their heartstrings and pleads for sympathy and sanctifies its own suffering? The men'll always be few who are willing to shoot down the rainbow and jump down the rabbit hole, confront evil on its own terms or break the rules and become the villain to build a more lasting right. Only so many are capable of striking through the mask."

"Against an enemy that lacks all morality, I imagine it'd be a mistake to not use every tactic at your disposal."

"You need every tool, and you need the far flank. Few things are more fated than its expulsion, the question is how to go about it. You can expose it and slowly disarm it, but the time will come to remove it, and that's when you need the men who have reached that lower layer and struck through the mask, who know what must be done and can step up and manage the purge. Because not everyone is capable. This time, though, you give it no chance to cry, to tell another fable or broadcast its lies to all again."

"My own mask is broken, sir. And I have to admit, it was more comfortable when I couldn't see what I do now."

"Here you are."

ED CLIMBED UP to the crow's nest as a leaner Shrewsbury sung farewell over the ranges and the light broke sparingly in over New Freedom like that of a day whose temperament had not yet been decided. Sergeant Stu became aware of his arrival in a trice and did a triple-take back, his expression of feigned shock as he slow-yelled what sounded like *Breach in the nest* and swiveled around in the chair, *Ka-pugh, ka-pugh, ka-pugh*-ing as he pretended to mow Ed down.

Hand to heart.

"Best spot in the caboose."

Ed confirmed with a thumbs up but left it at that, going about his business until the Sergeant called out a moment later. Ed's attention veered ahead and followed a finger to a fast-approaching sign, an eye-catcher, up the empty sweep of road. Blackeyed Susans waving them in, by and bye like greased lightning: the oxidized heraldic banner of George Calvert, 1st Baron Baltimore—*Founded 1634.*

MARYLAND WELCOMES YOU . . . ENJOY YOUR VISIT!

Across the Mason-Dixon Line on 45 were many a haunted nook or manor—darkened by landhell shadows, algae-wrapped like rocks on murky seabeds, driveways bending into the wooded unknown as an uncertainty fell over the landscape, a felt presence, an earthly mourning of snaps and whistles, soughs and whispers—whatever mysteries she wished to convey, from this dissenter of time's perch, more acutely felt. It was still so Northeastern, the arboreal blanket of crimson, gold, and shamrock. Candle-dripped willows and fro'd white oaks, hispid cones of juniper and redfire maples over round beds of fallen scarlet leaves. Green acres spaced by tubes of forest. Songs of whip-poor-wills. Then in view were estates with signs of life: smoke, livestock, people, a few: holdouts, older men, visible beyond steel-spiked gates. Standing on lawns with beaten stares. Arms lifting but not waving. Dogs barking and running along the confines with the tank. Parkton and Windtree lots with rain wells and biodomes and solar tractors and the other implements of autonomy required to make it out in the badlands.

"*Curshshk*," Sergeant Stu crackled, fist to mouth like a radio. "Captain's Log, Stardate: three-four-nine-four-one-five-dot-niner—*Yankee Rover* has discovered additional lost members of our tribe outside of the BeeTree Preserve Colony in Maryland Province—ourrr comrades appear weak and beleaguered but have not yet fallen prey to primitivism. Ground crew is requesting delivery drone with Idaho Earth Bars and other essential provisions. End of dispatch—*curshshk*."

On and on then the self-sustaining habitats passed before them and through their imaginations the stories of those living here lo these many years, simple curiosity it was above all as to why they chose to remain behind on this road guiding the way into the depopulated burbs north of Baltimore.

"Ever had to use that thing?" Ed, chinning to the gun.

Tongue-click, sideways headshake, exhale of disappointment, "Gimped a few in the Puerto Rican Surprise but that's about it."

"What was the deal with that?"

"We don't like to talk about it, Edward. Not much action out these ways anymore, though."

"Been noticing. How'd you end up on a mission like this anyway? You're a hardy guy, think you'd be closer to the action."

"*Tchuh.*" Sergeant Stu shook his head away sheepishly. "There are things I prefer not to talk about."

"Sorry, didn't mean to—"

"—How is it that a man can be judged by the departed?" The Sergeant bellowed this out dramatically as he took stride to the center of the nest. Holding a strong underclaw in front of him, he continued, "Is the self not the sole actor in the play of life? Are we not liable to but one, good brother? I knew not this man, but he hath borne upon me a mark of great confusion and scandal. Tell me, where are your jokes now? your pranks, jester? your flashes of merriment? Where lies your noble dust, turned to clay, '*swounds! I—*" He stopped suddenly, deflated, then hiked back and shrugged his way into a more casual demeanor. "Issues with the family footprint, Edward, I regret to say. Turns up some strange stuff and the higher-ups don't know what to think."

"Too bad."

"Don't get the wrong idea, though, I've seen plenty of heat—was scorching flyover metros at thirteen with the original Midwest War Party."

"What was that?"

"The Mid—oh it was nothing. . . . Just the most vicious crew since the Proud Boys. Rampaged from Milwaukie to Chicago, drove a million gangsters all the way to Little Rock, Lake Michigan Massacre they called it. Resurrected forms of capital punishment that hadn't been used for centuries—blood eagles, scaphisms, *poena cullei* here and there with a bad hombre and a couple copperheads, you dig. But we were disbanded after that."

"Why's that?"

"Bad optics."

REVELATIONS FLASHED ACROSS the clearscreen of the mind when new twists weren't taking the plot on detours from the comical to the puzzling to the downright frightening. Filling in the blanks could be arduous, with immersion-sessions in the optic artifice having the tendency to blow open ten doors for every one forced, in a compromise between wisdom and time, closed. Did this thing go deep or what. That there was a story with a couple sides on a spectrum and a reasonable middle ground between seemed an obvious and natural enough dynamic to go along with, but when it became known that that centerish-or-so area had been framed by foreign sociopaths trying to narrate both sides in their own interests and against your own, it kind of threw a wrench in the works. "They say for most people at first it's like really scary," Jennifer had put it at one point. "Then it's like super liberating because you like finally understand how everything works." Ed, by now, could arguably have claimed to have made it through those first two stages. "But then it gets like really, really scary once all the ramifications have set in. . . ." Away from castle comforts and mentorettes with primary qualities to temper any hard truths, traveling the empty roads of Postamerica with an Eastern fall chill settling in as someone who'd spent little time in geographic clines north of Lompoc, now an uncertified unit in a war . . . it could get there.

Lieutenant Millerson, crack shot he was, had in no time learned to augur an inquiry, which wasn't to say Ed was or had ever been the patient-in-the-fog type. Clearscreen disappearing off, head back against the seat, inching into the aisle, a barely audible gasp.

"What is it, Ed."

"Nothing."

"It's okay, say it."

"The frog, the Pepe, I just don't get it. People thought it was Egyptian magic?"

"I don't know if anyone really believed it."

"Stupidest thing I ever heard. I mean it's just so stupid. But what about the Hapastans, where all the people who got caught in the mix move to. L.A. was like that in a lot of places, hard to tell what anyone was."

"They were the casualties of the multicultural experiment, but their fate was intended for all of us. Our own who mixed out were the feebler among us, which was why they made the decision they did. But the rest of us didn't want that, or the resulting outbreeding depression and other health issues. The mule's no good, and shedding the weak makes the core stronger. Most of them are happy to move to their Hapastan anyway. Here they were caught between identities and suffered because of it, because of a primal wound that was caused by a choice they didn't make. There they can be with their own kind in their own country and create a real identity for themselves, one they share. It's a positive thing, Ed."

"Never thought of it like that."

"It's also a necessary part of the Demulticulturalization Plan."

Eyes straying out to Monkton and the northerlies of My Lady's Manor. Speed limit signs, ivy-sheathed. Flagpoles waiting for the new nation to come around. Bottomed-up runabouts, waterbound with a patch: jib to the Chesapeake squall again. Fixer-uppers and forever green, nooks under the floorboards of heaven. Small farms are making a comeback in neoagrarian New America. People are talking. Homesteaders are moving east this time and land's cheap, up for grabs, few early birds out already. Come back after winter maybe, pick one and dock. Scrap the fence, yank the tree off the garage. Get the grass mowed, hose the pool up. A good sunbeat spring it'll be stripping painting flooring roofing decking. Giver a salt-white gleam, cherry-red on the barn cause that's the law right. Snag some fittings from those Amish folk up the road, some of that modesty too this time around. Big garden for the missus, field of dreams for them love trophies, forget-me-nots for fairy crowns, barley back waving for miles, cows and chickens, collies and Maine Coons, out here growing till we're cycled through to our hereafters. . . .

"What's up, Ed."

"Wasn't a big deal."

"Just say it."

"So after the Ultrafascist Putsch—"

"—After we won, yes."

"When Neo-Imperialist Model policies were—"

"—The Hybrid New State Model, we call it."

"So then the Free State Liberation Movement was—"

"—The Structured Imperial Contraction . . . *potahto*."

"I'm talking about before the neopogroms—"

"—Fiction, Ed."

"Eeuh-*wuh*, all right."

"The war was against *us*, and we'd been jumping around from place to place pretending it wasn't happening for decades before we ever began fighting back—moving south, west, or wherever to escape the demographic wars being waged against us, only to see our cities get flooded again."

"People got tired of being targeted."

"We certainly did. Tired of standing by as we were pushed out of our own institutions. Tired of letting a foreign group label us the bad guy, classify us as a nonentity, and celebrate our replacement."

"People had to do something about it."

"We had to develop a plan and change the way people thought about themselves, their culture, their society, and their future. We had to make them aware of what was going on so we could start to reverse the damage, learn how to work together and stop behaving like a bunch of selfish individualists, so we could take power away from our enemy. We had to stop allowing them to pervert our culture, corrupt our politics, and control our money, we had to break the kritarchy and put an end to the Sackler Drug Epidemic, snuff out the pornographers and the pedo-normalizers, discredit the foreign-run media, take back the narrative, and build a new one."

"Why is it always about *them* . . . *this* people?"

"They had forced their way into every part of our society and arranged it to protect them and further their interests, while we couldn't even speak openly about our own without being condemned. *They* make everything about themselves, we were only ever reacting to that. It's them who see it as their right to live among us and rule over us and attack anyone who says anything critical of them. And as they pushed and we caved it became them who set the parameters of our social and political discourse, who set the cultural agenda, so ultimately it was them who had to be purged and removed—zionized. Only after that could our new plan be put into place and our new vision instituted."

"I get the case for Europe . . . but us? There's a case against us, isn't there?"

"Whatever the case may be doesn't matter. There will always be others willing to come and take it if we don't protect it, and few act in as good a faith as we do. We created this country and built its institutions, and we're taking it back."

"Who are *we*, though?"

"In a way we're still defining that, figuring it out. But we knew it before and we're realizing it again. What we know for sure now is what it's not."

"What's it not?"

"Something we should feel guilty about or ashamed of, something we let our enemies trample on or something we won't defend or fight for. Our identity will no longer be a burden that weighs us down or an-uh, the-uh . . . the thing—*the bird*, you know the bird they hang around people's necks, what's the name of that?"

"No idea."

THE BACKWOODS HIGHWAY SNAKED ON. *Yankee Rover* drifted casually under cloud and timber cover that with the aid of some hallowed ozonic filter imparted unto the otherwise melancholic terrain a peaceful grape blush. With no more than a mild drone they breezed by the provincial hazel-stone houses of Philopolis, among which stood still the schoolhouse of Lincoln's triggerman, until the decondensing trim gave steadily way to open canvas, the two lanes somewhere became five, and the road bowled them briskly out into the exurban clearings of Cockeysville. There the path straightened, the intersections ran up even, and into the strip mall sprawl they forged, entering an unearthly gauntlet speckled methodically with the old gas cartels' discarded filling stations, Wells Fargos and Ramadas, State Farms and Jiffy Lubes, Wawas and Rite-Aids, empty parking lots and fenced-in Señor Storage units, vile-brown office buildings and boundless emporiums—each and all unsightly orthogonal backdrops to the streetside instafood chains copping aristocratic themes in funhouse form, once serving up culinary ensembles even fungi knew not to touch. Block after block of it—*this* . . . this Late Capitalist wonder, with its branded-horizon aesthetic, the slow-passing lots' scallop-capped marquees rising like tombstones into skies of funereal ash, presiding in effigy over the abandoned corporate shell of Old America.

This went on. On for a while. Down through Lutherville-Timonium but becoming less bleak, less baron, less visibly forsaken along the way, and evincing in parts traces of rehabilitation that were spreading outward from some forthcoming hub—this being, it would turn out, the New Towson Protectorate. Continuing on the same road, in the same long-running groove, they motored into town. In outward appearance the New Towson Protectorate maintained a *Truman Show* [1998]-like veneer—clean but closed up, the show not yet begun, or begun and canceled after a single season—the trappings those of an ambitious satellite city whose plug was pulled when national policies of unlimited metropolitan expansion and diversity to diversity's end became those of gradual contraction and Demulticulturalization—the city, after the fall, having been caught somewhere in limbo between its sleepy humble past and the budding outer-*Wire* escape many high-minded developers had envisioned, and for a good while enjoyed the fruits of, dependent on population growth *ad infinitum* and diversity-boosting government loans funneled through its namesake university, "Until the Debt Explosion," Lieutenant Millerson was saying as they caught a one-sided glimpse of the Jacobean campus walls farther down the road, under the shaded face of which was suddenly no shortage of people: jogging, studying on the lawn, throwing frisbees. "Profit-driven universal higher education—another brainwashing and neobondage scam that under the foreign elite had diminishing returns and was set up to self-propagate at any cost—one of the many bubbles we had to prick the pin into and deflate."

"Looks like it's still going strong."

"After some modifications. Towson now has one of the best Reclamation and Remigration Planning departments in the new nation. Students here've been coordinating the Baltimore Recovery Project. Ways to go with that. City had quite a reputation before."

"Reputation like a bad one?"

"You'll see here in about," the Lieutenant, in a metaphorical gesture, glancing at his wrist, "five or so minutes. Aren't you supposed to be up front for that?"

"Think so."

Pressing on, the New Towson Protectorate short in the rearview, there came a stretch of historic districts like that of Anneslie and once-wealthy residential neighborhoods like that of Cedarcroft, lapsed Episcopal, Lutheran, and Catholic churches above whose doors at one time hung the MOG flag, while peppered about the streets were the surviving remains of what was left behind by those who tried to hold on, who thought they could keep it alive—their yoga studios and gourmet ice cream shops and hair boutiques and fusion bars and music workshops and vintage clothing stores—hanging on at the fringes with charter schools and abortion clinics and the stakes of the oriental vultures who swooped in with King Wok's and Fu Wa Carry-out's, around the appearance of which Ed was summoned back up to the captain's cabin to find himself poring over the more comprehensive view, of surrounding imagery that got worse, much worse, worse instantaneously, as the blocks condensed and ghettofied around them with rickety shotgun and row houses and rotting Victorian mansions and NO SHOOT ZONE ordinances tagged on cracked brownstone, a transition sharp and sudden from the modern to the colonial, from order's ghost to earthborn entropy, from white to black—Baltimore had arrived.

After decades, along imaginary borders pushed this way and that by factions too dense or civil to acknowledge the unworkable reality of their arrangement, in a tussle too gradual to incite full-scale war until time said enough, the lines had come finally to rest where they were on this day drawn, making for abrupt transitions from Italianate estates with ivy palisades and retail shopping deserts one could at least imagine being in another era pleasant, tolerable, even now possibly redeemable, to clogged urban sinks seemingly ravaged by tornados and earthquakes and the rest of the lineup the natural world kept on deck to let fly at its hide-riding barnacles at whim. But as Ed peered down the alleys of Pen Lucy and Sir Scott's Waverly ways it became apparent that what he was seeing was not the result of some unpreventable accident, but of a special kind of neglect.

Despite it all, the 18th and 19th century framework, colored dirty-off-white and wornout-red, still stood, and retained vestiges of exceptional architectural design: Athenian in parts, Early American everywhere, with Flemish bond brickwork and checkered formstone, white-marble steps to witch's hat turrets, a *trompe-l'œil* effect ebbing down the robust, high-density blocs. But the tenements were long derelict and the communities scarred with defunct dindu'd relics—one-time district crack dens and dump yards, nail salons and weave-service stores and bail bond firms, Darou-Salam Outreach temples and Faithtriumph Ministries, paled signs, signs with missing letters, the hood's various grub-stops belly up down the wilted line: U.S. Fried Chicken, Seafood & Subs Take Out, DuShon's Crab Sticks and Lake Trout—by the Boost Mobile, next to the Ill Cutz, down from McGee's Tax Outlet, below the 1800-LAW4YOU billboard—many bookended by muraled walls of swipple-commissioned art . . . *Long Live the Rose that Grew from Concrete.* . . .

Proving nature's law was *right*.

And when it seemed it couldn't get any worse, worse it got. The vicinity was awash with distractions, the ominous day made naught the merrier.

Hanging signs creaked above boarded doors, swings danced on empty play-grounds in the high-grassy distance. Sickly dogs rummaged through rubble, lampposts lurched into the road. Every side street vented open to lay bare a long cave to hell, their every move felt as if it might wake the dead. Green-mount was post-nuclear, nothing seemed where it belonged. Vehicles had been burned out, whole buildings razed. Slow and cautious, *Yankee Rover* slipped around a Charm City Circulator lying on its side near Barclay . . . *dis ear boi*—the remnants of the last Baltimore riot . . . no more space to destroy.

Downtown skyscrapers were visible through the gap when people began coming out of the woodwork, stumbling from back streets and out of make-shift shelters into the open, while more appeared along the sidewalks—pros-titutes and stoop-dwellers in drug-droops, looking old even if they were young, heads turning from under-tree shadows, rising when they saw them rolling through.

Ed's nerves spiked as more and more emerged, many yelling and waving and running after the tank.

"This normal, Captain?"

"Normal as boogies in the beak," Captain Ó Draoi, without moving, trained eyes ahead. "Nothing like it used to be, though."

Individuals up ahead paraded out into the street, flapping their arms and pointing at the sky like they were trying to flag down a plane from a desert island. *Yankee Rover* slowed, braking and eventually stopping in front of them as others caught up and moved in and surrounded the tank.

"Let's see what the issue is here," Captain Ó Draoi drawled. He grabbed the mic off the dashboard and held it to his lips. "Why aren't you all at the stadium?" his voice blaring through the streets. The group gathered at *Yankee Rover*'s bow began howling in unison, forcing the Captain to come speedily back with an addendum. "Hold it!" he shouted, "Hold it! quiet! One at a time."

A thin man in a larger man's pants, a white shirt, and an askew cap, took a step toward the front guard, finger to the sky. "We is waitin fohda drop-box," he yelled up at the windshield.

"Yey," said another, also moving forward, "wheyda dropbox at?"

"Well," Captain Ó Draoi sighed, "the dropbox might not be coming since you aren't supposed to be here anymore. What I have here," the Cap-tain said as he looked at one of his screens, "says the final pickup was yester-day. Why weren't you guys on it?" The group in front looked at each other, hands on their hips or scratching the tops of their heads. "Give me a minute here."

"Dropbox, Captain?"

"Aid we've been dropping in here. Don't want them to starve before they have the chance to get home, do we," sincerely enough. He then added, "Keep your eyes on them and let me know if anyone does anything stupid."

"Sir."

The Captain made a call. Ed, still unsure what was going on but not bent on making his ignorance a distraction, watched over the group. Beyond some odd, flamboyant gesticulating and hard-to-decipher banter, there was little of note going on—none of them, it appeared, eager or able to cause a problem and content to wait for the Captain's reply.

"Uh-huh. Uh-huh. Fifty at most . . . ," Captain Ó Draoi said before tak-ing a break from the line. "It'll be a moment," over to Ed.

"No problem, sir."

There was a long silence. The Captain whistled. He chuckled to himself and turned one of the knobs on the panel in front of him. "They'd always put them on the Tube playing doctors and lawyers trying to fool people. Trying to present them as these noble figures to make us think they were something they weren't, that that was normal, when the norm was, well, was . . ."

"Something more like that out there, sir?"

"Exactly. We pretended to believe it, agreed with our feet."

" . . . "

"Violent. . . . Committed a lot of crime, I mean. Most of it, in fact."

"They did, sir?"

"Yahp."

". . ."

"Media always covered it up. Tried to blame us."

"Big shock there sir right."

"Big shock. Reeal shocking."

" . . ."

"They have low IQs."

"Think I've heard that before, sir."

"Like the lowest. Used to say that was our fault, too."

"What did they ever say wasn't?"

"They're like this everywhere, though."

"Can't be our fault then can it, sir."

"Never was."

" . . ."

"Never. Was. We wuz. Ever see that—"

"—So are we allowed to talk about this subject now, sir?"

"Think it's okay now."

A call came back. Captain Ó Draoi answered.

"Uh-huh. Okay. Got it. Thanks." He picked the mic up and announced to the group: "Good news, they said a dropbox is on its way. They're also going to send another wagon through here later. You need to make sure everyone's on it so you can get down to the stadium. You don't want to get stuck here now, hear me?"

They nodded and waved and began to disperse, up with parting cheers, "*Aight*" . . . "*Yight*" . . . "Thank yawls" . . . "Preechatechuhs checkin" . . . So on.

Yankee Rover creaked forward and started onward again, but hadn't gotten much farther than a block when a loud siren belted through the streets. The tank decelerated again. Captain Ó Draoi highlighted for Ed a screen with a view of their rear. "Aircaid's fast these days."

In the sky a craft was soaring low up from behind them. They alternated views and watched as it passed overhead then appeared in front. It slowed to a hover at an intersection two blocks up. A hatch at the back opened and a giant crate slid out with a trailing ribbon that flapped in the lag. Ed and Captain Ó Draoi both flinched, ducking faintly where they stood as it collided against the pavement with a board-breaking climactic blast.

"Hear that?"

"Loud, sir."

"Swan song of the welfare age."

YANKEE ROVER GROWLED ON. The tower masts of Baltimore sprang into the cloudpressed sky ahead. Ed climbed back up top as they were rolling over the 83 expressway into the neighborhood just north of the downtown, Mount Vernon—the hip district all sizable Old American cities once had, and fine havens they once made, inhabited by the progressive urban bohemian who was destined to run out of space and time due to an apparent aversion to reproducing itself. The Truest of the True Believers, they were some of the last to give up hope since their hyper-individualized identities and tender-minded ideals were tethered to the theory that everyone aspired to be just like them; however, the integrity of such a delusion could suffer heavy losses when your hipster wonderland was a mere bridge-crossing away from a Monrovian hellscape, and as those capable of maintaining the caliber of law and order your attendant *mode de vie* required became fewer in number.

So down, on down Mount Vernon sank, supervised by departments of clockwatchers and sold at a markdown to foreign buyers to leverage down the line, left to various factions of occupiers who had no hand in its development and no interest in its improvement, who could brook and hold coop in the slum belt, pick away at the carcass and squeeze every last penny out of it, employ every tenable scheme and exploit every available loophole to get a leg up in the free-for-all, the multicultural sweepstakes the nation had come to be with its founders indisposed, loath to turn on the lights, to send the cockroaches scattering, to do anything at all, making it home to everyone and no one as it acquired year after year a more vacant grace, until the Helmand's ran back to Kabul, the Belvedere stopped taking reservations, and the contents of the Walters Art Museum found refuge somewhere up around Detroit, leaving the district's framework, most Second Empire, waiting for the next to come along. . . .

At the base of facades dense and baroque they rode North Charles toward the Washington Monument: middled, tall, and priapic at the end of the road, sliding through at a slow enough pace to absorb it, take it in like a spell cast by the midday shadows, sandwiched between massing and pilaster of resplendent high-styled design and sculptured detail at which the eye could only marvel, as the mind could only wonder, where it was architecture of such class and quality had gone. And wouldn't you know that as the stories grew higher and the corners quoined out of sight, so too could be found the first glimpse of the Baltimore Recovery Project. The business district was sprouting forth ahead. Autodars and other machines were out. Men in hardhats gave two-finger salutes as the tank sliced through the underlit spaces below the skyscrapers. It was one part eerie, riding high through a business district with no business, but it was one part magical, as well.

These buildings had histories and came to life in a time when aesthetics meant something, back when building was an art form that paid tribute to the best that came before. These buildings contained indescribable nuance countless millions had strode or ridden past in the many years they loomed over this commercial theater—scrutinized or ignored, admired or missed, looked upon with the highest regard or given a glance and turned right away from. Plenty paid no mind. The city moved fast. And the senses had their limits. But these buildings were monuments that represented something beyond the Old American Empire and its capitalist credo—they were embodiments of a people at their peak and eulogies to the cities those people came from, reflections of a *sui generis* spirit and an artistic energy that was against all unrivaled. Even with the plans in hand and the materials on-site, few others could re-create what stood here, in broken old Baltimore, and what did were the accomplishments of one people alone—symbols of their might to raise lasting beauty to the sky from the rock of the earth.

Saratoga to Lexington: Old Saint Paul's, founded in 1692, whose harvest time hues would come to reflect its self-immolation in the Era of Guilt. The Grand: a Rosslyn Chapel cover set under the caduceus from 1866 and a former Masonic lodge; and where were those guys, by the way? No last line of defense, it turned out. *As Above, So Below, Out to Lunch*. . . . The Fidelity: a wedge of Romanesque Revival designed by Josias Pennington and Ephraim Baldwin, the latter of whom furnished the former nation with nine children and 500 buildings from New York to Georgia. The Vault: a bank turned apartment complex that never received anything higher than a one-star review during the early days of the Googlopticon. Fayette to Baltimore: the S- and C-scrolls and broken pediments of the B&O Railroad Headquarters Building, constructed after the Great Fire of 1904 around the god Mercury. And 10 Light Street: 34 stories and 509 feet, whose space was up for lease long before its tenants were run out with a whimpering *Shalom*.

From City Center to Inner Harbor they stood on through it all, deteriorating nary a bit, padded with the brawn to brush aside the hard times. But past those few fair blocks was a line of demarcation, an architectural timestamp and a stark transition into that which arose after the Worst War and the Western Cultural Revolution, buildings that told the story of a city's slide into death, when it all became ugly and stale, tan and gray, steel beams and birefringent glass—be the skytracts cloudfree or sunproof, to the day's expire—welkin-marred with cubical atrocities: modernist, brutalist, internationalist, the Less is More corporate engineering plastering the jerry-built horizon with sated rows of soulless office cells. Something had changed, someone else had taken over, it wasn't the same as before. This wasn't an existence—this zone, no pinnacle of workaday life . . . this was designed to break you, to make you bear it—*here*, you slave, feed and toil and in sync lay siege to plenary highways for *this*, goyim.

The harbor-bay was clear as glass, white with silent light, so smoothly strewn, expanding into view on the left as they turned right out of the downtown. Ed turned with it and watched the city ease out. He could taste the ocean on the breeze. He watched white phantoms riding the air like loose plumes, singing their godly hymns . . . farewell, to man and bird and beast, farewell. Then he faced back to the front and set his eyes on Camden Yards.

Perched withal this unmerciful Disaster,
The departed city's Corvus master;
Her floodlights hang below heaven's door,
She shall move the chains, ah, nevermore!

"*Oh, Baltimore,*" they sang, and that about summed it up. Another beautiful city that had died long ago. Just died. Boom. Dead. *And they didn't know why.* . . . It was undoubtedly a mystery that would take historians decades to unravel and understand. Meanwhile, slipping deeper into the delusion, ever-ailed by this social pathogen, masking atrophy with rosy nicknames—*The Greatest City in the World*—like some cruel joke. Oh, Baltimore. . . . Oh, *America*. . . . Why wasn't it working anymore? Why were her cities falling? Why was she dying? This was supposed to be the Equalitarian Era, when the ruled became the rulers, the previously oppressed propelled by an allegedly organic force to equal footing with the rest, to prove that prosperity wasn't predicated upon *types* but *opportunity*. . . . It *had* to work, or it had to be *made* to work, even if that meant the ultimate destruction of everything, because *this* was how it was *meant* to be. They were sure of it. And what a magnificent fantasy it was. A grand illusion no less spectacular for the tamed warrior who had willfully given it up without ever bothering to ask: *Who's putting these ideas in their heads and why? Who's gaining here?* His desire to fight for *something* channeled through the dazzling temple *Yankee Rover* was now approaching, centered around what was, perhaps, the most important symbol of the nation, one that embodied its imperial decadence and degeneration as good as any: the Gridiron—Libancien coliseums where ex-slaves battled in front of men who wore their names proudly on their backs, the city-state emblems stitched tight across their hearts and chests, an acceptable substitute identity for the polite consumer on this new day of worship, his spiritual awakening arriving, with fortune and grace, sometime in the afternoon, depending on kickoff times and the amount of 4% suds required to permeate a cheese-lined gut.

"America."

"*Old* America."

Good riddance.

THERE WAS HEAVY TRAFFIC outside the stadium. Crowds were busying up the lots and lining the road around the perimeter. The tank trod a path through and around to the back and was flagged into a space and then the crew shuffled out and walked together toward the amphitheater. They were waved through an open-arched entrance and made two turns then went down a cool concrete shaft with a gateway of light at the end of which they were spit back out into the day near a pronged yellow upright. On the opposite side a carrier-pod was landing by a mass of people who were waiting to board. There were trailers and tents on the field and smoky pits and a fairground feel. Pungent barbeque smells were whipping through. A concert was taking place around the 50-yard line on the left side where people were dancing two-dozen rows into the stands. It was a celebration, one of the many Parting Suppers that had been taking place across Old-Am for years. In attendance were New-Am service personnel and members of the former African American community of greater Baltimore. They were saying their goodbyes, telling stories, and reminiscing about a shared past that, while consisting of many high points, was a prime example of the failure of diversity.

And through it all one of the true misfortunes was what the fallible hand of history forgot—what went missing from the pages at the backs of prudent scholars wagging their fingers to caution others about future mistakes, what got stricken from the record, intellectually laundered, or modified at the discretion of the new information management team, to disguise misconduct or simply pass it on to others. Several parties were to blame for the former African American community's dispatriation, but one in particular—the merchant class, dominant in the organized trade of human flesh from its dawn to this day—had failed to own up: a people for whom the virtue of honesty was as foreign as they were, had always been, and forever would be. But while the pen of history would remain in the hand of interpretation, and animus over events of the past would till doomsday supply its ink, the only equitable solution was a decree of self-determination for all, so that every group would be able to maintain governorship over its own future. This was fundamentally impossible under the auspices of the Libancien, but the multicultural catastrophe its doyen had foisted upon the people of the West was now moving, with time and a tough nudge, and on a track unbroken and invariable, into the historical registers of the past. . . .

After reaching a temporary settlement on the Gulf Coast, the members of the former African American community here would be transported to the new state of African American Africa, informally referred to in some circles as—many were insisting—Wakanda, on the southwest of their native continent. There they would join a burgeoning national project already in progress and together with their brothers and sisters rediscover, revive, and restore their natural identity and culture, marching onward into the future with their collective destiny back in their hands. Everyone knew that this was necessary and for the best—that it would ensure the greatest amount of long-term happiness for all and finally put an end to the exploitative practices of ethically impaired third parties.

"Wonderful sight, isn't it?" Lieutenant Millerson said to Ed as the others dispersed across the grounds. He placed the silver case he was carrying down and raised his arms to his hips, sighing "The Great Return."

"Great Return?"

"Yep. Warms the heart to see a people after centuries finally getting the chance to go home, taking the last step toward liberation. They were always out of place here anyway, it was never going to work."

"Why not?"

"This was an alien environment for them. The vast majority couldn't function in our society and we only made their situation worse by taking the most capable out of their communities and parading them around in our own circles to signal how open and tolerant we were. That was selfish and pathetic behavior on our part, and it didn't benefit either of us in the end."

"Why didn't this happen sooner?"

"Our enemy used the former African American community as their primary shock troops against us, a moral wedge. Families like the Lehman's and Monsanto's brought them here, then their descendants tried to pass the collective blame onto us, propagandizing them, controlling them through the welfare leash, and covering up the reality of their dysfunction. Before, we weren't even allowed to talk about doing what was right, which is what we're doing now—giving the former African American community their autonomy back once and for all."

"I never thought of it that way."

"You were never allowed to. None of us were. But things change." The Lieutenant picked the case back up. "Anyway. Feel like making a delivery?"

"What are we delivering?"

He slapped the outside, "The flux capacitor."

The route took them back to the concrete tunnel between the field and the outside, dense but empty, with dens on the left where the concessions used to be and high ceilings with big round spotlights that beamed down and bent into the unseen beyond with the faint turn ahead. A walk down an adjoined hallway and an elevator ride later, and they were entering a luxury suite. Two dusty-haired military men were sitting across from one another against a three-quarter wall that cut off most of the view to the inside. One rose as the Lieutenant marched to and made a statement. Ed stood back, courteously postured, as he supposed he was supposed to, till the Lieutenant signaled to follow him in, toward the glass at the end overlooking the field and around the three-quarter wall. The bar on the other side was desert-dry, the room had been stripped. Outlines on the walls evidenced where gladiatorial regalia once hung, markings on the floor where anchored furniture provided comfort to high command. Along the far wall were a couple of Redpill Machine-like dentist chairs, a table, some equipment, and a stout man with a slight beard who was slouched on a stool with his back angled mostly away from them.

Steps heard or company sensed, the man's head drifted around, followed by the rest of his body. "Eh, Millerson," he snarled in a post-Metropolitan accent, "thought I told you never to come in here."

Lieutenant Millerson introduced him as *Sizeable Dwight* to Ed, then Ed as *Ed* to Sizeable Dwight, before he went for the setup.

"This your first time going in, Ed?" Sizeable Dwight asked.

Ed shook his head. "In where?"

"Where, what where, into the time machine, where else? You're going in, right? He going in, Millerson?"

Lieutenant Millerson gave them half a face. "It's not a time machine."

Sizeable Dwight snorted. "It takes you *back in time* . . . doesn't it? That's like literally the definition of what a time machine does." He looked at Ed and scoffed at the Lieutenant behind his back. "Sounds like a time machine to me, sound like one to you?"

Ed, with impartial palms up, "I wouldn't know."

Lieutenant Millerson turned and made a crossing gesture with his hands, but quickly gave up on the demonstration. "A time machine has to go *both* ways—*back* to the past, and *ahead* to the future—and it can't be limited to only the recent past."

"Says who?" Sizeable Dwight in dissent. "Sorry, but I refuse to accept such a narrow definition of 'time travel.'"

"So what's it like in there?" Ed asked.

Sizeable Dwight stared into nowhere with a stuffed-face look, appearing almost as though he was about to cry. "There's nothing like it," he said at last, his voice cracking faintly. "I practically live in there, it's like a second home."

Just audibly from behind, "Don't ask what happened to the first."

"Watch it," Sizeable Dwight admonished. He planted a hand on the table and leaned into a stalwart pose. "It's a lifestyle to be honest, being trans-temporal, living in the expired days of life. No reward like it, though—tracking down traitors and agenda-setting elites. I find their itineraries, the little messages they pass on, homes and hideouts they keep around the globe. I'm a vintage guy, so maybe our coin-clipper's playing tennis on his compound in Malibu one day, or leaving a conference in Zurich, when one of my loopers, well—" turning and aiming a finger at the back of Lieutenant Millerson's head, "—*pop*. So basically what I'm saying is that I'm kind of like a time-traveling hit-broker . . . and I don't let anyone try to tell me otherwise."

"I wouldn't, either."

Lieutenant Millerson backed out and rejoined them, then he and Sizeable Dwight started talking shop, which prompted Ed to cut out and step over to the glass looking out over the field. Eavesdropping, of course, but how could he not, in and out between his own inner dialogue, which was rehearsing how he would politely turn down the offer if asked again if he was "going in." *Don't be silly.* He was joking, Sizeable Dwight, the guy wasn't being serious. This was business, weighty stuff, and Ed would only be wasting resources. Probably screw something up inside, too—disrupt the thing whatever it was the space-time continuum—so *no*. Nope. No way. Wasn't going to happen. Pleasing though it would be to confess to the occasional stranger or confidant that he, Edmund, *it was true*, had been in the time machine . . . even if it wasn't *really* a time machine; though of course it was. It went *back in time* . . . basic requirement filled.

Behind him they were talking about big fish and access points and virtual vortices and static erasures and post-time equalizers and a powwow in
Dimona and then they started whispering like they were talking about him
and Ed was getting nervous.

"So what do you say?"

"I don't it's not I mean s-say about what?"

NONE COULD BE CERTAIN whereto it all went, but Time after that first
and last trip in the time machine turned days to weeks then weeks to
months—ticking ever onward as it was obliged to do under universal con-
tract and enslaving the willing and un- to it, while on the living, gradually
running out. There remained no more foremost teacher of lessons, still, collectively learned and retained through inheritance, but from time to forgotten time painfully relearned in new trials by nature, who here on this earth
had no space for angels and awarded no second prize to power, and within
whose arena the strategy of the greatest savage, it would come to be known,
was as victim.

Sadder and wiser men we rise the morrow morn, with of yet no way
around the prosaic: life as usual. Meditations over the out-well, smart-
showers and first squares, then onto the business of the day. For Edmund
Loxley that had come to mean a job as a Junior Renovation Specialist, a
craftsman or master fix-it, manual laborer in no uncertain terms, for the
New-Am Historical Preservation Society. While most other able-bodied
men, loosely defined as the *functionally bipedal,* were busy in roles he was
unqualified for, the summer being still some months away, accommodations
could be made in the nascent and overstretched but blooming into its right-
ful own New Republic of America. The position had taken Ed to a place
he had with a helping hand from his simulated education never heard of,

Harpers Ferry, a historic town at the easternmost tip of West Virginia that had become in times of war home to a small military encampment staffed thinly and irregularly by men most long past their heroic days. It was close enough to several hotbeds, Ed supposed, a theory later confirmed through hints and then overt pronouncements, that he could be handed a Redeemer and sent into the inferno if need be, but the war had in large part by then begun to decelerate as the winter, entering sleepy and hushed itself, set in over the tri-state corner of paling-green Appalachia.

Ed had arrived in Harpers Ferry behind the blinds of night but was able to determine a few steps into the following morning's stroll that he had by windfall or providence landed at some crossroad of the terrestrial and divine, an initial impression that would be upheld and broadened in more ways than one later that afternoon when, with the sunlight breaking in thin radiant streams through the thickset cotton ball cloudage over town, he made it to the top of the Maryland Heights lookout point. There was the settlement built up around the island-hill, the point where the Potomac River split around it, and the dense trees overlaid throughout—unspoiled yet. And this was prior to Ed having any knowledge whatsoever of the history, a topic on which he was to become, and in short order, one of the nation's leading experts, owing to the nature of the job and the relayed wisdom of the man he would meet under the twilight of Church Street as that first day was drawing to a close, his boss to be, Pik Walton. The meeting got off to an embarrassing start when Ed, assuming the town wasn't a place just anyone could relocate to, asked Pik how the residential selection process in Harpers Ferry used to work. Pik didn't follow; and, as it turned out, Harpers Ferry had only lost residents year after year until the number dwindled to zero, making it akin to a ghost town museum of sorts, until even the field trips stopped coming.

Ed performed his duties the best he could and went above and beyond wherever possible in the aim to make the town again what it once was, his daylight hours spent gutting and refurbishing the Victorian homes, Queen Anne B&Bs, and various American Foursquares situated up and down the main couple drags, serving as the long arms, the easy-bending knees, the unsciaticized back of Pik, himself brittle and grayed by days. By Christmas-time Ed had repointed the mortar on St. Peter's Church and the Town's Inn, installed new weatherstripping on Provost Marshal and the White Hall Tavern, slated the roof of the Stagecoach Inn with New York red and unfading Vermont green imbrication, planed stacks of heartwood for the upgrade to the Harper House, which lodged on their trips to town both George Washington and Thomas Jefferson, and repainted the doors of the rechristened Reunification Armory where Meriwether Lewis, other half to Clark, in 1803 arrived to stock up on weaponry prior to the pair's coast-to-coast expedition, all while a chair-bound Pik lectured on to Ed's best-kept attention, "—Walked out that there door with 15 rifles and powder horns, 30 bullet molds and ball screws, 58 tomahawks and 24 knives—" Information he'd try to retain, positive the wayback machine had it but entertaining the idea, in keeping with tradition and all, that he too might find himself an old man prattling up at some ladder-wed duty-dodger, fastened, each passing day nearing firmly and forever, to the earth.

It would be Ed of all people who would nail the plaque to the unctuous John Brown on the wall at the back of the Armory, and be with hope one of the last of his generation to realize how important narrative control over one's history was to a complete and accurate understanding of it. While Harpers Ferry had in the previous era become a symbol of endless penance and glorified kinflict, it would be such a place no longer, but rather, and thanks in part to the steady hands of Ed, a symbol of reunified strength and the brother wars never to be waged again, along with an idyllically set rebuke to the misguided moral signaling, further aggravated by outsider myths, that had led to the sacralization of the Other over their own. It was the error of that logic—the equalitarian proselytizing and the global liberation ideologies, religious and secular—that had brought forth these late ruins. And though there were disagreements and clashes among the diverse populace of the New Republic, none to a man were over the big picture, or in dispute beyond petty grievance regarding the collective way forward.

Ed would on occasion stop by the town's couple-few haunts to mingle, not trying to be anything more than he was, which was someone still discovering his place in it all, but demonstrating in whatever minor way he could that he was a partner in this campaign and wasn't just over here hiding out, which was what most thought with him being, if the eyes of botwar-hardened veterans were any judge, better fit for monitoring an autodar combing through Trenton or blasting evacgas into Nuevo Phoenix than sopping up fresh air and grand views from pedimented rooftops . . . so he usually left out the part about being an absentee golf hustler. Shirt-off-their-back types who could be sparked after a few to go on about things that made Ed look forward to doing his part, exultations about securing the border from Boise to Bear Lake, holding up the whole of Cape Canaveral and moving the Kennedy Space Center to Nebraska, the Los Alamos labs to Wyoming, or the contents of the Met to the New England Remandate, about the Battle of Area 51 and the Wars for New Texas, and missions that took them to his old neck of the woods to dismantle the San Diego Naval Base to keep it out of Old-Am's hands and safeguard it from Chinese annexation.

It was hard for Ed to imagine what his life would have been like had he never left, but as awareness of the how's and why's grew clearer the more thankful he became to be where he was now, and would for as long as the future went the way it tended to, where he belonged. When others gave him the floor and he brought up Jennifer they'd tell him to make sure she wasn't one of those defeminized women of the past and he'd let them know she wasn't and then they'd say to quit dallying around and he'd tell them he was working on it when the situation had in reality escalated well past that, New-Am's cohabitation laws low hurdles for the leap of love, with regular visits and talk more purposeful, concerning things that would have once caused him to tilt a toe toward La Plata but that now made him grateful to be able to speak of any future at all. Because there *was* a point to all this. And they'd tell him about their own families, waiting back in Lincoln or Winnipeg, Cheyenne or Calgary, Springfield or Thunder Bay, and throughout the Old-Am-Can Orbit, their children, grown and up north or out west somewhere, raising families when they weren't depopulating Toronto or blockading the Rotten Apple or shaking them down someplace else. About how it wasn't easy being away, but expressing hope, for Ed's sake, that a greater peace would arrive by the time his own came along.

And so life pushed forward as an eerie-peaceful quiet spread across the rolling ridges and woodlands of Jefferson County. The trees entered their hibernal shed and the chill deepened over the landscape and the earth hardened into copper and the grass weeded into olive and it was like the world had gone to sleep, turned inward into idle peace. The weather became brutal as the winter progressed; seemed there were weekly discussions about the record lows being set. People could often be spotted trying to dodge it out in the open, twitching in it along building faces spared direct hits, even braving it with shields and body armor. Laments padded and extended for small talk value rang through the town's heated spaces but came only to bewildered rest between the ears of Ed, whose *winter*-winter experiences had until then been limited to a failed attempt in a dry-Andes freeze to board the wagon, and who thus found this expanse of wilderness nothing short of, and frequently in a magical space beyond, enchanting. Downtime and the general change had brought with it a feeling that ranged initially from gloom to mild fright but became with familiarity and growth soothing in a way he couldn't quite put a finger on—something approaching, he would periodically conclude, the intuitive or even religious, elusive but long-standing, as if he had been transported to a previous time and was becoming in this frigid backcountry, strange as it seemed, a reincarnation of his erstwhile selves.

One of those unexplainable feelings that came from deep down in this man: palpable, positively spiritual, left behind for comforts not all better for the whole of him, but endured over too many lifetimes to not have become knitted into his code and in turn longed for in absence and recalled through Hyperborean gateways upon his reentry into the wintered forests in which he struggled, to which he adapted, and from which he would emerge more inventive and determined than any other. Ed would whenever time allowed get bundled up and take to the trails, wandering off the beaten path and roaming the woods around Harpers Ferry on casual walks or prolonged adventures, escaping into the enclosed depths, getting in touch with that primordial consciousness, and imagining once in a while that he was a hunter or explorer, pioneer or the like, in some polar forest alone and against nature's indifference, without elective relief or ringport, and equipped only with a birch longsword that would double now and then as a makeshift 3-iron to strike in throwback to the glory days the occasional TaylorMade pinecone lost forever in the rough on the golf course of life. . . .

THEN IT HAPPENED one day at a still-dark hour before dawn—instigated by jet-like screaming: loud and gone then from memory departed. On the boundary of waking, conflict mounting between the real world and the inscrutable realm of dreams, the two fusing in the seam as roused senses pulled one way and languor the other. The room was dark and warm. The clock said all was still asleep. Ed crawled out of bed and wavered over the john with a slight headbang.

Afterward, with a spurt of energy, he put a jacket on and went outside. Standing on the porch in the cold-stinging air, waking not yet upon him, waiting for the battle to play out between the faction begging to go back to bed and the one saying *On to this day* until the latter was nudged across the finish line and his feet were stomping down the road under connected jerkinhead gables that rose higher overhead as the road sloped to lower ground.

Moonbeams through light cloudspray illuminated the path. Gravel crunched under his feet and water purled ahead, louder as he neared the Point, the river split, the confluence, the dry-land peak with a view down the barrel of a chiseled-out bosom-track of watered earth. Bridge rubble from another time jutted out of the river on both sides; little white rapids rippled in moonlit glint around the remains. Above and beyond on the left was the footbridge and the train tracks that ran parallel to it—under truss, over stream, and to the first hill of Maryland, whose hump lurched out of the darkness, unfaced by the light. On the right was Virginia.

Ed here decided that this would be as far as he would go. As he leaned into the railing he recalled the noise from earlier, the sound that caused him to wake, but it lapsed again from memory as his mind wished to ride every imaginative morning spark. Then thinking about how, were he around back then—the precise *when* being indeterminable and trivial—in the times Harpers Ferry was no more than a landmark with geographical placenames like "The Hole," he might have been across the river on that Old Dominion hill amid a westbound Annapolis war party with a heavy Pennsylvania longrifle across his back, chopping through branch and brush with some early iron mistress, half moon tomahawk, clearing out space for a fire then curling up beside it in a beaver fur sack until it was his turn to stand watch for black bears, Algonquin wolf packs, and Huron hatchet snipers. He'd be gone about this time next morning and eventually settle deep in the Piedmont, while decades later one of his sons, traveling with a band carrying a *veta madre* of deer skins destined for the homeland, would come through town just as Bob Harper was taking over the Virginia to Maryland ferry route. The loot would allow him to upgrade to a civilized life in Williamsburg where he'd meet a colonial Miss Guinevere and march with Patrick Henry, who would introduce him to Thomas Jefferson, the man he'd try to catch up with here in town years later only to find out he just missed him. "Kept going on about that rock up there . . ." *Know what you aughta name it.* Successive generations would make their way through on the B&O Railroad, board wagons to see John Brown hanged, then watch their brothers jockey for control and slaughter each other in a war over matters that would do little to benefit their descendants, who would themselves roll through later in their Model T's, their Econoline's, and then their autocars, each year in fewer numbers as Harpers Ferry became a memorial to their alleged victims and in the end a site their children and grandchildren and great grandchildren would visit and be told to be ashamed of all those men who came before. . . .

Ed was brought back around and out by the first light of dawn entering from under the cloudscape, and noise coming from across the river on the Virginia side. Something was afoot. Rumbling could be heard and glittering reflections seen, springing through the trees on the highway at the base of the Loudoun Heights hill: a convoy—hard to say, but maybe . . . a modern war party on the move . . . this time headed east.

Ed left the Point. He made the left turn then the right and then he met with a military truck that was on its way down the narrow street. He stood to the side and watched it pass. Away from it he turned right as the wheels squeaked. Then someone called out.

"Hey" then "Hey" again. A soldier was getting out, a heavyset man Ed recognized, a popular character around town, who was known simply as the Poet. He was on this morning wearing a crooked and unstrapped helmet and a five-day beard, chewing on an unlit cigar, his arms bare and hairy and sticking out of a thick red vest. Ed met him at a midway point on High Street.

"Guy on the roofs," the Poet said. Ed nodded. The Poet then turned and thumbed back at the truck. "Catch a ride in."

"Gotta work later."

A cloud of breath rose into the air as the Poet laughed; with a silver-toothed smile: "Ain't no work today."

The truck crossed the river and hit the road that ran parallel to the Potomac along the base of Loudoun Heights, then made a right turn into the backwoods of Northern Virginia, onto a two-laned road and into the skinny birch gauntlet, thinned further by the winter reduction, that was to take them into Washington D.C. Packed in the back of the truck with two half-asleep soldiers but the luxury of a window seat, Ed made himself comfortable and watched the scenery float by: the farms, the churches, the cemeteries, the traditional two- to three-story homes spaced out every quarter mile; not a flower bed short of ideal at earlier points on the timeline, but vacated and ominous now, murky and unshorn, posted principally up the left side, where rose a light slope.

It was difficult to tell where exactly the change occurred, but some miles into the trip through Loudoun County the homes became noticeably larger, nested farther from the road, visible mainly because of their great size deep in harvest-painted coves or on hills acres back—not sleepy, family-type farmhouses, either, but weekend homes, second and third homes, estates, on which once sprung lush orchards and vineyards, where lied still manmade lakes, split fenced manors, and the skeletons of equestrian obstacle courses—habitations that were too big to be seen and could only be judged by the tall rows of pine trees guarding the fore of the properties, and the elongated walls that met, sooner or later, at shrouded demesne drives.

The clouds ahead were icing over into a dense blanket that made the morning feel it was getting darker. A ghost-hissing wind blitzed outside, putting a shiver into the truck now and then and the country under a balletic spell.

The most obvious of epiphanies then arrived not in a clairvoyant thought but a transcendent feeling, like a mystery made manifest, formerly abstract but now ubiquitous, a realization, that the nucleus of the fallen Empire was near. As though passing through the wheat fields leading into Eridu, the ore mines of Memphis, or the olive groves of ancient Rome—he could sense it, see it in that taking shape around him—out here, the hinterland plantations and hideaways of the patrician class. Properties once belonging to senators and jurists, foreign lobbyists and dealers of all evil, the acquitted and the pardoned—if a just God was waiting: the forever damned—where money plundered by the high bidders of the State got entrusted into the mansions of Paeonian Springs, Shenstone Farms and Beacon Hill.

They were close. On the outermost ring. . . .

Tucked away in little locked-in heavens up long hackberry-brushed lawns a comfortable distance from the peasantries being lured in—the grencho landscapers here to spoil the plot to time's desire, who'd just be propagating exponentially down the highway in Leesburg, trafficking up the town and crowding in the apartments on Battlefield, spilling into neighborhoods and pushing the old residents out—bringing some El Salvador to town: storming the pool and Peleing it over at Ida Lee Park, McChillin or riding the wall at the Premium Outlets, collecting that untaxed scrilla and spinning those chrome hellaflush rims down East Market Street—the finest sampling of diversity Cuzcatlan had to offer, though, strangely, a cultural import whose value always seemed to rise in accordance with one's distance from it, a remote luxury less frequently afforded to members of the former working class who would be stuck with the lion's share of that which their charitable brethren up here living high on hog and hedged hill were such staunch advocates for, communities already strapped and fractured and poisoned with vices of a thousand and one encroached upon and overwhelmed and treated to a spike in crime and plunged into competition with their occupiers for the downward-trending scraps of the global economy, drawing base pay in the service industry after their jobs were shipped to Guangdong, mothers and fathers who would be forced to watch as their children's schools became mestizo dumping grounds, and who could only internalize their confused sense of loss, self-muted in fear of sin against the divine order of diversity, as those children grew up and bred out into an invading alien culture, or got strung out on Sackler pain management products. It hit those at the bottom the hardest, and gone was the class of men who would never have allowed it to get this far, men like Colonel Thomas Lee—from whom the 'Burg received its name via his son Henry "Light-Horse Harry" Lee, who was himself the father of Robert E. Lee—along with the other First Families of Virginia, who could never have imagined in their worst nightmares such a future when they planted here west of the river some of the earliest seeds of the Commonwealth. . . . Leesburg, on the periphery in times before but swallowed up in those thereafter by the Empire's bureaucratic creep—meaning that coming up fast was the Grid, the metro: Dulles.

The highway met with the helical loops of numbered others of unknown origins, crossing overhead and underneath and widening the path as toll roads and rail lines were tacked on, magically incorporated, suddenly *there*— the empty speedway like a bundle of fiber optic cables that grew thicker as they closed in on the hub, the Netplex, the infobahn corridor: a server farm and supercommtech nerve center acting as a base of operations for vendors, providers, and manufacturers of circuit integrators and cyber services, space-net sensors and magnetic actuators, semiconductors and quantum modifiers, whose sea-blue-glass headquarters were now rising every which way out of the earth—sinister below the pale of sky, windows flexing miragelike into nacre, checkered like the latticework of the Grid—a mega-city model and layout all too familiar to those who had spent their lives tiptoeing along its adjacent parkways and hunting for space in neighboring plaza lots when not at the office or home, the latter being more often than not located in one of the apartment complexes or condominiums whose headstone crests could now too be seen a squinting-inch above the treeline, residencies unaesthetic even on the rare occasion when efforts were made to make them appear otherwise—the Park, the Point, the Place, the Village, the Homes, the Ridge, the Oaks, the Court, the Crossing—from stints in which the more diligent would hope to one day upgrade to a nook in a centipedal subdivision, a townhouse or housing development with mirror-image homes, or maybe a yard-exempt unit in an edge city faux-urban village with an industrial park and commercial center built by a multinational real estate investment trust that contracted with the same companies to appropriate whatever was left after the housing payment, cents shaved off incrementally at the corporate sushi restaurant, the Brooklyn pizza joint, the sports bar, the southwest grill, the joe and tea stop, and the semi-organic market—all small-business trendy in outward appearance and with localish-sounding names but that were of course nothing of the sort and, as the wiser you had correctly surmised, were only given those chic veneers and alliterative one-offs because market research showed that chain stores were not to your yuppie liking.

"City living!"

Life on the Grid. But you'd made it: achieving high-commoner status in the new cramped and depreciated middle class—kudos, well done, hats off, *Slugger*. Then the first icy wind would arrive at the stern of the long year and the fall back would turn the days' ends into early nights and on eves more honest you would ask as you dragged your felt soles from the office and down the parking lot aisle and hit the teeming trail for home amid a procession of brake lights on lonely turnpikes under skies of blood-purple, bruised and baleful, if there was, perhaps, another way, or if this was it . . . *could it be?* But in the course of time you would arrive back at your midrise Town Center Parkway apartment building having forgotten you ever posed such a dangerous question, be in stride down the final stretch of cranberry-colored carpet while absorbing tacitly behind a labored smile the silent scorn of resource-competitor-neighbor Ming Sung Pan, enter with a turn of the key your bugman studio, and find yourself alone at last but for the invisible presence of the Googlopticon, ready to prepare for a standard evening of high-calorie fare *en plastique*, bargain Moscato, a middling dose of benzos, and a gradual expiration over the hours to come into sweet phantasmago-ria as you caught up on that unending TubeFlix fantasy series sprawled out on a misty-wheat sofa next to your American Shorthair Skeezer and Pro-fessor Dumbledore, the Scottish Fold. Life was great: same-day delivery on everything, Drumpf was gone, and you'd been chosen to be lead tolerance monitor at the diversity seminar next month, which meant that unlike some of the unfortunate others at the company you'd dodged the latest round of layoffs and wouldn't be training your replacement out of the batch of malo-dorous surrogates recently flown in from Uttar Pradesh—stressful eggshells once obstructing the path ahead swept, for the coming year at least, aside, making room for a future that looked, with children now likely out of the question, footloose and fancy free in terms of time available to campaign for equalitarian social issues and report Mebook hatespeech violations while rolling in forged absolution knowing you were too independent to be tied down, too good for just one, too wild for this world baby, and as an added benefit wouldn't be contributing to the overpopulation problem, though family members had voiced concern over what they perceived as an uptick in irritability which didn't make sense because you were happy, and that was all that mattered: *you.*

The same you who would on the downmost of nights cruise the neighborhoods of Fairfax, Tysons and McLean, crossing swords with the spiritual chasm growing in your soul but having not the slightest clue what it was or where it came from—at the root of it: being blind as a fucking bat as to how the world had actually become this way—cluelessness you most assuredly shared with those residing in the spectrum of opulent homes fading as if on glow-blurred carousels aft out of your peripheral vision as you drove tearfully deeper into the woods of Old Dominion Drive, Odricks Corner and Langley—each house unique, all a substantial fortune and forever out of reach, reserved for Inner Party or Chinese buyers, a distinction that was increasingly unclear as the national fire sale lingered on, exacerbated by these mysterious movers and shakers and profitable functionaries and corporate managers and partisan lobbyists and licensed usurers and Big Four bookkeepers and business intelligence operators and MIC contractors and software specialists who could hinge backdoors on backdoors—themselves too busy to philosophize, too ambitious to stir the pot, too in clover to care, and without a reason to sitting pretty in the spacious offices of law firms and think tanks and Booze Allen and the CIA. It was a war from the bottom to the top, and it was the predecessors of those now serving as imperial administrators both public and private who had failed the greatest: men who obeyed genteel customs and conducted affairs with Anglo courtesy among an enemy that mocked all such guidelines and behavior, and who would thus over time be bridled or bought out, handpicked for corruptibility, or in other ways corralled and made into subjects of the Empire, their loyalties reformatted to lie no longer with a people, a nation, or a civilization, but with a global machine that rewarded them for protecting and furthering the interests of the gypsy con artists posing as nouveaux aristocrats in their forefathers' place.

How the smart could be so unwise; at heart and by nature, for good and ill, just too damn naïve. Believing it was in their own interests, thinking their ideals and meritocratic approach would be adopted by all, broadcasting how great it was that the Potomac School was more Sinocentric every year. It was no different at these echelons; the ethnic power struggle was the same. It was merely being fought by different factions and under a mannerly pretense sly outsiders wanting a piece of a pie they could never bake themselves were able to mimic until in positions to appoint their own to these lofty perches and become the new leaders working out the details on Foggy Bottom or mediating the terms in offices on K Street or otherwise assisting in the forced diversification of the Old Stock living on depreciatingly peaceful streets hundreds of miles away, for whom fateful decisions were so effortlessly made. Most assumed they were doing the right thing, not realizing the future they were creating nor taking seriously their roles as stewards, but acting in the service and benefit of market share and quarterly returns and global security and desert fiefdoms, to the yay or nay of those with their hands on the greenback spigot and in perpetual fear of their clansmen ruling over the new public square where heretics and renegades were made examples of, conformity was enforced, and reality through lies and moral liturgy cast out unto all. What could they do? What would they do. Who would play the devil in this life and take his honor in the next? Who would step up and start the purge.

Gentlemen.

[. . .]

Gentlemen?

So the arms of the Empire stretched like the District Grid and grew like the Pentagon's war chest and scattered across the earth her battlestations and unraveled scrolls of legal code and rolls of red tape and invented impotent ministries to oversee it all while adding zeros on zeros to the gibs being handed over to the imported peasants sacking every once-pristine city across the nation so they could buy up more cut-rate feed and garb from the warehouses your 401(k) was tied to in this impossible-to-untangle web driven by the endless debt continuously issued to keep it all going—this Paper Leviathan, this merchant scam—whose Emerald City fronts stood from San Francisco to Seattle to Austin to Minneapolis to Miami to right here in Arlington where they rose over the Potomac watershed and guided the glassy way to the Roosevelt Bridge that slid straight into Constitution Avenue and opened at once, at last, *behold*: the former Imperial Capitol of the Old Republic of America. . . .

One of those things where, before you realized it, you were there: the National Mall, the Federal City L'Enfant. A park took up the right side. Wide sidewalks on the left attached to lawns that attached to the row of federal buildings overlooking the royal boulevard. At one time: the War Nation's Institute of Peace, the Drug Nation's Pharmacists Association, the Debt Nation's Central Bank, with memorials to plagiarists and other notable ironies. In the park, people were setting up for an event. Along the street were vehicles and men leaning against them. The truck pulled into a space and Ed and the others got out into the cold morning air.

The atmosphere was quiet. Maybe it was too early. Maybe there wasn't a whole lot to say. Ed stepped into the street and turned and took in the surroundings of the vast space: of the park, of the plot where the Washington Monument stood, of the neoclassical buildings along the grand avenue, then into the final rotation whereupon he came face to face with the Poet, whose head was tilted as he lit his cigar. After a few puffs and an upward burst of smoke he put his arm around Ed and took them on a short trip to the front of the truck. He pointed across a long lawn opposite the park and mumbled, "White House."

They were all white. Silent seconds amassed into a near minute. "So is it over?" Ed asked.

"For today, I guess. Guess it can be, I mean. Though it never is."

"So we won?"

"We won a long time ago. But you know. . . . This, mean what happened here, what happened to us, it's happened before. We know more now than we ever have. Seems unwise to point to one thing across the ages and say that's it, even if the same mark was left, the same people, the same result. But we know now. Because civilizations don't just fall like the history books say, they're destroyed from within. Only question is whether we'll learn this time."

Someone came up from behind them and started talking to the Poet, who looked back and nodded and said *Mm-hm* a time or two before lifting his arm up and off of Ed.

"We gotta take off. Think you can find a way back later?"

"I'll figure something out. Where are you guys going?"

"We're border guys, and something's come up a bit north. Some people are trying to get in."

"People?"

"Saying they've been persecuted."

"Who are they?"

"They're Jews."

Ed walked across the street to the park as a light snow began to fall over the new morning, over the new day. Over a new age. . . .

THE FLOORS SMELL of pine. She loves the cabinets, the backsplash, the powder walls. She can feel the summer breezes, visualize the placidity of the morning sun percolating through the windows, the particle dance in a Tuscan tinge behind light curtain shade. Her mind is rearranging furniture and filing through color spectrums, imagining perfect order, gauging aesthetic optimization. Because she has a knack for these things. This would be her castle, where she would live with her king—a serendipitous design: as it was, as it happened, as she always knew it would be. Men had to fight for their value; they had to build it, often from nothing. But she was born with hers. And communities were created around her to protect that, because she was the source of their future salvation. Within them, she would be safe. Within them, she would find him, not too early seen unknown, and known not too late. In the fullness of time, they would exchange a faithful vow on a spring day under a green arbor, with a dance of love to follow, the venerated spinning in a rich iridescent glow to a symphony of falling flowers, to laughter and the dreams ahead. Whisked away once the champagne has been drunk and the sun has gone down, off to somewhere distant, Sardinia or Santorini, somewhere with a balcony overlooking a beach, with quiet candlelit restaurants and fiery sunsets that plunge into an archipelago, silence between their embered eyes—*come, gentle night, come*—and DO NOT DISTURB—*fellas*—there's business to be done. Candy to be laid out for the stork, who'll drop something down the chimney in two-hundred and seventy days or so, erelong. Wrapped in a soft white sheet, plump and sourfaced, well, that'd be little Robin Hood Jr., the first of many, coming in tipping those scales at 7 pounds 8 ounces. And you wish you'd seen him there in his mother's arms—squinty-eyed, runny-nosed, pink-cheeked, pulling in his first breaths. A tiny vessel, a prince of our new imperium. . . .